Also by Bartle Bull

A Café On the Nile
Safari: A Chronicle of Adventure

The
WHITE
RHINO
HOTEL

Bartle Bull

CARROLL & GRAF PUBLISHERS, INC.
NEW YORK

for my son
Bartle B. Bull

Illustrations copyright © 1992 by Max Cutler
Maps copyright © 1992 by Viking Penguin

First Carroll & Graf edition 2000

Carroll & Graf Publishers, Inc.
A Division of Avalon Publishing Group
19 West 21st Street
New York, NY 10010-6805

Library of Congress Cataloging-in-Publication Data is available.
ISBN: 0-7867-0798-4

Manufactured in the United States of America

The Characters

Olivio Fonseca Alavedo The Goan bartender of the White Rhino Hotel in Nanyuki, British East Africa (Kenya)

Jill and Tony Bevis Young English settlers

The Black Tulips Exquisite Somali twins, courtesans

Ernst von Decken A German ex-soldier, son of Hugo von Decken

Hugo von Decken A pioneer settler in German East Africa (Tanganyika, Tanzania)

Anunciata Fonseca A woman from Portuguese East Africa (Mozambique)

Vasco Fonseca A Portuguese planter, brother to Anunciata

Lucy and Tom Gault New settlers, the parents of Anna

Jezebel and "Shotover" Graham Goldminers from New Zealand

James "Spongey" Hartshorne A British colonial official

Karioki Kitenji A Kikuyu ex-soldier, son of Chief Kitenji

Kina Kitenji A young Kikuyu girl, sister to Karioki

General Paul von Lettow-Vorbeck The German commander in East Africa in the First World War

Alan Llewelyn A Welsh ex-soldier, settling in Kenya

Gwenn Llewelyn A Welsh woman, the wife of Alan Llewelyn

Lady Penfold Sissy, the wife of Adam Penfold

Lord Penfold The proprietor of the White Rhino Hotel

Mick and Paddy Reilly Brothers, ex-soldiers with a criminal past

Anton Rider A young Englishman, raised by gypsies

Rack Slider An American white hunter

Raji da Souza A Goan moneylender

Victoria A Samburu woman

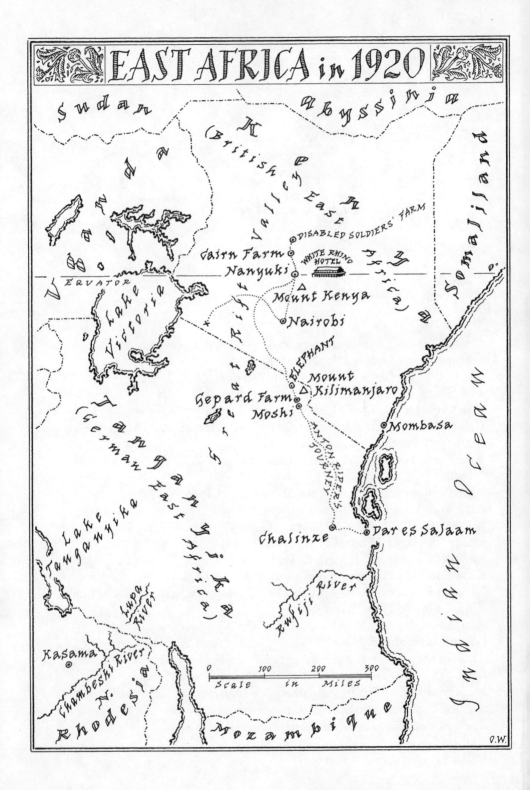

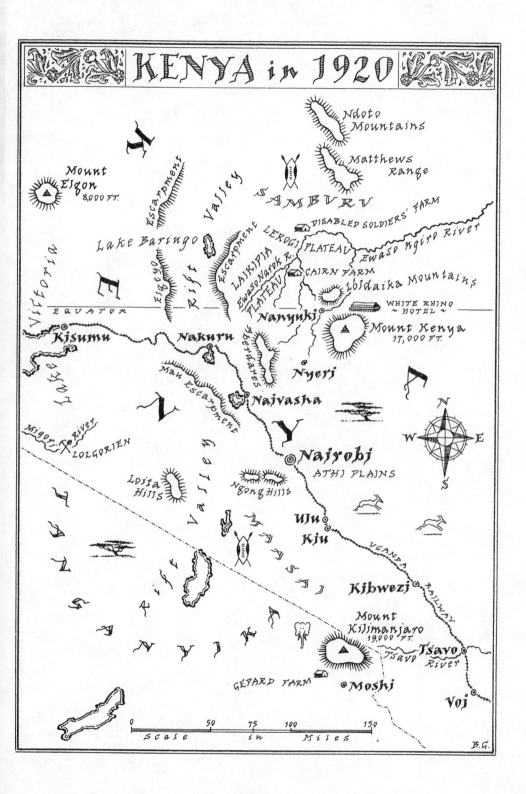

KENYA in 1920

PROLOGUE

12 November 1918

— *1* —

The White Rhino Hotel, Nanyuki, Kenya

Crab-like, Olivio scuttled up the ladder behind the broad lead-wood bar. He hauled himself up by his arms until his tiny sandalled feet balanced lightly on the shelf that ran behind it. The dwarf removed the linen towel tucked into the saffron sash around his waist. He advanced along the shelf to the end of the bar, studying its surface for the previous night's abuse of curry, cigars and claret. Cut from the planks of a pioneer wagon, each board retained the impressions of the iron elbow clasps that once secured them to the wagon floor. The carved provenance LUANGWA, NORTHERN RHODESIA 1902 was still visible through grime and wear and polish. Like the bed of a stream or the hide of an old Cape buffalo, the bar of the White Rhino Hotel was a diary in itself.

Olivio swept off ashes and the wire frames of spent corks. He reached one arm under the bar and ran his fingertips along the smooth rounded steel. The old Rigby elephant gun still hung in its brackets. The dwarf lifted a seltzer siphon and settled to the sticky work of wiping away the chutney and dried port. With the bar at last clean to the eye, he unscrewed a tin of Young's Rifle Oil. Olivio sniffed the odor of carbolic as thick amber drops spread on the towel bound around his hand. Working in expanding circles, his face held low to the surface, the little barman polished until a shine rose like the burnished shell of a tortoise.

He adjusted the few remaining bottles on the wall behind him, mostly Belfast Ginger Ale. A row of animal horns rose above them.

Some were straight or spiralled, others delicate or monstrous. All emerged hard and dark from the trim white bone plates of their foreheads.

Now the bar stood out among the ruins of the evening like a gleaming yacht floating in a filthy harbor. Only the yellow-brown panelling of the camphorwood walls was undisturbed. Overturned chairs, backgammon pieces and broken plates cluttered the floor. The upright piano rested on its side. A torn photograph of Kaiser Wilhelm was pinned onto the dart board.

It had been a long night for the newly defeated German emperor, 12 November 1918. His enemies, Kenya's colonial English, had been celebrating the end of the Great War. They drank all night with the same boyish gusto they had carried into the early days of the four-year battle. In 1914 the British had marched south to invade German East Africa, cheerful as schoolmates playing capture-the-flag, keen to do their part in the war to end all wars.

One sturdy table remained in place in the center of the room, exactly straddling the equator. A narrow trench cut its square surface. The dwarf stroked both ears with his fingers and recalled a long evening some years before the war. Lord Penfold, the hotel's proprietor, then in younger, stronger days, had raised a panga and slammed the heavy blade down to mark the middle of the world. As the lord remarked that night, the White Rhino was the only bar where one enjoyed a drink in one hemisphere and got rid of it in the other.

Olivio heard a whistle blast call to him from an upstairs room as a man blew into the empty brass cartridge of a 7-mm Mauser. The barman drew the last bottle of champagne from the cold locker, selected a rhinoceros-hide tray and gathered a bottle of stout and two glasses. Then he ascended the stairs to the guest hall, pulling on the rail with one small hand.

The keyhole of Number 3 welcomed the dwarf's eye at just the proper level. And not by accident. He thought back to the day the carpenters had asked him how high to set the keyholes. He placed his right eye comfortably against the small familiar opening.

"Not now, Shorty," an American voice said. "Just set down the black velvet. Go spy on Spongey next door. What's goin' on in there would blind a camel."

"Yes, Sahib Slider." Olivio moved to Number 4. He opened his eye wide and set it to the door. Two white robes were scattered on the floor. A musical tinkling, as of a thousand tiny bells, thrilled his ear. The Black Tulips, he thought. He moistened his lips and angled his head to catch sight of the bed. He was eager to study their work while the exquisite Somali twins performed their tantalizing specialty: leaving their client exhilarated and exhausted without permitting penetration. A boot crashed against the inside door handle, bruising the dwarf's temple. He heard a voice whine, "Off with you, you twisted little brute!"

From long experience in the Bombay Club and in British East Africa, Olivio knew it was time to withdraw. The English were sensitive about their relations with these Africans, as well they might be.

Vengeance would come later. Like most Goans, Olivio Fonseca Alavedo took a long view. The Portuguese had occupied his own land, the island enclave of Goa on the coast of India, for over four centuries. One day they would leave. In the meantime, he would reward this rude Englishman, Mr. Spongey Hartshorne, in his own way.

Only the English, Olivio reflected, would build this wretched hotel in the hills of central Kenya, a refuge for every red-eyed farmer and philandering ivory hunter from Nairobi to Abyssinia. What could such people know of civilization?

With only two thousand Goans in all of British East Africa, Olivio and his countrymen had built one of the first stone buildings in Nairobi, the Goan Institute. While these English farmers, three hundred and fifty years ago, were shivering in damp huts in their own country, huddled under thatched roofs like black savages, the masters of the Inquisition were purifying western India. Olivio's own father, he recalled with pride, was almost certainly the bastard son of Dom Tiago de Castanheda y Fonseca, the late Archbishop of Goa.

Olivio imagined his distant relatives, powerful and rich, not aware of his existence, going about their privileged lives in Portugal. The dwarf dreamt what his legacy might be.

Born in the shadow of a sixteenth-century Portuguese cathedral on an island where Hindus and Moslems had battled and bred for centuries until the viceroy Don Albuquerque killed every last Mohammedan in 1511, Olivio knew barbarism when he saw it. Just now he heard its voice from the verandah, as the dice clattered on the backgammon table.

"Java! Coffee!" the hoarse voice said. "Quickly, boy! *Pesi pesi!*"

Olivio walked slowly towards the broad wooden verandah. He absorbed the bar's lustre as he passed with the dark Kenya coffee. He stepped through the doorway and paused to breathe in the cool sharp-scented breeze of the African morning. He listened to the crested hoopoes calling. The birds flapped leisurely about, hunting worms and lizards on the lawn. Sometimes, like a Hindu, Olivio's heart lay with the lizard. Sometimes, like a conquistador, his spirit was with the hunter.

He observed the all-night backgammon contest. Olivio knew at once what the stakes must be: land. Money would not keep these coarse farmers up all night, and they were not playing for fun. The loser, ruined, Olivio hoped, desperately sought to recover his farm, ten acres at a time, by doubling the stakes once more.

Wherever they went, the dwarf had learned, the English took the land. Always the land. Even Africa would not be large enough for them, although sometimes you could walk for days and hardly see a man. If they possessed land at home, these English ventured to India and Africa to find the money to keep it. If they had no land at home, they went abroad to steal it. Soon, with the war finished, they would kill one another for the land.

Olivio returned to the backgammon table. He bowed slightly and presented a folded bill to the winner. The seated farmer waved at his departing friend over the white wooden rail of the verandah. His corrugated face was flushed and exhausted. The man rubbed his eyes and drew a slip of paper from a stack of crumpled vouchers.

"Money's impossible, Olivio. I'm a farmer." He surprised the dwarf by signing the paper and handing it to the barman. "You settle up for me. Pay my account. In exchange, take this chit for yourself to help you remember the end of the Kaiser's war. Ambrose's damned land ain't worth a farthing anyway. Who'd want to live up there?"

Walking a tour around the hotel, Olivio came to the white English rosebush at the rear of the two-story structure. He leaned into it until the thorns pricked his cheeks. He closed both eyes and inhaled. How few men, he thought, ever used their noses! The dwarf plucked off each insect-damaged leaf. He cracked the white shell of an invading snail with the toe of his sandal, mercilessly pursuing its slippery occupant. He ordered the garden boy to water the sturdy plant as if it were the last of his father's maize.

Seven years before, Olivio recalled, as the hotel went up but with the tin roofing not yet arrived when the April rains flooded the rooms, Adam Penfold had planted the rosebush himself. The root ball and a sack of English soil came from the family gardens in Wiltshire. Months later, alarmed by its sparse growth and weak hold in the land, Penfold ordered a hole dug at the foot of the plant. He led over a sick ox, its nostrils dripping with brown tick fever, its flanks bony like an open fish. His lordship shot the beast behind the ear with his Webley .45 and shoved the dying animal as it fell. The ox collapsed into the waiting grave before Penfold packed in the earth himself. Olivio nursed the plant like a puppy until finally it flowered, his lordship forever proud that four hundred pounds of walking fertilizer had saved this corner of England.

Olivio put aside the memory and reached into his sash. He drew out the farmer's wrinkled voucher.

I.O.U. and hereby transfer to the bearer, he read, *ten watered acres of Eland Ranch at my bend of the Ewaso Ngiro River.—Richard Ambrose, 12 November 1918.*

One day he might find it useful.

Olivio approached the open kitchen doors at the rear of the hotel. Two slender figures slipped out, holding hands. White cotton robes covered the backs of their heads and offered a suggestion of pointed breasts. Each wore a tight necklace of small silver bells high against the smooth dark column of her neck. What symphonies those bells had played! As the two women emerged, apparently hurrying to avoid the dwarf, a barefoot rickshaw boy drew up his light two-wheeled carriage and took his place between the long shafts. The twins, ignoring Olivio's smile, assumed their seats.

Tall spoked wheels turned. The rickshaw rolled away as the boy leaned into his work. The ladies settled back under the sheltering canvas hood of the vehicle until Olivio could only see two arms gesturing, graceful with silver bracelets and long brown fingers. Pursuing the Black Tulips with his eyes until the rickshaw was clouded by red dust rising from the curved drive, the dwarf opened his mouth.

He suspended his thick quivering tongue between his lips, like a lizard. Inspired by the Tulips, his mind turned to a different woman.

Frustrated, Olivio looked behind the kitchen to the Kikuyu village that extended back under the acacia trees. Only the few young girls drew his interest. His deep-set eyes narrowed while he searched the busy scene. Where was she? Smoke floated up from fires that smoldered among flat cooking stones. Women wove baskets. Boys set out to watch the cattle. Several men hung about the round straw-thatched huts, waiting for wives to bring them gourds of the thick mead they called *njohi*. Olivio spoke to one man, who at once ran to get the chief, a pleasing reminder that the villagers were in thrall to the dwarf. They knew the barman controlled the opportunities and largesse of the hotel.

Chief Kitenji emerged from his hut after an annoying delay. Lean and angular as a locust, he was bent over a carved mahogany staff. The old man advanced to the undefined line in the dirt that separated hotel from village. Olivio watched the African lower himself onto a log. The rancid savage had learned not to provoke him by looking down upon him. The dwarf was aware that Kitenji and the villagers referred to him as *Chura Nyakundu*, the Yellow Frog.

Olivio prepared for the wily African's daily attempt to secure the dwarf's favors without surrendering his own property or influence. Doubtless today the chief would find the answer he found every morning: give the dwarf the gift of another man's things. Olivio, however, had a richer bargain in mind.

"I salute you, great *Baba,* father of my village," said the chief when Olivio advanced to him, leaving not a footprint as he moved across the dust.

"Where are my special hides, old man?" the dwarf hissed. "Where are the kongoni hides? Where are the baskets your hags owe me?"

"Hides? Baskets? What are these, my Baba?" The chief raised his voice and rolled rheumy eyes. "Yesterday I gave you beans and fat pumpkins. Hides? Where am I to find hides? My people are not allowed to hunt."

"You will find hides on the antelope. Take them. Cure them well. Give them up to me, or you will draw no water from the lord's stream," whispered Olivio sharply. He remembered how he had learned to bargain as a hungry youth in the frantic bazaars of Bombay.

Did this stinking scoundrel think to haggle with him! With Olivio Fonseca Alavedo, who at fourteen had bartered his master's cuff links for pearls, and pearls for Chinese silk, and silk for his first young girl, enough of it, twenty yards, to overcome even the child's revulsion for his attentions?

"Water? Without water my children cannot serve you, beloved Baba. What of the men I gave you when this war began? Think of them, Baba. Eighteen strong porters to carry for the English soldiers. They walked long, far into the land of the filthy savages, the evil Maasai, the land of lion and sickness. Have my brothers come home? Are their children fat? Are their wives warm? If they return, will they honor their chief, after they have suffered with the English, carried and starved, died many times? How will their eyes look on me then, divine Baba?"

"Did I make this war, old man?" The dwarf thought of his own obsession. "Did I take your men? Do they carry for me? No. It is the English. Wives? If the women are alone, show them to me. Yet they carry babies as before. You owed men for the war, twenty-five, but I saved seven for you, pleading with the lord's friend. So you owe me seven men, or three very young girls, or perhaps a single special one."

Olivio detected resistance building in the old savage as the dwarf unveiled his purpose.

"Your daughter Kina." The dwarf spoke more slowly. He watched the fingers of the African stiffen and his eyes grow hooded. "Only she can save your wretched son, the foul Karioki. Already she is nearly twelve. Her breasts are fresh and proud. It is time—"

Kitenji interrupted the Yellow Frog as he mentioned the one thing the chief still denied him. Kitenji turned and called to another villager. "Ngeri!"

For an instant Olivio thought back to a day before the war, the morning Karioki had intervened while the dwarf was playing innocently with the African's adorable sister. How patient Olivio had been since then, waiting and waiting while the child ripened!

Ngeri came over slowly, silent. Olivio understood his reluctance. The man knew what Kitenji would ask. Considered by the District Officer to be a vicious native poacher, to the villagers he was their finest hunter, part Kikuyu and part Nandi, always more adept in the bush than the agricultural Kikuyu. "Come, Ngeri, bring for the Baba our last skins, the two fine ones, the only ones we hold."

At that moment Olivio heard a motorcar drive up to the hotel. He listened to the engine as the vehicle slowed. The old Napier saloon. He fixed Kitenji hard with his eyes. The horn sounded twice. Lady Penfold. He must put his own work aside. Spared for the moment, the chief inclined his head with respect while the dwarf moved away and entered the kitchen.

Olivio knew too well what his demanding mistress would require.

Ever since Lady Penfold had learned that, with suitable preparation, it was possible for the dwarf to insinuate his entire hand into her vagina, she had given him no peace. Even this morning, he was certain, while she drove home after an exhausting night, she had closed her eyes in the motorcar and imagined Olivio's tiny fist, small and perfect as an infant's, but wonderfully active, opening inside her like a tropical flower.

Long ago, the barman reflected without regret, he had set aside all hope of being loved. That, ordinary men could have. Instead, at the White Rhino, he was mixing a cocktail of revulsion and desire.

Finding early in life that the person less desired physically must do the sexual toil, Olivio had trained himself to relish the extremity of this inevitable role. The more revolting women found him, the more skilled and pleasing he must be. Other men gained women through appearance and power, money and charm. Most men, whether English or Kikuyu, approached women intent on their own brief pleasure. He knew that few, especially Englishmen, considered how to give pleasure to a woman. The dwarf, however, thought of little else. By giving women what other men did not, occasionally he became the creature of their fantasies.

Olivio advanced into the hallway and bowed as Lady Penfold swept by. Tall, more thin than ever, she declined to look at him but dropped orders as she passed, faster than a Kikuyu flung seeds in a furrow. "Gather the accounts. Call for my bath. Prepare yourself. Wash carefully, Olivio, and come to my sitting room."

Years of private service from the Malabar Coast to the highlands of the Aberdares had taught Olivio how to please, and how never to please completely. He obeyed slowly. He waited until the bath softened her before presenting himself through the steam to Lady

Penfold, like a genie, he thought, with his accounts in one small hand, her warm massage oil in the other.

Olivio's grey eyes became flat and distant. In a few moments he would be Lord Penfold. But why, the dwarf reflected, remarking her flushed, bone-hanging skin with distaste while he thought of another, far younger woman, am I always welcome at the wrong door?

— 2 —

Windsor Great Park, Berkshire, England

The old jack hare stood erect and majestic on heavy hind legs. It sniffed briskly. Its long white whiskers feathered in the sharp November wind. Shifting weight to advance one leg closer to a juniper bush, the hare left the track, narrowly missing the loop of braided green fishing line that lay in its path. The tawny animal browsed on the stiff, sharply pointed leaves of the plant. Step by step it moved deeper into the vegetation, leaving the snare behind.

Pressed flat to the ground between the strong roots of yew bushes thirty feet away, the boy studied the hare. A knot twisted in his stomach. Frozen with concentration, the hare seeming huge before him, his will sought to direct each step the animal took. Whenever the wind died, Anton could hear the stiff leaves snap as the hare took them. He admired the thick winter coat and considered the shilling the hare might fetch in the Windsor market. One bob for eight pounds of stew and fur. But how slowly the old gent picked and ate his lunch. Patience, the boy forced himself to remember, thinking of his gypsy mentor, patience.

But time was dangerous, for Anton knew he too was hunted. The gamekeepers, priding themselves the sharpest in England, made Windsor Great Park a perilous haunt for poachers. Wily and keen-eyed countrymen themselves, they held a particular dislike for snares. Nearly eighteen, Anton would be beaten, not prosecuted, and the keepers knew him too well to spare him. He dreaded another humiliating thrashing. Worse, they would bring more trouble to the gypsies, hounding again the Romany families with whom Anton shared a life. The gypsies, in turn, would hound him.

Hunting and hunted, the boy slowly shifted his weight, the acorns printing impressions on his hard stomach. He followed the hare with cornflower-blue eyes and prayed silently while the animal moved back closer to the track. The wind died, shifted, rose again. Turning, hopping twice with a thump that seemed to shake the land, the old jack pointed both black-tipped ears towards the new wind and stared into the yews with wide-set prominent eyes designed to see to the side. Knowing that another slight wind change would carry his odor to his prey, the boy stopped breathing when the hare hopped once more, landing back on the track beyond the snare. In a moment the hare would be away, leaping at right angles in fifteen-foot bounds to interrupt the continuity of its scent as it returned to its bed-like form in a thicket of briar and gorse. Now must be the time.

Deep in his throat Anton uttered the low cough of a stoat. The sound of an enemy jolted the hare's heart. Instantly the animal turned and bolted into the loop. The young silver birch, no longer bent back like a bow, released and whipped straight. The hare shot into the air, dangling and spinning helplessly.

The boy darted forward as the hare ground its teeth and screamed like a child. He seized the squealing animal by the ears and struck it on the back of the neck with the edge of his hand, knowing not to use his knife lest a bleeding body be harder to conceal. The hare twitched and became still. Anton suppressed the sense of respect and regret that stung him whenever an animal died at his hands. He untied the snare from the birch and coiled it inside the lining of his cap. He slipped the body into the oilskin pouch in the back of his corduroy jacket, gulped a deep breath and ran for home.

A bearded figure leapt out from behind an oak and slammed Anton in the chest with the stock of a shotgun. Falling, stunned, the boy heard bells ringing in the distance. He sat up, dizzy and gasping. The gamekeeper held the gun over him.

"You again," the man said.

Anton coughed and swept the straight straw-colored hair back from his eyes. Blood pumped in his ears. The bells grew closer, louder, until Anton recognized the answering peals from the stone church tower at the edge of the forest. Then, from the artillery park beyond

Windsor Castle, they heard it. The rolling boom of light cannon as the Royal Horse Artillery celebrated the end of the World War. Anton searched his captor's face.

"It's a lucky day for England, and so for you too, my lad," the old forester roared. He clapped Anton on the shoulder and felt the warm burden in the small of the boy's back. He smiled, his weathered face creasing in layers like a sailor too long at sea. "Keep your dinner, and make it a fine one. There's plenty of men for whom these bells ring too late."

"Thank you, sir," Anton gasped, feeling light-headed.

"A breath of advice for you, my handsome lad. Never come back. You're good at this forest life, too good. The best I've caught in forty years under these trees. That thievin' black-faced tinker taught you too damned well. But this forest'll never be yours, nor mine neither. Aye, leave Windsor, leave England. On this island you'll not be free. But there's Canada, Australia, maybe East Africa. Plenty of land there, and gold they say, and game enough for everyone. Run now before I blast you."

In the evening the gypsies breathed frost while they laughed and drank to the music of a fiddle. Anton sat by himself on the steep narrow steps of the *vardo,* the Romany wagon that was gathered with others at the edge of the wood. The caravan door was at the front so passengers could chat with the driver while the wagon roamed. On either side of him a horse shaft stretched to the ground. Before him the remains of the great hare simmered in an iron pot suspended from three wooden poles that met over the dying fire.

Anton raised the collar of his jacket over the knotted red *diklo,* his gypsy neckerchief, and stared into the campfire, then into the sky. He squinted to find favorite stars in the thin air of the northern night. In his right hand he held a circle of gold that hung from a leather cord about his neck. It was the earring of Lenares, his teacher of the forest. Unwed, Anton's mother had taken Lenares as her gypsy lover when Anton was born. After Lenares was killed, she often disappeared to London, leaving Anton alone in the old caravan the three had shared. To find a new start, she explained tenderly, she had to be on her own for a while. The last time, she had not returned. Perhaps she had tried, he hoped, but had lost track of the small tribe as it wandered. He imagined the different ways his mother might have been detained, finding new, more believable reasons for her absence. With his mother gone, Anton would never learn who had been his father, whether he was handsome or strong, or whether he liked to fish or hunt.

Remembering Lenares, Anton thought about their days and nights fishing and poaching together, and how he had learned to hunt without a gun, as poachers often must, and to fish without a line. Always it was patience, silence, being death-quiet. Growing, Lenares told him, into the land. Lying on a dew-chilled riverbank at dawn, just below the dream-like haze of the morning fog, his right arm was extended into the icy water, his hand rubbed with bacon grease to protect against the cold and to lure the fish. He waited for the trout to move against his palm, touching them gently, tickling them slowly with curled fingers, until they eased. Then he tossed the slippery fish up onto the bank, their silver sparkling briefly like new coins. He fell on them before they flipped back in, his right hand too slick with grease and stiff with cold to hold them. Always he left one trout behind, hanging in a tree, to make certain more would be awaiting his return.

Now Lenares was dead, never found after his company was blown aside at Mons in the first days of the war. Before Lenares signed up, he had removed his single earring, for the only time.

"My granny's wedding ring, made for her by my grandfather when he was sixteen, from coins he stole himself, luckier than a cat's tooth." Lenares smiled with dark eyes and pinched his left ear. He kissed the ring and gave it to Anton.

The morning the troop train pulled out, Anton watched young men in coarse khaki queue up at steaming tea carts on the rain-wet platform. While others cried goodbyes, Lenares made Anton his brother, a *phral,* almost a *Rom,* a member of the tribe. Opening his pack, Lenares removed a frayed leather sheath and slipped from it a long Toledo blade. Slightly hollow near the point, it was a *choori,* the weapon of the Latin gypsy. Lenares gave the knife to Anton without speaking and took his penknife in exchange. He kissed the boy on the lips and turned to Anton's weeping mother. Perhaps now, at last, Lenares had found the freedom every gypsy sought. But curse it, Anton thought, why did everyone disappear?

He rose and stepped to the edge of the fire, the *atchen-tan* that was the center of each camp. There he crouched with a handful of coarse salt and read the fire as others might divine cards or tea leaves. Unclear images formed and vanished in the flames and embers. The lower in the fire they appeared, the farther in the future he would find their lessons. For an instant he almost saw what he sought. The ancient signs of travel: a boat, a kangaroo. Uncertain, Anton felt rising within him the skepticism of a *gaujo,* a non-gypsy, reining back his instinct.

Concentrating anew, releasing himself, Anton closed both eyes and cast the salt into the fire. The coals flared. For a moment he saw glowing before him the golden-yellow image of a long key. The sign of opportunity. A new path.

Memories flickering in the darkness, following the sparks that disappeared into the crisp misty evening, Anton thought of all the schoolboys across England tonight celebrating the end of the Great War. Boys with a classroom schooling, homes and the family he would never have. Tutored by his mother, Anton was the only child in the gypsy camp who could read, and the only one not trained to steal. The other children, darker, often barefoot, with parents intent on protecting their ways, mocked the young gaujo whenever they saw him with a book.

Feeling himself an outsider among outsiders, Anton would sit hunched on the steps of the high-wheeled caravan and lose himself in his private pages. His library was a shelf nailed above the carved door of the vardo. On this board were the tales of Charles Dickens, the one writer, his mother told him, loved by every sort of Englishman.

Early one evening he had run home through the woods, eager to pick up his favorite book from the step of the wagon where he had left it. Its characters were his family: Peggotty, Em'ly, Mr. Micawber. He arrived breathless at the vardo and looked about for the book.

David Copperfield lay in the mud beneath the little stairway. Anton knelt and touched it. Tears clouded his eyes when he picked it up. The front cover was burned away. The pages were charred through, curled and black-edged, exposing the inside of the back cover. There, drawn crudely in charcoal, he found the images of an arrow and an alligator, Romany signs of bad news and injury. His jaw clenched. Why could they not leave him be?

Gazing into the fire, searching for better memories, Anton considered all that he had learned instead of schoolwork: the secrets of Lenares, the trades of the gypsies. Sleight of hand, horse-dealing and fairground boxing, how to make a knife whistle when it flew, the mysteries of dice, cards and fortunes, trick shooting and wood carving. Best of all, an affinity with nature. How to release one's senses like an animal, and how to wander and always be at home.

But gypsy schooling had its price. Anton pinched the bump on the tall straight bridge of his nose. Two months before, Anton remembered with anger, he took a hard beating from the farm boys at the Needham Market fair. They always used their fists when he outsmarted them. He had nearly tricked them all at the rifle booth, competing against them with a .22, the youths not knowing from his fair looks that he was shilling for the gypsy stalls. Carefully, narrowly, Anton beat them one by one, winning their pennies as he drilled the targets, never shooting too well, just well enough to win, betting casually with the boys around him. Then one lad, insolent, a fine shooter, pushed Anton to the test. He grouped five shots near the bull's-eye.

"Who can beat that?" the farm boy said.

Taught to have a gypsy's scorn for farmers, Anton seized the rifle. He bet two bob, then more, and took his turn while the boys crowded about. Forgetting his Romany training, he revealed his skill, deliberately firing each shot just inside one of his rival's, echoing his pattern. Anton ended with a perfect bull's-eye. He collected on his bets and pridefully looked his opponent in the eye. Suddenly the boy recognized Anton as the youngster who had helped erect the gypsy stalls. Furious, the farm boys were on him fast. Better with their fists than with a rifle, they beat him bloody and broke his nose. He was left to lie bleeding and crying after they emptied his pockets and gave him a few final kicks.

Anton lay in his blankets under the wagon with the earring smooth in his hand. He smelled the two mongrels that lay warm against his back. He heard one dog crack the bones of a hedgehog between its teeth. The other dog raised its head and licked the greasy kettlebox that was bolted under the rear of the vardo. Above Anton were the blunt iron hooks that held the pans and chicken baskets that swung freely as the wagon journeyed. He peered out between the wooden wheel spokes and the short legs of the grazing donkeys. He listened to the dark-faced gypsies sing poems of loneliness and talk of going home, of mending the caravans and crossing to Europe. He tried to force from his head the thoughts of beatings and the memories of his mother. The gypsies knew that after great events their brothers, too, would be drawn back to the old places, to the mountains of Spain and the dark woods of Roumania, that it was time. Time to go, Anton thought, time for me too. For in the forests of England, I will never be free.

— 3 —

A *The German Camp, Kasama,*
Northern Rhodesia

splendid morning for making war, wouldn't you say, Captain?" Adam Penfold sniffed his coffee and observed the early light brighten the dew on the bush eight hundred miles southwest of the White Rhino Hotel.

"Every day is satisfactory for making war, my lord." The German officer grunted and bent to loosen the strap of a leather puttee.

For Lord Penfold and Captain von Decken, the Great War was not over. Penfold was propped on a stretcher in khaki shorts and a frayed bush jacket of the East African Mounted Rifles. He tried to ignore the small fires in his bandaged right leg, painful still from shifting fragments of shrapnel. He pushed back his greying hair and pressed down his moustache and the long eyebrows that rose like wings above his hazel eyes. Then he turned his high-beaked nose and craggy face to study the enemy officer.

The Captain, heavy-set for a man still yellow with malaria, sat back, filling his canvas camp chair. He passed both hands over the bone-smooth ridges of his scalp. Unable to lead the raids and scouting parties that had won him the name Bwana Sakarini, the Wild One, von Decken was now in charge of the captives who marched with the German column.

As the senior prisoner, Penfold represented the captives in dealing with the enemy. The Englishman had learned to relish these breakfast conferences.

"What will you do afterwards, Captain?" Penfold tried not to think of his own future.

"After what?"

"When the Kaiser's war is over."

"First it'll be home to Moshi, where I was born, in the high country near Kilimanjaro, to take an apple schnapps with my old papa and see what's left of the plantation. Perhaps a little shooting, a few women."

"And then?"

"Then, my lord, I will grab my share of Africa. How is the leg today?"

"Your lads are better at banging the metal in than they are at getting it out, Captain. That Bavarian medicine man promises I'll have these last little bits with me forever, which makes damned fine news for the gin trade."

Penfold tasted the luxurious coffee captured from the Portuguese planters in Mozambique. He watched von Decken concentrate on his maps while the Burungi cook removed the German's right boot. Both boots were already slit open in several places to ease the pressure of the leather. The African carved incisions under the officer's toenails, splashed on a few drops of paraffin and began cutting out the chiggers. Penfold abandoned his attempt to ignore this delicate procedure and enjoy his morning coffee. The cook scraped the knife clean between his teeth and turned aside politely to expectorate. It appeared that, however painful, the German enjoyed these quiet displays of what was, he must realize, English sangfroid.

The previous morning Penfold had seen two nails removed to permit access to the dreaded burrowing insects, but the officer's feet were still swollen with infected flesh. Female chiggers, preferring to burrow into the scrotum and armpits, had begun to ovulate beneath von Decken's skin. There they fed off the damaged tissue they had manufactured.

"Have you thought of recruiting elephants, Captain?"

"Elephants, my lord?" Von Decken did not flinch or change his tone when the cook flipped a discolored nail into the dust with the tip of his knife.

"Of course," Penfold said. "Elephants. Hannibal used war elephants and African soldiers to defeat the finest armies of Europe. Surely your emperor could do the same?"

"Hannibal's elephants were Asiatic, Major Penfold, simple to train, like your Indian troops. Here in Africa, everything is more difficult."

Penfold understood. He had trekked with the Schutztruppe for eight months and had endured three operations in the field. General von Lettow-Vorbeck, the enemy commander, had led this colonial army across Africa for four years, often on foot, sometimes mounted on a white mule or a bicycle. He always evaded the British forces that pursued him across German East Africa, Northern Rhodesia and Portuguese East, as the English called Mozambique. Today Penfold watched von Decken consider again his commander's greatest ally, the immensity of Africa. Sometimes Penfold had to restrain himself from helping the German, for von Decken's right eye had been slashed by elephant grass.

Coffee finished, Penfold was carried to the field hospital. Occasionally, when the pain screamed in his leg, he would disappoint himself and ask for precious alcohol or morphine, knowing he would be increasing another soldier's pain.

Like many prisoners, he preferred the German doctors to the British, who seemed always too busy with amputations to change dressings. The jelly base of ointments came from the fat of elephant and hippopotamus. Bandages were made from softened bark and the torn uniforms of the dead. At first Penfold had been distressed to find his leg bandaged in the shirt of an old friend. Now, if he was alone, he sometimes spoke to it as if his brother officer still wore it.

Every European suffered some combination of wounds and illness. Today the lucky ones, like him, received bottles of Portuguese wine instead of medicine.

As Penfold waited his turn, the man before him stumbled to one side. Wet with fever and leaning on a black comrade, the young German opened his trousers with trembling hands. He urinated blood in thick inky spurts, splashing himself. Blackwater fever. Penfold tried not to embarrass the man by watching. He knew that here malaria and its consequences were beneath medical attention. Penfold turned his head and the bearers lifted his stretcher.

"No, bwana!" an African voice said as Penfold was carried past a hospital tent on his way back from the dispensary. His medicine, a surprisingly sweet white port, an Alcobaca, lay beside him on the stretcher.

"Only for operations!" the voice protested.

The sound of two blows followed. A swarthy figure in a soiled linen suit burst out through the tattered canvas flaps and blundered into Penfold's stretcher. Flashes of pain burned through the Englishman's leg. The bearers staggered and paused.

"What's the row, Fonseca?" Penfold asked his fellow prisoner. He saw Fonseca's hollow cheeks draw in. He found no apology or sympathy in the deep-set dark eyes that looked down at him. Not for the first time, Penfold wondered how this churl with the peculiarly high, rounded forehead could have such a ravishing sister. "What's the row?"

"Nothing. Blasted kaffir's getting in the way." The Portuguese planter tightened one fist around several small objects. His wide lips curled over tobacco-stained teeth when he spoke. Penfold noticed the man's boots. Typically upper-caste Latin, too delicate for the bush, and just a trifle too pointed and high in the heel.

A medical orderly emerged from the tent. Blood dripped from one corner of the African's mouth. His khaki puttees were rags, his boots cracked. Stains of dried gore layered his shirt. The man spat blood to the side and spoke one word: "Morphine."

"Show me what's in your hand, Fonseca," Penfold said.

"It's not your affair." The Portuguese jammed his fist into the side pocket of his jacket.

"I'm responsible for the prisoners."

"I'm not part of your English rabble."

"Show me at once, or by God I'll have you before the General."

Vasco Fonseca removed the hand from his pocket. He trembled with anger and opened his fist, squinting at Adam Penfold with narrow cruel eyes.

"The opium's for the dying, not the decadent." The Englishman noticed the man's long nails as he removed five glass vials from the dirty hand and passed them to the orderly. Penfold raised himself on his elbows and spoke in a low clear voice.

"One more thing, Fonseca. You are not in Portuguese East. Do not ever strike another African. If my lads knew you'd beaten a medical boy they'd have your hide. If I were up, I'd cane you myself."

"You and I will be in Africa a long time, Penfold. I will not forget this."

"Nor shall I," said the Englishman. Mercifully, after the war he would never see the beastly man again. But what about his sister, Anunciata? One day, he hoped, she might come to the White Rhino.

Penfold remembered what Anunciata had told him of her brother. His cunning. The tales of cruelty. Most of all, the obsession that kept Vasco Fonseca in Africa: his dream to become a *prazero*. The relentless ambition to build his own *fazenda,* or *prazo,* a great estate in new country, where Fonseca could rule like a prince in his own way, as his ancestors had done in Amazonia and Mozambique.

Penfold clenched his teeth and clasped the bottle of port to his stomach while the bearers carried him back to von Decken's tent.

"Will you join me, Captain, while the cook checks my leg for guests?"

"Hate to see an old soldier drink alone." Von Decken opened the Alcobaca and splashed half of it into two tin cups. "Shame you picked such a young one. You English don't know how to drink wine."

"Perhaps I could learn." Penfold thought of the fine clarets he had been able to afford in his youth.

The cook knelt and examined Penfold's good leg. There, on the inside of the calf, the white head of a worm emerged slowly from an open blister. Like a lazy boy stretching in the morning, the worm arched and wiggled gently when it encountered the air and light.

"Out she comes now!" said the cook with delight. "Maybe she is fine big one. Two, three feet, with many sisters!" The German watched with the hint of a smile, quaffing his port like beer.

Penfold reflected on the long year he and the parasite had shared since her larvae had penetrated the lining of his stomach. Mating inside him, fertilized, her dead male discarded, the incubating female had migrated down through his body, feeding freely off her host as she trekked. Rather like these Huns marching through Africa.

"Matchie?" said the cook.

The German officer handed the African a waxed wooden match. The man wrapped the head of the guinea worm around the matchstick. Aware that von Decken was watching him, Penfold tried to sip his port with a steady hand.

"Slowly," von Decken directed the cook, "*pole pole*. More port wine, Major? Your worm looks thirsty." He emptied the bottle into the cups.

"Thank you."

"Patience is the hunter's greatest weapon," the German reminded Penfold. "Whether with women or regiments, worms or elephants. With patience you draw out a few centimeters of your guinea worm each day. But if you pull too sharply, my lord, it will break and the living segment will retreat into your body."

"Have you considered leaving stone markers behind, Captain, like the Seventh Legion?" Penfold glanced about the sprawling camp and raised his cup.

"The Seventh Legion?"

"Romans, you know. Rather like you chaps." Penfold felt the wine reach him. "A bit serious, always charging about on the remote edge of empire, fancying themselves the last outpost of civilization. Learning the ways of the barbarians and all that. They always left markers, in your country and in mine, saying, 'Here was the Seventh Legion.' "

"We leave different monuments." Von Decken's eyes turned to the hillside where an African burial party was piling low mounds of rocks and pounding in rough wooden crosses.

Penfold did not reply. One by one the old Kenya hands had been left behind. This wasn't a war for old farmers, he'd learned. Like so many things in Africa, war was a young man's game. Whenever they broke camp and the bearers raised his litter, Penfold noted the thickets of crosses and knew they would not last. Sometimes he said a prayer before looking back to see high-shouldered spotted hyenas already scraping away the rocks.

Thinking of Rome, Penfold pined for his Gibbon, his own bickering notes written in beside the historian's. When life was sour and incomplete, when rust killed the wheat and his wife, Sissy, complained, he still found a welcome in *The Decline and Fall of the Roman Empire*. Like love and farming, two indulgences Penfold knew he would never understand, war was always reduced to the simplest things. Would she welcome your touch? Would water fall from the sky? How many steps could a hungry soldier walk in a day?

Lying awake at night, his leg throbbing to the beat of the cicadas,

Penfold would close his eyes and shut out the mesmerizing sky. Then, if the Portuguese girl did not come to him, he reviewed on the campaign maps of his mind the long marches of the Punic Wars.

Penfold watched the tent boy shave von Decken's face and scalp. Shots and cheers rose from the riverbank behind them. Soon an askari, a native soldier, came running.

"Bwana Sakarini!" The man saluted von Decken. "Hippopotamus! Many great fat ones!"

At last, Penfold thought, the men would feast together again, perhaps for the final time. Each hungry man craved a different food. For von Decken, he suspected, it was plump dumplings and *Preiselbeeren,* the small tart currants of the Rhineland. For Adam Penfold himself, it was the hot *samosas* of the White Rhino, each triangular Indian pastry carefully filled with his favorite spiced stuffings. Chopped brussels sprouts, or the ground meat of Thomson's gazelle, or, after the rains on Mount Kenya, tiny forest mushrooms baked in eland marrow, with just a dash of homemade tamarind chutney. And perhaps a little grouse paste on a biscuit. He closed his eyes.

Often the Germans, askaris and prisoners shared near-starvation. They baked loaves from yams and rice. They burned mangrove shrubs to use the ashes as salt. They chewed on strands of leather cut from the belts of hide that held up a suspended bridge. Penfold supposed there was nothing that, properly chopped and mixed, could not be built into a loaf of bread or, better still, into a cigar. He had seen long-range patrols stagger into camp, Germans and askaris indistinguishable in their wretchedness. Each man was parched like a raisin, unable to speak. Some had sipped their own urine, or the blood of birds.

Every day Adam Penfold was carried along by relays of cheerful stretcher-bearers. The men, black and white, would be strung out in columns miles long, their rifles slung butt backwards, chanting their marching song "Haya Safari" while they forced their way through bush and swamp. Even many captives shared the spirit of the march.

Sucking pebbles to allay his thirst, his litter swinging with the twisting movement of the dusty game trails, the Englishman would close his eyes and feed on the beauty of his distant farms. England and Kenya, Wiltshire and the White Highlands blended together.

Penfold often considered the post-war life that waited for him like an overhanging cliff, a cliff too steep to climb. Secretly he dreaded the challenges of peacetime. The debts, the endless work, the struggle to hold the land. Could he manage it, just getting along, avoiding obvious failure?

Once the war was over there would be no excuse for not proceeding with one's life. Already, seeking to make his fortune in Africa, he had lost it in England. Did Sissy know they were too poor to go home? Year after year he had sold family land in Wiltshire for money to work the land out here. But at least in Africa he could still manage a decent life. Land and servants and sport were cheap enough, and the shabby edges of life did not show as they would in London. If it was properly cut, a frayed jacket would serve in Nanyuki, but not in Belgravia.

He wondered how to use the lessons of this wartime trek, how to improvise and endure. If only, Penfold thought, I could manage my farm and the White Rhino as these Huns run their military safari. At least, once these devils are beaten, there should be more opportunity in Africa. Then the scramble would really begin, like boys breaking out of school onto a playing field. Perhaps Kenya, Tanganyika and Uganda would be nicely patched together into one proper colony, more like India or Canada, rather the way America should have been.

Penfold watched each day as the Schutztruppe was further reduced. The army of white officers and loyal Africans, laced with German settlers and sailors, was originally supported by companies of Arabs from the coast. Like a starving animal, the Schutztruppe had lost its soft tissue first, as many Arabs melted away in the early fighting. Now it was honed down like an old blade, razor lean from long service, and sharper than ever. Penfold estimated that one hundred and fifty Germans still marched, the survivors of three thousand. In addition, five thousand askaris and camp followers, including babies born on the march and African boys belonging to the Arabs, were scattered in camps along the river. Today the Schutztruppe would feast, having captured from the Portuguese more wine and schnapps than they could carry.

"I see you've stopped taking Portuguese prisoners," Penfold said to von Decken.

"Better to let them run off into the bush like guinea fowl. As prisoners, they eat better than they march." The German paused to belch. "At least you British can walk. But why is it, my lord, that your officers decline to fraternize with our Portuguese prisoners?"

"Because of what they carry, Captain."

"Carry? I've never seen a Portuguese carry anything. What do they carry?"

"Syphilis."

"True, but Portuguese vices are German assets. After three centuries of peonage and the chain gang, their Africans welcome us like liberators."

Penfold heard shrill joyous cries from the riverbank. Carried to a slope above the Chambeshi, he looked down upon the slaughter.

Two wounded bull hippos, still more alive than dead, plunged and thrashed in the swirling reddened water. Kneeling askaris fired their Mausers. The animals' wounds blossomed like pink flowers in the stream. Four other hippos, fatally hit as their protuberant eyes peeped above the water like periscopes, settled to the bottom. In three or four hours their bodies would float to the surface. One only, a female, shot while it rushed to its sanctuary, lay dead on the bank, its vast jaw agape. The round yellow ivory of its curved canines glistened with blood.

A bit upstream, the water ran pink where men washed bandages in the river.

Penfold observed the scene, drawing on his port. An African courier hurried to him and handed him a note.

> My Dear Major Penfold:
> I request the honor of your Lordship's society this evening at a Special Mess to celebrate the occupation of Northern Rhodesia, the first British territory to be invaded by Imperial German forces in this *Weltkrieg*.
> We also welcome to our table your Portuguese companion-at-arms, Senhor Vasco Fonseca, and his sister.
>
> P. von Lettow-Vorbeck

Penfold saw the bodies of the hippos in the afternoon. Bloated with gas from the fermenting grasses that stretched their stomachs, they bobbed one by one to the surface of the river like toys in a bathtub. Each three-thousand-pound beast meant not only meat but vast quantities of the white fat so favored by the Africans, a lard so pure and rich that Penfold had seen it melt like butter in the sun. Sometimes, if no one was looking, he used a handful to polish his boots and belt. Occasionally he employed the rib of a hippopotamus to bone his boots.

On the march, lunch was often hippo fat smeared on old bread. Hippopotamus hide, an inch thick and tougher than a rhino's, provided belts and boots and whips. Some men carved false teeth from the hippo ivory, more durable than the tusks of elephant. Others marched with lengths of hippo tongue swinging from their belts.

Now askaris waded out with ropes to haul the carcasses ashore, wary of crocs and covered by the weapons of their comrades. At once the blades were out. Pangas sawed incisions the length of the stomach, then up the throat to the chin and down the inside of each leg. The skinners cut back the hide from the flesh, separating the underside of the skin from the fat and meat beneath, as if a different creature lived inside. Each open body became a meat market, swarmed over by cutting, hacking men, sticky and shiny with blood. They scooped out the three-chambered stomach and chopped off the head and legs. They carved and tore the ruined bodies until nothing survived but offal, stomach grass, severed tails and pools of blood. Each askari ran back to his company's fire with slabs of slippery meat and fat slapping against his shoulders. Bowls of liquid fat were gathered for drinking. Dishes of blood were heated and stirred until they grew warm and thick as liver.

General von Lettow's cook waited by the body of the youngest hippo. Refreshed by the spectacle, his eyes shone when he smiled up at Lord Penfold on the slope above him. Eager cook boys stood behind him with canvas sacks.

The cook stepped forward with a bayonet as soon as the body was open. He jostled aside hungry rivals, loudly proclaiming, "For the General!" He cut the heart free with rapid strokes and lifted it out with both hands like an offering. He propped open the animal's mouth with a shovel and cut out the tongue, his commander's favored delicacy. He dropped both organs in a sack and ordered a boy to guard them as he would his own. Finally, he cut free the ribs and both front legs, thicker than the animal's hind legs because of the immense pear-shaped head they supported.

At least in Africa a man knew what he was eating, Penfold thought. In London no one knew what dinner looked like before the cooks got to it.

Back at his fire, the cook shovelled hot coals into two pits dug as ovens to bake the feet. He cleaned the remaining hide from the legs and rubbed them down with the last of the salt. He covered them in wild onion grass and lowered each into a hole until its four toes stood on the coals. Filling the pits with hot ashes, lest coals burn the meat, he built a fresh fire on top of each and left the legs to bake. Then the cook turned to the tongue.

Hungry, his wine finished, Penfold asked his bearers to carry him to his place near the General's tent. There he found his enemy preparing for dinner. More spare and hawkish than ever, von Lettow took between his fingers the frayed edge of the immaculate but slightly yellowed white mess jacket laid out on his cot. Only the Iron Cross, personally dispatched to Africa by Kaiser Wilhelm, decorated its left side.

"Have I told you, my lord, that I danced in this coat with Baroness Blixen on the ship to Africa in 1914, *The Admiral,* and why I wear it in the bush?"

"I'm not certain you have, General. No doubt your coat has an agreeable history." Penfold thought of his own thirty-year-old suits.

"I wear it, Major Penfold, to remind my men of German standards. It is a stronger tonic than a flogging or an execution."

Captain von Decken strode up and clicked to attention. Two askaris waited behind him with a prisoner and a motorbicycle. "My General, we captured this English dispatch rider on the trail south. He carried this sealed message."

"At ease, von Decken." The commander examined the officer and his equipment. He removed an envelope from the dusty leather satchel, cut it open with his penknife, and twice read the single sheet of paper.

As von Lettow turned and entered his tent, Penfold thought he heard him whisper, "So it ends."

Properly kitted out in his regimentals, von Decken straightened his heavy shoulders and limped ahead of Penfold's stretcher to the officers' mess, this evening a clearing among the acacia trees. Ammunition boxes served as camp chairs. The bamboo flagstaff was planted between two fires, the black eagle of Hohenzollern fluttering gently.

Penfold was relieved to see drinks waiting on the wooden door that served successively as operating platform, bar and dinner table. The officers were accustomed to standing about each evening while the gory stains were scrubbed down with sand. What bounty had the Portuguese provided tonight! Wine, madeira, port, more than even the soldiers could drink.

Men gathered at fires while the sun eased down through the trees, hugely round and red in the settling dust. The African night swiftly stretched an immense blue-black canopy above them. Each soldier had made himself as presentable as conditions would permit. German eagles flashed on brass buttons normally covered with dried mud to avoid reflecting. No uniform was complete. Some men were too weak to stand. But, as the General always insisted, every officer was shaven. The Englishman caught the lean faces of his companions in the firelight and reflected on each man, knowing some too well.

"Welcome to you, Major Penfold." Von Decken bowed slightly to the Englishman. "May I offer you a cup of your own ruby port, Herr von Sueca? How are the ancient allies getting on this evening?"

"Well enough," the Portuguese said. Penfold saw the man turn hard dark eyes on the German officer before he spoke again. "Fonseca." The cunning planter had a gift for conveying his languid arrogance even when speaking in a language not his own. "But may I ask why, Captain, in this stinking wilderness, you and I converse in English? And why, Lord Penfold, you English learn every native dialect but never a civilized European tongue?"

Von Decken drank without replying.

"I congratulate you on your grapes, Fonseca." Penfold rose on his elbows and smacked his lips. "I say, Captain, let's spare another glass for the wounded. Can't have these civilians pinch all the drink. How are you enjoying the British empire, von Decken? Do you find it rather hot?"

"We Germans, my lord, must get used to every climate."

Not for long, you won't, Penfold thought, confident how the war must end.

Servants cleared the door-table. Ammunition cases and one camp chair were ranged about it. Von Lettow and six men prepared to sit. Penfold's litter was set down behind the seats to the General's right. Other guests sat about the fires. Standing at the head, with the empty chair at his right, von Lettow said, "Where is our lovely guest?"

"Senhora Fonseca is nursing the wounded, General," the surgeon said before Fonseca could speak for his sister. "She will join us after she has washed. She asks that we begin."

"The lucky wounded," muttered Captain von Decken. Fonseca glared at him.

Penfold noticed Fonseca's fingers toying with the gold fob watch the man had won from him at cards. A gift from Sissy, the half hunter still worked a few hours each day. The English major had a weakness for gambling. He had learned that this Portuguese, perhaps more skilled at cards than any gentleman should be, had an eye for weakness. A trusting man himself, Penfold had realized too late that Fonseca preferred to cut a deck with men suffering from fever or exhaustion.

Silence held the hungry table. Men tore the fresh camp bread and gulped down the full red wine of Estremadura. Then came fried apples and crisp broiled pork, reminders of Germany, and the last of the herd of swine driven with the Schutztruppe from Portuguese East. Soon the young pig was gone. More bottles were opened. Penfold smelled the rich familiar odor of hippopotamus when servants brought the baked flesh to the table. The General stood and pulled back the chair beside him. Penfold squinted into the shadows.

A long-legged shapely figure, extremely womanly in patched military trousers and a taut khaki shirt, emerged into the firelight. Once again, Penfold was stirred like a boy by the promise of her full lips and thick dark hair.

"Forgive me, General. Have your officers left anything for a lady to eat?"

"Of course, Anunciata." Von Decken smiled eagerly into her enormous deep brown eyes while he reached across to fill her tin cup.

The waiting hippopotamus shank soon received the table's attention. The General himself carved the tongue into thin slices. Penfold noted that as usual the Portuguese took more than his share, particularly of the succulent marrow. Von Decken leaned forward on his crate and addressed Fonseca at the foot of the table.

"The wine and the swine may once have been Portuguese, but the hippopotamus, after all, was Rhodesian, an English hippopotamus, and so is now a German prize of war. Perhaps you have had enough, von Sueca."

"Fonseca." The Portuguese sucked the marrow from his fingers. "Fonseca."

"As it may be. A question for you," said von Decken. "In German Africa, we have proved, even to a man as incurably violent as myself, that the childlike disposition of the native is made more productive by civilizing leadership, rather than by excessive cruelty and indolent example, if you take my meaning. But on your plantation we found whips, blacks in punishment irons, and not one Portuguese at work. Do you find all this efficient, von Sueca, or merely enjoyable?"

"Fonseca, Captain. Efficient? What is efficient? Would you not work harder if I put the bastinado to your back each time you stopped? A little pain helps. But you Germans know this secret. Have you not shown a taste for killing blacks?"

"We kill when we must," said the German.

"For you a black is always a black." Fonseca pointed at von Decken with his fork. His voice rose. "But for us, an educated African is a Portuguese. In Lourenço Marques I take my *mulatina* to the most fashionable cafés and houses, and she is received. But you Germans, and these British, you don't let black women wait on your tables."

"Pass the wine," said von Decken.

"We Portuguese take a long view, von Decken. For centuries my family has advanced our interests in Africa. And we will continue, I promise you. We grow sugar. You eat it. What do you grow?"

"At least we do not grow little tan *totos*!" Von Decken laughed loudly and grinned down the table with his mouth open.

"Excuse a foolish woman," said Anunciata Fonseca in a throaty Latin voice. "What have you Germans or British built in Africa? Dar es Salaam and Nairobi are villages. Our Lourenço Marques has museums and grand cafés, a cathedral and a bull ring. After your war is over, gentlemen, my brother and I will do whatever we must to restore our family's place in Africa. You Germans came yesterday. You may leave tomorrow."

"I am German," said von Decken. The humor left his heavy face. "And I am an African. You will find that I, too, am staying."

The diners turned back to their drink and food. Von Lettow whispered to an orderly. The man passed from fire to fire. Soon the flames flickered alone. Hundreds of men, white and black, Arab and askari, some on crutches and others supporting invalids, gathered in a circle among the shadowy acacias and spreading fever trees.

Von Lettow stood, his jacket stark and ghost-like against the darkness. The firelight was sharp on the drawn lines of his face. Silence fell among the soldiers. Adam Penfold saw the General look over his men with glistening eyes before he gazed up at the four bright stars of the Southern Cross. For a moment Penfold heard only the shrilling of the cicadas and the barely audible grunt of a distant lion.

"This evening, our war is over," the General announced into the night, his message on the wind. "I have word that peace has come to Europe. But we in this camp are not defeated. Tonight we drink to his Imperial Majesty, Kaiser Wilhelm."

From his stretcher Penfold heard scores of voices echo the toast through the trees: "The Kaiser." Vasco Fonseca stood silent, his sister Anunciata seated. In the deep shadows to the General's right, behind the woman, Penfold whispered, "God save the King." As he emptied his cup, his other hand met the olive-skinned fingers that reached down and caressed his bare leg. Penfold closed his eyes.

"You and I will miss our cruel trek," he heard the General continue. "With all its pain and loss, we will not know again such comradeship, such closeness to this magic land. Perhaps one day we Germans will fight again in Africa. Tomorrow each of us begins a new adventure."

BOOK I

1919–1920

— 4 —

Gwenn Llewelyn raised the collar of her worn army greatcoat and leaned into the corner of the abandoned chapel, one of hundreds in the hills of Wales. Through the thick khaki she felt the damp reach into her from the wet grey stones of the wall. She tightened her scarf with stiff fingers and raised her pale green eyes to glance through the open roof. Clouds of mist gusted past against the hillside, filtering through the door and windows of the chapel. The moisture seemed permanently suspended in the air, without the descending pattern of rain, as if its course had no beginning and no end. Gwenn licked her lips to taste the freshness of it.

In France, during the war, she had prayed for days like this. Prayed for the cold wet cleanness of Denbighshire, for the spongy soaking grass of the rocky hills instead of the deep muddy ruts of the Western Front.

She would never forget the noise. The groans and cries of her slippery cargo, the strain of the engine, the unceasing pumping of the French 75s, and the churning of wheels behind her as she lowered the gear uselessly and the overloaded ambulance dug itself in like a good soldier. Usually one of the walking wounded sat beside her, strangely shy and respectful, ready to help if a single man could. Once she had picked the wrong boy, not realizing how he bled. After a time, when the Renault lurched on, he fell forward, loose as a doll. His face struck the windscreen. His body died. She looked down and saw the mud of his boots glistening darkly with fresh blood.

Now it was over. Never again would she see a human body torn open by wounds. And Alan, too, although damaged, had survived. He was still in hospital abroad.

Gwenn twisted the wedding ring on her wet finger and reached into the pockets of her coat. She withdrew the sealed envelope of a telegraph cable and the nubbly woollen mittens knitted by her Gran. She opened the faded yellow envelope and took out the cablegram. The typed words of the text were glued onto the sheet in long grey strips. Here in the hills the short horizontal page seemed such a foreign creature.

The distant messages of wartime always made the relationship still more remote, whether a cable from the War Office announcing Alan's wounding in Mesopotamia, or even the occasional censored letter from her husband himself. Without these dispatches, she could have held together an active memory of how things had been, as their sensibilities began to mesh during the six weeks of marriage they had shared before the war. Jarring, impersonal, untimely, these messages never met her on common ground. She stretched open the creased paper in the deepening gloom.

OUT OF HOSPITAL NEXT WEEK AND DEMOBBED IN BOMBAY
FEELING BETTER SHIPPING ACROSS TO BRITISH EAST AFRICA
TO TRY WIN US A FARM ITS OUR BEST CHANCE GWENNIE
SOLDIER SETTLEMENT SCHEME IS GIVING AWAY FINEST
LAND IN AFRICA THROUGH LOTTERIES AMONG OLD
TOMMIES WILL CABLE FROM NAIROBI PRAY FOR US HOPE
YOU ARE FINE ALL MY LOVE—BWDD WYCH—ALAN

Gwenn drew on her mittens and remembered the afternoon of their first assignation at this abandoned chapel. It was one of those startling spring days the Welsh wait for all year. The soggy heather and the bogs steamed while they resisted the unexpected heat. Even the lichen that covered the stones was unsuited to the sudden warmth. She had watched Alan's slender figure climb slowly to meet her.

Always late, he hurried his steps when he came to the humped stone bridge. He looked up and waved. Climbing, he was distracted by the stones. She smiled when she saw him pause. He touched with

one palm the shiny-smooth slate flagstones that ran past the end of
the bridge. He studied the iron-grey monolith that brooded halfway
up the hill, one of a line that ran north to the Irish Sea. As Alan
came to her he bent and lifted a smooth oval rock. He wiped it on
the heather, cleaning from it dense black sheep droppings and tangled
shreds of wool. He kissed her cheek and offered the stone with an
awkward smile.

"Another man might have picked me bluebells or a primrose," she
said.

"Stones last forever." Alan swept back his long dark hair and
regarded her with poet's eyes. "We'll set it here and add one each
time we come. Then, if you'll have me, Gwennie, our grandchildren
can carry on till it becomes a proper cairn."

He spoke of his grandfather, a quarryman who had made his life
cutting limestone from the valley walls, each day coughing the hard
grey dust of the rock rather than the black grit of the coal pits. From
this one hill, his grandfather taught him, you could see in the stones
below all the history of the Welsh. The monoliths of the Druids, the
Roman road on the valley floor, the distant Norman fort, the abandoned hill chapels of the Dissenters. And the steep dark mountains
of rocky slag from the mines, surrounding some villages like the
black walls of a fortress in hell.

While that warm night descended, Gwenn had asked Alan to stay
out with her, to shelter in the chapel and watch the stars come, as
one rarely could in Wales. If the dawn was bright enough, they might
see the sea. It wouldn't be right, he said, and they had walked down
holding hands. They watched crescent-winged swifts swoop through
the darkening sky and hunt insects with long knife-like dives.

Now again it was dark. Gwenn crouched on her heels in a corner
of the chapel. She worried about Alan's wound and how it might
affect their life together. She shivered and looked out through the
faint lightness of the empty doorway. She stood and beat her arms
against her body, tingling briefly when her nerves came to life. Later
Gwenn sang a schoolish hymn favored by the choirs of her valley.
She thought of the tight tribal life of the village and wondered what
everyone would do when the rest of the men got home. Already
there were strikes in the pits and steel works. Deferred resentments
were coming due. Everywhere returning soldiers looked for work.

What could Alan do here? And what about herself? Gwenn wondered. If Alan won a farm, what would her days be like in Africa?

She thought of the grinding mining-valley life that had made her mother old. Scrimping farthings for each stew and shoe, waiting for the men to come up from the pit, dreading the shrill mortal piping of the steam whistle signalling another accident. And the thing she and her mother hated most: the evil black dust that waited for them snake-like even between the folds of the laundry and the stacked plates in the kitchen.

After the challenges of France, Gwenn feared village life would be an even more spare and limiting confinement. She clenched the cable that was folded in her pocket and felt a surge of excitement as she imagined the possibilities of Africa.

One thing she knew. Come what may, come the devil himself, somewhere she would build a family with a secure place of their own.

Numb, hugging her knees with her hands clasped together, Gwenn let her eyes close as she began her prayers.

After a while she saw lean Druids stalk the valley walls and haunt her among the stones. They brandished long staffs. Their cloaks billowed like bracken in the wind. A flock approached and a ewe bleated when a wolf cut off a trailing lamb. The shaggy long-jawed animal turned to Gwenn, loping towards her with its head close to the ground. She smelled its warm breath when it leapt on her.

Gwenn jumped awake as a tongue licked her face. A sheepdog. A friend. She hugged the animal and rose stiffly. She stepped to the door of the chapel. The sheep, fat and curly grey, were sheltered tight together in the lee of a wall. The morning fog filtered away. The driven clouds parted at the valley's end. A black plume of smoke rose where the dark open wagons of a coal train snaked through the low green pastures. The hard angles of the Norman tower emerged and stood out firmly at the edge of the land. The beginning of the endless grey sea caught her eye and beckoned.

"Damn your eyes, boy!" the pier foreman yelled at Anton through the thick gloom of the harbor's dawn fog. "Stop roving about staring at them crates and get your bleedin' back into it."

Anton bit down hard. He hated being yelled at but could not risk getting tossed off the dock. He gazed along the wall of wooden packing cases that extended into the mist down one of the stone piers of Portsmouth, or Pompey, as the tars called it. From this dock, the old hands told him, the world's first battle tanks and Britain's first canisters of poison gas had sailed for Cherbourg and Le Havre. Now the cargoes were different, and the destinations were Santiago and Sydney, Calcutta and Cape Town. This load was bound for Mombasa, British East Africa.

"Aye, sir." Anton's mind was alive with what the future held for each crated implement and condiment. He saw stacked above him the heavy tools and small comforts of empire, each one boxed and labelled by consignee and contents. To Karimjee Jivanjee Ltd., Nairobi, a Riley's Full-Size Billiard Table, Phosferine Sleep Tonic, White Buckskin Tennis Boots and Tinned Herrings in Tomato Sauce. To the Central African Trading Company in Mombasa, Canon Iron Kettles, Gold Prospecting Pans & Picks, Primrose Cream Separators and Kynock Brass Cartridges. Anton wondered if they were finding gold in Kenya. Farther along, he saw Fordson tractors and Cockshut maize planters lashed to wooden pallets.

For three days Anton and the other dockers had unloaded the bounty of East Africa. His back ached, but his mind buzzed with hopes of what lay before him. All day the booms reached out from the twin masts of the *Guildford Castle,* lowering nets of cargo to the dock. First ashore was a scrawny black-maned lion, listless and rank and disdainful in a tight filthy cage. Saddened by its confinement, Anton turned away to study the packing cases that followed. He examined each black-painted label with wonder: sesame seeds and cedar slats, pecan nuts and antelope hides, ostrich feathers and ivory. Their odor distinct, fifty-pound bags of coffee were piled to one side. Each sisal sack bore the stencil of a mountain over the words MT. KENYA COFFEE, LTD. Anton stared at the image of the majestic twin-peaked mountain. One day he would see it.

Even the shippers were magical: wattle bark and wool from Equator Ranch, horned trophies from Newland & Tarlton, tea and flax from Goshawk Plantation, every case neatly stencilled with the dark profile of a hawk in flight. Anton felt the fierce freedom of each short-winged bird. A scrap of transparent beige packing paper was folded in his pocket, bearing his careful tracing of the hawk. He considered how to make the bird his.

Now this Royal Mail steamer was empty and the job was to repack the holds with all they could carry. As the foreman said, only the rats made the round trip. Nearly invisible, a deep shadow in the mist, the *Guildford Castle*'s sister ship lay in the nearby drydock. Anton heard the echoing sounds of repair while riveters and machinists patched up the pre-war vessel.

Soon the *Garth Castle* too would be bound again for Africa, and Anton would be among people who did not know him as either a gypsy or a gaujo.

Above Anton's head the empty net descended through the fog like a webbed shroud from the heavens. Gathered at the center, the net swung from the loading hook. He looked up just in time and stepped aside.

"Spread her out, lads. Hop it, we're late," said the foreman. "One tractor and the coffee pulpers into the net first. The light muck and the tin roofing on top to hold 'er steady."

Finally the edges of the net were bound up around the cargo to the hook. Anton and a senior docker climbed atop the heavy load, their boots anchored in the frayed rigging of the net. Excited by the work, Anton held a guy rope secured by a seaman on deck. His other hand gripped the loading hook at the top of the net. The grey-haired docker, holding a long gaff, raised his free hand and described two circles in the air. Anton squinted up into the fog when the ship's steam winch engaged and the hook began to rise. He enjoyed the sound of the stretching ropes. The net strained and tightened.

The load rose four feet above the pier, then paused. Under Anton's feet the galvanized corrugated roofing slipped to one side. The cargo rocked. Settling, the lowest corner of the net steadied inches above the dock.

"Away she goes!" the foreman hollered after checking the load. He raised his hand, and the winch began to haul.

Fifty feet above the pier the sheets of tin shifted once more. Separating in layers like a deck of cards, the lower sheets shot down one side of the net. The elder docker lost his footing. The netting beneath him unbalanced and jerked higher while the other side swung down. He dropped his gaff and fell free with a scream. Anton released the guy rope and clutched for the falling man.

For a moment Anton's right hand grasped the docker's belt and waistband. The loaded net, free of the guy, twisted and spun wildly. Beneath the two men the sharp edges of the roofing cut against the rope netting when the winch stopped with a jerk. Anton heard the ripping of the cords as the net tore open. Dockers bolted for safety. Tractor, crates and sheeting crashed to the pier. One man was caught by two falling crates. Another fell mutilated when the slicing blows of the corrugated tin struck his shoulder.

Oblivious of the scene below, Anton clenched the hook with his left hand while the man he held grabbed the tangled spinning net and made himself secure.

"I'm owin' you a rum, young Rider. You've a grip like a freight-car hitch." The grizzled docker smiled down at Anton and the zebra-skinned tattooist seated at the back table of the Old Pompey Cafe. The man led by the hand a young weary-eyed woman, still pretty but seemingly separated from her youth. "And I've brought you a gal to swill it with. If you let Hetty treat you her way, you won't feel them needles old Zebraman here'll be darnin' you with."

"Thank you," Anton said, feeling embarrassed and not knowing what to make of the praise. Hetty caught his eye. She smiled, as if sharing something with him. Anton looked down, more nervous about the girl than the needle.

The wrinkled bit of beige paper lay on the table, facing Zebraman. The hawk was pinned flat by four squat bottles of ink. Anton coughed in the smoky air and watched the tattooist. Broad black and white zigzag stripes covered the ageless face and bald head. They continued down the man's neck, disappearing into a turtleneck jersey and reappearing to cover his wrists and hands.

Anton gripped the far side of the much-carved table with both hands, wondering how much it was going to hurt. His bare forearms stuck to the beer-soaked surface. The woman drew up a stool behind Anton and rested her hands on his shoulders. He stiffened when her fingers touched his neck. What was she going to do?

Zebraman opened the camphorwood lid of his brass-cornered needle case. He selected a whalebone needle. He opened bottles of black, grey and dark blue ink. He stretched the skin tight with one striped hand, and Anton braced for the pain. Zebraman punched the needle into Anton's right forearm while the woman stroked her fingers down Anton's sides to his hips. Concentrating silently, rejecting the ongoing pain, Anton fought to ignore both sensations while he followed the craftsman's work.

Alternately dipping the needle into the inks and jabbing Anton's bleeding skin, Zebraman moved continuously without looking up from his work. The girl pressed her lean body against Anton's back. She lifted a glass of Pusser's Navy Rum and held the dark drink to his lips. Her other hand slipped into one pocket of his trousers.

"You're one of the quiet ones," Zebraman said to Anton while he tightened the caps on his inks. He splashed rum over the tattoo, wiping off the blood and alcohol with a hard hand when he rose. "Some blokes, the weepers, make a lot of fuss when I stick 'em."

Pleased and proud, Anton studied the scabbing, blood-bordered bird. Hetty moved to Zebraman's seat.

"Why did you have that beautiful hawk put on your arm?" she said. "When you move your muscles like that it almost flies."

"I did it so I'll not forget why I went to Africa." Anton prayed he would be glad he went. He was abandoning the familiar life of the forest and the gypsy camps. For nights now he had lain awake, trying to imagine how Africa would be.

"Why are you going?"

"I want to see the animals and be free and make my fortune. There's no good work in Pompey. Every time a fellow gets hurt, ten old soldiers fight to take his place. One day I want to ride my own horse, on my own land."

— 5 —

Welcome home, Bwana Lord!" The turbanned doorman of Nairobi's Muthaiga Club bowed.

"Still on parade, Havildar?" Adam Penfold rocked on his crutches and clapped the old Sikh on both shoulders. The white-bearded sergeant wore the striped campaign ribbons of distant Victorian wars.

"Hurry along, won't you, Treasure?" Lady Penfold called back as she entered the hall ahead of her husband. She examined the wall mirror with cold pale eyes. Her thin lips pursed. She smoothed the flowered print dress that hung from her angular shoulders.

"I gather a few members won't be back to hand you their rifles and sun helmets," Penfold said to the doorman.

"Nineteen died, my lord, in the King's service." The straight-backed Indian cast his eyes down the drive, where a border of Flanders poppies encircled the Muthaiga's memorial cenotaph.

"Sad news, Havildar. Only lions and malaria've cost the club more, if you don't count the fellows drowned by Gordon's gin.

"At least we paid our dues," Penfold muttered to himself as he entered the wide doorway. "We heard 'the bugles of England blowing o'er the seas.' " He knew Kenya's Europeans, seven thousand strong when war came, had lost a larger proportion of men than any other territory in the empire. Of the first two hundred to leave to fight in France, seventy survived. Of all Muthaiga members, over half were casualties.

"Thank heavens they haven't tarted up the place and redone the chairs." Penfold sank into his favorite seat with a groan. Deep and comfortable, its familiar cracked goatskin was mercifully free of repair. He groped for a pipe in the pocket of his bush jacket.

"If I must endure this dreary bar," his wife's voice said, "I do hope you won't spend the entire evening drivelling on with some old bores about how to murder sheep parasites and coffee mites."

"There are no coffee mites."

"Before the war it was those endless lion stories," Sissy said, not hearing him. "Then for four years it was nothing but who bagged the most Huns. Now it's locust control. Why must you farmers always be slaughtering something?"

"Won't you have a Pimm's, dear?" Penfold tapped a crutch on the parquet. He called for drinks and monkey-nuts and realized why he preferred the Muthaiga over his London clubs. The sense of reassurance and ongoing friendship, the preservation of one's little customs, were the same. But there was something else, a tolerance for excess and boyish wildness, the knowledge that while it was all still English, it was not England, that here one could chuck the billiard balls about and smash things up if the crops were bad, or good.

Penfold glanced across the room to the massive fireplace that had befriended so many evenings before the war. Carved in stone in Swahili were the words *Nakupa Hati Nzuri,* I give you good fortune. He thought of old friends and schoolmates he would not see again. He looked to the bar when he heard a man chortle, "Ronnie's heart's back in Africa, but he left his legs in Belgium."

Lady Penfold's thoughts were elsewhere. The tinkling of her ice became her only conversation. She watched her husband empty the dish of unshelled peanuts onto the center of the table. He hadn't changed. "All men are boys," Sissy's mother had told her repeatedly. "All they want are flattery and sweets." There were several types of sweets, Sissy had learned.

How astonishing, Sissy thought, looking about the drab room, deploring its green and cream-colored walls, that her dependable husband, still an attractive man, held no charm for her needy body, while that vile dwarf made her ache with delight. Nor, she had to admit, did Adam seem to have much use for her. He preferred to play with his toy soldiers. When the Penfolds shared a bed, their very body temperatures lowered to the grave. But even to think of that ghastly Olivio was to grow wet as the heat raced through her. Small men, her mother had advised her, made the best lovers, but surely this dwarf was unimaginable.

"You don't suppose they've made that fellow a member?" Penfold said when he saw Spongey Hartshorne enter the bar. He looked away to avoid catching the man's eye. Sissy ignored her husband when he continued.

"No club's ever small enough. That lounge lizard hasn't paid for a drink since he came out. Worse than a Frog. Club should give 'im some sort of prize."

When he noticed Sissy wasn't listening, Penfold grumbled on. "One of those chaps who has the wrong school tie and wears it every day. Always dressing carefully, but not well. Usual government type. Little too shiny, if you know what I mean." Penfold separated the peanuts into two unequal piles, the normal two-nut shells to his left, the special one-nut singles on the right. There was one three-nutter. He hesitated, then ate it first.

Typically, Hartshorne was achieving an eminence in Nairobi that would have eluded him in London, Penfold thought with a dash of jealousy. Worse, Spongey had not heard the bugle's call. Thanks to his service in the Colonial Office, Hartshorne had enjoyed a quiet war, very quiet, occasionally pulling on his gloves to welcome train-loads of sick and wounded when they pulled into Mombasa or Nairobi, and always advancing his influence over land policy, the key to Kenya's future.

Himself a member of the Land Commission, Penfold understood that game. The commission was charged with the tricky job of allocating the land of Kenya, four times the size of England, among the whites and forty-two tribal groups. Blessed with every habitat, from deserts to glaciers, at first Kenya had held land enough for everyone.

Penfold remembered the first morning he had ridden up to the central highlands in '07. He smelled them on the wind before he came over the last of the approaching hills. His mare tossed her head and danced with impatience. The crisp freshness of a Scottish breeze brushed down from Mount Kenya and the Aberdares. But it was a richer softer air, with the promise of warmth within it and the pungent breath of star grass and wild flowers, sagelike brush and cedar forests. How young they all were then.

Cool and green and healthy at six thousand feet, the highlands seemed ideal for European farming, for wheat and sheep, with the hope of tea and coffee at just the right altitudes. Soon Penfold had built a wattle and daub cottage, sold more farms at home, and sent for Sissy. He had been confident she would love it too. And what a paradise it would be for children.

In the evenings the game, the most splendid and varied in the world, wandered past their porch like friends. Best of all, the highlands were white man's country, with no need to dispossess the blacks, for the place was virtually empty, with more antelopes than Africans. Only the haughty Maasai occasionally drifted through, the land too high and cool for their cattle and their way of life.

To Adam Penfold and his fellow pioneers, Kenya had offered the prospect of Eden. But the reality, he remembered, proved cruel. Most were not strong enough for Africa. Others could not adapt. Illness and disease struck every family and crop and herd. Toil and investment were unending. Then came the struggles over land. African traditions of communal ownership, seasonal migration and right of conquest were inconvenient to the settlers. Ancient tribal customs and disputes were overridden by European notions of ownership and the demand for certainty of title. English farms became buffers between the lands of warring tribes.

The 1914 war suspended every issue, deferring painful judgments, returning farms to virgin bush as the men left to fight. Now, in 1919, with the war over, the leading settlers were struggling against the Colonial Office to carve out Kenya's future, trying to reconcile opportunity for old soldiers with a land plan that could work. Penfold, representing the early settlers, but with a sympathy for the Africans that many had yet to learn, understood too well the difficulty of starting up and the need for families with both tenacity and capital. Neither money nor energy was sufficient on its own. He himself, he had learned, didn't have enough of either.

Spotting the Penfolds across the bar, Hartshorne moved to join them, smiling with his soft wide face, his mouth never quite closed, his eyes always a shade too open and prominent, as if constantly staring.

"Evening, my lord, Lady Penfold."

"Hartshorne," Penfold said.

Sissy provided no discernible acknowledgment. In the absence of something more interesting, however, she considered Hartshorne briefly, annoyed by his polished fingernails. She closed her own hands and looked at the man more carefully, noting the large ears and sloped shoulders. There had to be more to this pasty piece of work than met the eye. Too loud and hearty for a pansy, yet devoid of manliness or muscle, she detected in Spongey Hartshorne a craftiness that gave him depth. An ineffective man, she judged, yet always up to something and burdened with that tiresome need to be liked, an ambition she herself no longer nourished. What could he want this evening?

"So tomorrow's your big day," said Penfold without enthusiasm. He looked at Hartshorne over his gin. Now the man was eyeing his nuts. "We'll soon learn if you Colonial Office wallahs know what you're about. Either this Soldier Settlement Scheme'll make this country, or it'll bugger it up for good."

"Right you are, my lord. The greatest land lottery in the history of Africa. We'll be settling fifteen hundred of your old Johnnies on three million acres of raw bush, most of it rough vacant land a hundred or more miles north of here, up past the White Rhino. Should bring you some fun, eh?"

"Have a nut. It won't be a party for these new chaps. They'll need a lot of help." Penfold hoped Hartshorne would not take the last of the single monkey-nuts, a nice fat one.

"They won't be getting any help," Hartshorne said, scorning the nuts. "They're too damned lucky as it is, and now the Colonial Office tells us the interests of the savages are meant to come first. 'Native Paramountcy,' they're calling it in London."

"Hard to say who're the savages," Penfold said. "But at least the Maasai've got their bit. Fifty thousand of those Nilo-Hamitic rustlers wandering about on a reserve bigger than Wales."

"And they're still complaining. Meanwhile the other tribes say it was all their land. Can't win with these filthy sods. If we weren't here, they'd be eating each other."

"We're not so bad at that ourselves." Penfold thought of the Kaiser's war. He polished his pipe on one side of his beaked nose. He watched Hartshorne checking his nails, extending his fingers, the tips up, instead of curling them into his palm like a man.

"Must you smoke that filthy thing?" Sissy Penfold said to her husband without looking at him. The fulfillment some women found in children or the piano, he thought, Sissy found in complaining. Rather like that peevish shrew Xanthippe, Penfold reflected with good humor, thinking of the quarrelsome wife of Socrates.

Penfold looked at his wife. Could this be the same girl he'd met at a jolly Hampshire weekend, everyone madly young and celebrating New Year's, 1900, the first day of a new world? Slightly horsy even then, one had to admit, but schoolgirl fit and in the saddle graceful as a dancer. On New Year's Eve she had cantered with him on the carriage path under a crisp midnight moon whilst the church bell rang in the village. It had never been the same again. Now all they could look forward to sharing were the irritations and afflictions of old age, and even for those they would have to wait a bit. It might have been different if they'd had a child.

Sissy heard a loud American voice and turned her attention to the bar.

"Double whisky on the rocks."

It was Rack Slider, the Yank white hunter. Tall, unavoidable, Slider arched his back against the bar and looked about the room, cocking the worn-down heel of a cowboy boot over the brass foot rail.

"Ready to roll 'em, Spongey?" he called cheerfully to Hartshorne. The civil servant rose to take the challenge.

"For the usual stakes." Hartshorne lifted the leather cup and rolled. "Kindly call me 'James.' "

As five ivory dice tumbled out along the bar, a woman entered, escorted by a dark-faced man in an excessively tailored white suit. Long tan legs, thick chestnut hair and an elegant linen dress draping high buttocks and a voluptuous figure drew every man's attention, and Lady Penfold's instant resentment. For once, Sissy sensed an animal reaction in her dormant husband. He seemed too startled to move when the woman advanced smiling to their table, leaving her companion at the bar.

Penfold stood and extended his hand. Anunciata Fonseca kissed him, leaving a blush of lipstick on his cheek.

"My dear," said Penfold, reddening and turning to his wife, "let me present Miss Fonseca, a wartime friend from Portuguese East. My wife, Sissy Penfold." He stroked his eyebrows nervously. Over Anunciata's shoulder he saw Vasco Fonseca greeting Hartshorne at the bar. What could that swarthy scoundrel want in Nairobi?

"A pleasure, Lady Penfold. Your husband meant so much to us all when we were prisoners of the Germans on that endless march."

"I'm sure," Sissy Penfold said with narrow lips. She noted the woman's poreless olive skin and rich dark eyes. Scarcely a creature designed for bridge and gardening. "What a very unusual campaign. May my husband order you a drink?"

"Thank you, but I must join my brother. He's talking business with a friend."

Penfold watched Anunciata helplessly as she walked away from him. She was even more lush and sparkling than the image of his memory. He recalled stroking her leg while she stood against his stretcher the first evening, Anunciata carelessly unbuttoning her shirt before she leaned over him. Now she was speaking with Hartshorne and her brother at a small table. How typical of the Portuguese to do business in a club. Penfold picked at his pipe.

"What could that Hartshorne friend of yours be doing with those foreign people?" Sissy said in a tight voice.

"Must be some sort of mischief to do with the land scheme." Penfold watched Fonseca open a map and point something out to Hartshorne. "Those two make a charming combination. Worst of both worlds."

After a time, as the bar filled and the noise of drinks and laughter crowded the room, Hartshorne returned to his game with Slider. Finally the American turned the leather dice cup upside down. He emptied his whisky and slapped Hartshorne on the shoulder. "They're all yours, Jimbo. Sure hope you know what to do with 'em."

Waiting in a Muthaiga Club guest cottage, two young figures donned school uniforms. They buttoned white shirts and pulled on grey flannel shorts. Drawing on long green woollen socks and matching sweaters, carefully knotting green and yellow striped ties, the two tied the laces on their practical brown boys' shoes. They gazed into the mirror and adjusted their school caps over one eye. Smiling into the reflection, they turned to one another, nuzzling and hugging, licking and sucking each other's ears. One slipped a hand inside the back of the other's shorts. They heard a key turn in the door. Who would it be? the Black Tulips asked each other. The wild American hunter, or that pale soft-faced Englishman with the sickening tastes?

The Theatre Royal stood out proudly among its shabby, tin-roofed neighbors on Nairobi's only thoroughfare, its uneven boardwalk and tall wooden marquee reminiscent of a Dodge City saloon. Generally the scene of amateur theatricals and public meetings, the Theatre Royal was still celebrated for its chaotic opening-night performance of *The School for Scandal*. Today, it would be home to the first land lottery of the Soldier Settlement Scheme.

At five in the morning, although the doors would not open until nine, Alan Llewelyn and four hundred other white men stood in line, each desperate for a piece of Africa. Exhausted by treks from the bush and the coast, others slept in the ox carts and high-wheeled wagons that extended down the dusty street and into the blue gum trees past the edge of town. A few had walked a thousand miles from Northern Rhodesia. Some, like Alan Llewelyn, stood squinting in the early light, studying the Land Office bulletin posted at the theatre door. Beside it he read posters announcing the East African Boxing Championships, the Repertory Theatre performance of *Are You a Mason?* and Charlie Chaplin's comedy *The Immigrant*.

"What sort of farming have you done, mate?" the man behind Llewelyn said.

"None." Alan sought to keep his weight on his left leg. He felt his pelvis like a hot stone in his body. "I lied to them. I used to be a miner."

"And the C.O. thinks we're all farmers. I was a postman," the man said. "Still, they say the land's so rich out here all you've got to do is chuck in a few seeds or tea bushes and watch the stuff grow like money in the bank. Steady, mate, you're not looking too well."

Alan leaned against the wooden wall and closed his eyes. His body went wet with sweat. Urine trickled uncontrollably down one leg. He felt himself sliding down until he sat on the splintery boardwalk with his legs straight before him.

Alan remembered sitting like this in a horse-drawn ambulance cart on the retreat to Kut after the abandoned march on Baghdad, clutching the rough wooden sideboard in a hopeless effort to hold his lower body steady while the bone splinters moved inside him. For three days the springless wagons bounced along the stony track, pursued by sand flies and mosquitoes drawn to the wounded. Each morning the carts were clean, the blood washed away by the freezing night rains of Mesopotamia.

Alan felt the pain soften and his sweat go cold. He stood and rested against the wall. He thought of Gwenn and his valley in Wales. There men of his family had worked underground for three generations, the hard black dust permanently fixed in their pores and lungs, as much a part of them as their ribs or kidneys. Regularly they lost fathers and brothers to cave-ins and chest troubles. As his friends had joked in the Welsh Fusiliers, at least in the trenches you died in the fresh air, unless the mustard gas got you. For Alan, with a slight build and an injured pelvis, any life must be better than the coal. Lucky to be in Bombay when war ended, he had shipped straight across the Indian Ocean to Mombasa. He knew Gwennie would hold on and give him a chance to see if they could start a life in Africa. Today he would find out.

Like Alan Llewelyn, virtually every European in Nairobi had abandoned his home and come thousands of miles to find land in East Africa. They said there was no business, no crop, no estate in Kenya that would not be affected by the disposition today of the first of millions of acres of Crown Land. Added to the five million acres already officially alienated to Europeans, by the end of the drawings five percent of Kenya's land would be permanently white. Much of it was the best in the colony.

Many Africans, too, recognized the stakes. For years the principal chiefs had struggled to secure their tribal interests: some, like the Maasai, from positions of favor in European eyes; others, like the Wandorobo and Waliangulu, without a strong voice. Few in number, remote, shunning contact, content to gather honey and track game in dense forests of bamboo and cedar, the Wandorobo avoided recognition. The Waliangulu, wiry and tireless, skilled elephant hunters, the finest archers in Africa, always kept their distance. For them, Nairobi was as far as London. Avoiding the white man's process, these tribes and others maintained their customs but in time would lose their wild homelands. When the English claimed the land was empty, they rarely counted these small elusive nations.

Only the Kikuyu understood how to play the white man's land game. Adaptable, instinctively mercantile, often willing to work for white farmers and businessmen, they were benefitting the most from the peace and commerce brought by the Europeans. For generations the Kikuyu had been pillaged and driven from place to place by more warlike tribes, as the Nandi and Maasai burned their huts and stole their children and cattle. Now the Kikuyu, like Chief Kitenji and his village behind the White Rhino Hotel, were settling onto the European farms, obliged sometimes to work but cultivating their own plots and secure for the first time.

This morning, huddled around a low fire at the edge of town, a party of Kikuyu joked quietly about the foul-smelling Maasai they could scent passing nearby, each slender figure wrapped in its blanket cloak and stinking of ochre and animal fat. With luck, these cruel enemies would lose the Kikuyu lands they had stolen.

The sun rose and dawn shadows stretched across the street. Two lamplighters extinguished the oil lamps outside the stone government buildings. The line behind Alan grew. The waiting men became the center of every activity. Crowds gathered to watch, clustered by race and tribe. Arab traders offered ivory and silver trinkets. Indian merchants directed their tea wallahs to hawk biscuits and tea from red copper trays. Nairobi's first photographer trotted up on his pet zebra with a camera bearer jogging behind. Reporters from the *East African Standard* and the Associated Press offered drinks for interviews, hailing this as the greatest real estate bonanza since the Oklahoma land rush.

A grey-bearded Sikh scribe, dignified in a white turban, set up his table under a jacaranda tree and spread his ink and pens and umbrella upon it. A client, writing home to Bombay, bent over and rested one elbow on the table, pinching his lower lip, his chin in his palm.

He looked up to the sky and conceived his romantic dictation, trusting in the scholarly Indian to embellish it.

Cheers went up when four women were passed along to the head of the line, V.A.D.s, the only ladies allowed in the drawing. Like Gwenn Llewelyn, they were Volunteer Ambulance Drivers, female veterans of the Great War. Hardened to slogging overloaded Renault and Ford wagons through the shelling behind the muddy lines of the Western Front, habituated to arriving at sprawling dressing stations to find their bleeding cargoes mingled with the dead, these women were prepared for Africa.

As nine o'clock neared, James Hartshorne arrived in the governor's car, a gleaming four-door convertible Hupmobile. Its top and windscreen were folded down. The silvery spokes of the spare wheels were in perfect polished trim. The leather straps that secured them shone like a guardsman's belt. Stiff and important, Hartshorne was attended by two young assistants from the Colonial Office bearing a fat wicker barrel. Eight black constables, impeccable in creased shorts and polished leather, held the line back from the double doors as Hartshorne approached. The land officer was tightly packed into a three-piece tan linen suit, striped tie and compressed-cork pith helmet covered in white drill.

"Excuse me please, sir, could we see a map?" one soldier asked him. Hartshorne glanced at the man without speaking. He ignored the questions that others urged on him when he passed. After the constables forced the doors shut behind him, Hartshorne examined the hall, irritated to see wide-eyed Africans watching him through every window. A narrow stage crossed the end of the room. Long beams held up a flat ceiling. With chairs in the boxes and dress circle, and benches in the stalls and pit, the Theatre Royal was built to seat two hundred.

"Set tables by the door," Hartshorne said to his nervous aides. "Be certain each man shows his demob papers and a certificate from the Selection Committee. Can't trust this rabble. They'd kill for a scrap of land."

Once all the candidates were approved, the soldiers would draw one by one from the revolving barrel on the stage. The losers would draw blank cards. The winning cards were numbered in order from one to four hundred, denoting the sequence in which the winners would select their plots from the catalogue of farms prepared by Hartshorne's office. Each catalogue listing indicated the farm's acreage, altitude, rental, development conditions and recommended use, whether "agricultural and grazing" or "flax and coffee." No mention was made of resident Africans or native claims, for the major tribes were now assigned their own large reserves, and most smaller tribes still lived about at will.

The farm plots were divided into two categories. There were three hundred and twenty-five small farms of up to one hundred and sixty acres. These were free, except for a modest annual rent of one rupee per ten acres. In addition there were nine hundred and seventy-five larger farms to be sold at three acres for one pound sterling, or thirteen rupees. Of the thirteen hundred farms, seven hundred were to be allotted at drawings in Nairobi, and the other six hundred at lotteries held at the Overseas Settlement Office in London. All the farms would be granted on nine-hundred-and-ninety-nine-year leases and would require investment in permanent improvements and on-site residence by an owner or manager.

Alan Llewelyn had positioned himself to qualify for a large farm, after five days of gruelling bargaining with Raji da Souza, a plump Goan moneylender.

"There'll be one loan for the farm itself, you see, backed by your land title," da Souza had explained to Llewelyn, wagging his finger while he dictated two notes to the Sikh scribe, "and a second loan, at a higher rate, of course, for the monies you shall require to develop it. Your medical pension will back that debt, though it will never be sufficient."

With Indians and Goans forbidden to acquire property outside the town centers, da Souza and his countrymen were obliged to enter the land business indirectly. He himself acted as banker and broker for many Asian lenders and merchants. These included his countryman, the dwarf of Nanyuki, Olivio Fonseca Alavedo. The investors were committing their savings to the land scramble by using debt, not title. In time they would find a way to own the land itself.

Typical British fair play, da Souza thought. They brought thirty thousand Indian coolies to East Africa to build the railroad, thousands of them dying on the job. They allowed the better caste of Indian or Goan, like himself, to set up in business. But they denied Indians and Goans the real riches: land. And all this on the pretext that Asian landholders would upset the Africans. A gifted dissembler himself, da Souza could not help but admire this pretense. The useful British notion of Crown Land also amused him. The fantasy that land in Africa, and indeed all around the world, belonged in the first instance, by fundamental right, to the unseen island king.

Watching from across the street, trying to distance himself from the chattering throngs of filthy Kikuyu, Raji da Souza studied the waiting line, particularly Llewelyn and his other clients. How could these English soldiers let those four women go first?

Da Souza worried about Llewelyn. Too thin and frail for the hardships ahead, with the drained battered look of da Souza's more deprived countrymen, Llewelyn would bear watching should he win. At the same time, the scrawny veteran was incurably earnest and naïve. If he won and brought out his wife, he would work endlessly, his head low, like a circling donkey at a well. "Sometimes," da Souza's grandfather used to say, "the thinnest ass walks the farthest."

In India, the Goan recalled, the British took the money and didn't care who owned the land, as long as Indians did the work. Here in Africa, da Souza would flip the coin.

"Open the doors, let the mob in slowly," Hartshorne said at precisely nine. The straggling line condensed forward. Hard-pressed constables struggled to admit each man in turn, until the hall was packed with four hundred feverish applicants. Hundreds more remained in line outside, obliged to confirm their qualifications at the tables by the door and then wait in an anxious stirring mass while the job went on.

"Lieutenant George Hennell. Captain Henry Duberly. Surgeon Harold Fitzgibbons." James Hartshorne called out each name to an aide as the cards were drawn. Cheers and groans filled the theatre and carried into the street. As winners were named, the odds worsened with every draw.

By late afternoon, it was nearly done. Hartshorne, well nourished backstage with lager and sandwiches, supervised the recording of the winners. Gazing over the shabby pressing crowd below him, Hartshorne wondered why he must do the work and they should get the land. Was he, too, not entitled to his share of Africa? He would get his bit, even if he had to keep some bad company to do it. He thought of the planter from Mozambique. The man fancied himself a Portuguese aristocrat, if there was such a thing. As a foreigner, Fonseca would need help with the Land Office. For a price, he might get it.

"Alan Llewelyn," Hartshorne said, nearing the end. Stunned, Alan gripped his winning card and turned to leave the hall.

Across the street, Raji da Souza stood next to the scribe, questioning the Sikh about the letters dictated that day. Da Souza had watched with distress while four of his five candidates slipped away in defeat, retreating across Victoria Street to the overworked bar of the New Stanley Hotel, already a jostling scene of dismay and jubilation.

Da Souza looked over and saw Alan Llewelyn emerge blinking into the light. Llewelyn spotted him and held up the numbered card. Da Souza had a winner! Even good fortune, however, seemed too much for this Welshman. His pale demeanor was unchanged. His dark hair fell over tired eyes.

Da Souza led Llewelyn down the street, lending him coins to telegraph his wife and swiftly chaining him with debt. At the same time, the Goan reminded himself, Llewelyn must be helped to think the farm was truly his own. Why else would a man toil ceaselessly for nothing? Just to keep things honest, however, da Souza would place an African, Arthur, on the Llewelyns' household staff.

Now the job was farm selection. Llewelyn was entitled to choice No. 47 among the larger plots. The trick was in knowing more than the land catalogue revealed.

Rarely had da Souza heard anything in life honestly described, even a basket of curry powder. He knew from his friends and debtors among the government clerks, most of them Indians and Goans, that today there would be few exceptions to this ancient rule. With their help, he had devised a ranking of his own, not perfect, but truer than the catalogue's descriptions of the plots. As the first forty-six choices were made, the Goan crossed each off, cursing some and nodding at others.

"Now it is our turn!" da Souza whispered fiercely to Alan. He seized Alan by the sleeve and was alarmed to feel the bone of the man's arm. It was nine-thirty in the evening. The lamplighters had just finished their rounds. "If you want my monies, Mr. Llewelyn, you will select farm Number Eighty-eight. It has water and will make you rich."

Exhausted, his wound pulsing, Alan Llewelyn nodded without speaking. He reentered the Theatre Royal. Thinking of Gwenn, he chose farm No. 88. Two thousand two hundred acres set on the Ewaso Ngiro River. Seven hundred and thirty-three borrowed pounds for his family's future in Africa. He would try and do his best.

— 6 —

The S.S. *Garth Castle* steamed south past the coasts of France, Spain and Portugal with four hundred and twenty settlers and other passengers crammed into her aging decks. She sailed east through the Straits of Gibraltar and the Mediterranean. After a coal-bunkering stop at Port Said, she slipped through the Suez Canal and steamed south down the hot passage of the Red Sea, making steadily for the open waters of the Indian Ocean and the East African ports of Mombasa and Dar es Salaam.

Anton Rider worked as an under steward, earning his passage by swabbing out bathrooms and dining halls on the well-worn vessel. Forced to sign on for the round trip, he omitted to tell the recruiting officer he planned to jump ship in Mombasa. Through the stink and slop of his job, all Anton could think of was walking free into Africa. Now eighteen, tall and whipcord fit, he had the arms and shoulders of a prizefighter after a year as a stevedore on the Portsmouth docks.

At night, his duties done and the plank decks alive with heat-struck passengers, Anton would climb to the cage-like lookout's nest on the forward mast, avoiding the smoke that streamed aft from the ship's single raked black funnel. Far below him the crowded vessel vibrated with the drive of the steam boilers, and the sea spread to the edge of the sky in a perfect dark circle. Anton would lose himself, trying a cigarette and watching the moon and the stars hang over

Africa. The night sky grew ever more broad and clear as they sailed
past the Sudan and Ethiopia.

One evening, after more than three weeks at sea, the white vessel
hugged the coast and made the turn south around the horn of So-
malia. The phosphorescent ocean glowed and sparkled. A perfumed
hot wind blew off the desert and brushed the water. Anton smelled
Africa.

He closed his eyes and remembered the diaries of the old African
hunters he had read by lamplight in England. Frederick Selous,
nineteen, setting off alone on a thousand-mile walk with a double-
barrelled rifle and two pounds of tea. Gordon Cumming diving into
the Limpopo with a knife and a leather rope to secure a wounded
hippopotamus. Would he find the life they knew? Was he ready for
it? Sometimes a knot grew in his stomach when he thought of it. He
remembered the tale of Selous as a schoolboy in England, sleeping
on the wooden floor by his bed. Found by his headmaster, Selous
explained, "I am going to be a hunter in Africa, sir, and I'm hardening
myself to sleep on the ground."

Anton breathed in and saw already the dusty dry bush, the endless
landscapes and the incredible animals that awaited him.

His dreams were interrupted by singing from the deck below.
Hearty Irish voices shared an old tune from the trenches.

> She was young, and she was tender,
> Wictim of a willage crime.
> 'Twas the squire's 'orrid passion
> Wot robbed 'er of 'er honest nime.

Anton learned the *Garth Castle* was built in 1910 for the long run
between Southampton and Bombay. At 7600 gross tons she was
designed to carry two hundred and seventy passengers in two classes,
first and third. Refitted as a troop ship in 1914, for four years she
hauled to England her share of the million Indians who fought with
the British army, faithfully returning the wounded on each voyage
out. The dark men who made it back to Bombay bore two memories
of empire: the mud-deep trenches of France and the rusting hospital
cabins of the *Garth Castle*. In 1919 the Colonial Office needed a

ship to transport the soldier settlers and their families to Africa. The *Garth Castle* was just the vessel.

Berthed in the lower decks, where the perpetual trembling of the engines shook rivets from the bulkheads and kept the hammocks swinging, Anton's shipmates talked about the Indians.

"If you batten these portholes," a seaman said one night, "you can still smell the gangrene and the stinking curry. Some of 'em must be down below there yet."

"And when you button up," said his mate, "I can hear them wounded cryin', and that chatterin' Hindi racket from the old cabins by the shaft."

In addition to married passengers, the ship carried forty-five betrothed women going out to Kenya on their own to meet their fiancés in Mombasa or Nairobi. The unmarried veterans were paying court by the time the *Garth Castle* passed Gibraltar.

Anton looked down one evening from his crow's nest into an open lifeboat. The stout wooden hull was painted white with black trim. It was suspended by chains and pulleys. The boat hung over the edge of the sea like a giant wooden crib. Nestled inside, an impatient bride-to-be was entangled with a soldier on the bottom of the boat. The girl's blouse lay crumpled in the bow, the man's trousers beside them. The girl gazed up towards the sky across the man's shoulder, astonishing Anton by smiling and waving at him behind her lover's back.

The next afternoon the lifeboat girl, pigeon plump and friendly, stopped Anton on deck. "Was that you sitting in the sky," she said, "or was I dreaming?"

"You were not dreaming, miss."

"For heaven's sake, how do I know if my Charlie's still waiting?" the girl said, defending herself. "A girl's got to worry about her future. I don't want to get to Africa and find myself without a man and a farm, now do I?"

"I guess you don't."

"My girlfriend says it's her last chance to have fun. Maybe you'd care to meet her."

Anton blushed as she looked him over with friendly eyes. Nervous, he thought how white and inviting her full bare breasts had been in the night.

"I think she'd like you," the girl said.

Later, spotting the girls together, Anton found himself feeling disinterested and avoided the introduction.

Gwenn Llewelyn pulled the woolen shift over her head, relieved that her cabin mate had gone on deck. Naked save for her corset, stockings and shoes, she caught her reflection in the cracked mirror that was secured to the wall. Gwenn rarely possessed the time or inclination to study herself. But for the first time since the war began, on the *Garth Castle* she sometimes had a few hours to herself. She was concerned about her new life, and her husband, and how attractive she would be to him. Gwenn seated herself and looked into the glass.

Mercifully, she thought, the light was dim. Forgiving, if not flattering. Gwenn did not feel her best. She did not sleep well in the airless interior cabin. The dining hall and the public rooms were crowded and smoke-filled. There was no privacy. It was difficult to bathe. Only the deck and the ocean gave her pleasure. And even on deck she found it hard to be by herself. There was one man who never left her alone. One of two brothers, both heavy drinkers and rumored to be violent, he frightened her with his persistence. Claiming to be a soldier friend of her husband, the big Irishman followed her about, denying her peace. Always, she sensed, he was on the edge of making some advance.

Gwenn stared at the mirror and recalled her mother's preoccupation with growing old. She began to examine herself.

Thanks to the voyage, her face and hands had color. Her clear skin rose over high cheekbones, but her cheeks themselves were still a trifle gaunt. Her full lips seemed pale. The circles beneath her eyes had not quite disappeared. The war, she saw, had not yet left her. Would this be true of Alan?

She straightened her back and noticed the slightly boyish shoulder bones that were set squarely below her long neck. Her breasts had not changed. She covered one with her hand and held it, enjoying the touch. Not so large as some girls', but still high and firm and shapely. Her lower ribs were a bit prominent, almost bony above her flat stomach and tapered waist. Gwenn frowned. When she was thin, her ribs were always a problem. I could use a few pounds before Alan sees me, she thought, but I'm not too bad for twenty-seven. Sometimes she felt unused and wasted, as if her body missed a man and children.

Gwenn moistened her lips. She bit the edge of her lower lip several times and watched it redden. She arranged her tawny hair with her fingers. Gwenn turned her head from side to side and gazed into the glass with her chin high and her mouth closed. Light and almost straight, her hair nearly touched her shoulders when she released it. She tried to look into her eyes, always her best feature, her Gran had said, but she could not make out their color.

She heard a sound at the door. Gwenn stiffened, feeling her nakedness. She stood and snatched her dressing gown from the narrow bunk. A loud knock rocked the metal door. Too late, she raised her hand to slide the bolt closed. The handle turned. She hoped it was not him.

"It's me," an Irish voice said as the door pushed inwards. "Mick."

Gwenn stayed where she was in the narrow entrance. She belted her robe in a tight knot. A large red-haired man filled the doorway. Gwenn blocked his way. He leaned over her and clutched her shoulder as he stopped himself.

"I asked you to leave me alone, Mr. Reilly," Gwenn said, pushing his hand from her shoulder. She smelled the alcohol and the sweat of his body.

"We'll just sit on yer bunk and take a drink together." Reilly smiled and drew a bottle from one pocket. She tried not to notice the uneven yellow teeth. He reached for her waist with his other hand.

Gwenn flinched but held her place on the threshold, fearful he would enter and shut the door. She moved her arm to ward off his grip.

Steps echoed towards them down the passageway. Gwenn recognized the first mate approaching with two sailors.

"Goodbye to you, Mr. Reilly," she said in a loud voice, drawing the attention of the men. "Goodbye."

"No worry, girl," Reilly said. "I'll be back." He patted Gwenn's cheek and left her.

———

Each day Anton searched out crewmen with knowledge of Africa. Most seamen knew only the ports, Mombasa or Lourenço Marques, Port Elizabeth or Cape Town, and held no more than the memory of a few lost days ashore. Only the ship's doctor seemed to know about Africa as it might be.

"Life won't be any easier in Mombasa than in Pompey, my lad," the grey-whiskered physician told Anton one evening as he stirred his whisky with his middle finger. "And the jobs you know, the hard physical sort, are all done by the blackies. Work's hard to find for a white man, except on the farms, and that's killing and useless unless the land is yours. Can you do anything else?"

"I can hunt," said Anton. "What about ivory, or gold?" He thought of the gold coins so loved by the Romanies, each one both an adornment and a store of treasure.

"So far the gold's only a few lonely grains here and there, though they say miners are coming out on every boat, poor sods. And there's no money in ivory anymore. The old days are gone when you could find big tuskers everywhere and live like a lord on their teeth. Today you might scratch a wee living selling lion skins and antelope meat, and a few tusks, but there's no future in it. Even the racket of leading rich visitors into the bush, safari hunting, has shut down tight since the war. Now no one has the money."

"I'll find a way," Anton said. Whatever he faced, it couldn't be worse than the confinement of life in England.

One night, after a long talk with the doctor, Anton descended a metal companionway that connected the passenger deck with the lower decks. Suddenly he heard a woman scream. He paused to listen. Anton heard a second muffled, horrified cry. He ran down the long passageway to the door of an isolated cabin.

He burst in. A large red-haired man was bent over a woman on the steel deck. The woman screamed and thrashed hysterically. The man hit the woman open-handed across the face. Her head knocked back against the deck. The woman's blouse lay torn and crushed under the man's bare knees. Her long skirt was gathered high over her stomach with her ripped underclothes. A man's trousers and belt lay on the deck. The red-haired man was still inside her.

"Get off her!" Anton yelled, stepping towards them. "Leave her alone!"

The man returned his hand to the woman's naked chest. He pressed roughly against one breast to hold her body down. His other hand gripped her wrists above her head. The woman yelled and writhed. Her green eyes stared with fury through wildly tossing sandy-colored hair.

Stunned, hesitating for an instant, Anton felt a surge of rage. His muscles tightened.

"Get the hell outa here!" the man roared.

Anton seized him around the head. He felt the man's sweat and spittle wet against his arm. He inhaled the stink of the panting body. For the first time, Anton smelled the odors of sex. The man's face was caught in the joint of Anton's right arm. Anton twisted violently. The man grabbed Anton's belt with one hand and fought to pull him down. Anton heard the cracking of cartilage in the thick neck. The man screamed. The heavy body was wrenched from its victim. Freed, the woman rolled into a ball against the edge of the bunk.

The enraged man struggled to his feet. Belted with muscle and fat, his heavy white body was spotted with pale freckles and matted with moist red hair. Anton stepped in front of Gwenn. He crouched and faced the rapist with his gypsy knife. The man lunged. He missed Anton with a club-like blow. Anton's blade cut a fine line along his jaw. The man turned in the narrow space. He watched the sharp choori from small tight eyes. He put a hand to his jaw and cursed when it came away red with blood. He glared into Anton's steady blue eyes and paused.

"More?" asked Anton.

"You'll pay for this, boy. I'll not forget you." Blood slipped down the front of the man's neck. He hauled on his trousers and made for the door. "And if you ever speak of it, I'll kill you."

Anton covered the crying woman with a bed sheet. He felt the smooth warm skin of her shoulder under his hand when he helped her onto the bunk. There she turned moaning to the cabin wall. She struck the metal bulkhead with the side of her fist and shrank away when Anton sought to comfort her. Feeling intrusive yet wanting to help, he went to the door and looked back at her. The woman sobbed and gasped. She was still beating the steel plate with her fists.

"I'll get some water," he said quietly. As Anton left, Gwenn retched and vomited against the wall.

Returning with a bucket, soap and a towel, he put them inside the cabin door and urged the speechless woman to bolt it after him. He glimpsed her naked torso when she reached for the towel. Slightly ashamed, he closed the door and hurried down the passageway.

The next afternoon, making his round of chores, Anton spotted the heavy-set Irishman standing on the open deck below him, joking with a group of Tommies. Among them was another, even larger, red-haired man. Brothers? Anton wondered. The man with the wounded face glanced up. Anton met the small eyes for the second time. The man stared hard and Anton turned away.

That evening Anton saw the woman sitting alone in the third class dining saloon. Startled by her beauty, he remembered her skin and her smell and her young-girl's breasts. Feeling guilty to find her attractive, at first he could not believe it was she.

Her eyes were the clear luminous tone of light green apples. Tall and graceful, with rounded cheekbones, perhaps six or eight years older than himself, she was too perfect. The bruise on one side of her face did not mar her. Embarrassed to be staring, Anton continued awkwardly across the room with a stack of filthy trays. The second time he did this, she rose and approached him.

"I must thank you. It was a nightmare. I can't believe it happened." She looked up at him. Anton saw tears in her eyes. "And you're so young. My name is Gwenn Llewelyn."

"I'm Anton Rider."

She paused and sought to compose herself before replying. But the shock of the rape rushed back at her. Rage and anger filled her. Gwenn felt herself flush. She could not speak.

After a moment she gathered herself, determined not to be dominated by the horror. She added calmly, "I'm on my way to join my husband in East Africa. You must never speak of this, never. On your honor. That man who attacked me, Mick Reilly, knew my husband during the war. They say he and his brother killed two men in Galway the day before they signed up. Watch out for them."

Busy with his duties, Anton felt excitement build on the ship as Christmas and Mombasa grew closer.

"For these families," the doctor said one warm evening, stirring his whisky, "it's more important than for you. You're just going out like one of those besotted hunters in the old days, with your scruffy cap set for freedom and adventure. You're a boy, though a damn big one. But these families've sold everything at home. Many ain't so young. For them, Africa's the last drink in the bottle."

Caught up in the intensity of expectation, Anton one afternoon turned down a narrow passageway on a lower deck. He recognized the huge man coming towards him, the deck companion of the rapist. Behind him Anton heard heavy steps echo along the metal deck. After twelve months on the docks of Pompey, Anton was no longer surprised by violence. He slipped out his knife and put his back to the bulkhead. He felt his stomach harden. He turned his head and recognized Mick Reilly coming up behind him.

"There'll be no more carvin', you young cock." Reilly lifted a fire extinguisher from the wall. The other man rushed forward. Reilly swung the brass cylinder across Anton's shoulder, paralyzing his right arm. The knife fell to the deck. The two men opened the door to the donkey boiler room. They dragged Anton inside as the boy struggled. He slammed the head of the larger man against the steel doorframe, but they held him and shut the metal door behind them.

The two men looked around in the dim light of three small portholes. The bigger man pulled Anton towards the steampipe that powered the ship's windlasses and winches. Reilly found a stretch of exposed pipe where the protective plaster and sackcloth lagging was frayed and hanging loose. He slapped the bare pipe with his palm.

"This'll do the job, Paddy." Reilly winced. "She's flaming 'ot."

Paddy dragged Anton over. He twisted Anton's good arm behind his back and ripped off the boy's right shirt sleeve from the shoulder. He pinned the inner elbow joint against the hot pipe.

"Just look at 'is pretty tattoo," said Reilly. "Let's leave a little grilled meat for that bird of 'is to feed on."

Pain seared through Anton. He kicked out, jerking wildly, and caught Mick Reilly in the crotch. The other man clubbed him on the side of the head. Reilly was bent over, cursing, on his knees. Paddy returned Anton's arm to the steampipe. Anton smelled scorching skin and flesh. Blood ran down his arm from the edge of the smoldering wound. Paddy lifted the burned arm from the pipe. Skin and blood adhered to the rusted metal. The big man examined the wound.

"Is he cooked?" Reilly asked, rising.

"Not quite done." Paddy pressed Anton's arm to the pipe for the third time. He held the open wound tight against the metal. Anton fainted.

"That'll teach 'im for now," Reilly said. "Best not do any more on the boat. But if I ever catch the bastard ashore, I'll kill 'im."

The men flung Anton down. They left the auxiliary boiler room. Paddy collected Anton's knife before they hurried down the passageway.

The pain woke Anton. The inside of his arm was a charred mess of blackened dry blood, wrinkled raw flesh and gory blisters. He got to his feet, gasping with agony. He searched vainly for his choori, then lurched to the doctor's cabin. The physician opened the door in his dressing gown.

"You're growing up too fast, my fine lad, but the *Garth Castle*'s seen worse." The doctor handed Anton his whisky glass and examined the wounded arm through his spectacles. "And to think it's almost Christmas. How did you earn this?"

"I can't tell you, sir." Anton flinched, then struggled to be silent while his friend dressed the wound. Determined to keep the rape a secret, Anton would say no more, even while he and the doctor finished the whisky. Later that night, with the pain molten and throbbing like a drumbeat, Anton did not sleep. Damn, he thought, he had left England to put the bastards and their beatings behind him. And now even here he was getting beaten once more. It would not happen again.

In Africa, no gamekeeper, no foreman, no steward would tell him what to do. But would he find his world of freedom and adventure? At last he should be free to walk and ride and wander like the old hunters, with a rifle in his hand. He would stalk and sleep where he willed. He'd have a bit of money in his pocket and a friend or girl to share his fire. He thought of the peaks of Mount Kenya, stencilled on the coffee sacks in Portsmouth.

Anton avoided Gwenn all the final day. His right arm ached in its sling, and he was anxious to avoid recounting what had happened.

The boat stayed awake all that night, celebrating Christmas Eve. Union Jacks were garlanded between the masts. Soldiers and their families talked and sang under tan canvas awnings on the crowded decks. Anton noticed several prospective brides in the shadows, taking passionate or tearful leave of shipboard loves. Married that morning by the ship's captain, the lifeboat girl and her new husband were not to be seen.

Copies of A *Christmas Carol* were passed from group to group while families gathered under deck lamps to read aloud. A party of children, carolling beside the lifeboats on the port deck, sang the old songs of an English Christmas. Filled suddenly with loneliness, remembering gypsy winters by campfires in the frost, Anton was not the last to cry.

He paced up and down the starboard deck, looking west towards the coast he could not see. Anton sat on a ventilator near a lamp and drew a book from the pocket of his corduroy jacket. He searched for the passage.

> *It was a long and gloomy night, haunted by the ghosts of many hopes, of many dear remembrances, many unavailing sorrows and regrets. I went away from England.*

"What are you reading?" a woman's voice asked.

"*David Copperfield.*" Anton looked up and rose to his feet. How lovely she was. "He's just left home."

"What happened to your arm?" Gwenn raised her hand.

"I fell on the companionway." Anton hesitated. "It'll be fine."

"Is that really what happened?" She touched his sling with her fingertips.

God rest ye merry, gentlemen, the singing voices interrupted. *Let nothing you dismay.*

Anton looked down to where Gwenn still touched his arm. He saw the long fingers, straight and slender, and the clear veins on the back of her hand.

"Would you like me to read your hand?" he said, surprising himself. "It's beautiful."

"I'm not sure." Gwenn hesitated before she turned over her right hand. "Well, yes, why not? I'd love you to."

Anton took her hand for the first time. He felt almost light-headed touching its smoothness. He led her closer to the light. Carefully he squeezed the edges of her palm together. The lines deepened between the ball of her thumb and the bottoms of her fingers.

At once he knew it was a mistake. He glanced up without speaking and looked into her eyes, less green now, almost smoky grey in the uneven light of the deck lamp.

"Tell me what you see," she said, putting lightness in her voice.

"Perhaps we shouldn't do this on Christmas Eve."

"Please tell me the truth."

"Most important is the line of head." Nervous himself, Anton was surprised by her relaxed hand and calm demeanor. He resigned himself to telling the truth.

Anton cupped her fingers inside his left hand. He pointed to the horizontal line that crossed her palm. "Yours is straight and clear and deep. You have intelligence and purpose. But it's not quite connected to the line of life that circles the mounts of Venus and Mars here at the base of your thumb. That means you're independent, and daring, with a purpose you will not yield."

"And my heart?"

"Your heart line rises between the first and second fingers, there, from the corner of Jupiter. Your affections are calm and deep. You will sacrifice yourself, and you don't expect too much." He paused to look at her face as he felt her warm hand easy in his.

"And the future, Anton?"

"Your fate line rises directly from your line of life, here, so at first your life will be hard and difficult. Then it continues on its own, towards the top of your hand, so you will prevail. One day you will be happy, but . . ." He recognized the threatening island that broke the fate line on her Plain of Mars. He knew what the drooping curve of her marriage line meant in gypsy lore.

"But?" she asked. Gwenn's face paled when Anton reluctantly released her hand. "Don't be afraid to tell me the truth."

"But first you will suffer."

For a long moment Gwenn looked him in the eye. Did she understand?

"Well," she said, trying to smile, "I certainly hope you're wrong."

She turned, and they both gazed over the port rail to the swiftly brightening sky. Gwenn looked forward along the deck. She saw Reilly drinking and laughing with his brother near the bow.

Gwenn felt herself chill and grow nauseous. She felt dirty. Humiliation and anger boiled within her. She could kill him. How would she feel, she wondered, if she murdered such a man? Would the humiliation and the hate be gone?

With the children at last asleep, snuggled together like puppies in clumps around the deck, a broad arc of light hovered on the horizon to the east. The *Garth Castle* altered course on a westerly bearing toward the coast of Africa.

Anton and Gwenn watched in silence. They stood side by side with their hands on the rail, Anton intently aware that they were almost touching. He glanced down at their hands, wanting to put his over hers.

Mombasa's Kilindini Harbor opened wide before them as the early sun struck it. Coconut and mango trees, bright chalk-white walls, red roofs and Arab houses welcomed them. The ship dropped anchor outside the reefs. Scores of small-boats and lighters swarmed towards her from the shore. The wide sandy beach was crowded as all Mombasa turned out to greet the settlers.

Dumbstruck, overwhelmed by the reality of arrival, Anton looked down over the gathering boats. At last he was in Africa.

"Where will you be living?" Anton asked after a time.

"Up near Mount Kenya."

Anton was caught by a thrill of recognition, thinking of the stencilled coffee sacks.

When he did not reply, she looked up at him, taken for an instant by the vivid blue of his eyes against the morning sky. How alive this young man was, how different from the quiet husband she remembered.

"Our farm's on a river north of Nanyuki," she said.

"I think we'll meet again." Anton thought of the twin-peaked mountain. "I may jump ship at Dar es Salaam."

"Good luck, and happy Christmas."

"Happy Christmas." He bent and hurriedly kissed her cheek. "Goodbye."

"All ashore as goin' ashore!" a bosun hollered from the gangway.

Surprised by the kiss, sensing his nervousness, Gwenn smiled.

"Goodbye," she said. "Perhaps one day we'll see each other in Africa."

Gwenn left Anton. She took charge of her tin boxes and worn leather trunks. She climbed down the gangway and stepped into a pitching surfboat. The small vessel moved off and crashed through the breakers towards the beach. Gwenn felt the fresh wind clean her. She turned once and waved, tossing her head. He could not see her eyes, but her tawny hair rippled with the wind.

"Don't think of goin' ashore, Rider," the chief steward bawled at Anton. "There's work, and we're late for Dar. And you new lot don't get paid till we're home in Pompey. Now get yerself below and swill out those cabins."

What brings your brother and you up to our desolate part of the country?" Olivio heard Lady Penfold ask Anunciata Fonseca. He detected a rare effort at insinuating friendly curiosity into her voice. Clearly the lady suspected her husband had resumed a wartime intimacy. Perhaps she had spotted his lordship slinking down the hallway. Why else would she show interest in another woman?

If only Olivio himself could be Lord Penfold with his master's mistress, instead of with his wife. How sublime that would be. In a moment he must go upstairs and examine the baggage of these Portuguese guests. With the war over, things were getting interesting at the White Rhino. Who knew what mischief was at hand? Particularly with his lordship away at the coast, greeting the new settlers.

The dwarf lifted the empty coffeepot and slowly wiped the table while the two women ignored him.

"Vasco is looking over some properties a bit to the north," said Anunciata, "and invited me to join him. He thinks there might be a future up here."

"That would be a surprise," said Sissy Penfold.

The dwarf retreated with a small bow when the women rose and stepped down from the verandah of the White Rhino. He tightened his nostrils and tried not to inhale the stink of horses as he passed the stable on his way to the Penfold bungalow. He himself always avoided the towering beasts, fearing their long-legged menace and resenting the artificial stature they added to other men.

"Do you ride frequently, my dear?" Sissy asked Anunciata while the two women strode to the stable.

Sissy noticed how flatteringly her borrowed twill breeches covered the Portuguese woman. Her derriere was high and round enough to grip the male eye, yet tight enough to be a woman's envy. Still worse, her belt was cinched in more than when Sissy herself wore it. Yet the woman filled her shirt like a bursting fruit. How old could the swarthy tart be? Trying to appear twenty-six or twenty-seven? But tiny suggestions of lines around the eyes and mouth suggested thirty, perhaps thirty-two, even thirty-three or thirty-four. These olive-skinned bitches lined later, Sissy's mother had warned, thanks no doubt to their oily skin. Once they began to fall apart, mind you, they were nothing but bags of runny dark suet.

Certainly, Sissy thought, she had every right to snuff out any lingering liaison her husband might enjoy with this dusky vampire. Whatever her own indulgences, and one couldn't count the absurd dwarf, it was impossible to have her husband fiddling about at the hotel itself.

"Sometimes we rode at the plantation in Mozambique," Anunciata said, "but Vasco scares me when he rides, and he's hard on the horses."

"I'm sure. Why not try Mercy here? She's not too high and she has an easy trot." And quite a gallop too, Sissy thought. She had chosen the mare with care. Coffee planting and training these hopeless servants rarely amused Sissy, but when it came to dogs, horses and intimate distractions, she acknowledged herself a wizard. She remembered Mercy as a three-year-old in the Somali Handicap at the Nairobi race meeting just before the war. Hysterically competitive, the mare strained from the drop of the flag, ignoring her Arab jockey and closing to a heart-bursting second place. Soon, Sissy thought, she would see what those perfect Portuguese legs could do with something other than a man.

Sissy glanced up before mounting her hunter. She saw the curtain flutter in her bedroom window. Was that Olivio peering from the window, his peculiar round head shadowed inside the sill? Was the wretched creature interested in her, or in this Portuguese? The syce, her horseboy, lengthened Anunciata's stirrups. Three prancing whippets joined the riders when they set off down the dusty drive.

So the mongrels were going too, Olivio observed. He remembered the day the hideous beasts had arrived from England. It was the last time he had seen the lord and lady share a pleasure. Alight and giddy with excitement, they had romped like children with the slobbering hounds. The worst of the beasts, Guinevere, had twice knocked Olivio down on her first day at the White Rhino. Exhaustingly friendly and nervous, Guinevere had jumped up, making the dwarf ridiculous. Insulting him before the servants, she leaned her front paws on his shoulders, soiling his uniform and smearing his face with her long thin tongue. After a few days he had been obliged to poison her, using a rather slow and painful mixture, the better to simulate illness. Only the evil cook, Olivio suspected, guessed whence justice had come. But the other dogs understood and had learned to leave the dwarf alone.

He turned away from the window.

The two women climbed through the cool hills behind the hotel, trotting between rows of coffee plants and shade trees. Foamy white blossoms lay scattered about as the ten-year-old coffee trees came into berry. Little though she cared, Sissy recognized that some plants were robust, with pairs of glossy evergreen leaves and clumps of hard berries. But most bore only wizened raisin-like dots where shiny green and red berries should have flourished.

From the corner of her eye Sissy saw Anunciata posting easily. How could Adam sleep with such a tramp? The woman's thighs were firm in her breeches as she rose smoothly with her horse's gait. Her form lacked discipline, of course. She slouched slightly, with her small feet too level to the ground, but the Portuguese had a feline smoothness as she moved with her eager mount.

The whippets were a more serious problem. Even for whippets, they were now too lean, too short-haired, too nervous, all their taut virtues strained to excess by this noxious land. Their prominent ribs showed through like the bars of a bird cage under a nighttime mantle. Lancelot, the leader, carried an ugly scar across his wiry grey shoulder. The survivors of fourteen, once the finest whippet pack in Wiltshire, the hounds, like most things from home, were too good for Africa. Bred for generations to put up stag and hare, too swift and keen to abandon any chase, here their breeding was destroying them.

Four had died in seconds before her eyes, hunting lion. Coursing across a valley after a great dark-maned beast, in a scene she conceded compared favorably to a wild Irish hunt, the pack finally exhausted the lion's patience. Turning at bay, the dogs snapping about it, the lion let them close. Faster than any creature she had seen, the lion slapped out once with a paw, sending one broken dog flying like a shuttlecock. It rushed in and killed three more before Adam, never a really satisfactory rifle shot, dropped the beast with his .375. Even with his Holland & Holland, the finest rifle in the world, it took him four messy shots to get the job done, and one bullet accidentally finished off a mangled whippet.

Two more dogs, she reckoned, were killed by hyena when they vied to bring down a wounded antelope sheltering in thick bush. Another was plucked by a leopard from the very edge of camp. The other whippets refused to follow when their brother cried out and the snarling cat dragged it off. The remainder were tiresome, undramatic deaths: sickness, a broken leg, snakes.

Just now the three survivors, not gifted with the vigilance of memory, darted about ahead of the riders, left and right, sniffing and running, searching for a chase. Sissy used her spurs, prompting a canter when her mount leapt forward to close with the dogs. She saw Mercy shift gait abruptly to keep up, catching Anunciata off balance. Soon they were cantering fast while the dogs began to bay. Mercy fought the bit, working to seize the lead.

Sissy spotted it first: sleek and fast, a dark arrow flying low to the ground. Its ebony and silver back stretched and its thick tail flowed as the jackal tore into the bush beyond the coffee. Now was the time to see if the trollop could ride. Sissy pricked with her spurs.

She saw Anunciata give her horse the wrong signals. The woman rose slightly in the stirrups and leaned forward, low over the horse's neck, to keep her balance when the mare plunged from side to side, avoiding holes and rocks. Mercy, feeling the saddle unweight as if a jockey rose for the gallop, gave it her heart.

Jackal, whippets and horses tore madly through the bush. Rather like a proper hunt, Sissy thought, only without the promise of decent English food and drink to celebrate the kill.

First streaking, then jinxing from side to side, the jackal used every gully and bush for cover, every rock and tree as hazards for its pursuers. The whippets held their narrow heads low and pointed straight before them. Their deep chests pumped like bellows. Rowing forward, powerful hind legs reached in front of their shoulders and pulled and drove the animals through the wild country while they flowed through every obstacle. The hook of a wait-a-bit thorn lashed across Lancelot's long nose and whipped his left eye from its socket. Without a pause, the dog flashed on through another thicket with his brothers baying beside him. Sissy encouraged her horse to keep the pace. The experienced hunter picked his route with care, galloping hard on the clear flats and cooling imperceptibly in the thicker bush.

But Mercy knew no restraint. Her coat glistened. Her mouth foamed. Her eyes were huge and alight while she held a straight line after the hounds. Anunciata appeared intent not on controlling her but on staying aboard and, to Sissy's knowing eye, perhaps in leading the chase. The hounds split around a tall thorn tree. Sissy edged her own horse to the side, encouraging Mercy towards the oncoming tree. She saw Mercy gallop straight on close beside it. Anunciata ducked a heavy limb and pressed her cheek flat to the horse's sweating neck. But her left knee caught the trunk. Anunciata screamed and was scraped from the saddle.

Sissy reined in sharply in a tight circle and came back to Anunciata. Lying stunned, evidently numb with pain, the injured woman moaned and pressed her lips together.

"Are you all right, dear?" Sissy looked down at her. "I'm worried about the dogs."

"I think so. But my leg is hurt. Go on, leave me here and catch my horse."

Sissy frowned with concern and went after Mercy and the dogs. This should keep the slut in her own bed for a few weeks. Sissy thought of her own dreary life at the White Rhino. It was time she began to think of herself for a change.

The fingers of Olivio's square fleshy hand worked through the pockets of the crumpled white jacket. He replaced each object with the care of a watchmaker reassembling a movement. A sense of alarm thrilled through him, and he recalled the single occasion he had been caught. As a boy in Goa, misshapen and unwelcome, he did not play in the alleys with the Indian urchins or in the courtyards with the Portuguese scholars. Instead, his chosen game was to rifle through a desk or chest, memorizing each article and leaving every page and scarf folded precisely as before.

Only once had he indulged. In an apartment at the Bombay Club, working as a hall boy, he found a pigskin memory book beneath a pile of silk shirts. Passing his fingers up and down their luxurious rainbow, he chose a deep blue shirt, smooth to the touch like the inner thigh of his first young girl. He unbuttoned the shirt with care and drew it over his ill-fitting uniform. He turned up the long sleeves that insulted him, the cuffs hanging like the arms of a scarecrow. But the collar buttoned neatly about his brief thick neck.

The young dwarf looked directly across the surface of the dressing table into the glass to admire the dark globe of his head floating on a sapphire sea. He raised his chin and smiled. Then he turned back the cover of the scrapbook. Absorbed by distant English scenes of lawn teas and country shoots, wedding parties and pony rides, Olivio had the pages spread on the campaign chest before him when the tall officer entered the room, unbuckling his sword belt. The man's eyes flashed and he cursed. He became a giant, filling the room with rage. He struck Olivio across the face with the belt, cutting the dwarf's forehead.

Although the officer would never know it, the flogging that followed was not the end of this awkward incident.

For Olivio, who had the gift for revenge that some have for friendship, justice had been a simple matter. Remote but effective, it lacked only the satisfaction of personal observation. But it gave the little man a regard for the diverse uses of the Royal Mail.

Olivio steamed open the soldier's next letter to his young bride in Cornwall. Into the envelope the dwarf added two love notes and a flattering drawing from the officer's Bihari concubine, together with several bills for her presents. In time, when the mail packets crossed the oceans and returned, the brute learned that his wife had attempted to poison herself. She survived, but their unborn son did not.

This experience also impressed on Olivio the need always to ferret out the useful lesson. In this case, not to abandon spying, but to do it better. As other men with swift certain hands might tie an artery or play an ivory keyboard, so Olivio could search a room or empty and repack a trunk. Too proud to steal, but too inquisitive to leave a case unopened, he garnered information as others might count or harvest. This morning, when he cleaned the bar, he had found the linen jacket of a guest.

The pockets yielded a wrinkled heavily-marked map of central Kenya, four cigars in a worn leather case, one deck of cards, a gold fob watch, and a handful of coins, Indian, English and Portuguese. And in an envelope, two faded sepia photographs. He turned over the watch. A half hunter, its glass cracked, it was Lord Penfold's own! Olivio smiled when he opened it and read the engraving, *Forever, your Sissy.*

One photograph showed a splendid villa with terraces and columned porches set in a hilly vineyard. Figures bent over round baskets set among the vines. Others were bowed slavelike under large baskets of grapes carried on their backs. The second picture, very old, all four corners flaked off, was of two men. From their heads, they might be brothers. Wide noses, thick lips and small hard eyes under high brows dominated the camera. One man stood tall in a white military jacket hung with decorations and a sword. A Portuguese officer, Olivio guessed, with the easy haughtiness of Senhor Fonseca himself.

The tall man rested one hand on the hilt of his sword, the second on the shoulder of his companion, a far shorter person. The other man's entire neck was consumed by a clerical collar that pressed against his chin. He seemed familiar to Olivio. A large cross of bright metal hung about his sturdy shoulders on a heavy chain. The exalted robes and tasselled sash of a prince of the Church fell to his buckled shoes. The vestments of an archbishop? The dwarf stared into the man's sunken determined eyes. He wiped the picture with his cuff. He returned both photographs to their envelope and turned it over before returning it to the inside pocket. Olivio hung the jacket over a chair in front of the bar.

The dwarf climbed the ladder to his shelf. Polishing the leadwood counter, he reflected on the envelope he had just replaced. On the back flap was a crest and the word *Fonseca,* Olivio's own middle name. Was it possible? Could this be his family?

"Hold tight, memsaab!" the cheerful African boatman said when the bow rose and the surfboat surrendered to the rushing water.

Already, Gwenn realized, Africa was a physical adventure. No longer was she an observer, waiting for her husband's telegram, sitting on deck, staring out over the rail while men brought up her baggage. The white rowboat struck the wind-brushed surf. Four oarsmen chanted in Swahili and pulled in unison. Gwenn felt the broad bow rise, then slap down as the shallow-bottomed vessel angled in between two coral shoals.

Wide-eyed, appreciating the trim white uniforms and red cummerbunds of the crew, Gwenn gripped the wooden seat with both hands and glanced up at the wheeling gulls. Warm spray drenched her wool cloak. She thought of the mist and rains of Wales. Gwenn laughed with her companions and licked the salty water from her lips. She glanced back at the *Garth Castle* but could not see the awkward boy who had kissed her goodbye.

Forty yards from the beach the surfboat ground up on the white sand and gave Gwenn the choice of every new arrival: to wade ashore or be carried in on the shoulders of the gleaming-wet Africans who grabbed the boat, smiling while they held her steady. She took her shoes in one hand and jumped over the side. Her long skirt ballooned out around her waist like a water lily. She pushed through the sea and scanned the beach for Alan.

She saw the friends and families of other passengers welcome the travellers ashore, hugging and talking, sweeping up children in their arms. Twice Gwenn walked the long beach searching for her husband, trying not to stare at the excited couples who held each other close. Disappointed, she began to worry. Was Alan too weak to come? Had he not tried? Finally accepting that she was alone, she sought her baggage in the luggage stacked under the giant palms at the head of the beach.

Her first euphoria chilled, Gwenn knew her dream of raising a family in Africa would not come easily. She sat on a battered leather trunk and dusted the sand from her feet. She laced her heavy shoes and walked up onto the hard red earth that began behind the line of palms.

There she found the Mombasa trolleys, six small gharries or wagons rattling to a stop on narrow-gauge rails, each topped by a striped canvas sun roof and seating four passengers on back-to-back benches facing fore and aft, like a funfair railway. The pride of Mombasa, the trolleys shuttled from port to railway station, propelled by teams of chanting Africans in sailor suits. The men hopped on board whenever the gharries began to coast. The luckier passengers, those met by experienced friends, with servants helping and their baggage in hand, crowded aboard. The overloaded trolleys glided away.

Gwenn searched in vain for her second trunk. Already she was being followed by a friendly African.

"I am Mulwa. I will help you."

The man looked at her closely with lively intelligent eyes. She noticed his wide nose, strong jaw and regular features while he stood before her in a frayed blue jersey of the King's African Rifles. Below it he wore khaki shorts, a twist of cloth knotted about his waist and cut-off boots with the toes open.

"My people are Wakamba, memsaab, far away. I can do work. I need food or money."

Mulwa gathered her tin cases as she found them. Unsure where to go, Gwenn turned to a young couple who were supervising the loading of a two-wheeled ox cart. The man's empty right sleeve was pinned neatly to his shoulder.

"Could you help me, please?" she said. "I'm Gwenn Llewelyn."

"If you'll hop in the tonga with us first and come be my bridesmaid," the girl said.

Still dizzy with arrival, the stocky blond girl introduced the well-starched man at her side. "This is my fiancé, Tony Bevis. I'm Jill and we're going straight to church, aren't we, Tony? Aren't we, Tony?"

"Of course, dear," Bevis said. His brown hair was parted in the middle and dipped in two arcs over his forehead.

Gwenn abandoned her lost trunk and climbed onto the seat with Jill and Bevis. She wondered where the driver was to sit. She knew the betrothed girls were to be married at once, most the day they arrived. It was unthinkable that a decent girl, unmarried, would travel either alone or with a man. Mulwa loaded up Gwenn's things, careful and proprietary in his work. The turbanned Indian driver, disdaining baggage handling, spoke only to the Englishman.

"All in ready now, sahib? Churchie?" the driver said.

Jill giggled and Tony Bevis nodded to the Indian, admonishing his bride. "It ain't so funny, dear. These devils speak four or five more languages than you or I."

Straddling the heavy pole that separated the two oxen, snapping in Hindustani, the driver brought his animals to life. Gwenn winced when the man pulled on the rope that passed through holes in their nostrils, serving efficiently as reins, halter and bit. Mulwa followed at a distance, twirling his mahogany *rungu*. The throwing stick was heavily knobbed at one end. The smooth tip of its handle was carved in the form of a penis.

The Anglican church, Gwenn found, was today a marriage carnival. Wooden, painted white, with pointed gothic windows, the church was straight from home. Almost the very shape and size of St. Chrysostom's in Denbigh, where she had married Alan five years before. The windows of the narrow nave were open. The sweet breath of frangipani and hibiscus washed through with the breeze. Varieties of wild white lilies dressed the altar.

Fifteen buzzing wedding parties crowded the church. Gathered in clusters, each awaited its moment. The color of virginity harmonized conveniently with tropical dress as each bride and groom wore at least some white. Several women had borrowed white topees. The wide-brimmed cork sun hats were hung with white puggarees, pleated muslin scarves that replaced the discreet lace veils of England. Gwenn and Jill and Tony sat in a side pew near the front.

Sadness left her when Gwenn watched the hurried services begin. Three couples were married at a time. Gwenn found herself smiling, sharing their hopes. The portly minister garbled names when the couples paused before him. "Do you, Harold, take this woman, Lydia, to be your lawful wedded wife?"

"Actually, I don't. Mine is Rosemary."

Gwenn grinned and Jill giggled nervously. One veteran whispered to a chum, "You suppose they'll let 'em get divorced three at a time?"

The Bevises' turn came and Gwenn stepped to the aisle with the couple. Tony paled and turned to Gwenn.

"Crikey! The ring!" Bevis said to Gwenn with horror. "Dear God, the ring. I'm most awfully sorry, have you got a ring?"

"A ring?"

"Of course, a ring. I can't marry her without a ring!"

"Oh, I only have my own. But you can borrow it for today," Gwenn said, overcome by the romantic enthusiasm around her. In another moment, however, a cold dread of bad luck chilled through her.

She stood before the altar and licked her wedding finger, thinking guiltily of Alan. With difficulty Gwenn pulled off the thin gold band for the first time. The service proceeded. Unsettled, she watched Bevis force her ring onto Jill's chubby finger.

"Where shall we go now?" couples asked their friends when they emerged squinting into the bright sunlight. Accommodations were scarce in Mombasa, Gwenn had heard, and mostly uncomfortable.

"Won't you pop over to the Mombasa Club with us to celebrate?" Tony Bevis asked Gwenn. "We've an introduction from a chum up-country."

Gwenn joined the newlyweds, feeling herself an awkward extra but not knowing where else to go.

The club was set on the waterfront of the old Portuguese harbor. A black-barked casuarina tree, hung with cardboard angels, warmed the gloomy entrance hall with its drooping tufted foliage. The bar and verandah welcomed them. Elegant oryx heads and brooding Cape buffalo looked down at Gwenn from the walls with glass eyes. She felt the red-faced members, most dressed for dinner in black trousers and short white mess jackets scalloped at the back, study the new arrivals over the tops of venerable English newspapers.

Gwenn and the Bevises began on champagne and giant broiled shrimp. The wagon and Mulwa waited outside under the massive sixteenth-century walls of Fort Jesus.

Just as the eland curry was set before them, at precisely seven o'clock, the young Somali coffee boy, dashing in a white fez, paraded through the club. Enjoying himself, important, he swung a bell with one hand and displayed in the other a small blackboard: NO LADIES PLEASE. At once a steward handed Bevis a chit. The Englishman looked up, fork and knife in hand. The steward explained that all ladies must retire from the club by seven. Astounded, mumbling "Of course," Bevis dabbed chutney from his chin and signed the name of his host. Still thirsty and hungry, they left and made for the Grand Hotel.

Optimistically named after its dignified European cousins, but shabby after twenty hard years, the Grand was kept alive only by its competition. A street arcade prevented light from entering the front windows. Dirty peeling paint revealed cracked walls. Gwenn and Jill waited in the dark hallway while Bevis stepped to the desk. Gwenn wondered what size must be the spider that wove the immense web that shrouded one corner. A regular approached from the bar with a tall drink in either hand.

"If you don't mind my saying so," the red-faced man said, pausing to look over the new ladies, "it's not as bad as it looks. It's worse. During the rainy season, there's more rats than waiters. And some of them, the water rats, come bigger."

Tony Bevis was told the hotel was full for the night but that blankets were available on the floor of the billiard room. Bevis asked the ladies to wait in the bar while he checked the other hotels, the Africa and the Cecil. Gwenn went to the door and gave Mulwa a florin. She and Jill sipped gin and Indian tonic at a table in the bar and tried to ignore the attentions of the male guests. If Alan had come, she wouldn't have had to put up with this nonsense. It would be a long trip to Nairobi.

Outside, Bevis climbed wearily into a two-wheeled camel cart. The Indian driver smiled, stretching his dignity, when Bevis asked that he run him down to the Hotel Africa. "If you get lost, sahib," the driver said, "you can always find the Africa with your nose. Not by the one smell, but by the many."

Built with the stinking wood of mangrove poles, the Africa waited for them like a dusty toad resting by the side of the road, low and wide. Sewage, spoiled food and old garbage gave up their odors. The well, already burdened with unmentionable contributions, was filled to the top with thick shark oil, useful for hardening work boots and protecting the bottoms of Arab dhows against boring worms. Bevis entered the reception hall and found three seamen drinking gin from a bottle. The men were seated on stacks of antelope hides. The edges of the skins were tan and white and slightly curled like the layered parchments of a giant ancient tome. Bevis approached the dozing clerk and asked for a room.

"He's deaf now, mate, and he don't speak English," said one sailor, "and if he had a room, it wouldn't have a door, and you wouldn't want it."

Tired of the search, cranky as his lost arm began to ache, Bevis decided to spend his wedding night on the billiard table at the Grand.

Several drinks and some buffalo stew later, Gwenn turned to the Bevises. "If you don't mind," she said, exhausted, "I'll read on a chair in the bar."

Taking an oil lamp, blankets and a bottle of brandy into the billiard room, the newlyweds left Gwenn. Still irritated about Alan, annoyed by a frustrating day passed amidst the joys of others, she directed her thoughts to the future.

As her eyes closed, Gwenn smelled fragrant pipe tobacco. She thought of her father and heard steps and a cane approach along the wooden floor.

"Excuse me, please," a friendly voice said in crisp well-educated English, "but this will never do."

She looked up with a start to see a distinguished grey-haired man leaning on a bamboo cane. The man took the pipe from his mouth. His eyes crinkled when he smiled and introduced himself.

"I'm Adam Penfold. I reckon I'd do better in the bar, and you'd do better in my room." He extended a hand to help her rise.

"You're very kind. I'm Gwenn Llewelyn. I came in on the boat this morning, but my husband wasn't here to meet me."

"Must be up with the other new settlers, waiting for you in Nairobi." Penfold lifted her small bag. "We tried to keep 'em there so the boat trains wouldn't be overloaded. I'm on the Land Commission. Just nipped down to Mombasa to keep an eye on things. Tomorrow we'll get you on your way."

We're on two different ships," the doctor said to Anton one evening. "The passengers are on one *Garth Castle*. The crew is on another."

A few crewmen, Anton noticed, remained loners, clinging to the isolation that drew them to sea. Most found steady companions to drink and gamble and talk with, usually grouped by their watch or job: stokers and engineers, stewards and cooks.

Anton learned that every watch had its cardplayers, men who gambled all they owned, who lost their pay before they saw it. Two days at sea and the gamblers knew who had luck, who would pay, who was sharp. Weeks of toil were lost on a card. Whist, gin, poker, double demon, it was a life Anton understood.

"Watch the other players," Lenares had told Anton when he was twelve. The wiry gypsy used his quick hands expressively while he spoke. He mesmerized the boy with sad dark eyes as he turned cards and told of fortunes gained and lost. "Watch their mouths, their eyes, their skin. That, few men can control. Does it perspire? Does it draw tight? Most of all, watch their hands."

Some men gambled for excitement and release. But the gypsies had taught Anton differently. For them, it was a stalk, a hunt, a blend of instinct and discipline, understanding what it means to be hungry, yet patient. Knowing the tricks, and when not to use them. To watch, to lose a bit, and never to win too much.

By the time the *Garth Castle* sailed from Mombasa's Kilindini

Harbor and steamed south overnight to Dar es Salaam, the old capital
of German East Africa, Anton had won nearly as much as he dared.
Long ago he had been taught the value of gold. Perhaps in Africa
he would find his own. At every opportunity he converted debts to
cash, then cash into gold sovereigns, often taking far less in exchange.
Sewn in his money belt was £40 in gold and folded fivers.

So far Anton had avoided playing cards with the other stewards.
Wary of his boss, the chief steward, he waited for the right moment.
Tonight, late, with most passengers debarked and the work done,
he knew the stewards would be relaxed, and fat with tips and pay.

During mid-watch he stopped at the lavatory. He unbuttoned the
high frayed collar of his white service jacket and soaked his face and
hair in the tepid water. He blinked away the sticky salt water and
looked into the mirror with clear eyes. For luck, he knotted his red
diklo about his neck and left the collar open. By now, he reckoned,
the game should have boiled down to one table of big winners. Anton
felt a thrill, knowing they shouldn't be much harder to beat than
English farm boys.

He entered the first class dining saloon, late at night the refuge
of the stewards. With chipped mirrors and battered chairs, it was
run-down but comfortable. Six men still played at the corner table.
Glasses, old tobacco and money were spread before them like a messy
meal. Other stewards slept around the cabin, dozing back in chairs
or slumped on tables.

"Excuse me, gentlemen," Anton said, approaching the round table
when one player gestured him to the empty chair on the dealer's
left. "What's the name of this game?"

"Poker. Nothing wild. Table stakes. Pot limit." The chief steward
spoke without looking up, a cold moist cigar in his teeth. "If you
want a hand, drop your quid on the table, you idle bilger."

Anton emptied a pocket with his left hand, his right arm painful
in its sling. He counted four pounds in shillings and half-crown coins
onto the table and pulled up the chair without speaking. A second
steward passed him the deck. The round-faced man to Anton's right
cut the cards.

"Down the River," Anton announced. He always preferred stud
games. With some cards dealt face up and others down, he learned

more about the other players. He dealt each man two down and one up.

"Jack bets," Anton said. The betting began. He curled up the edges of his cards, glanced at them, and left them face down before him.

By the time the ship's whistle blasted twice and the *Garth Castle* turned in to port, of the five players left at the table, two were winners. Anton had been careful not to be the bigger. But he had thirty-four new pounds before him, including the last two weeks of his boss's pay.

"One last hand." The chief steward lifted a shot glass and spat his cigar butt into it. "Cincinnati. Up the ante. Five bob for everyone."

Another man, with less than five shillings left, rose from the table, leaving only four. Too few for a good game, Anton thought, since several generally folded before the final betting. He stood.

"Sit down, Rider." His boss picked a dark flake of tobacco from his front teeth and scraped it off his finger on the edge of the table. The other two players pushed five shillings forward. "Sit down."

Anton took his seat and put two half crowns into the pot. He felt the stale mood of fatigue that bound the other men. A dependable ally, he thought, all to the good.

The steward gave each man five cards down. He dealt five more face down into the center of the table.

Anton reflected that in Cincinnati it would take a strong hand to win. Probably a Full House or better, since each player could use the best five of the ten cards seen by him. There would be five rounds of betting, one after each center card was turned up. He looked at his own hand: three 4's, a Queen, and a 5. Trips on the deal. A strong start, but still carrying with it the risk of being second best.

If he could make the most of it, this could be the hand. He remembered the advice. If you hold a strong hand, don't reveal it by betting early. Sandbag them. Appear uncertain. Let another gambler start the betting, then strike.

The five common cards lay face down in the center of the table. The chief steward, as dealer, turned one card face up. It was a 5. The card completed Anton's Full House of three 4's over two 5's.

Anton considered the situation. If other players stayed in to the end, at least one hand might equal or better his own. At this early stage in the betting, the pot totalled one pound. Anton watched the others.

"Check," said the round-faced man, declining to bet.

Anton checked too. Let's see what the others do, he thought. The man to Anton's left, "Hooker" to his mates, was a long-server with olive skin and a narrow hooked nose. He checked. The chief steward, who had dealt, checked and reached to turn over the second common card.

Blast, Anton said to himself. No one's betting, and the pot's too small. But a big bet would frighten everyone out. The dealer turned up a 6. No help for Anton, and maybe someone else's hand was strengthened.

All the players checked around again. Double blast. The dealer turned up a third card in the center of the table, a Queen. Interesting, Anton judged, viewing his Queen in the hole, but no real help, even though he now had a Full Boat, three 4's over two Queens.

The round-faced man took one quid from the money in front of him and threw it into the pot. The three others did the same. Now the pot held five pounds. The game was getting richer, thought Anton. All the players had paid to see another card.

The fourth common card was a 4. Anton's heart skipped as he saw the case 4, the final 4 in the deck. Now he had Four of a Kind. A killer. He remained calm and disinterested. He kept his face loose. The round-faced man checked.

Anton checked again, holding back, calculating that another player would bet.

Hooker stroked his nose and slid a fiver into the pot. A pot-limit bet, observed Anton. Hooker, too, must have a strong hand.

"I'll see your five and raise you two." The chief steward threw seven pounds into the pot.

"Too classy for me." The round-faced man folded with a curse.

The chief steward looked at Anton with sharp red eyes. Without comment Anton dropped seven pounds in the middle of the table. Hooker pushed in another two, building a pot of twenty-six. What were the other two men holding? Anton worried.

"Pot's right." Anton's boss turned over the last common card: another Queen. The chief steward's expression changed almost imperceptibly. The skin tightened around his mouth as the muscles of his face contracted. The common cards now showed 5, 6, 4 and a pair of Queens.

"My bet, pisser," the chief steward said to Anton. He looked closely at the remaining pile of money in front of Anton. He counted four white five-pound notes into the center of the table with a look of satisfaction.

Except for the snoring from scattered tables, the cabin grew silent. Anton fingered his money. He had very nearly thirty pounds left before him. The bet would nearly tap him out. He held four 4's, almost certainly a winning hand. He paused and tried to read his opponents' hands. With a Queen and a 5 in his own hand, Anton knew his boss could not have four Queens or four 5's. It seemed very unlikely there was another Four of a Kind. Chances were the second common Queen had improved the head steward's hand, and that he was now betting a Full House with Queens high instead of 5's or 6's high. A strong hand, but one that would lose to Anton. But what about Hooker? Could he have the winning hand? Hooker seemed a bit too disinterested in the confrontation between Anton and the chief steward. Anton hesitated. Unconsciously, he twisted the diklo at his throat.

"Always," the voice of Lenares said, "leave something behind. Leave the forest or the table so it will welcome you back."

The ship's clock chimed eight bells: *ding ding, ding ding, ding ding, ding ding.* Change of watch. Four in the morning.

"Your hand." Anton nodded at the chief steward and rose. He tossed his cards face down onto the table. "I fold."

The chief steward leaned forward and started to rake the pot towards him with both hands.

"Just a moment," said Hooker wearily, pinching his nose.

The chief steward flushed and pushed the money back into the center. Anton felt the table's concentration. Hooker placed his cards face down in a tight pile. He looked intently at the chief steward and then at the five upturned cards in the center of the table.

"I'll see you." Hooker counted twenty pounds in coins and bank-notes from the stake in front of him and pushed them into the middle.

The chief steward's face changed again and he scowled. Reluctantly he turned over his cards: two 5's, a 3, a Jack, the Queen of Spades. The gypsy "death card," Anton thought, relieved he was no longer in the hand.

"Full House, Queens over fives," the chief steward said.

As Anton suspected, his boss had been betting with three 5's up until the final card, when his Full House improved to Queens up.

Hooker turned only three of his cards over: all 6's.

"Four sixes," Hooker said, nodding towards the 6 in the center as he drew in the pot. "A nice hand, I must say."

Very nice indeed, thought Anton, thanking Lenares.

He still had twenty-five new pounds, but one more problem awaited him, Anton reflected while he climbed the steel companionway: jumping ship. Then he would be alone again.

He made his way to the starboard end of the wide flying bridge and waited for dawn to brighten over Tanganyika. Watching the light change, his heart bursting with expectation, Anton waited to see the land. He remembered another early morning, in England three years before.

Naked save for his tweed cap, he had stood shivering by the frost-fringed edge of a small lake in the Midlands. His toes curled tight, he squinted into the first light and made out the high leafless branches of the elm trees that rose from the island in the center of the ornamental lake. In the upper limbs the dozen nests of the heronry began to stand out like dark baskets against the brightening sky. Early nesters, the herons should have laid their eggs already. Anton bit his lip and entered the fog-covered water. In a few months it would be summer, he thought, and he could set his trimmers, leaving the small wooden floats scattered about the lake, each one suspending a fishing line and hook. Then it would be fresh pike, baked and stuffed with pudding.

Anton walked into the water and swam the short distance with a slow breaststroke, careful not to splash. He stepped out and began to climb a tree, wishing they were oaks, shorter and better-limbed for climbing. Shivering, he looked up and saw the long-necked waders flapping away as he approached the nest. Inside were four large blue eggs. Anton put two in his cap with a protective handful of the small sticks with which the nest was lined. He climbed another tree and did the same. Then he entered the freezing water with the cap clenched in his teeth.

Swimming quietly, he looked across the water's foggy surface. He was surprised to see a figure emerge from the woods near his pile of clothing. Anton trod water. A redheaded boy, also about fifteen, stripped quickly to his shorts. He put one foot into the water and inhaled with a whistle. Anton laughed, startling the other lad as Anton grabbed for his cap when his mouth opened.

"Beat me to it, have you?" the red-haired boy said cheerily. "Who are you?"

"Anton Rider."

"I'm Stone. Fourth Form, Rugby." The boy examined the eggs while Anton pulled on his rough clothes. "Where are you at school?"

"Do you collect eggs too?" Anton said, embarrassed by Stone's question. "Would you like one of these?"

The boy dressed quickly and picked an egg from Anton's cap. He drew a slingshot from his hip pocket. Then Stone sat on a log and carefully tapped in a neat hole at each end of the egg with the sharpened tip of the handle of the catapult. He blew into one end, forcing out the dripping egg at the other. He licked his lips and used his shirttail to wipe the egg and his freckled chin.

For five weeks, Anton and Stone met before dawn every Sunday. They went bird's-nesting for magpies, rooks and missel-thrushes. They trapped and skinned water rats and moorhens. They collected their blown eggs in a hollow ash tree.

Sometimes they played duck-on-a-rock in the forest and talked about their own adventures. Stone was always eager to relate the troubles and excitements of schoolboy life. Unwilling to disclose the frights and humiliation of being driven from village to village, Anton spoke instead of trapping and hunting, or taught his new friend how to pitch a knife.

"What're you reading in school?" Stone said one morning while he piled smaller and smaller rocks atop each other.

"Dickens."

"Me too. What's your favorite?"

"*David Copperfield*, but I lost my copy." Anton was still angry at the memory. He picked a good rock and waited for his turn to throw.

On the morning of Palm Sunday they met for the last time.

"Next week it's Easter hols," Stone said, uncertainly. "Maybe you'd like to come down to Manton for a few days? Two other Fours are coming."

Flattered, tempted, but knowing he would be an outsider, Anton was not certain what to say. They could share the woods, he knew, but not Manton Hall.

"I can't. I've got to be with my family," Anton said, wishing it were true. "I'll see you after Easter."

" 'Fraid not, I'll be playing cricket, got to win my cap." Stone took a book from his jacket pocket and presented it to Anton. "Thought you might like this."

Six months later, working the gypsy horse fair at Northampton, with manure sticking to his boots, Anton saw Stone again. Taller, elegant in black cutaway and waistcoat, Stone was swaggering by with two schoolmates, their top hats at jaunty angles.

Behind Anton, gypsy horse-copers displayed two prancing mares to wary farmers. Only weeks before, Anton recalled, the same horses had been tired screws, their patchy coats and listless eyes betraying hard use. But after a fortnight of making up, the mares shone. One gypsy, swank in tall boots, plush vest and a long black coat, casually began to grind a handful of pebbles in one hand under a mare's nose. The horse's eyes came alight. She twitched and tossed her head with the animation of a yearling. Each day the same horse faker had rattled pebbles in a tin bucket beneath her nose until the horse grew crazed. The other animal snorted smartly and riffled her soft nostrils, her clear breathing provoked by the rosemary that had been packed into holes drilled into the insides of two teeth. This morning Anton had seen the copers slip slivers of ginger up the anus of each horse, certain inducements to a prancing stand and high carriage of the tail.

Now Anton dreaded an embarrassing scene if a farmer exposed a gypsy ruse with Stone nearby.

Stone spotted Anton and smiled awkwardly. He stepped apart from his friends and called out.

"I say, Rider! How's our collection?"

"Someone broke all the eggs." Anton held up two dirty hands to avoid a shake. "Probably a pine marten."

He watched Stone turn his back and wave over his shoulder. In a moment he was gone, like all of Anton's friends. To the gypsies, Anton thought, I'm a gaujo. To Stone's friends, I'm a farm lout or a gypsy. Tears of humiliation burned his eyes.

In Africa, Anton hoped, as in the forest, none of that would matter. But even as he dreamt of his fresh start, a knot crept into his stomach while he watched Tanganyika take form in the early light.

Desperate to get ashore at Dar and aware that stewards were no longer so needed, Anton had told the first mate he was an experienced dockhand. The mate seemed confident Anton would not jump ship, knowing the boy had not been paid. Since the youngster had one arm in a sling, the friendly officer assigned him to direct one of the unloading gangs when the vessel tied up.

Shortly after daybreak the *Garth Castle* was secured along the end of the old German pier. The stone surface was still pitted by the shelling of the British cruisers that had attacked von Lettow's garrison in 1914. Anton saw narrow-gauge tracks leading to the base of the pier. Light cranes waited to help. Gangs of shiny-muscled Africans stood about, ready for work.

In minutes the hatches were open, winches were grinding, and the ship's booms were lowered and swinging as men discharged crates of paraffin engines and giant spools of copper telegraph cable. At dockside, Anton was assigned an Arab headman who spoke some English, and a team of twelve strapping Africans to sort and stack the goods before the importers signed the bills of lading. It made a hard hot day's work. At the end, the mate called Anton aside.

"Time for a glass, young Rider. Then I'll show you what's on for tomorrow," the man said. Anton slung his jacket over one shoulder, making certain Stone's *David Copperfield* was safely in one pocket. He followed the mate past the Kaiserhof Hotel and along a row of whitewashed stores fronted by thin wooden columns. Indian and Arab proprietors offered beaten copper trays, lengths of patterned cotton and carved ivory figures when the Englishmen passed. Stepping up onto a boardwalk, the mate led Anton through a curtain of colored beads into a cool room illuminated by slits in the thick stone and plaster walls. They found the ship's doctor seated on a brocaded cushion, stirring his drink with one finger and admiring a tray of silver bracelets held by a veiled Arab lady.

"Welcome to Ramzi's," the doctor said, stroking the woman's ankle while she appeared to ignore him, "the pride of the Dar waterfront in peace and war."

"What do they sell here?" Anton asked when they joined the doctor at a low copper table.

"Everything a healthy lad might dream of." The physician eased one hand into the loose fold of striped cotton that draped the woman's substantial rear. Did she mind? Anton wondered, particularly with whisky on the doctor's finger. "And they never close. Even when the shells were falling. While the Huns bolted out the back door, leaving their steins on the tables, old man Ramzi held the beads aside and his new Brit customers charged in the front. Whisky?"

"Beer, please." Anton was startled by female laughter from another room.

"Shall we slip into the next room, boyo, and check on the state of play?" the doctor asked while Anton drank.

"I reckon we'd best prepare for tomorrow's work, my young pup," the mate interrupted. He finished his drink and rose before Anton could reply. "Otherwise this old rascal will lead us all to hell."

Back in the dusty street, the officer led Anton to a long narrow warehouse. They banged on the brass-studded door and were admitted by an aged Arab with a pointed white beard. The man was clothed in a white djellaba belted with a silk sash. His hood thrown back from a lean pockmarked face, the Arab held an oil lamp overhead while he examined the visitors. The mate introduced himself.

They followed the Arab into the warehouse. Anton's eyes adjusted and he noticed rows of iron rings set into the walls and extending down the length of the vast structure. Rusted chains and hinged manacles dangled from the rings. Some hung low to the ground, with lighter manacles suitable for children. Shallow stone troughs ran along each wall near the ground, reminding Anton of a milking barn.

"Slaves," the Arab said with an old smile. "Black gold, but those times may be gone." From a hook on the wall he lifted a long flexible whip that narrowed to a hard-edged point.

"My father's favorite schoolteacher, effendi, cut from the tail of a devilfish, a giant ray." The Arab moved his wrist. Dust flew. Invisible, the tip of the lash snapped like a gunshot against a ring set in the wall.

"In my father's day," the man said, gesturing with the weapon, "these troughs ran with thick gruel. No drop was wasted. Every place was taken. Hundreds. Each collar and bracelet. Burungi, Ngoni, even Wagogo took their turns. Only when the fast slave dhows came from Zanzibar were the irons cold. But then your Queen's navy stopped the trade. How sad it is like this. Now we have only white gold, ivory, and with your infidel war, even that we could not move."

"You can move it tomorrow," the mate said when the Arab raised the lamp.

Bats fluttered to distant corners. Anton saw light glitter over rows of ivory tusks, arrayed like slender ghosts, white in the shadows. Hundreds and hundreds, perhaps thousands. Some were piled ten deep. Others, the longest, were stacked like sheaves of wheat in huge bundles, standing on broad hollow ends. As varied as people, Anton thought. Some fat and short. Others lean. Many thick and long, the tips often rounded or chipped. A few were stained yellow or brownish grey, like the teeth of an old pipe smoker. Forty yards down the lanes of ivory, Anton saw the polishing wheels and worktables. Soft wooden vises gripped the tusks, patiently waiting for chisel and knife.

The Arab displayed his finest pair, almost perfectly matched and exceptionally tall and thick. Anton held one upright. The bottom two feet were lighter in color and coarser than the rest of the tusk. "That part was inside the face," the Arab explained. The balance of the tooth was almost exactly Anton's height, six feet two inches. The Arab invited Anton to lift it.

Anton hefted the tusk in both hands, surprised by its weight, about a hundred and seventy or eighty pounds. As he stroked it, feeling the pearl-like smoothness and the lines and grain, the ivory was alive under his hand. Chilled, feeling disrespectful, he turned his mind to the elephants themselves. What would these giants be like? What if all the elephants whose tusks were here could be living again, hundreds of them, making their way slowly through the forest, bellies rumbling, snapping branches and sniffing with their trunks, trumpeting calmly while they advanced?

Retreating at last to the door, the mate promised to return next day to negotiate a shipment.

"Too much death in there for me," Anton said, shaking his head.

"Back to Ramzi's, my boy, otherwise the Doc will do all the damage without us."

"If you don't mind, sir, I think I'll just cut back to the ship."

"Then it's good night to you, laddie, and a happy New Year!"

With that, the mate hurried on to Ramzi's and Anton strode towards the docks. After a time, he stopped and looked up at the Southern Cross. Then he turned and walked away from the sea.

— 9 —

Money! Money! I have rupees, I have pounds and pence!" the Indian called repeatedly, his cry a beacon in the swirling chaos of Mombasa station.

Gwenn looked about and saw old lorries and ox wagons arrive with more settlers. Porters jumped down from the gravel platform to help. Somali train staff, crisp in white cotton uniforms and red fezzes, sold tickets, first class for the European carriages. African women hawked mangoes, pawpaws and bananas from wide flat baskets. European ladies from the church offered tea and orange squash from a cart while their servants helped to pour and keep an eye on the cups.

The scene reminded Gwenn of Kipling. She could almost see Kim darting about among the crowd.

Concerned about the exchange, Gwenn bought Indian rupees from the money trader. She purchased a ticket and bought cashew nuts wrapped in a banana leaf. She spotted Adam Penfold at the far end of the platform. He was helping a couple gather their belongings by the goods van.

Gwenn admired the pre-war carriages, smartly repainted in the cream and pale chocolate of the Uganda Railway. Steam clouded out between the great wheels of the American Baldwin locomotive as the train prepared for the three-hundred-and-thirty-mile run to Nairobi. She climbed in and found her seat. She lowered the window and stood looking out with her arms resting on the sash.

"Hope you'll make Nairobi," Penfold said to her, smiling up from the platform and raising his cane in salute. "This old Baldwin's had a pretty hard war. Von Lettow's mines blew her off the track twice, and she's been leaking steam ever since. Probably feels 'bout the way I do. Hasn't the heart anymore for the climb from Nairobi to Lake Vic, so they just use her on the Mombasa run."

"I'm sure we'll get there. Thank you again for the room last night. You should've let me pay for it."

"Sorry I can't join you, but I've got to wait and see the next lot off. Might catch you on the way north after Nairobi. There's only one way to go."

The engine whistled twice. The couplings groaned. Slowly the train pulled out, the four small cars crammed with ninety-five weary settlers. Gwenn watched other passengers wave and felt her loneliness as she saw Mombasa diminish behind her.

Old hands after three days on the coast, glutted with advice from hours in the bar of the club, Gwenn and the Bevises had picked their seats with care. Dust was the first plague. For much of the route, the tracks were laid with insufficient ballast to stabilize the ride. In the wet seasons, farther inland, the train sprayed arcs of mud when it advanced, rocking from side to side, pounding the rails into the murky black cotton soil that turned to swamp in the rains. In the dry seasons the same ground hardened to a corrugated rock-like surface that bounced the wheels violently as they passed.

Now, in the dry weather near the coast, crossing the red lateritic soil of the Taru Desert, the penetrating red earth painted the inside of the old carriages even with the windows closed. The last cars got the most dust, enveloping the rear passengers in blinding clouds for miles at a time.

Unlike the modern corridor trains coming into service at home, the carriage compartments, known as "horse boxes," opened directly out the sides of the train. At night each compartment unfolded into four bunks. On the crowded boat trains, however, the occupants either had to share bunks or sleep upright on the thirty-hour run to Nairobi. Besides the Bevises, Gwenn found herself sharing a forward horse box with the Gaults, a nervous London couple with two young girls. Mulwa, apparently a permanent part of the household, Gwenn reflected, was in the goods van at the rear, lounging among piles of

crates and trunks with the other Africans and a few penniless
Europeans.

The Gault girls, eight and ten, eyed Gwenn's banana leaf when
two cashews fell to the floor. The elder one drew designs in the red
dirt that painted her sister's face.

The locomotive showed its age as it climbed onto the coastal pla-
teau. Gwenn unfolded the leaf and offered nuts to her companions.
She watched the dry scrub country expand in the distance while the
Baldwin slowed on the ascent.

Forever thirsty, inefficient in converting firewood to steam, the
old engine challenged its engineer. One hour outside Mombasa the
water gauge dropped and the tired seams began to sweat. They passed
blackened patches of bush where the sparks of locomotives had
started grass fires. The engineer braked for a water stop at the Mile
70 cistern.

Gwenn saw a long pipe descending from a waterhole ninety yards
away. It supplied a raised wooden tank near the track. The firemen,
pouring with sweat from stoking the furnace, jumped down to fill
the engine. Doors opened all along the train. Passengers stepped
down from the footboards onto the hard earth. For most of the
Europeans, it was their first taste of the African bush. Gwenn savored
the pungent smell of it, the fresh brush-scented wind, like sage, and
the clean odor of the dust.

The Gault girls exploded out of the compartment in rumpled tartan
skirts. They dashed alongside the train and chased two boys who
were hurling stones at a ground squirrel. "Look, a snake!" one lad
hollered. Mrs. Gault hurried down the track, crying out in alarm.

Mulwa ran after the children and swung his rungu, pinning a green
snake to the ground. He lifted it by the tail and showed the wriggling
serpent to the children. Parents yelled at him in fear. The snake
twisted its head round and round, winding itself into a corkscrew.
The end of its tail snapped off and the snake slipped free into the
bush.

"Not to worry," said Bevis, calming Mrs. Gault. "It's only a hissing
sand snake. They feasted on our trench rats during the war out here.
Ate better'n we did. Almost harmless. It's the mambas you want to
look out for. They run faster than a man and knock you flatter than
a Mauser."

"You shouldn't have hurt him," ten-year-old Anna Gault said to Mulwa, shaking dusty blond pigtails at the African. She looked up crossly, blue eyes flashing, and snatched the stub of tail from his hand. "He was beautiful with his tail."

"He still has a tail, missy." Mulwa turned to Gwenn and grinned.

Three hours later they pulled into Voi station beside the dining bungalow, an open shed with rough wooden columns supporting a tin roof. Gwenn was surprised by the contrast of wild surroundings and luxurious service. Two hundred yards on, a cluster of single-story buildings was Voi itself, one of four sparsely settled landmarks between Mombasa and Nairobi.

"I am Nazareth and I welcome you." The Goan proprietor bowed and stretched his arms wide when the travellers entered his shelter. Good news for Nazareth, Gwenn saw, was bad news for his staff. Exhausted from serving the first two boat trains, but still smart in soiled white gloves, his Indian stewards helped the ladies and children to the first sitting. The men, more thirsty than hungry, took bottles of Tusker lager from tubs of water and wandered off a few paces into the open country, looking at the wide brief sunset in the western sky.

"Damn sight sportier hereabouts in the old days," Tony Bevis said to a group of first-timers while he drank from their bottle of Sandy McDonald whisky. "Back in '99 an Italian, a German and an Englishman shared a sleeping coach at a siding up the line here at Tsavo. With a door open for the breeze, the German bedded down in an upper bunk. The Wop stretched out on the floor, Eye-tie style, if you know what I mean. The English chap sat by an open window, watching for a man-eater they'd come to bag. The Italian woke up to find the hind feet of the lion braced on his back as the cat reached up to seize the Englishman.

"The Kraut jumped from his bunk," Bevis said, taking a drink, "and fell on the lion, which took the English bloke in its mouth and leapt through the window to enjoy a nice feed in the fresh air. Mark you, the cat was a specialist, a man-eater of the old school."

"Is it true," one soldier said, his eyes wide, "that lion prefer white men to Africans because we're saltier?"

"Wouldn't you?" Bevis said, finishing the bottle. "Mark you, those Tsavo man-eaters developed a taste for wogs. Before they got knocked off, they gobbled up twenty-eight coolies in one spot. They always begin with one's arse, licking off the skin with those sandpaper tongues, then lapping up the blood before really starting in. Would you mind passing me a Tusker?"

Nazareth lit the gas lamps that swung over the tables, drawing fat-bodied moths and clouds of mosquitoes to the dinner. Anna dipped her fingers into the eland-tail soup and removed a flapping moth. Gwenn watched her delicately hold the struggling creature down by its abdomen and pat it dry with her napkin, blowing on it gently. The girl frowned when tiny fragments of the mottled wings clung to the cloth like old parchment.

"You wouldn't want him to drown, would you?" Anna said irritably, looking up.

Less successful, Samantha Gault pressed another moth deeper into a greasy lump of tinned Bombay butter. "Don't worry, my dear," another mother reassured Mrs. Gault, "that rancid mess is the better for it. Older than the train and quite disgusting."

"Fortunately," Bevis said while other men rummaged in luggage and returned with flasks and bottles, "no old Tommy travels without alcohol, especially in these filthy countries."

By the time the men got their turn, the soup, the pawpaw pudding and the beer were finished. With the children asleep in the carriages, Gwenn and the other ladies chatted in the shadows, speculating about the future, missing England but excited about the next day and new homes.

The men attacked the stew and roast guinea fowl the stewards set before them. "I've heard about this impala meat," one diner said, "but damned if this isn't the finest brisket I've ever tasted."

"Actually, it ain't impala, and it's nobody's brisket." Bevis leaned across his neighbor to help himself to Gault's gin. "It's goat. Tops. Angora, I'd wager."

With the alcohol finished, the scene stilled while the stewards cleaned up and the travellers crowded back into the train for the night. A few men stretched out on the packed dirt floor of the dining shed.

Unable to sleep, sitting by the window in her compartment with Anna's head on her lap, Gwenn Llewelyn gazed out at the night and rubbed her bare ring finger. Would she find Alan in Nairobi? What had the war done to him? Would that instant of recognition be happy, or awkward and empty? Could she tell him she was raped? Sometimes that horror seemed so far away.

But often at night, or if she saw a man with Reilly's shape or face, the unspeakable violence attacked her again. The disgusting insult of it when he ripped open her clothes and ran his rough hands over her body. The stink of alcohol and sweat when he forced his face close. Her maddening helplessness while he used her, and the impossibility of cleaning herself. She shivered and prayed that nothing more would come of it. Even without this, there would be enough problems trying to begin again. She knew the rape must be her secret.

Gwenn tried not to think of Anton's words. "First you will suffer," he had said as his blue eyes looked into hers.

She lifted Anna's head and stroked the petal-smooth skin of the child's cheek. She stood up and rested Anna against her small bag. Gwenn remembered moving her own younger sister every night after the girl fell asleep, shoving her back to the far edge of the bed so she herself could climb in.

Gwenn stepped down into the night. The dining shed and Voi were on the other side of the train. She walked away from the carriage. The train grew smaller as the immensity of the African night spread above her. Gazing up, awed by the depth of the blue-black sky, dazzled by the intensity and individuality of each star, Gwenn thought that never before had she truly observed the night above her. She distanced herself from the train until it was only a dark wall to one side, punctuated here and there by the glow of burning tobacco.

Gwenn closed her eyes and prayed for a happy life, determined to build with Alan a family in Africa. But after so long apart, would things still be the same with Alan? Did he want children as much as she did? Suddenly she heard a cackling bark and opened her eyes, instantly fearful.

"*Fisi,* memsaab, hyena. No good," said Mulwa's voice behind her. "Back to train, please."

On New Year's Day, 1920, Anton watched the sun rise by the old German road three miles west of Dar es Salaam. His back rested against the rusted-out fender of an abandoned Daimler. The seats and every usable part were gone, but Anton, gypsy-trained, had slept easily in the back of the open lorry. Waking once, his dream about Gwenn Llewelyn naked in a lifeboat was interrupted by an animal rustling through the tall sword grass. He recalled his revulsion at the rape, and found the dream disturbing. "Why do I keep thinking of her like that?" he muttered to himself, inevitably returning to the thought.

Distracting himself, Anton lay looking up at the night. He identified the sharp light of Sirius and remembered rainy days in the wagon of a crippled gypsy astrologer, the *phuri dai,* the sage woman of the tribe. The low walls, ceiling and door were pasted over with ancient star maps printed in Bucharest. Ropes of garlic, a chain of castanets and the skeleton of an immense bat dangled among the stars. "Never marry a girl who can't cook garlic," the phuri daï had told him.

At first the wagon was unutterably gloomy, the black walls a prison. But as the old woman taught him, and he helped her cook and clean, it became a magic chamber, each bright point a friend. The names themselves peopled his imagination: Castor, Betelgeuse, Bellatrix.

Lying in the truck in Africa, Anton studied the southern heavens he could never see in England. One by one he recognized shining companions from the wagon walls.

"Hello, Phoenix, Peacock, Al Na'ir," he called aloud with a friendly wave. Soon the celestial families stood out in familiar patterns and the southern constellations filled his night.

In the morning Anton instinctively reached for the gypsy knife habitually at his waist. He missed stropping the blade on the side of his boot. One day he'd find that Irish bastard and have a chance to get back his choori. He tried not to hear his stomach grumble.

As he fingered the empty sheath on his belt, his arm stiff and painful, Anton determined to start making his way north to British East Africa, until he found the twin-peaked mountain where the goshawk flew. He'd buy a rifle and travel overland, like Selous, stopping to make money where he could and avoiding any border towns. With only a seaman's papers, and long wary of authority, he feared for his reception.

The sun rose higher and warmed him. He stood and slipped his right arm through the sling and began to walk with the sun on his back. After a time Anton heard a motorcar approach noisily down the pitted road. He turned to see a filthy Rugby Durant rattle to a stop beside him. Its tail of dust caught up with it and enveloped him. The rear of the old automobile had been converted into a short flatbed. The wooden spokes of the wheels were splintered and bowed. On the battered door Anton saw the painted profile of a cheetah, above it the words *Gepard Farm.* Wearing grey German military trousers and a cracked leather jacket, a heavily built, hard-set man stepped down.

"*Deutsch oder Englisch?*" the man said in a loud voice.

"English, sir. Can I help?"

"I am Ernst von Decken." The man examined the load on the back of his vehicle. "Step around the other side, young fellow. Quick, now. Quick. Pesi, pesi! Check those ropes. If you can't tighten them with one hand, you're not strong enough to be useful. If you can, I'll give you a ride."

Anton did not reply. Unable to see over the top of the load and unaware that the driver was heaving on the same line, he pulled hard on a rope with his left hand, binding the German's fingers against the wooden crate.

"*Ach! Halt!* What do they feed you, boy? Just make it secure and jump in. What do you call yourself?"

"Anton Rider."

"You don't have much to say for yourself, do you?"

"No, sir."

"Where are you headed, *Engländer?*"

"Mount Kenya."

"That's five hundred miles north of here. How will you get there?"

"I thought I'd walk."

"That will do you good."

Ernst drove northwest through vast neglected fields of white-flowering sisal. The spiky sword-like leaves resembled giant artichokes. Each plant, the German told Anton, was rich with the world's prime hard fiber, the raw source of binder twine and carpets, ropes and sacking. They came to a stream that crossed the road. Ernst drove the Rugby Durant off the shallow ford into deeper water. He switched off the engine.

"Five years ago," Ernst said with a gesture towards the sisal, "my old papa, trying to make us rich at last, from Bielefeld ordered two stitching machines, designed to make Africa's finest sisal bags from the tow of these plants. The stitchers arrived in Dar in '14, one week before your cursed navy. Then von Lettow stole every vehicle in port and nothing could be moved.

"Now the precious *Nümaschinen* have spent five years rotting in these crates, and my papa has lost his taste for commerce. All the old man wants is to rub against his kaffir girl and walk alone in the bush with his double-barrelled rifle, waiting for the lions to get him, if the guinea worms don't clean out his insides first."

"Why've you parked the lorry in the river?" Anton was hungry.

"After four years killing English with that madman von Lettow, I'm owed a barrel of schnapps and a month being scrubbed by the girls in Baden-Baden, not fourteen flaming hours a day rebuilding that blasted plantation."

"Why have we stopped in the river?"

"To give the spokes a drink. Can't you see they're all dried out and shrivelled? Why did you think she was rattling so?"

Midday they stopped at Chalinze by an old German army storehouse, one of a chain, Ernst explained, built by von Lettow to permit rapid troop movement without resupply. Made of stone, it operated now as an Arab shop, a restaurant and a warehouse.

"*Kaffee, Herr Effendi?*" The Arab bowed to the older man, evidently surprised to see a German and an Englishman travelling together.

"Of course. Four eggs each, meat and beer, potatoes, onions, bread," the German boomed. "The beer now. Clean the table. And show my quiet friend your best knives. An empty sheath is dangerous."

The Arab wiped the table and brought two beers.

"*Prost Neu Jahr!*" Ernst raised his drink. He downed the first three without a pause, belching and calling for another when each arrived. He wiped his mouth on the back of his hand and began to eat with equal efficiency. His hands were large and square, the fingers and palms about the same length. Dependable, healthy, uncomplicated, Anton recognized.

"What happened to the arm?" Ernst tilted his plate and scraped it with the side of his fork. He leaned back and gestured at Anton's sling with the implement.

"Someone tried to teach me a lesson."

"Did it work?" The German speared a small piece of meat from the edge of Anton's plate and looked at the younger man.

"I don't think it did," Anton said. For a moment the memory flared up: the Reilly brothers and their filthy faces, but they were far from here. Anton finished eating and pushed his plate towards Ernst. He rose and stepped into the shop. He examined the knives the Arab had laid out. Seeking a good blade that might fit his sheath, he took two Solingen knives outside into the light. He removed his arm from the sling and balanced each German knife in his right hand.

"I'll buy you breakfast, boy, if you can stick one into that baobab tree," Ernst called from the doorway. He stretched and wiped his mouth against his palm.

"Where?"

"In that great fat tree, I said, you young English idiot. If you miss, you walk."

"I meant where in the tree, Mr. von Decken?"

Ernst hesitated. Anton threw the knife. Turning over twice in flight, it stuck deep into one of the young baobab's spindly bare branches.

"Typically English," Ernst said. "Almost missed it altogether."

The second knife was already in the air. It lodged two inches from the first.

"Easy enough with good German steel," Ernst grumbled, "but you only get one breakfast."

A red stain grew on the shirt sleeve that covered Anton's bandaged arm. He went indoors and bought the first knife. The German paid for breakfast and they left, motoring north for Moshi.

— 10 —

The rising light sparkled the dust of the window and woke Gwenn early. She heard the firemen stoke the engine, building steam for the day's run to Tsavo, Kiu and Nairobi. Stiff and dirty, the passengers stepped down from the carriages. Following tradition, the men went off to the port side, the ladies to starboard. Nazareth's stewards offered tin bowls of hot water for shaving. The men stood about in the bush with cutthroat razors. Promised that breakfast would be waiting at Tsavo, the travellers accepted cups of strong tea and tinned milk, then climbed back in among the dozing children.

Gwenn watched the morning's dust dim from red to grey as the land became thick with leafless stunted trees, tangled underbrush and wait-a-bit thorns. Looking across Anna to her left, she made out the grey and white tip of a mountain hiding in the distant western cloudline. Probably Kilimanjaro across the border in German East Africa. Suddenly the thought occurred to her: Where would young Anton Rider be this morning? She hoped he'd made it ashore in Dar es Salaam. She was thinking about Anton, she realized, catching herself. What about Alan?

Thirty miles on, the train came to the Tsavo River, its swift waters bordered by the thorny branches of lofty mimosas. They stopped at the edge of the small town for a solid English breakfast: fresh warm bread, eggs and crisp sausages. Gwenn watched Anna and the other children toss stones into the river while the engine took on firewood.

"Used to be a deal spicier along this stretch of the line," Tony

Bevis said as the train slowed two miles past Tsavo and passed the ruins of the old camp of the railway workers. "Anybody have a biscuit?"

Gwenn wondered if he was about to present another horrific tale, like a schoolboy enthralling his friends with ghost stories.

"Twenty years ago the Tsavo lions developed a taste for Indian coolies," Bevis said, nibbling. "Finally two thousand of the little buggers walled themselves in, just over yonder. Three weeks behind barricades of tin sheeting and railway supplies topped by thorn branches. Wouldn't come out and work till two man-eaters were destroyed. Every night they wore out the camp tarts, Lumbwa girls bought from the villages and slick little Arab boys from the coast. The wretched coolies slept in trees like pigeons or in pits dug under their tents. Covered the sleeping holes with logs while they buggered away down below. Rest of 'em stayed awake, banging kettles, feeding fires and waiting for the lions to hop in."

"I wonder why the lions liked the poor coolies so much." Anna snuggled closer to Gwenn. "Wasn't there plenty to eat outside?"

Bevis glanced at the child without replying.

Forty miles later, the vegetation became greener as they climbed between the Chyulu Hills and the Yatta Plateau. The thirsty Baldwin pulled to a stop at a waiting cistern. Finding the tank empty, the firemen began checking the feeder pipe that linked it to the distant waterhole. They followed the pipe back towards its source, knowing that animals often disturbed it, separating the joins so that no water came through. The passengers dismounted reluctantly, stretching and complaining about the delay. Anna and Samantha, followed by other children and Mulwa, wandered down the pipeline after the firemen. Just before coming to a donga, a gully thick with bush that held the pool, the firemen stopped to reconnect a bend in the pipe.

Anna ran on to the top of the slope above the donga. She looked down and turned and waved both arms at Gwenn and her mother.

"I found the water!" the girl yelled. Gwenn could not hear her words.

Anna ran down into the donga, sliding and scuffing her shoes on the dusty slope. At the bottom she stopped and knelt by a bush to study a large tortoise. Her plaid skirt dragged in the dust. She moved one hand and stroked the high-backed mottled shell.

Directly above the tortoise a large moth reposed on a branch in the shade. Its yellow wings were folded slightly apart. Anna admired the moth's stout body and feathery antennae. Farther along the branch, only an inch away, she saw a slender grey lizard. The lizard bore one small horn at the end of its snout and one just before each eye. A chameleon, she guessed. The long-toed feet of the lizard remained in place, gripping the branch, while its body and head stretched forward towards the moth.

Before she could warn the moth, the long tongue of the lizard flicked out and wrapped itself about one wing. The moth flapped frantically with its free wing while the chameleon drew the first wing into its mouth. In a few seconds the lizard had gulped in the wing, and its mouth rested directly against the fat thorax of the moth. For a moment neither creature moved.

Spellbound, Anna watched a second, slightly larger lizard move out along the branch from the trunk of the bush towards the other side of the moth. The second lizard opened its mouth, lashed out with its tongue and secured the free wing. Both lizards were jaw to jaw, with the moth pressed between them. The body of the moth twitched while the chameleons struggled. The larger lizard pulled back its head, and the moth came with it. The first lizard blinked one eye and lay still on the branch. Moth fur covered its lips. Just then Anna smelled a horrible odor. She lifted her eyes and looked through the thorny grey acacia branches.

She stared into the amber-yellow eyes of a lion. The animal rose on its extended talons. Its tail stood straight in the air like an iron rod. Anna screamed and raised her hands.

The lilting duet of two tropical boubous woke Anton in the final moments of darkness. Curious to see the conversing birds, his body prickling with the pre-dawn cold, he stepped naked from his cot to the door of the cottage. He watched the sky soften. All at once a brilliant patch of silver glittered alone high in the western sky, suspended against the darkness like a giant moon. For the first time Anton saw the snowy crown of Kilimanjaro. Gradually the rising light gave the peak roots in the endless plain below.

Hurriedly, keeping his eyes on the emerging mountain, he pulled on his trousers and boots. He flexed his arm and left his sling behind. At last he was free to walk alone in the bush. Anton wished he had a rifle. He set out, trotting towards the mountain through the well-tended orchard that spread below the plantation house of Gepard Farm. He noted the small circle of raked raised earth that surrounded the trunk of each apple tree.

Many years before, Ernst had told him, Hugo von Decken had determined to bring to Africa three reminders of his German home: an orchard, to yield shade and fruit, schnapps and *Apfelstrudel*; a house; and a young blond wife. The old family shooting lodge was disassembled. Each log and plank was numbered and shipped to Africa. Cases of new German nails, pegs and screws escorted them. While Hugo von Decken hunted ivory to pay the bills, Gretchen supervised the reconstruction. When he returned from the bush, each carved window box was bright with tulips. The Bavarian cuckoo clock chimed again on the inside wall of the dining room. In twelve months Ernst was born. A year later Gretchen was dead, after wasting cruelly from malaria. She had disappeared a bit each day like a candle burning down under her husband's already lonely eyes.

Anton paused in the orchard to eat three tart Rhineland apples. He pressed both palms against the wet morning grass and wiped his face with dew. He ran on between meticulous rows of sisal, a domesticated relative of the wild sansevieria that Ernst said was beloved by elephant. Anton smelled the crisp scent of the bush replace the sweetness of the orchard. The warming air rose and a morning breeze swept down from Kilimanjaro.

Virgin bush waited at the end of the planting. Clusters of thornbush and umbrella-like fever trees sprinkled the patchy coarse grassland. Anton felt the hard dusty ground under his boots. The curved hooks of wait-a-bit thorns tore at his thick woollen trousers. He walked toward a spring, scaring off a family of wild pigs. The warthogs trotted off, grey and solid, regimental, tight in line with heads and tails proudly in the air. The three youngsters darted down a hole. Their parents followed, entering backwards, the prickly old boar last. Six long warts rose randomly on his wrinkled face. His uneven yellow tusks glinted when he glared out from his fortress.

The shallow pool was set in a broad pan of dried mud, soft and darker near the center. Anton, astounded, crouched by the water.

There, within yards, were the spoor of more types of game than existed in all of Europe. Taught to spot a few russet threads of a fox's fur caught on a bush, the bead-like droppings of rabbits, the occasional tracks of deer and badger, Anton was dazzled by the density and variety of the prints before him. He traced their impressions with his fingertips. He rolled different pellets of dark dung against his palm, guessing at their age by their dryness, curious about the diets they suggested. Not knowing which belonged to each creature, he admired the spoor of wildebeest and zebra, eland, topi and rhinoceros, leopard and impala, giraffe and jackal. And many more, print covering print, some hard and dry, others damp and fresh. Two he recognized: the two-toed track of the wild pig and the bovine footprint of buffalo, far larger, he noticed, than its domestic English cousins.

Anton stood and turned to run back, reluctant to depart, wanting to lie in wait and watch each print come to life when the game returned to drink. But work began early on Gepard Farm, and Anton wished to be helpful. Hungry, he ran back between the neat rows of sisal and saw lines of cutters moving among the plants. Long-bladed pangas flashed. Men severed each leaf at its base and sliced off the sharp spiny tips. Ox-drawn harvesting carts followed, spaced out in line like skirmishers, loading bundles of the four-foot leaves. Far more orderly, Anton observed, than hay wagons on an English farm.

Anton heard the old Benz engine warming up. The uneven coughs as it came to life signalled that Hugo von Decken was once more at work. The operation of this engine was the only chore to which the old planter still lent himself. Stripped out of German East Africa's second Daimler truck when the exhausted vehicle collapsed around it, the engine was now mounted on a throne of mahogany. Bolted onto its heavy timber frame, it turned a single ten-foot shaft. Like the engine on a cobbler's workbench, the spinning shaft drove four leather belts, each stitched from strips of eland hide. The belts powered the decorticator wheels that scraped the white plume-like fibres of the sisal from the rough green shell of the leaves.

Nearby, within von Decken's vision, two men were preparing new belts from an eland hide. Like an apple perfectly peeled, with its skin in one continuous circular piece, so the enormous pelt was being cut into one long strip. Starting at the edge of the skin near the neck, the men cut the belt in diminishing concentric circles until they reached the center of the hide. Then the sixty-foot strip was tied taut between two posts. A round piece of hard apple wood, split like a giant clothespin, was dragged back and forth along the belt to scrape the hide clean. After several days the strip of leather would be supple and hairless.

Hugo von Decken looked at his pocket watch, silently reminding Anton of his tardiness. Beside von Decken sat a lean African with a patch of tight white curls above each ear. His face was deeply lined, as if perpetually squinting into a brilliant sun. The man's only hand ladled grease onto the unpowered end of the shaft where it spun in the center of an old truck wheel. Himself wrinkled like an aged bull elephant, his blue-grey eyes slightly watery, von Decken turned to consider his guest. Anton felt the old man assessing him.

"Already today you have been to the bush, I perceive. Yes? Is it not now time you dressed for Africa?"

"Been to the bush, sir?"

"Your boots carry fresh red dust. Your foolish English trousers are torn. From the British only one thing I have learned: always in Africa to wear shorts. All the rest they have learned from me. In shorts, the thorns do not stop you, and there is less noise when you stalk. Your skin is not important. It will mend itself. Yes, I will send the girl to make you shorts. Since Gretchen died, I have always a girl for sewing and for this and that. This man is Banda, my gunbearer. He is even more old and wise than I."

Anton extended his hand with a smile. Banda gripped it in leathery fingers without speaking. Anton turned away to supervise the unloading of the first sisal cart. Von Decken watched wagon follow wagon, nodding whenever Anton himself used a wooden pitchfork to rake up the spilled leftovers and feed them into the decorticator.

"Each plant, young Englishman," von Decken said, "must be watched more than a child. After two years in the nursery, the healthy ones are still lower than your knee. Two years more and they can be cut for the first time. Not until seven years are they truly ready, the same age a boy should hold his first rifle."

Finally the bell rang from the verandah. Anton and von Decken went up for breakfast. Anton smelled the feast as they approached.

His mouth watered. They found Ernst reaching into the platters, coffee and beer at his side, his large plate not seen under cold roast pork, sausages, sliced fried apples, eggs, thick fresh bread and pan-roasted chopped potatoes mixed with onions. Anton saw a basket of green farm apples resting in the center of the heavy wooden table. They were the color of Gwenn's eyes.

Von Decken bent stiffly and sniffed the potatoes. "Be certain, Ernst, that this filthy cook prepares the *Rösti* to your mother's recipe. Every day you must teach them once again. Otherwise everything falls apart and our lives have been for nothing. First the potatoes will be chopped too fine, like this one here, useless; then tomorrow nothing will work and Gepard Farm will be finished."

After the meal each of the Germans selected and ate a raw apple with his coffee. "Freshens the mouth," said von Decken, "cleans the teeth." Anton chose one. He remembered what the old astrologer had told him: eating an apple will arouse a woman; eating a pear will arouse a man.

Anton helped break open the crates that contained the stitching machines. Hugo von Decken watched from a distance, frowning, his arms folded. Ernst and Anton prized out the nails and loosened the old boards. Whenever an African stopped to watch, von Decken ordered the man back to the fields.

"Careful, don't bend the nails," von Decken said when Ernst ripped one loose between the teeth of a small crow. "These boards and nails could be more use than the blasted old machines."

Finally one stood free on the floor of its crate, a black block of latent perfection, neat and solid and oily as the day it was shipped. The words KOCH & ADLER, BIELEFELD rose on the heavy metal base. Von Decken stepped over and wiped off some of the protective grease with his fingers. He rubbed it between his palms and smelled his hands.

"She's still perfect." Von Decken looked at his son and turned away. "How could we lose the war?"

He picked up a walking stick and beckoned to Anton. "Come down to the sisal with me and I'll teach you to be useful."

Back on the verandah that afternoon, taking coffee and a drink after lunch, the three Europeans sat on the steps gazing out at Kilimanjaro. "Germany's tallest mountain," von Decken called it with pride. Tired, enjoying his beer, Anton listened to his hosts speculate what the post-war British administration might do to their occupied country.

"Maybe they'll give Kili back to Kenya, now that Queen Victoria's dead," said the father. "Victoria only gave it to her grandson, old Kaiser Wilhelm, so he'd have his own mountain, since England already had Mount Kenya. And I hear the British may steal all these German farms. 'Enemy Property,' they're calling our land."

"Why not? They've already stolen everything else for Kenya. And now gold's been found out here, that'll be next." Ernst drained his apple schnapps and glared at Anton.

"Gold?" Anton said, excited.

Ernst ignored him. "First you British smuggled out our sisal bulbils and suckers. Then you pinched our coffee plants. From China you stole the tea trees. Now it's all growing in Kenya on land you stole from the schwarzes."

Anton stood up. "I heard all this 'German' sisal was nicked from the Florida Keys about thirty years ago."

"No need to fight the war again just yet, you two. We stole a bit of land ourselves, Ernst, praise God." Hugo von Decken got to his feet slowly and looked at Anton, perhaps curious, Anton guessed, as to which of them would win a brawl. "Why don't you walk with me, young man?"

Von Decken stepped into the house and unlocked his gun case. He selected a Mannlicher-Schönauer and removed it from an immaculate green felt partition.

"My first rifle." Von Decken wiped it with an oily cloth. "A two fifty-six. Light and deadly, perfect. Gretchen always used it."

He replaced the Mannlicher and took down a 7-mm Mauser and a double-barrelled .450 Gebrüder Merkel. He put the bullets for each rifle into a different pocket of his faded bush jacket. Outside he handed the Mauser to Anton, keeping the shorter heavier weapon for himself. They walked down through the rows of sisal.

"I never shoot at the first water. Want to keep them coming back." Von Decken's stride picked up, his step lighter as he entered the bush. "Sometimes, when I walk out here, I forget how old I am.

"When you hunt," he said, loading his heavy Merkel and handing a single 7-mm bullet to Anton, "if you can't do it with one bullet, don't try it. Do you know what to do with that thing?"

"I believe so." The rifle was comfortable in Anton's hands. It had the clean oily smell and feel of a well-tended weapon. He checked the barrel and saw the brilliant sky through the spotless rifled tunnel of the gun metal. At last he was hunting again. He felt his senses come to life as they used to in the forest. Sharpening, they tingled with the excitement of a hunt, like the blood-fed muscles of a race-horse twitching before the start. He felt von Decken's eyes on him as he loaded the Mauser. The old man understood.

They walked in silence. Anton was astonished by the variety of thorns that attacked his clothes, each little plant devilishly clever and defiant, often shielding small white or yellow blossoms behind its sharp defences. Von Decken pointed with his rifle at a line of prints wandering before them.

"Fresh topi tracks," the German whispered.

Anton had already noticed the sharp-edged prints at the edge of the open plain. Each was divided into two tear-shaped impressions, not unlike an English fallow deer. One hundred yards farther on a swarm of smaller but similar tracks obscured the trail.

"We've lost him under these blasted impala," said von Decken.

Anton walked a small circle and gestured to von Decken. He pointed out the topi tracks and waited for the old hunter to resume the lead. With the breeze fresh in their faces, Anton knew the antelope would not smell them.

A hundred and twenty yards off, they saw it. A single large male, nearly four feet at the shoulder, with a glossy rufous coat, casting a purplish hue, and thick ridged horns. Von Decken put his arm around Anton's shoulder and drew the boy down as he knelt. "Why don't you get him for the pot?"

Anton nodded. Patiently he watched the animal graze away from them. The topi raised its head from time to time and scraped the ground with a front hoof. Anton crawled to his left until an acacia bush separated him from the antelope. He stalked slowly forward in the shelter of the plant, unmindful of his aching arm. He was totally concentrated, aware of each branch and smell and movement. Whenever the topi grazed, he advanced. If it paused, he lay still, always reflecting the animal's attitude, like a partner in a dance, Lenares had told him.

At fifty yards Anton slipped off the safety catch. Kneeling, waiting for the creature to turn, he pressed the Mauser into his shoulder. The topi stepped once and forked up the ground with one front hoof. It turned in profile and raised its head. Anton squeezed the trigger and ran forward as the antelope fell.

Von Decken joined him. He examined the wound and the dead animal. "Foolish. You might've lost him trying to get so close. You certainly aren't ready for bongo. See where the leopard clawed his haunches? He was lucky that time. All that scraping with his hooves was to mark his territory, trying to lure the ladies. Just like the rest of us, only instead of money and a fine house, he uses scent from his foot glands."

"What's a bongo?"

"A giant red antelope that hides in the mountain forest in Kenya. Shy as ghosts. Many men hunt a lifetime and never find a bongo. When you get one, you'll know you're a hunter. Now we'll hurry back and send some boys to bring in your topi before it gets dark and the hyenas are into him."

As von Decken spoke, Anton quickly ran his knife down the animal's stomach from breast to anus. With his own choori, he could do a neater job. He scraped out the coiled sausage-like intestines. Without looking up he cleaned the chest and stomach cavity and cut off the head. He stood and balanced the heavy body across his shoulders. He held two legs crossed in front of his chest with one hand and his rifle in the other. He enjoyed the feel of the hard smooth-haired legs in his grip while he followed von Decken home to Gepard Farm.

"Well, well," Ernst said, waiting for them on the verandah, schnapps in one hand, cigar in the other. "Our young Engländer got lucky, did he?"

"Don't know about luck, but the boy creeps like a Frenchman in a cathouse," said Ernst's father, "and he keeps a sharp knife." The old man watched Anton peel back the topi's hide with the edge of his blade. Anton drew no blood when he separated the underskin from the membrane and flesh beneath. Then he carried the carcass to the kitchen.

"You're fortunate that boy wasn't hunting you on one of those long trails in the war," von Decken said to his son.

"We killed a few hunters," Ernst said.

Anton washed his hands in a bucket and went down to the cottage. Surprised to see the flickering light of an oil lamp in his window, he entered the small room cautiously. An African woman lay on his bed, dressed in the off-white smock of a house servant. She sat up, swinging long black legs over the side of the bed, not young but conscious of her voluptuous attraction.

"Come make shots," the woman said.

"Shots?" Anton stood awkwardly near the door.

"Yes, shorts. First I measure you." She removed one of the two lengths of string that hung about her neck. She came close to Anton and drew the string around his middle while her heavy breasts hung against him. Suddenly nervous, he smelled the warm appeal of her body. Her fingers felt him slowly from the small of the back, around the sides to his stomach. She tied a knot in the string, tightening it between her teeth as she looked up into Anton's eyes with a smile. He flushed. Taking the second string, she held it against Anton's buttocks, then slowly moved her hands around his hips to the front, cupping him. Again she knotted the string.

"Now I know size. Very good. Papa Deckie too old." The woman smiled when she saw Anton's rising embarrassment. "Maybe you too young?"

The lion ate her!" Samantha Gault screamed as she ran to her parents.

Mulwa emerged from the donga carrying Anna in his arms. Gwenn saw the child's body hanging like a torn blood-soaked doll.

She helped Mulwa lay the girl on a blanket in the carriage. Wailing and trembling, Mrs. Gault sat on the step clutching Samantha. She stared up at Gwenn with her mouth open.

"Best not look at her now," Gwenn said to Mrs. Gault.

Gwenn examined the injured girl. She saw the fresh, still pure wetness of Anna's blood. Gwenn felt herself go cool and enter the dead calm detachment that had kept her sane in France. She remembered the shining soaked floor of her ambulance when the last body was emptied out.

Anna's skirt and blouse were shreds. Her face and hair and ripped clothes were dark with dust. Her lower body ran with blood through the torn tartan skirt.

"Tony," Gwenn said to Bevis as Gault held back his wife, "draw two buckets of water from the engine. Filter them through a bit of clean cotton until the water's clear. Have Tom keep Samantha and her mother in the next compartment. Then collect any medical supplies you can find."

Gwenn used a soldier's knife to cut away Anna's clothes. She studied the young naked body. Life as a Volunteer Ambulance Driver had made her difficult to shock, but she was horrified by the child's wounds. The deep open cuts in her thighs and hips might have been made with a carving knife. Gwenn filtered the rusty engine water once more through a strip of gauze and washed the unconscious child.

While Gwenn worked she thought of the first day she had been dragooned into a surgery tent. Her first month as an ambulance driver had been horror enough. But that afternoon, at a dressing station behind Neuve-Chapelle, every unwounded person was forced to help. Intended as a minor field hospital to give temporary care to the lightly wounded, the dressing station instead became the first refuge from a slaughter that left thousands of trees and men and horses in blackened splintered ruins across fields of mud-filled shell holes. A young English doctor with sunken crying eyes stepped from a tent. His surgical coat was splashed like a butcher's smock. He ordered Gwenn and four other V.A.D.s to join his work. While he spoke she saw his hands shaking. Screams howled through the canvas behind him.

The upper half of Anna's body was almost free of damage, except for two shallow puncture wounds on her stomach from the lion's teeth. Her right thigh, bleeding heavily, was savagely raked by the cat's claws, always, Gwenn knew, the carriers of festering infection.

"How the devil did this happen?" she heard Bevis ask a fireman outside the carriage window.

"We run to the donga top when the children screamed," said the soot-covered Indian. He pointed towards Mulwa. "I saw this man run after a lion with a girl in its mouth. A thin lion with a bad leg. This man's club hit the lion and it dropped the girl and run off."

"Pile back in and fire her up," Bevis said to the stoker. He turned to the engineer. "And make your damn best time for Nairobi."

"It'll take her a good nine hours," said the engineer. "We've hills to climb and old Baldie ain't what she was."

Gwenn worked silently in the front compartment. Bevis watched and did what he could. She was surprised and relieved by his silence. She swabbed out the puncture wounds with carbolic soap and boiled water. The talon cuts, some deep, were foul with decomposing animal waste lodged in the predator's claws. Gwenn cleaned the cuts and prepared to place crystals of permanganate in the wounds. Worried that the salt and acid base of these infection killers would damage the healthy tissue, she crushed the crystals between two coins and pressed small fragments of the ground permanganate into Anna's open flesh.

"Till we get her to hospital," Gwenn said, "this loss of blood is even more dangerous than infection. Can't we go faster?"

Whenever pressure was removed from the right thigh, small rushes of blood pumped out from a thin tear in the femoral artery. Gwenn knew the delicate surgery required was beyond her training, and the rocking of the train made fine work impossible. To stop completely the flow of blood to the lower leg would risk losing the limb. To let it pump out for nine hours must mean death. Gwenn hoped the bleeding might ease if moderate pressure were maintained on the damaged artery. She held a thick dressing against the wound.

After an hour, Anna stirred. Gwenn feared the girl would wake and thrash about in pain. She gave her an injection of morphine and a whiff of ether.

The locomotive did not take easily to the ascent towards Nairobi. The approach to Kibwezi, still over a hundred miles from the capital, was a struggle of rushing descents and dragging climbs. Like a tired cyclist, the engineer sought to gather speed downhill, but not too much, to assist him on the next ascent. Eight miles from Kibwezi the boiler pressure dropped. Gwenn watched helplessly while the train slowed. Beside her, the upholstered seat was wet with fresh blood.

She felt the train lose headway as the engine's power was overcome by a long climb and the drag of the load. The train hesitated just before the crest. It began to slip backward. Gwenn heard the wheels screech when the engineer tightened the brakes. Wheels locked, the train glided slowly backwards to the valley floor. She saw Bevis run forward to speak to the engineer. He conferred with a group of ex-officers who at once took charge.

Eighty passengers climbed down. Small children and severely crippled veterans remained aboard. The engineer reversed power and the train backed up the preceding slope. With a rush it descended again and climbed the next hill. Walking rapidly along the track, the passengers were back on board in twenty minutes.

Three passenger cars and the goods van were uncoupled and shunted aside at the Kibwezi siding. Wood, water and fuel were loaded. Bevis gave the stationmaster a cable for Nairobi. A few families crowded into the remaining compartments. The others waited for another locomotive.

"Bad news!" The Sikh stationmaster ran over just before the train pulled out. "The cable did not go through! Our line is down. Must be giraffe, or those Maasai dogs stealing the wire for jewelry. Unless you go so very fast, pesi pesi, you will meet another train on the track!"

The locomotive, fuel tender and single car swept out of Kibwezi.

Anna, repeatedly on the edge of consciousness, was kept numb with morphine. Alarmed by her pallor and loss of blood, Gwenn applied a full tourniquet to her upper right thigh. The leg began to lose color.

Four miles from Ulu, the last fuel stop before Nairobi, the train braked again. Gwenn leaned out the window. A giraffe lay dead across the track. Copper telegraph wire was tangled insanely about its neck. The firemen and every able-bodied passenger jumped down. Hauling on the legs, the men and women dragged the two-thousand-pound animal to the side.

At Ulu firewood was loaded and the telegram sent. Gwenn wiped Anna's face. The girl was still unconscious. Gwenn turned her own eyes to the window.

The train crossed the Athi Plains for the final run and Gwenn saw at last the Africa she had expected. A grey-green landscape sprinkled with acacia trees, and everywhere animals. Ostrich, giraffe, zebra, Thomson's gazelle, other antelopes for which she knew no name, all roamed before her in the vast open garden of the plain. She prayed Anna would live to see it. The child's heart was still beating, but always more faintly.

Late in the afternoon, the train pulled into Nairobi station. Families and friends crowded the platform. Beyond them, all Nairobi seemed gathered around the little station, in wagons, on horseback and on foot, in open cars and rickshaws. A makeshift Chevrolet ambulance, its wooden box body painted white, backed up to the train. Two European nurses and a doctor stood ready. Gwenn looked down at Anna's blanket when they lifted the child onto a stretcher. Horrified, she saw a small mass of dried blood where Anna's lower back had rested. Another wound.

Dusty and stained, Gwenn stepped down onto the platform and helped place Anna in the ambulance. She glanced nervously down the platform, suddenly aware of her messy appearance. She pushed back her hair with soiled hands. Gwenn saw a man staring at her, a slender dark-haired figure in loose-hanging clothes. Oh, God, could that be Alan? She hesitated, confused that he looked so much older and thinner. Finally she ran to her husband as he walked stiffly towards her. Gwenn hugged him, crying, rocking him. She felt the bones of his back. Alan put his arms around her and hugged her weakly, but at least it was affection. She closed her eyes.

"Thank heavens you're here," she said. "Are you all right?"

"How was your trip?" he asked as she spoke.

"You can't imagine what happened on the train. That poor girl was attacked by a lion. She's bleeding to death. I've been trying to help her." Gwenn bent her head back and looked up into Alan's face, hoping to find something of the lover she remembered.

"We have it, Gwennie, our farm," he whispered in her ear while she clung to him again. "Two thousand acres on a beautiful river. Ours, what you've always wanted. And there's our wagon."

"How could we afford such a farm?" Gwenn leaned back with her hands on his arms and looked at him. He didn't seem to care about the injured girl. His eyes were different. Deeper, lonely, no longer a young man's eyes. She must have changed too. She wondered how much the war had done to them.

Gwenn turned her head and saw the splintered wagon loaded high and drawn by four mules. Beside it stood an African and a fat Indian, richly dressed. "We must follow the ambulance to the hospital and make sure Anna's all right," she said.

"A new friend helped with the money. Here he is, Mr. da Souza, and this is Arthur." Alan took Gwenn's hand to help her up to the wagon bench. Gwenn nodded at the bowing Indian. The caked blood on her fingers drew Alan's attention to her hand. "Where is your wedding ring?"

Anton woke himself before dawn. He rubbed his eyes and made a low twittering sound, repeating it slowly until he had it just right. He called to the boubous, at first quietly, then with insistence.

One bird answered, beginning the morning's conversation. Another joined in.

Anton rose and drew on his heavy shorts. A faded field grey, they were cut from old tent canvas. You couldn't get proper leather shorts in Africa, Hugo von Decken had grumbled, and these were next best. Von Decken himself saved his lederhosen for the evenings, the thick grey leather of the German shorts never washed in thirty years. Seated on the doorstep in the dark, Anton pulled on his new boots, short and too heavy for his taste, but durable. He took the Mauser from the corner, checked it and trotted down through the apple orchard. True to von Decken's injunction, he carried two bullets. One to hunt with, one to come home with.

The sky lightened. Anton climbed up into his favorite cranny in the kopje, a jumble of boulders near a waterhole deep in the bush. Piled together as if by the hand of a giant at play, the rocks gave a useful view of the oasis below, both for Anton and for the predators that shared his interests.

He observed a scatter of porcupine quills on the rock just before him, too many for anything but the death of their owner. Anton reached out and picked one up. He admired its perfect architecture and alternating grey and white bands. Hollow and sharp-pointed, lightweight yet remarkably rigid, it seemed more suited to its work than the finest copper-tipped bullet. It was sufficiently light to be carried and released, yet strong enough to penetrate and wound. He put the quill in his shirt pocket.

Anton passed his fingertips over the rock where the quills lay. Nothing but the dust of the veldt clung to them. He moistened his fingers and did it again. They bore a suggestion of red drawn from the dry blood that must be there. Nearby he saw large droppings of chalk-like dung. Hyena, he knew, each calcium-white pellet the efficient distillation of a victim's bones, ground to fragments by relentless jaws. But the porcupine was probably too troublesome a prey for these scavengers. He looked again and found a mass of smaller white droppings. Perhaps one of the lesser cats, he thought, wishing he knew more, possibly a civet.

Just then he heard the bushes rustle below him. A long narrow face parted the acacia branches, searching right and left. A tall fawn-colored antelope, a hartebeest, emerged and waded into the shallow water and began to drink. A strange creature, dumb-faced, with widely spread horns and humped shoulders far higher than its rump, it seemed to Anton devoid of grace. Another hartebeest followed. Then many more, perhaps eighty or a hundred.

Astonished to see such plenty, Anton thought back to the Cheviot Hills of Northumberland. There each animal was a precious sight. He could still taste the tension that bound him when he poached red deer with Lenares in the freezing dawn mist that rolled down from the Scottish hills near Coldstream. To avoid capture by gillies and keepers, Lenares allowed himself only one shot with a light-calibre rifle, always in a tight valley to hold the crack of the explosion, and never after the day was light.

Stiff and numb after a night on the ground, Anton and the gypsy lay on their blanket among the bracken and bog myrtle. They watched a wide-antlered stag emerge from the forest edge. It looked about and stepped warily across the open haugh to the stream. This stag, they knew, was beyond them, a twelve-pointer, royal game, reserved for other hunters. Like a tempting expensive menu posted in a res-taurant window, it was too desirable and valuable, too dangerous a prize. Finally a young buck stepped from the wood into the water. Lenares passed the .275 to the thirteen-year-old boy. Overwhelmed by the trust, Anton took the rifle. Failing to steady his breathing, he fired high and forward, taking the young deer in the shoulder. The crippled buck staggered deeper into the stream. Lenares fell on it with his knife, trying to slit its throat. Animal and man rolled in the icy bloody water.

Anton remembered watching from the riverbank as the deer flung off the hunter and fought back to its feet. It staggered across the river, gathering strength and breaking up the far bank with the choori still buried in the lower part of its neck. Lenares and Anton charged through the cold rushing burn. They followed the bleeding animal up the next hillside, running on rocks and slipping on fallen leaves. They paused on the crest, gasping for breath, and scanned the terrain below them. Morning fog covered pockets of the lower land. They spotted the deer emerging into a misty glade, its legs invisible, swim-ming in a cloud. The animal paused at the far edge of the opening while the air cleared. The buck stood on three legs. It tossed its head desperately, trying to free itself of the blade still set in its bleeding neck. Then it limped into the private forest that lay beyond.

Anton and Lenares followed the trail of blood. The morning brightened and the mist burned off. Dark fir trees crowned distant hills to the north. Lenares, nervous, trotted with his head low, watching the ground, anxious to finish the kill and recover his knife before the nearby villages came to life. Once more they saw the red deer in the distance, moving more slowly, with the hilt of the knife higher as the blade worked free. Gradually the forest became less wild, park-like, thinner. Old oaks and yews stood pruned and healthy, without the dense clutter of underbrush that harbored the smaller animals. The two hunters went on. Anton felt Lenares growing less at home, wary whenever they emerged into a clearing.

Suddenly Lenares raised one hand in alarm and dropped to the ground by a thick copse of young birch. Anton lay flat beside him. Their shoulders touched. Anton felt the tension in the gypsy's body. Lenares rested the .275 between them and put his mouth to Anton's ear.

"We can't shoot. If anything happens, forget me and run for it with the rifle. Remember, as long as they don't catch me with a weapon, it can't be too bad. If I've got a rifle, it's prison."

Anton heard the murmur of approaching voices.

The wounded deer limped into view, walking towards them, a light wind behind it, fleeing back from the human scent and the voices that grew slowly louder. Blood trickled from the animal's shoulder and ran down its foreleg, leaving a cluster of drops on the ground whenever the buck paused. Lenares' knife was almost free. The top of the thin blade gleamed wet as it swung to and fro with the movements of the deer's neck. The creature paused near the copse, twisting its neck and tossing its head sharply. The knife shook loose and rose into the air. Captivated by the sight, disturbed by the animal's suffering, Anton saw the blade shine magically for an instant in the light at the top of its ascent. The knife fell among the leaves and acorns.

Lenares leapt up and grabbed his choori. The deer ran off on three legs.

"There 'e is!" yelled a strong voice. "After 'im, lads!"

Lenares threw the knife towards Anton. The blade sank to the hilt in a tussock inches from the boy's left hand. Anton lay frozen, the rifle in his other hand. For an instant Lenares crouched in the clearing, a fox deciding where to flee. Then he bolted. Anton rolled deeper into the thicket and slipped the knife into the side of his belt before covering his legs and lower body with fallen leaves.

Three men burst into the clearing. Foresters, one carried an axe and another a pruner's billhook with a long curved blade. The unencumbered man, the youngest, tall and well set up, dashed after Lenares.

"A dram if you catch 'im, Rupe!" the axeman hollered after the racing figure. The older foresters sat down in the clearing. They settled themselves and drew clay pipes from the pockets of thick tweed jackets.

"Probably one of them blasted tinkers," the heavy man with the billhook said, lighting his shag. "Always coppin' and snitchin' what's not theirs. Never any honest work. Time we flushed 'em out for good."

Anton smelled the fragrant smoke. He felt himself sweat and shiver with fear. For the first time, Anton understood. Like all the gypsies, whenever he hunted, he was always hunted too.

In a few minutes Rupe was back, driving Lenares before him with hard cuffs to the head and shoulders. The gypsy's face bled from a cut below one eye. His thin black coat was torn where the half-crown buttons had been ripped away. He carried his boots in one hand, making a second flight unlikely. Anton had never realized his friend was so small and slender.

The heavier man stood and passed his pipe to the axeman. He approached the gypsy.

"This is for wounding a young buck and leaving 'im to bleed to death." The man grunted as he plunged a fist into Lenares's belly. Lenares bent over with a gasp.

Anton tightened his grip on the rifle, wanting to help, but scared. Should he jump up and threaten the men with the weapon, hoping Lenares could escape? Fearful, he remembered Lenares's orders, knowing, too, that menacing men with the rifle would be another crime.

"An' this is for muckin' about in our woods." The heavy man

punched the gypsy twice on the side of his face. "For the trouble you and yer lot cause us." Lenares collapsed. Anton, near panic with guilty indecision, was afraid to try and protect his friend.

Lenares curled his knees up to his stomach when the first kick caught him in the side. The gypsy screamed. Too weak to help without using the rifle, Anton closed his eyes. He heard the heavy thuds as the forester kicked Lenares in the chest and legs. The gypsy groaned again and again. The blows stopped. Anton opened his eyes.

"Keep away with yer bloody stealing and witching!" the heavy man said, short of breath, growing excited. He stamped one heel on Lenares's left hand. The gypsy's scream cut through Anton. The other foresters dragged their companion away from the fallen man. Anton watched the three figures disappear into the woods.

Crying, ashamed he had not helped his friend, Anton ran to Lenares. The gypsy sat on the ground, moaning and clutching two broken fingers with his right hand. Anton pulled on Lenares's boots. In silence, they made their way back to the encampment.

Today, Anton thought, still troubled by his conduct, would be his first day hunting alone in Africa. He must make a cleaner kill.

He waited until all the hartebeests had a chance to drink. He studied the more numerous females and their young, watching for habits that distinguished the hartebeest from the other antelope he saw each dawn. He isolated a large male that stood alone under a tree, rubbing a shoulder against the rough bark.

Anton fired. The male fell and the antelope scattered. Anton reloaded and ran down to the waterhole. Passing the pool, he noticed human footprints under the antelope tracks. He bent over the twitching body of the hartebeest and sensed a movement on the branch above his head. He looked up and saw a spotted tail. The long swaybacked body of a leopard rose on the limb.

Their eyes met. Anton saw the vivid spark of the cat's ferocity. He raised his rifle. The creature sprang. The leopard crashed into the Mauser as the weapon fired. Anton, rifle and animal fell to the ground. Almost too fast to watch, the frenzied cat scrambled after Anton in the dust. Its teeth bared, the leopard snarled viciously. Blood poured from its shoulder.

As Anton drew his knife, he saw an African dash up behind the leopard and stab it through the side with a spear.

The leopard turned, the weapon lodged through it like a spit. The cat caught the black man with its forelegs and dragged him down. Encumbered by the spear, it clawed frantically for the man's face and worked at his shoulders with the thumb-like dewclaws on the inside of its front legs. Anton rushed forward and wrenched the spear. The cat jerked its head, gnashing furiously at the weapon. Its green eyes blazed. With all his strength Anton drew his knife across its throat in a single powerful swing.

Suddenly the scene was still. The leopard's throat was cut through to the neckbone. The small round head hung loosely. Anton's left arm was soaked to the shoulder in blood, some of it his own. He bent over the African. The man sat tight-lipped on the ground examining his wounds. A patch of his scalp hung over one ear. His right shoulder and chest were torn open to the bone, skin and flesh stripped back as if chopped free by a hatchet. Deep cuts bled on either side of his stomach. Anton helped him stand and they walked to the waterhole. The African dipped himself once. He stood again, and clean blood ran from the wounds.

"Thank you." Anton stripped off his shirt and held it to the man's shoulder. "You saved me. Let's get you back to the farm."

The African nodded.

"My name's Anton."

"I am Karioki, Karioki Kitenji," the man replied in English.

They struggled two miles back to the plantation. Anton supported Karioki with one arm while he carried the rifle and spear in his free hand. As they entered the sisal, the African collapsed. Anton bent down and lifted Karioki across his shoulders, carrying the rifle in one hand but abandoning the spear. He staggered through the orchard and came to his cottage. He laid the bleeding man on his bed and ran to the house for help.

"Looks like you've finally met Africa," Ernst said from the breakfast table, a large sausage in his fingers, as the shirtless blood-soaked Englishman dashed up the verandah steps. While Anton gasped out the story, Hugo von Decken examined the three parallel cuts in his upper arm. Ernst strode to the cottage with a medical kit, yelling for the cook to bring boiling water.

"This one's probably had it," said Ernst lightly after swabbing out Karioki's wounds. "But you never know with these damn schwarzes.

He's a powerful-looking brute. Here, hold his head while I stitch up this mess. Won't be anything fancy, just my usual bush darning. But at least if he lives, it won't make us sick to look at him."

Eager to help, not wishing to appear squeamish, Anton clasped the sides of the African's head between his hands. The sweat and blood and dirt prevented him from getting a secure hold. He wiped his hands on his shorts and seized Karioki's head once more. Anton felt the man stir weakly. He recalled the gypsy rule against letting anyone be born or die indoors.

"Best gut there is," Ernst said while Anton and von Decken held the African still.

Anton was surprised by the unconcerned manner of the Germans. Both men acted as if they were filling a pipe or slicing bread. Was it the war that had made them this way, Anton wondered, or just daily life in Africa?

Working swiftly, Ernst patched the scalp and stitched back a wide flap of skin and muscle along the collarbone. He took out his penknife and trimmed off the ends of the heavy surgical thread. "Cut this stuff myself from the sinew that runs down the inside of a cheetah's backbone. Also makes the best bowstrings. If they used this in Berlin, those fat-bellied burghers would never wear out.

"Not a bad piece of knitting, I must say." Ernst rinsed his hands in a bucket and admired his work. He gripped Anton's upper left arm and began to clean the cuts with firm movements.

"I'm glad you didn't make my shorts." Anton tried not to flinch. When Ernst finished, Anton emptied the bucket of pink water outside the doorway.

"He doesn't look like one of ours, very likely a Kuke," said von Decken as his son went through the pockets of the African's torn khaki shorts. "And those are British army pants the munt's got on him. Must've been down here when the war ended."

Ernst held up a dented brass button and several empty rifle cartridges. A lion decorated the button's curved surface, and with it the raised letters K.A.R.

"The black bastard was with your King's African Rifles." Ernst flung the button to Anton. "If I'd known that, I would've stitched up something else."

"Thank God for my apples." Von Decken led Anton and Ernst to

the verandah for some schnapps. Anton cleaned the Mauser and
recounted what had happened at the waterhole.

"You made two mistakes, my young Englishman." The father
rubbed ointment on Anton's cuts. "When you spot a leopard, never
look it in the eye. If your eyes meet, or if you wound them, they
always attack. Every time."

"I see," said Anton, rolling the porcupine quill between his fingers.
"What else did I do?"

"You blinded yourself with concentration," von Decken said.
"When you hunt, you must concentrate like a gemsmith cutting a
stone. That, you do. At home, it would be enough. But here, at the
same time you must be wary like a rabbit in a field of foxes. In Africa,
the gift of danger is always all about you."

"Anything else?" asked Anton, with no annoyance in his voice.

"Yes. You took away a porcupine quill. That, of course, brings
bad luck."

Anton took his leave and walked to his cabin, thinking back to
the gypsy preoccupation with luck and fortune. His thoughts returned to the deer hunt with Lenares, and how he had failed to
protect his friend.

"For many years," old man von Decken said one evening as he rested
on the verandah and gazed out towards Kilimanjaro, "I dreamed of
making my fortune in Africa and going home rich as a prince. To
buy a grand estate above the Rhine and dance with the ladies. Like
your Clive of India, I thought, only he saved time by stealing from
the maharajahs. No?"

"Yes." Anton thought of his own dreams: freedom to roam, hunting in new country, his own land under his horse's hooves. Perhaps
even finding gold. He seated himself on the top step with his back
against a cedar pillar and looked into the night.

Ernst sat nearby, crushing bits of sugarcane and carbolic soap in a
coconut shell. He passed the poultice to Anton and interrupted his
father. "If you want to stay useful, boy, better smear this on those
festering thorn cuts. Lettow's balm, we used to call it."

"Fortunately, I never made enough money to go home," von
Decken continued. He drew three dark cigars from the cartridge

loops of his shirtfront and handed two to the younger men. "Finally I learned that if you worry about money, it makes no difference how much you have. More money will not free you. You will always want more and more, and always worry, like a banker. So instead, I walk in the veldt with my Merkel. But when Ernst was twelve I sent him home to school, to make a proper Prussian of my little savage."

"And I hated it," said Ernst. "It was too late. At school I lay in my narrow bed and dreamed of Africa. I closed my eyes and smelled the bush after the rains. The masters read us animal stories at bedtime. My friends were entranced. But at nine I had climbed an acacia near camp and watched two lion pull down a young buffalo, like butchers hacking at a living ox. Tearing it open while the buff snorted and raged, just too young to use its horns. Finally the lioness jumped on the buffalo's back and began ripping open the shoulders. The other lion reared up and belted the buff across the face with one paw, breaking its neck. What could bedtime stories tell me?"

"When I was a boy in Germany," Ernst's father said, "the Black Forest seemed an immense ultimate wilderness, a myth, teeming with mighty boar and deer. But when I went back, after Africa, it was like visiting my old schoolroom. Even the animals were small and few. After the veldt, the greatest forest in Europe was a park."

As the evening went on, von Decken spoke about the elephants and squinted into the darkness, searching for the great bulls in the shadows. Ernst rolled his eyes and disappeared into the library with his schnapps. Settling in with a cigar, the old man answered Anton's questions about the early days in East Africa, when Dr. Karl Peters carved out an empire for Germany, breaking the tribes and provoking the British to move in to the north, creating Kenya.

"In 1890 I met the last of the old elephant hunters," von Decken said, "Afrikaaners and English, Viljoen and Pretorius, Hartley and Finaughty, men who knew Africa when it was young and wild, before we ruined it."

"What were they like?" Anton tried to seem comfortable with the strong cigar.

"They were hard men who understood how to be alone. Lifetimes they spent following the big tuskers north. First the Transvaal and Bechuanaland, then Mashonaland and Nyasaland, finally East Africa, Uganda, the Sudan. No one killed and loved the elephant like they did. And in the end, one way or another, the elephant killed them all. Trampled. Exploding rifles. Buffalo. Malaria. Snakes. Loneliness."

"Tell me about hunting with them." Anton was relieved his cigar was out.

"The Afrikaaners first found me camping in the miombo forests along the Rufiji River," von Decken continued, as if no one else had spoken. "In the beginning I was a leper. They hated to see me. They were jealous lovers, believing Africa was theirs alone. But at least I wasn't British. Slowly we became almost friends, or at least I was someone to talk to. In time I became like them. I saw each new white man as an intruder stealing a piece of my Africa."

The old planter left his rattan armchair and slowly stepped down from the verandah. Riveted, Anton saw his white hair stand out like a gleaming helmet against the blue-black sky. Von Decken threw down his cigar and put both hands on Anton's shoulders. He stared into his eyes.

"Can you imagine how it was, boy, to be young out here back then? All day we walked and ran after the old bulls, sometimes away from them. Twenty, twenty-five miles in thick country. Day after day. Carrying only our beautiful heavy rifles while the thorns cut the clothes from our bodies. At the end of the hunt we'd camp where the bulls fell. At night we sat by the fire with our boots off and rubbed our blistered feet with sand. We cut thorn sticks and toasted fresh slices of elephant trunk in the flames. The smell itself was a feast. Pieces of the animals were all around us, almost alive. Legs. Hearts. Trunks. The blood was drying in smooth dark pools. We were part of the animals. The ivory was laid out on scraps of old tent canvas in the shadows, five, six, seven feet tall, often a hundred pounds or more a side. Some of the boys were sucking oil out of the honeycomb bone above the elephants' eyes. The gunbearers were cleaning the rifles, the other boys gorging and laughing by their fire, and these old bush pirates would drink and smoke and tell me the tricks. God, how they missed the wild days before the governments came."

Anton's shoulders ached as von Decken gripped them. He felt the pain of the three cuts on his arm. Behind the old hunter, fading into the night like the ghosts of his youth, Anton saw the white sisal fibre shift and ripple in the wind as it hung on the rope drying racks.

"Before light we were off," von Decken said. "Hunting at the streams and waterholes. At home the *Dummköpfe* say the lion's the king of beasts. But when an old bull elephant comes to the water, the animals know who's king. All of them, lion, buffalo, rhino fade into the bush and let him drink alone.

"After a time the bulls knew we were coming, even in new country. Every year there were fewer of them, the old hundred-pounders, and the hunting was harder and harder. The boys would follow after us, so as not to scare the game. Dozens of them. Almost mad, obsessed, like us, by the elephant and the life. They stayed with us for the meat. Each man carried one tusk, wrapped in antelope hide, with his tobacco and charms stuffed into the nerve hole. At the end, when we came home, we'd be either death lean with fever or fit as gods. The boys paraded through the villages, painted like demons, ostrich feathers in their hair, swaggering under the ivory. It wasn't the wretched missionaries who opened up Africa, or soldiers, or traders. It was the elephant."

"I wish I'd been with you," said Anton. "What was your best elephant?"

"Elephants are like women." The old hunter's grip relaxed. He grinned like a boy and tucked both thumbs in the top of his grey leather shorts. "The best one is always the next one. But tell me, young man. My black girl, my soft schwarze who keeps me warm. She says you do not like her. True? Or did you think old Papa Decken would be mad?"

"I don't know, sir. I wasn't sure what to do." Anton blushed in the shadows.

Before going to his cabin, Anton walked to the fire where Karioki was talking with von Decken's gunbearer. Karioki was mending faster than Anton thought possible. The uneven pink scar along his collarbone was vivid against the gleaming black of his skin. Now Karioki was speaking of going home to Mount Kenya. Von Decken had warned Anton that if he himself was thinking of walking north, he had better find a dependable man to accompany him.

"It'll be three or four hundred miles on foot, like the old days, and there's a lot more than leopard out there," von Decken told him. "That Karioki's just the sort you're going to need, smart and hard to kill. Surprising for a Kikuyu. Seems he was released by your army and was on his way home when you found him. He plans to leave soon. In the meantime, I'm having old Banda teach him how to look after you."

Squatting on his heels by the fire with the two Africans, Anton greeted the senior man first.

"*Jambo,* father Banda." Anton rested a hand on Karioki's arm. "How is my friend here?"

"Karioki is stronger," said Banda. "But you stupid boys must learn not to wrestle with leopards. Not even the ugly Maasai do that. The leopard always likes to wound before he dies, so we remember him."

"This stupid boy, Tlaga, the Watchful One, saved my life," said Karioki.

"I thought he saved my life," Anton said to Banda. He squeezed Karioki's arm.

"Use this whistle the next time you need me." Karioki handed Anton one of the empty Enfield cartridges he carried in his pocket.

"You know, father Banda, that Karioki and I leave soon," Anton said.

"Yes, and my bwana says at the beginning he and I will safari with you, so you children may learn from the men."

Anton grinned and rose to leave. Karioki stood and spoke to him.

"If we walk together, Tlaga, I must warn you. First we cross the land of my people's enemy, the stinking Maasai. And when finally we come to my father's village, by the hotel of the great Bwana Lord, a devil waits for me. He is very small, Chura Nyakundu, but evil, and more cunning than a leopard."

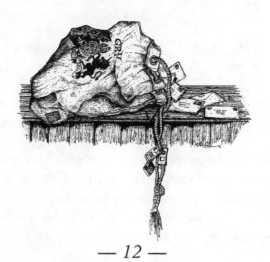

— 12 —

Gwenn and Alan spent a week under canvas at the Soldiers' Camp on the outskirts of Nairobi. Tomorrow they would leave for Nanyuki and the Ewaso Ngiro River.

They had checked lists of equipment, studied booklets on coffee and flax, and joined the Old Soldiers' Association. Gwenn visited the European Hospital each day. Alan accompanied her twice, pacing in the hall while she sat by Anna and held the child's hand. In the evenings Arthur cooked and she and Alan dined by the tent.

Not once did they make love. Frail and cool, Alan resisted her affection. He avoided letting her see him when he undressed. One morning she glimpsed scars on his lower abdomen. Alan would only say he had been wounded in the pelvis. When they were alone and she touched him, he was lifeless and silent. At first she was cruelly frustrated and upset by his coolness. Then she recalled how variously the soldiers in France had reacted to their wounds. Many injured men grew tortured when their bodies and their spirits were no longer in harmony. Resigning herself, Gwenn saw it would take time.

First there had been the welcoming tea on the lawn behind Salisbury House under the vast garden party tents reserved for Empire Day and the Royal Birthday. The event took Gwenn by surprise. She and Alan were still as nervous together as newlyweds. Straight from the train and the hospital, they found themselves locked in a line of vehicles on the dusty road beside the government buildings. A white pennant hung between two telegraph poles: B.E.A.

WELCOMES H.M. SOLDIERS. An African came forward and held the heads of their mules. People stepped down from lorries and horse carts, farm wagons and old motorcars. Ladies from the welcoming committee, wearing Union Jack sashes, greeted the arrivals. Gwenn looked at her hands and the rust-colored stains on her blouse and skirt.

"Wouldn't you like to come inside and wash before tea, my dear?" an English voice said. "I'm Florence Delamere. Welcome to Nairobi."

Gwenn jumped down and introduced herself. She took fresh clothes from her bag and followed the lady into a stone building.

"Do I look better?" Gwenn asked Alan with a smile when she came out.

"Wonderful." Alan looked up at her from the step where he was seated. He hesitated before taking her hand and suppressed a moan when he rose.

After a brisk welcoming talk by the Governor, servants uncovered the tea tables. The settlers looked in wonder at mountains of tiny sandwiches, biscuits and finger cakes. While they hesitated, Gwenn saw the scattering of old Africa hands, tan and at home, move swiftly to the tables and set to work. Established farmers, government officers, merchants, they swarmed about the platters.

"Better pitch in, Gwenn, before the locals scoff it all." Tony Bevis emerged from the scrum with a handful of sandwiches. "The Colonial Office rarely opens the door, and when they do, you've got to charge through like a rhino."

"Do you suppose I could have my ring back now?" Gwenn asked Bevis.

"That's rather awkward, actually. It's so dreadfully tight."

"Tight?"

"Jill can't get it off, even with soap. I don't know how she ever got it on."

"A girl can always get a wedding ring on," Gwenn said, annoyed. She felt Alan looking at her. "But I'm afraid you'll have to shop for your own."

Gwenn piled a plate with triangles of well-buttered white bread. She scraped each piece dry against the edge of her dish, accumulating a small pale-yellow mound at the side of the plate. She gathered the butter on the fingertips of her right hand and turned to Jill Bevis.

"Excuse me, won't you, Jill, but may I help you get my ring off?"

Jill held out her left hand and stared at the ring. Her lips closed and tears gathered in her eyes. The two husbands looked on without speaking.

Gwenn took Jill's left hand in hers. She smeared butter along Jill's ring finger. Steadily, more and more firmly, she turned and pulled the gold band. Jill bit her lip. Gwenn yanked hard.

"Ouch!" Jill cried. The greasy ring popped free. Gwenn wiped the ring on the corner of a tablecloth and slipped it on.

"What's that blasted wog usurer doing here?" said James Hartshorne. He stood near the Llewelyns, his white topee under one arm. "The fellow should be passing biscuits."

"Not so loud, Spongey," said Hartshorne's companion. "The fat bugger'll hear you and double your interest."

Gwenn turned to see Raji da Souza advance smoothly through the throng.

"Good evening, my excellency," da Souza said to Hartshorne, holding a steady smile, knowing better than to extend his hand.

"Evening to you, Souza. Don't worry, you'll be hearing from me shortly."

"There can be no doubt I will, my excellency." Da Souza bowed by drawing his bottom backwards. "May I introduce to you Mr. and Mrs. Llewelyn?"

Hartshorne acknowledged Alan Llewelyn and looked at Gwenn with admiration. He held her fingers briefly in his soft hand. Before excusing himself, Hartshorne said to Alan, "You were one of the luckier ones, weren't you, Llewelyn? On the river, are you not?"

"We believe so, sir." Alan brushed a long lock of hair back from his forehead.

While the two men spoke, da Souza took Gwenn aside. "Mr. Llewelyn seems some bit weak from the war, and there will be so very much work to be done. Do let me know how the farm goes, dear Mrs. Llewelyn. I have a friend nearby who can help you, Mr. Olivio Alavedo of Nanyuki. That is a hundred and fifteen miles north of Nairobi, and some thirty miles before your farm. Always I will be thinking of Mr. and Mrs. Llewelyn."

With the Governor and the sandwiches gone, the party ended. The settlers were on their own. Many went to buy supplies, trusting as far as possible to the old military goods sold by the Salvage Commission. But Alan told Gwenn that da Souza already had done much of their outfitting at minimum expense. While many settlers paid too much for each shovel and tent peg, da Souza had led Alan from shop to shop and stall to stall, haggling without mercy, swelling in size while his opponents lowered their prices.

On their way to the Nairobi encampment the first day, the Llewelyns had stopped at the hospital to enquire about Anna. Alan waited in the wagon. Looking into the child's room, Gwenn found Mrs. Gault collapsed in a chair. The woman looked up with red eyes. She spoke quietly to Gwenn.

"We should go home, all of us. We're not meant to live in Africa."

Anna was unconscious. Her face was pale and small. Gwenn looked down the bed. Her gaze came to the sheet that covered the child's lower body. She stiffened in horror, then bent and kissed Anna on the cheek. She rushed down the hall to the nurse. "What has happened to her?"

"We had to cut off her right leg," the woman said. "And I have worse news. The lion's teeth punctured her spine. The doctor thinks she'll be paralyzed below the waist. He was astounded you were able to keep her alive."

Back at the Soldiers' Camp, Gwenn and Alan sat on folding canvas chairs while Mulwa and Arthur raised the tent. Alan, she felt, still held himself a bit apart, as if he were not quite with her. Was this the man she married?

"I hope things work out the way we've prayed, Gwennie. We're so lucky." Alan rose. "Please don't mind if I lie down. I'm still a bit off, you know."

In the tent, on the narrow cot next to Alan's, Gwenn held her husband's hand and lay awake. She heard laughter and excited voices through the canvas as other families prepared for their adventures. She remembered lying awake in her wooden bed in Denbigh. Hungry, her bread and beef tea finished, with her sister curled next to her, she listened to the rain and imagined a sunny life of flowered skirts, porch swings and poetic lovers. Through the door she heard her father choking with his miner's cough while he argued with her uncle.

"Go to New Zealand or Argentina and become a sheepman, while you're still young enough to start," her father urged his younger brother. "Once you marry, it's too late. You'll be a slave in the mines forever. Finished, like me, with children to feed. You'll never be free."

Gwenn moved her hand up her husband's arm. He groaned in his sleep. She recalled her wartime lessons and worried about the wound. His obvious pain suggested damage to the pelvic nerves that led from spine to penis. It could mean impotence. She feared they might never again make love. But if the nerves were merely injured, not dead, they might recover after many months. Lack of nourishment, she knew, would only make things worse.

She remembered looking out her window as a girl, drawing hearts on the cold pane with the tip of her nose, waiting to watch Alan when he walked to school. Different from the other boys, she always thought, with the slender look and fine head of an artist or a gentleman. Now she felt his arm, its thinness. It was barely warm. She moved her hand along his side, touching his pale smooth skin, but her husband remained asleep.

Gwenn woke early the final morning. She pulled on a long skirt and sturdy shoes and stooped to leave the tent. Arthur crouched by a fire preparing tea. Mulwa was feeding the mules. Gwenn admired the ease with which the two Africans already had defined their roles. All these two men seemed to expect was to be fed regularly and given a few shillings or rupees.

In an hour they were reloading the wagon, seeking to balance the heavy weight. Sacks of seed, farm tools, cooking supplies, Gwenn's trunk and cases, all crowned by a grey zinc bathtub.

In the distance she saw a large man pushing through the crowded camp. She stopped working and looked more carefully. She recognized the shape of the heavy frame. A shudder of revulsion chilled her.

Rigid with hate, wanting to kill him, Gwenn could not speak when Mick Reilly approached and insisted on helping. The man stepped forward and clapped Alan on the shoulder as Gwenn's husband struggled to lift his end of a packing case.

"How's the old soldier?" said Reilly. With one hand he helped

Mulwa ease the case in place. He brushed against Gwenn when he leaned back. She recoiled, shivering when the red-faced man touched her.

"Did they patch you up good, matey?" Reilly asked Alan with a wink.

White with the pain of his effort, her husband gathered himself to reply. Gwenn put an arm around his waist. She swallowed her disgust and ignored the Irishman. "Arthur," she said, "please help Mr. Llewelyn up onto the seat. Mulwa, pack those last things in the sacking and tie them in the back."

"You're still not so friendly, luv." Reilly opened his mouth and grinned, revealing dark irregular teeth. Gwenn turned to face him behind the wagon while he continued.

"You'll be seeing a lot more of me up-country. Instead of joining the gold rush, me and my brother'll be workin' up there for this greaser swell, Mr. Fonsici, that's gettin' some estates together where the water's good."

Gwenn paused in her work. She looked directly into the close-set eyes buried like raisins in the great pudding of the man's florid face. Sickened and enraged again, she remembered him heaving and panting over her.

"If ever you speak to either my husband or me again," she said evenly, "I will see you jailed, Michael Reilly. I do not care what it costs me. And after that they will send you home and hang you for what you did there. Don't forget, I have a witness."

"That's no witness. I saw you moonin' about with that one on the boat. Want me to tell Alan? If I see your bleedin' boyfriend in this country, we'll fix that pretty young bastard so he'll never talk to anyone. We already gave 'im a taste on the boat. Next time I'll kill 'im."

Reilly softened his voice and smiled at her as Gwenn moved away to climb on board. "You'll see, luv, you'll get used to me."

Arthur led the mules through the busy scene as the wagon left camp. Mulwa walked behind, waving his rungu to a small boy seated on a water cart drawn by three oxen. Alan held the reins loosely in one hand. Gwenn sat on the bench beside him, thinking of Reilly's threat. It was her fault they were after Anton. So they had hurt him, and he hadn't told her. Somehow she would have to save him. She couldn't be responsible for hurting him again.

Passing back through the edge of Nairobi to pick up the road north, they drove slowly past the Norfolk Hotel. Men drank coffee and smoked under the arched facade of the long raised porch. Their talk stopped when they looked down and watched the new settlers move past.

"Good luck to you!" an American voice called down. The rangy man caught Gwenn's eye and tipped his wide-brimmed hat.

"They'll bloody well need it!" Gwenn heard his companion respond with a chuckle.

Olivio welcomed the mail pouch like a lost son. Each Tuesday and Friday it came to the hotel by rail and wagon, forwarded from the post drop at Nanyuki. On one side the canvas bag bore the regal G.R. V above the lion and unicorn of England, on the other the formidable profile of a white rhinoceros. A small padlock deterred prying hands.

For the guests and owner of the White Rhino the post was a simple matter, Olivio realized. Each person waited for his own. To the dwarf, however, all the mail was in fact his. During eight years of service at the hotel, Olivio had learned to assess the appearance of the mail sack as a farmer might judge a new lamb the instant it dropped. From its very weight and shape, from the way it fell upon the bar, he could reckon its value. Often there was no need for him to read a letter's contents. The envelope, its bulk, the postal mark, the demeanor of the recipient said it better than the writer.

This morning the pouch promised a feast. The dwarf's key opened the lock. He arranged the contents on the leadwood bar. For Lord Penfold, the news, as usual, could not be good. In addition to the customary bills from tradesmen, there were two letters from bankers in Nairobi, another from London, and a thick envelope from the estate manager in Wiltshire. One letter was for Lady Penfold, a return, written by her to a former male guest of the hotel, but posted back from Florence, the party unknown at that address. This, no doubt, she would like separated from her husband's mail.

O. F. Alavedo was himself an addressee, the letter sent by R. da Souza of Nairobi. The juicy plum in the pudding was a heavy buff-colored envelope for *Senhor Vasco de Castanheda y Fonseca.* At the bottom of this envelope was written the irresistible invitation. *Confidencial.* This letter came from Lisbon itself, dispatched by one *António Gama, Notário.* What mischief could this be? The dwarf thought of Fonseca's faded sepia photograph of the two men in Portugal.

Olivio descended the bar ladder and stepped into the hallway that separated the stairs from the dining room. He ignored the massive black buffalo head that scowled down at him stone-like from the wall. The spread of its horns, a near-record forty-nine inches, was three inches more than the dwarf's own height. He sorted the letters into the boxes mounted on the wall. Then Olivio climbed onto the third step of the staircase and examined himself respectfully in the hall looking glass.

Flawless leather sandals, smart pleated pink sash, immaculate white uniform, and his head. That was it! His head! His perfect round head! A thrill flashed through him. He felt his body moisten. Olivio had seen the short priest in the picture before! It was him! Olivio himself! How many such strong faces could there be? How many called Fonseca? This must be the archbishop, Olivio's grandfather!

The dwarf calmed himself and made his way back to the bar. He noted with annoyance the dusty prints of bare feet that one of the boys had left on the polished planks of the hallway. He climbed the bar ladder and opened the letter from his banker. It was written in a careful round hand on the crested notepaper of the Goan Institute of Nairobi.

My dear Olivio Fonseca Alavedo,
    I greet you with good news. Although things must go slowly, and it may be many years until this land is ours, our money is at work. Mercifully, the toil itself will not be ours. A simple British couple, the Alan Llewelyns, will open the land and do our work.
    The Mr. Llewelyn is weak from the war, but seems patient and capable of effort. I do not know how sick he is. The wife seems a strong one. You must become their

friend and see to our interests at this farm. If it collapses too soon, never will we see either our money in our pockets or the land beneath our feet.

I remain your faithful banker,

Raji da Souza

By the seventh day Gwenn felt at home. She walked ahead with Mulwa, absorbed by the vast land that opened around her. She wanted to come on each new view herself rather than see it from the wagon between the twitching ears of recalcitrant mules.

Gwenn did not believe such a climate could exist. She had imagined a baking colonial heat as the alternative to the penetrating damp of Wales. Instead she found fresh sun-warm days and cool evenings. The air glowed about her while she walked. The scents shifted with each breeze. Instead of the tight enclosed valleys of Wales, each new slope revealed an ocean-wide landscape. Gently rising hills waved on for miles. To the sides the horizon seemed farther than eyes could see.

But the road itself was rough and slow. Pitted with deep holes, set with stones, carpeted in six inches of red dust, it was lower in the center and bordered by high banks. The straining mules suffered fresh yoke galls on their necks.

She paused, smiling at Mulwa when he pointed out a buck grazing on the next hill. She and Mulwa waited for the wagon to catch up. She looked at her husband with sadness. Her experienced eye told her Alan was more ill than he disclosed. His hands gripped the edge of the wooden bench. His eyes were shut. For him it was a different sort of journey, a punishing trial to endure. The wagon pulled off the track and stopped. Gwenn and Arthur helped Alan down. She tried not to notice that the front of Alan's trousers was wet. He rested with his back against a hard red anthill.

"Sorry, old girl, I'm really all right," Alan said in a quiet voice. What must she be thinking of him, he wondered. He must seem so useless. "Is it time to stop for supper?"

Arthur gathered firewood. Gwenn took her husband's rifle from the wagon. Alan showed her how to load the Enfield and said, "You're an old soldier, Mulwa, why don't you show Mrs. Llewelyn how to use this?"

When they returned an hour later, Gwenn carried the rifle and Mulwa had a small gazelle slung over his shoulder.

"Well done, Gwennie!" Alan said in a stronger voice while Arthur clapped and grinned.

"No, it's Mulwa's. I didn't do very well. They seemed too pretty to shoot, and I kept waiting until they ran off. When it started getting dark, I gave Mulwa the gun."

"Memsaab not yet hungry enough. When she hungry, she kill." Mulwa set to work with his bayonet while Arthur put up the tent.

Chunks of meat, onions and unpeeled sliced potatoes were soon stewing in a three-legged iron pot. Arthur disappeared. He returned with small brittle branches covered in grey-green leaves. He crushed and rolled the leaves in his hands, then threw them into the black pot. He raised his palms and Gwenn smelled the pungency.

"Wild rosemary," she said.

Alan brightened while they watched the stew simmer. He told about shopping with Raji da Souza. "If you buy, please, the pot with three legs," the large Goan had advised as he picked the cheapest vessel, "then he can't fall over and waste your dinners, you see."

"We must try and find his friend Mr. Alavedo when we get to Nanyuki." Gwenn entered the tent to get a shawl.

"Do I smell venison for supper?" a cheery English voice called from the shadows by the road. A tall angular man in tan jodhpurs limped into the firelight leading a horse. He removed a brown felt terai hat and introduced himself to Alan and the Africans.

"How do you do? I'm Adam Penfold. If you can spare some grub, I can spare the whisky."

"Please join us," Alan said.

"Adam! Welcome!" Gwenn stepped from the tent and clapped her hands together. "I'm so happy to see you! I think we owe you some supper." She took her husband's arm and said, "This is the kind man who gave me his room in Mombasa."

Their guest unsaddled. "Hungry, Rafiki?" Penfold rubbed the horse's nose. He removed the bridle and hung it from a branch before feeding the animal a handful of oats from a saddlebag. He found some decent grazing and brushed down the horse and tied the animal loosely with a neck rope. The two European men drank from Penfold's battered silver flask. Arthur served the stew in tin plates. Gwenn watched Alan eat hungrily. For a moment no one spoke.

"This is the best food I've ever tasted," she said.

"It's a fine handsome stew, ma'am. Just needs a smidge of Marmite," Penfold said. "But if you come by Nanyuki, stop and dine with us at the White Rhino, and I'll see if we can top it. Someone said we've got the best table between Nairobi and Khartoum."

"The White Rhino?"

"Yes. That's my hotel. My final folly, my dear wife says, if we're lucky. I've tried all the others. Ostrich feathers, wattle bark, antelope hides, cattle, ground nuts, barley. Idleness is next. Fortunately I'm too old and feeble for gold mining."

"We're just coming up to settle by the Ewaso Ngiro," said Alan. "What would you suggest we farm? Flax or coffee, perhaps sheep?"

"If you take my advice, young man, you won't take my advice." Penfold smiled and passed the flask. "But you can probably count on being too low for coffee, too high for flax, and too far from the railway for mutton and wool. Now I'm going to tuck in Rafiki and do the same meself. I'll be off early. Hope to see you both up the road." Penfold saw the weariness greying Alan's face as he continued. "Just keep Mount Kenya on your right and you can't miss the White Rhino. Good night, ma'am, and my thanks to you both for a nice din'."

"Good lord, it's a dog." Gwenn watched a ragged creature drag itself towards them the following afternoon. Behind her, Mulwa and Arthur continued to unload the crippled wagon.

She picked up the Enfield and walked through the bush towards the dog. When she came to it, she looked up at the high vulture that had caught her eye. The bird floated patiently above its prospect, engaging every drift of air, first one wide wing higher, then the other. The dog whined and moved its tongue while it pulled itself in a tight curl against Gwenn's feet. Its left eye socket glared red. Blood seeped from the torn edge of the socket down to the dog's mouth. An old shoulder wound, reopened like a worn seam, revealed the pink fibre of lean muscle. The dog's black muzzle was split down the center, the base of its nostrils opened like a dark clam shell. The upper lip was ripped wide and exposed the top gums.

Gwenn lifted the unresisting whippet across her arms. Gripping the rifle in one hand, she carried the dog back and rested it on an old blanket in the shade of the wagon.

"Help me, Mulwa." She took her medical kit from the pile of supplies that cluttered the side of the trail.

Alan pressed a hand against his side and sat on the ground watching.

"Hold his body between your legs and his head tight in your hands, Mulwa." Gwenn prepared the curved surgical needle and sponged the animal's face with water and a towel. She remembered the identical advice given by her father and a military surgeon: if you have something unpleasant to do, don't do it tentatively.

Only the dog's snout appeared between Mulwa's hands when Gwenn forced the needle through the dry black muzzle. She sowed neat stitches between the whippet's nostrils.

She left the dog beside Alan. He squeezed water onto its tongue from the towel while Arthur and Mulwa removed the last supplies from the wagon. The two Africans worked at an unhurried steady pace.

This broken cotter pin, Gwenn thought, was one blow too many. As the wagon jarred against a rock, the rusted pin had snapped, freeing the right front wheel to slip from its axle. The wagon collapsed onto one corner. Alarmed by the crash, she had looked back to see Alan tumble off to the ground.

"Just like the war, memsaab. Wagons break every day. We fix soon. Please don't worry now," Mulwa said. With the wagon empty and light, he and Arthur forced crates under the sloping axle until it rested off the ground. They took grease from the rear axle and smeared it into the center of the lost wheel. The wheel was set in its place and Mulwa walked into the bush with an axe.

The sound of the working axe came to them. Mulwa returned with a dark inch-thick branch. "Ironwood," he said. He shaped the heavy wood with a panga, tailoring it to replace the broken cotter pin. Once in place he split each end until they widened and held the wooden pin secure.

Late the next morning, walking ahead of the wagon, Gwenn paused at a fork in the road. She glanced up at the massive rise of Mount Kenya to the east before reading the dusty wooden signs. To the left lay Nanyuki, to the right, the White Rhino Hotel. She turned and waved at Alan, then took the uneven track to the right.

— 13 —

They were walking north in the early morning, following the elephant tracks on the edge of the swamp country beyond Kilimanjaro. Ernst and Anton were together. Banda and Karioki studied the trail ahead. Hugo von Decken followed slowly with the cook and six men bearing supplies. Eager to feast on fresh meat, the Africans walked lightly under their canvas-wrapped burdens.

From time to time the hunters gathered without speaking and studied the ground. Anton tingled at the first sighting. He squatted and touched the corrugated impressions in the dust. Remarkably round, unlike any other sign.

"How big do you reckon she is?" Ernst said. Without allowing a reply, the German spoke again. "About seven feet at the shoulder. Twice the girth of the front foot. They're the big feet, because they support the head and the ivory. See how she sets her rear foot right inside the print of the front foot?"

Karioki knelt beside Anton. He spoke after Ernst moved on.

"There is more than one, Tlaga," he said quietly, before standing. "They are clever. The followers place their feet over the prints of the one who goes before. Perhaps four, five."

"When did they come by?" Ernst said when Anton caught up to him. Anton crouched again. He noticed the tiny undisturbed pattern of dew over the prints. He observed the small mounds of sand gathered by ants within them as nature began to reclaim the path. He stood and walked along the tracks. Fragments of acacia bark and

broken branches lay along the route, the leaves already shrivelled.
The amber sap that had leaked from the wounds of the branches felt
glazed hard and dry.

"Yesterday evening, I'd say."

"Not bad, for an English drifter." Ernst nodded. "Remember to
watch for saliva on twigs and acacia pods. That's where they chew.
If the spittle's wet, you'll need your rifle, because you're right on
top of them."

Anton examined some smaller prints to one side.

"These're all calves and females. Mature bulls only go with the
girls when they're mating," Ernst said. "The ivory keeps growing till
they die. The bulls with the best ivory are too old to have fun, usually
loners, or else roaming around with a couple of other old-timers.
But the young bulls go about in small bands, fencing with one another
when they feel sexy, like the university boys in Heidelberg. Then
they break off on their own to mate."

Karioki picked up a block of dung, the outside dry and laced with
fragments of coarse fibre and splinters of bark and branches. He
broke it open like an egg and showed it to Anton. The interior was
dark and moist. Seeds and acacia pods nestled in the rich fertilizer.

"Look inside, Tlaga—" Karioki said.

"She's an old cow," Ernst interrupted as if the African had not
spoken.

Karioki dropped the block of dung and turned aside. Remembering the feeling, Anton understood Karioki's resentment.

"Her food's barely broken up," Ernst said, "because her teeth are
worn down, worse than my papa's. Means she can't get much nourishment. Unless a hunter gets 'em first, they all die when their sixth
set of molars wears out, 'bout sixty years old."

"Excuse me," Anton said to Karioki, pointing to the dung. "How
old is it?"

"Two hours," said Karioki to Anton.

"We'll camp up ahead on the edge of the swamp," Ernst said.
"After the others find us, we'll walk in and lie up by the water."

They took their positions late in the afternoon. Nestled among
the reeds and grass on the steep bank of the river that ran through
the marsh, Anton and Hugo von Decken waited with their rifles.
The German cradled his old Merkel. Anton lay on his stomach with

Ernst's Sauer & Sohn. It was an over-and-under double-barrelled rifle, without the fine balance of the Merkel's side-by-side barrels. An unusual, slightly difficult weapon, rather like Ernst himself, Anton thought. How would it perform?

Whenever he lifted one of the double rifles, Anton was struck by its massive perfection. Densely heavy, yet each moving part exquisitely fitted, they were built to contain thousands of violent explosions without the slightest change or damage. Even the way they opened was a marvel. Anton gently broke the rifle open, pushing the top lever to the side with his thumb. He checked the two brass .450s that waited, their rims set perfectly into the recessed edge of each barrel. Despite the razor-fine tightness when the metal came together, the hinge worked easily as he closed it. He felt the cool, slightly oiled smoothness of the gunmetal and the worn comfort of the walnut stock. Compared to the rough weapons of his youth, it was a jewel.

Close before his eyes, the sharp-tipped blades of coarse swamp grass formed a dense green palisade. Each stand of grass contained a village of its own. A bone-white snail shell, empty and large as his fist, rested against the stem of a tall lily. He could smell the yellow blossom in the still air. While he watched, the spiralling scalloped shell became a magic staircase for tiny red ants that coursed up it like a moving ribbon. He saw their goal. A knot of eggs or larvae rested atop the shell, their grey smoothness sheltered in a gauzy film, scant protection from the rending pincers of their attackers. Anton squinted to follow the assault.

The entire shell rocked under his eyes. Two broad-spread twitching antennae emerged, followed by a narrow black snout, then two long three-hinged arms attached to a round head. A massive, hard-shelled orange-and-black body covered in pointed spines drew itself from the shell and began to climb the lily. As the beetle paused to chop neat bites from the stalk, Anton recognized it from his studies in the library at Gepard Farm: a weevil, a vegetarian, probably an iron beetle.

He looked up. Thirty yards across the river an elephant stood at the edge of the water, the sound of its advance drowned by the stream. Slowly it flapped its ears. Dust rose from its shoulders as the uneven ears slapped against them, loose sails rippling against a mast.

Unhurried, apparently hearing no disturbing sound, the animal raised its trunk. It directed the curving tip first upstream, then down, casting for scent. Anton thought of the stag coming to water. But instead of the wild grace of the stag, he saw primeval majesty. He watched a line of followers shuffle down to the water, huge grey blocks moving in the evening light, their pace stately, unlike any other animal, as if on an unending dignified march.

The big females entered the water to their knees. They dipped their trunks, flushing them with a fine spray. Then they drank. The very young elephant moved in among them, leaning against the legs of the females, splashing and experimenting with thin, bugle-like trunks. Anton rested his rifle on the grass with the safety on and stared while one baby stumbled in the mud. It struggled to get up. Its pointed mouse-like face was dark and messy. A young female moved to help the calf, righting it with her trunk like a fallen stool. Uncertain how to drink, the baby tried to use its trunk. Water dribbled out before it reached its mouth. The mother insinuated her own trunk into the calf's mouth, giving water. She sprayed the calf with fresh water and rubbed it with the side of her trunk. After they drank, the young elephant began to play, splashing and tumbling like puppies. The older females showered water over their own shoulders, cleaning and cooling themselves, ignoring the childish commotion beneath them.

As the afternoon darkened, Anton sensed movement behind him. The ground vibrated under his body. He turned his head slowly and discerned von Decken five yards to his right. Calmly, obeying his own injunction against hurried movements, the old hunter held out one hand, palm down, and gestured to stay in place. It was too late to bolt.

Anton leaned on his right shoulder and looked up through the grass behind him. An immense grey wall was advancing towards him. A line of elephant extended as far as he could see. Forty, fifty animals. They eased forward, several abreast, incredibly silent, the beasts in front raising their trunks when they smelled the water. From the river the drinking elephants began to trumpet. Welcome, or war? wondered Anton.

He lay frozen, prepared either to shoot or to roll into the water. Trying to disappear into the ground, he felt the gold earring on its leather cord press into his chest. The first elephant paused twelve yards to his left, a towering black mass against the darkening sky. Anton moved only his eyes. He remembered Lenares telling him never to stare at an animal when he wished not to be noticed. Like a man or woman, the beast would sense it was being watched. Anton looked down while the elephant resumed its march. He heard each footstep when the animal passed him. Coming to the riverbank, the elephant stiffened its front legs and slid down to the water with its forelegs straight and hind legs kneeling.

Soon the river was dappled with elephant. The arrivals approached the earlier drinkers, knocking their tusks gently together, bumping shoulders, entwining their trunks and trumpeting. Two young females put the tips of their trunks into each other's mouths.

Finally it became too dark to see, and Hugo von Decken beckoned to Anton. They crawled back to find Banda and Karioki, not speaking until they were on the way to camp.

"That was the beginning of the world," Anton said. "I'm glad we didn't shoot."

"It was getting dark for these old eyes, and I don't like shooting females," von Decken said. "But tomorrow, we get our ivory. And the boys want their meat."

At dawn the hunters were back. They walked upstream where the river eddied into shallow pools under the branches of wild fig trees. Banda found the spoor of several males. The hunters lay waiting for them on the bank under a canopy of dark green leaves. Von Decken drew ashes from a pouch and let them fall from his fingers. The air drew the ash behind them, away from the river.

"If I point to you, you shoot first," Ernst said to Anton. "Remember, go for a heart shot behind the shoulder. Those bony heads are too tricky for beginners. The brain's bigger than yours, of course, the size of a nice loaf of pumpernickel. But it's buried a foot deep, and you'll never find it."

Before Anton could reply, three bulls came to the water. From his position to the right Ernst pointed to Anton, then tapped his own teeth. Searching for the heaviest ivory, Anton studied the animals while they drank.

Two males began to tussle. They stiffened their ears and made sham charges. They touched trunks, stepped back and crashed together. Their tusks clacked when they met. It was violent, but not desperate. The heavier animal pressed the other farther and farther back. Each time the smaller male backed off, then gathered itself to try once more. A thick dark fluid ran unevenly down each side of its face from small cracks midway between its ears and eyes. A glandular secretion, Ernst had warned Anton, generally indicating a period of sexual arousal, when bulls grow more dangerous to the hunter.

The larger animal caught the other in the side, lightly puncturing its hide with a tusk. Anton raised his .450. The smaller elephant screamed and turned. Anton slipped off the safety catch with his thumb. He squeezed the trigger. There was a violent crashing sound where Banda was kneeling in an opening in the reeds to Anton's left.

Anton saw an enormous male hippopotamus strike Banda with its open jaw. It tore at Banda but missed with long curved canines. The man fell under it. The animal dashed for the water. Instantly on his feet, Ernst swung his rifle. He was unable to fire with Anton in between. Astonishingly swift for its immense bulk and short legs, the hippopotamus lunged into the water with the noise and violence of a locomotive. Anton fired his second barrel. His shot took the hippo behind the ear as it plunged into deeper water.

Rushing to Banda, Anton suddenly remembered the elephants. He looked up. Two had climbed the far bank. The third and largest, hit hard, was walking slowly after the others along the edge of the streambed. Blood seeped down its side. It approached the steep bank and tentatively raised one leg to climb. It paused with one foot on the bank and gave an echoing groan. It shook its head and swayed its trunk from side to side. The elephant it had been sparring with reached down and touched its trunk with its own. The third elephant descended the bank. Lowering its head against the wounded animal's side, it pressed its forehead against the big bull until the bleeding elephant wrapped its trunk around a tree and hauled itself up onto the bank. The three animals moved off, the wounded elephant in the middle.

Anton, Karioki and von Decken knelt over Banda.

The man's lower body was pulverized. His shorts, stomach and pelvis were an inseparable mass of flesh, cloth and crushed bone. Banda's one arm lay across his eyes. His fist was clenched. His mouth moved. Unable to help, sickened, Anton watched von Decken put one arm under the man's head and lay down beside him. Their cheeks touched while von Decken listened for his friend's words.

"Today we have taught these foolish boys never to stop on a path of the hippo," Banda whispered. "I wait for you one more time, my old bwana, at the next fire."

Karioki and Anton turned away. Von Decken lay holding the dead man in his arms. The German's shirt and leather shorts darkened with blood.

Finally von Decken rose. Anton moved to help, but von Decken lifted the body in his own arms and carried it to the fig trees. His eyes were red. His cheeks were wet.

"Help me dig here where it's cool, Karioki," von Decken said. "Deep so the hyena will not come. Your Englishman and Ernst must finish the hunt. Send four boys after them."

Anton and Ernst waded across the shallows, watching for the hippopotamus in the deeper water. At the far side Anton paused and looked back, unable to let go of the horror. They climbed the bank and followed the wide trail of broken branches and crushed bushes. Ernst bent down and wet his fingers in the elephant's blood.

"Bubbles. You got him in the lung. Be careful. They'll know we're coming."

For an hour the hunters walked rapidly in silence. After a time the blood became plentiful. They found it smeared against branches and gathered in dusty bubbly puddles like scarlet porridge. Emerging from a cluster of thornbushes, they saw the elephant sixty yards ahead.

The three were pressed together, the wounded animal supported in the middle. The elephant paused, aware of the hunters. The smallest one took a step towards the two men, rocking forward as it hesitated. Its trunk rose in the air. Its ears spread to the sides and stiffened. Behind it, unsupported, the wounded bull fell onto its front knees. Anton fired, hitting the dying elephant in the forehead. It collapsed to the side without a sound. Its young companion charged. With surprising speed the animal crashed through trees and thornbushes, trumpeting shrilly, its ears spread wide, its trunk extended straight ahead. Ernst fired into the ground in its path. The young bull came on. Ernst fired his second barrel. The bullet struck the elephant between the eyes. The animal crashed down five yards in front of him. The third bull cried out once, then turned and disappeared into the bush.

In moments the camp men joined them. Ernst sat on the ground and smoked a cigarette while they cut off the tails and chopped out the tusks with axes. The skinners slit open the belly of the larger animal and cut out the heart and liver. Despite the death of Banda, the men grew excited while they worked, laughing and joking as they sliced belts of fat from under the skin and long strips of meat from the shoulder.

That night they camped under the fig trees. The Gepard Farm cook served Ernst a plate of dumplings and elephant meat. Karioki began to make a meal for Anton and himself, preparing the meat in his own way. The other Africans feasted by a second fire.

Karioki built his fire over a circle of flat stones from the riverbed. He laid strips of liver and heart over the glowing-hot stones and covered them with wild herbs and hot ashes. Anton chopped farm onions and Karioki threw them in with the potatoes that hissed in a pan to one side. He and Anton ate a heavy meal.

Only the old German did not eat. He walked back and forth to the river, declining Anton's help and gathering rocks that he placed over Banda's grave.

Later Anton lay in his blanket, thinking about Banda and the elephant. For the first time Anton was unable to find satisfaction in a hunt. He thought of the wounded bull leaning on his comrades, his friends patient despite the deadly pursuit. Not many men would have waited and helped as they did. He remembered how he had watched Lenares take his beating. Before Anton's mind lost hold, hunters and hunted became the same. Like the leopard, and the gamekeeper in Windsor Great Park. While you hunt one creature, another hunts you.

In the morning Anton rose to find von Decken still sitting by the grave. Anton brought him coffee in a tin cup. The old man stood stiffly and tried to smile. His age was in his face.

"It is done now. It's time my boy and I went back to our farm. I'll accept a present of the ivory, young man, since you won't want to carry it."

"Of course, Mr. von Decken. I meant to give it to you anyway."

"And you must accept two presents from me. Here's the first." Von Decken handed Anton his Merkel and three cardboard boxes of Uttendoerfer Nitro Express .450s, the final sixty of his precious pre-war cartridges.

"She should bring you luck and help you remember an old hunter," von Decken said hurriedly.

Not able to speak, Anton accepted the gift. He knew the old man would never hunt again. And he himself would not shoot another elephant.

The hunters washed in the river before breakfast. A short way downstream, the hippopotamus floated on the surface, its body wedged among the rocks. The skinners cut out the two large lower teeth while the cook made breakfast and Anton and Karioki got ready to walk north. Each of them carried a blanket and a grey German army rucksack, faded and patched. The packs contained coffee and tobacco, salted elephant meat, maize and sugar. Ernst took a small parcel from his father and added it to Anton's pack.

Anton ate slowly, reluctant to end his last meal with his friends. When he was finished he drew his knife and sharpened it on a boot. He carved his initials and a Union Jack on one of the hippo teeth. He and Karioki lifted their packs and said goodbye to each of the men. Ernst stepped up and gripped Anton's hand. "Good luck, my young Engländer. Keep your blade sharp."

Anton picked up his new rifle and approached von Decken.

"Thank you, sir, and please take this." He handed von Decken the carved ivory.

"I wish I were marching with you." Von Decken gripped Anton's shoulders in almost-strong hands. "Just keep Kili behind you and walk west-northwest. You're right on the border now. You will find your way."

— 14 —

The dwarf heard the irritating clatter of a horse approaching up the drive. He stepped to the door and saw his master descend stiffly from the saddle.

"Welcome home, my lord." Olivio remained on the verandah while he clapped his hands for a syce to come and take the horse.

"Good morning to you, Olivio Alavedo."

Penfold tossed the reins over the rail of the porch. Olivio handed his master a bamboo cane.

"Home at last," Penfold said. "Have you been a loyal steward, my little rogue, like Eumaeus to Odysseus?"

"I manage your household as if it is my own, your lordship." The dwarf bowed and clapped his hands with impatience. Who was this man Eumaeus?

"How're my soldiers? Are they on parade?"

"Each brave warrior is in his place, my lord. Last night I dusted them with my own hands."

"Are the Portuguese still with us?"

"They are. Senhora Fonseca is downstairs. Her brother is taking coffee with two companions in his room, Number Four. I believe they speak of business. The room is covered in maps. Senhor Fonseca kept his friends waiting. This gentleman does not rise early, my lord."

"No doubt. Even von Lettow couldn't get that devil to see the sun rise. Help me off with this boot, won't you please, Olivio? And chase up some samosas and a cold lager. This dashed leg doesn't work without a drink."

Penfold saw Anunciata sitting gracefully at the end of the verandah. She sat in an unpainted wide-armed wicker chair, wearing an ivory pleated-linen dress. Her left leg, the knee stiff in plaster, rested on the tin-cornered tea chest before her. Penfold limped over and kissed her olive cheek.

"What happened to your leg?" he said.

"An accident while I was riding with your bride. She enjoys a hard chase, for a lady her age."

"Quite." Flustered, Penfold wondered if Sissy had done it on purpose. "I'm dreadfully sorry."

"Rather like old times, my sweet lord." Anunciata stroked his cane with hers. Her eyes grew warm.

"I hope your stick will be less permanent than mine." Adam Penfold stared at her like a schoolboy. Olivio appeared with a servant in a long white kanzu carrying a table set with lead soldiers and tiny square bottles of enamel paints. Lord Penfold shook one bottle, eager to display his skill.

"Who are those lovely strong men with the long spears?" Anunciata said.

"Macedonians. With one phalanx of these, and a few score Thracian slingers, our friend von Lettow could have conquered Africa." Penfold dipped a brush and touched a two-inch armored figure with fine strokes of silver paint. "What's kept you and Vasco in darkest Nanyuki?"

"Vasco's onto some land scheme up here. I've never seen him work so hard. He says it'll make us rich again."

Sharing their moment discreetly through the tilted slats of a louvered window, Olivio leaned on the end of the bar and rolled a leather dice cup in his fingers. He observed the movement of the woman's breasts as she breathed. He thought of Kina, and his fingers tightened.

He had waited too long. Three years ago, at the age of eight, smooth and glossy with health, Kina had arrested his eye. Exactly his height, generally almost naked, she had a more fresh odor and finer skin than other African girls. For years now he had watched her as she came and went about the village behind the White Rhino.

From time to time he gave the child one of her ladyship's thin English mint chocolates, taking the opportunity to place his small paternal hand on the girl's shoulder or side. Below her straight back she already carried the perfect bottom of the better women of her tribe, prominent, yet wonderfully high and hard. Once or twice, by accident, he had contrived to touch it. The following year, at nine, Kina's breasts had started to swell, not with their future richness, but with promise, set high and wide apart so that he could see them under her arms from the back.

What other man would have been so patient?

Now he must make the girl his before the savages circumcised the child and prevented him from using Kina's own delight to enslave her. There was not much time, for by twelve or thirteen most Kikuyu girls were married. At the first sign of puberty they were circumcised, to make the little harlots faithful, for without a clitoris, few women found much pleasure in sex.

Most men, to whom women came easily, used sex to satisfy themselves. Olivio, to secure a woman, had been obliged to take a less selfish path. He had learned, over the thirty years since his first girl, to attend with consideration to every corner of a woman's body. Rather the way, he thought, a poor farmer worked to extract the richest yield from every inch of his only field, or the way a butcher quartered a calf and dressed each cut for its highest use.

Some wise men reached a woman's body through her mind, but Olivio reached their minds through their bodies. Instead of leaving a woman with the tiny resentments that sometimes linger after sex, the dwarf left them, he believed, astonished at what he had uncovered in them, their "other woman," as he liked to call it. While he pondered, Olivio began to breathe harder. His thoughts shifted, following the line of his eyes as they made naked the Portuguese before him.

On most European women, he knew, the creamy linen dress would be conventional, even dowdy, but on this creature its coolness emphasized the hot promise beneath, like snow on the shoulders of a smoldering volcano. No doubt this was his master's wartime mistress. Why not? Only self-interest or a taste for the bizarre could force a man to Lady Penfold's bed. His needy master shared the direct unrefined tastes of every English farmer. And most Englishmen, he had observed, only made love when they were slightly drunk. In Anunciata, on the other hand, Olivio recognized a fellow connoisseur.

Her flesh spoke to him when he watched her. Honey-tan and luscious, a woman of his grandfather's race, for a moment she put young Kina from his mind. Could this Portuguese woman be his cousin? That would make it so much better.

Even when she returned from the riding accident, her filthy face sweat-streaked and death-pale while she gripped the mane of that dreadful horse, Senhora Fonseca was a living invitation. As the house-boys carried her into the White Rhino, the dwarf had thought how it might be. With the woman bedridden, he might slowly train her to his touch. At first just brushing her hand with his own while he laid the tray across her legs. Then, he thought, offering a simple massage when she grew stiff in bed. Bored and uncomfortable, the Portuguese woman would accept, thinking him beneath notice, harmless.

But if once he could begin, if her smooth skin felt his moving fingers, she would recognize and soften to the magic of his touch, understanding that he knew her. Finally the desire would leap from him to her, like an invisible frog. She would revel in the unmentionable while he tormented her, first with small oiled fingers, at last with his tongue and hand.

Anunciata, instead, was up at once, hobbling about the White Rhino, settling with languor in the lounge or stirring the bar to life with dancing brown eyes.

Meanwhile Olivio was obliged to watch her brutish brother drink and gamble. The dwarf tried to observe the man play, uncertain why Fonseca so often won. Cards, dice, backgammon always went his way. His habit, smoothly managed, was to win cash and lose on credit. And when it was time to pay or tip, he was meaner than any Scotsman. The smallest coin screamed as it passed through his fingers. His chits were piled in the bar drawer like rice in a sack. Not since Goa had Olivio endured such Latin contempt. Commanding a drink, the man spoke as if the servant were not there.

Presently, Olivio reminded himself, it would be time to serve lunch. The Penfolds, of course, would eat in the hotel with the guests. The dwarf walked across the uneven mahogany planks of the dining room into the kitchen, always a chaos of Africa, India and England.

Baskets of yams and casabas, ropes of bananas, shaggy piles of coconuts, and bowls of fine-ground curry covered the rough wooden counters. He peeked through the open door of the larder. A kitchen boy was tacking up the sheet-lead lining stripped from a tea chest, using it to armor the larder against the attack of rats and a thousand noxious insects. Tins of Birds Blanc-Mange and Chivers Custard Powder climbed to the ceiling. He stared for a moment at his master's revolting favorites: Pan Yan Pickle Sauce, Bovril, Travers Signal Brand Worcestershire Sauce, and Maconochie's Bloater Paste.

On a special table lay the produce of the lord's English garden, the well-bred Anglo-Saxon seeds grown to mad opulence in Africa. Outsize carrots, immense runner beans, and a virtual tree of brussels sprouts, each the size of a lime, ready to be boiled in the English way, boiled until the leaves flaked off. Wooden butterball paddles waited to one side in a bowl of cool water.

Olivio saw the cook stiffen and shrink into silence when he sensed the dwarf behind him. The Kikuyu stepped back and Olivio approached the oven. Thick homemade bricks framed a long box-like hole, busy with hot coals and pans. The oven was topped with a beaten-metal roof fabricated from a door of Penfold's old Ford. The chromium-plated handle served to shift the stovetop on which a large pot warmed. Handing the cook a plate, Olivio raised the lid. Clouds of spicy steam welcomed him. The dwarf's lips moistened uncontrollably when he smelled the Tommy curry. His nostrils widened, and he lifted a dinner plate. He stirred the dish with the fingers of one hand. He sucked them clean and sifted through the pot, plucking out favored morsels of the gazelle.

"Save this for me," the dwarf said.

"Olivio!" he heard Lord Penfold holler from the porch. "Guests!"

Olivio stepped from the kitchen. The cook spat thickly into the chosen plate of curry.

At the verandah the dwarf found an unpleasing spectacle. More penniless English settlers, the sort of shabby arrivals that promised work but no reward.

An overloaded battered wagon, attended by two filthy blacks. One of them, perhaps Kikuyu, pressed his vanity in a threadbare British army sweater. A thin white man, looking young and old at once, had not yet alighted from the wagon bench. Olivio saw Penfold limp over to greet a better sight. Warm and dusty, too skinny for pleasure, but with encouraging slender ankles, a young woman, not yet thirty, smiled at the welcome with startling green eyes.

"Lancelot!" Lord Penfold suddenly said with the enthusiasm Olivio's master reserved for dogs. To his horror, the dwarf, too, now saw the dormant whippet in Alan's lap. At least, Olivio thought, this must be the last of those high-strung pests. Thankfully the other two had never returned from the bush. "Lost at sea," the lord had said.

Ignoring all else, Penfold stroked Lancelot. The dog raised its head and licked Lord Penfold's hand. Olivio watched its stringy rat-like tail batting against Alan.

"Won't you please come and take a bite of lunch with us," Penfold said to the Llewelyns while he lifted the dog. "Olivio, be a good chap and find these boys something to eat, and have someone see to the mules."

Penfold limped onto the verandah with Lancelot in his arms. Ignoring Anunciata, Sissy stood on the porch with her back to him, opening a parcel of new victrola recordings from home. The awkward package was forcing his Greeks towards the edge of the table as Sissy tore loose the cardboard wrapping.

"Must you get paint all over the hotel when you're playing with these silly toys?" Sissy said when she recognized her husband's limp behind her. She tore impatiently at the paper covering, breaking a nail, and held up a record: Jack Hylton's Dance Orchestra Plays "A Pretty Girl Is Like a Melody" at the Savoy. "Heaven!" Sissy said.

"I thought you'd want to see Lancelot," Penfold said. "Some friends found him by the road. He's rather badly off."

Sissy spun about quickly on her high-heeled sling-back shoes. Three Macedonians, ensnared in the string of the wrapping, were caught by the sudden movement and fell to the floor. One soldier lost his long curved shield, another his head.

"Thank heavens!" Sissy stroked the dog's side as it flinched. "Look at the poor thing. But what can you expect in this filthy country?"

She watched in annoyance as Anunciata, under Adam's admiring eye, leaned far out over the side of her cane chair and recovered the decapitated Macedonian.

— 15 —

Do you want to stop and take some water, Tlaga?" Karioki said, feeling the tightness growing in his own calves. For five days he had walked hard, twelve hours a day or more, waiting for the white boy to slow the pace. When he was a youth Karioki had done this, always winning, walking and running with the young men of his tribe until the others dropped out one by one.

"Not yet, Karioki, unless you're tired." Anton was not displeased by the question. "Why don't we go on to that second set of hills?"

They were marching almost due west, looking for the great valley they knew lay before them. The land was uneven. Often rough and rocky, then green and shaded, only the thorns bound it together. In the dry country the thornbush was grey and low and brittle, the chosen diet, Karioki said, of rhinoceros and gerenuk. These diminutive, long-necked, giraffe-like antelope drank no water and stood on slender hind legs to browse, lean preachers at an outdoor service. The gerenuk were almost too delicate to shoot with Anton's .450. As the two men walked on into less dry habitat, the thorny scrub became trees, tall and green, inviting instead of hostile, welcoming giraffe and elephant.

Like cactus, the thorns always survived. Each was perfectly contrived, Anton observed, with tiny hooks or three-inch spikes to fend off certain hungry animals and to permit others to browse. After a time Anton became oblivious to their sharp punishment, as if strolling through an English rain. His legs and forearms a canvas of cuts

and scabs, he followed Karioki, at first in silence. Then the two would talk, mixing English, Kikuyu and Swahili, as Karioki used his wartime lessons and Anton's ear picked up the chanting tones of Africa.

When they found human footprints, Karioki crouched and studied them with care. Spitting the single word "Maasai" when he stood, he would lead Anton away from their direction. Twice they found tracks of masses of cattle, and once an abandoned boma. The thorn-branch enclosure was paved with cattle droppings and spotted with low dwellings fashioned from branches and packed blocks of dung. Only flies welcomed them. The insects rose slowly, tired guardians, their lifeless buzzing reflecting the vanished energy of the deserted village. Anton crawled into one hut through its single low opening. He found no sign of habitation, only a swarm of fleas and a stale presence that made him an intruder.

"Nothing smells worse than a white man," Karioki said one afternoon as he smeared Anton's back with a cake of moist elephant dung. "Especially to intelligent animals like elephant. If you wish to get in among the *ndovu,* Tlaga, you must clean your smell with this."

"Who taught you about elephant, Karioki?"

"As a boy, I learned the tales of the old hunters, before the guns came. They had to kill the bulls who ate their millet and tore up the banana trees at night. The bravest hunters made themselves into elephants, using dung and musk. They lay like leopards along the limbs of trees and punched heavy poisoned spears into the necks of bulls that passed below.

"My grandfather's father was torn from a tree by an angry bull. The wounded elephant, with the spear sticking in its neck, took him in its trunk and slapped him against the tree like a rag. It smashed him to the ground and placed one foot on his chest and ripped off his legs with its trunk."

"Terrible," said Anton. He paused. "But wouldn't you kill someone who stabbed you with a poisoned spear?"

"A man must kill anyone who attacks him with a weapon."

Anton sat to pull on his boots, but Karioki pinched his nose and frowned. Naked and armed, they walked through the bush to the waterhole, a shallow brown pool set among mounds of dark and fissured rocks. The two men lay side by side under the low arch of three joined boulders.

"Snakes?" Anton whispered while he settled into the cramped space, annoyed by the sticky shards of dung fibre that scratched his stomach. Curious, he thought, that his comfort depended on how well an elephant could chew.

"I think not, Tlaga. Here we watch for *inge,* the scorpion."

A Romany sign of danger, Anton recollected.

Sharing the last belt of elephant meat, Karioki and Anton chewed slowly without speaking. In four days it would be February 14, Anton's birthday. He was pleased he had waited to open von Decken's parcel. As usual, he did not expect many presents. If he were lucky, the package and a good bush feast with Karioki would make it a party.

Anton remembered another birthday, his fourteenth, when he had needed a friend. With Lenares dead and his mother away, he was alone in the vardo. He listened to icy rain strike the wagon roof and was glad for the coal fire that glowed in the small iron stove. He looked about the cozy space, compact and densely furnished like the cabin of some exotic ship. Richly tasselled scarves and beaten copper plates brightened the walls. Pleated satin folds followed the arch of the vaulted ceiling. A one-faced tambourine hung above the bunk. A sad-mouthed lover was depicted on one side of the drum skin. On the other was painted a swollen heart torn by an arrow.

Anton heated potatoes and blood sausages in a pan. He listened to the pork fat sizzle and pop. He called out "Happy Birthday" in a loud voice and began to eat directly from the pan. Later he lay on his bunk, propped up on his elbows, warm and full, humming to himself and reading *Hard Times* by lamplight.

Sleepy, he was surprised to feel movement, as if someone outside were hitching the wagon. Soon the narrow vardo began to rock from side to side. Anton jumped up and peered out the tiny dripping window. A gang of gypsy youths braced themselves against the caravan while they rocked it faster and faster. The dark laughing faces ran with rain. Seeing him at the window, the boys chanted, "Gau-jo! Gau-jo!"

Enraged, Anton pulled on his trousers. The oil lamp swung violently on its hook. Pans and books fell and slid about the floor. He felt two wheels leave the ground. The wagon rocked up onto the opposing wheels, hesitating, nearly in balance before it crashed back down. The lamp smashed against the wall, spilling drops of flaming oil down the carved wooden panelling.

Anton threw open the top and bottom sections of the door. The steps were gone. He yelled "Fire! Fire!" and leapt down, barefoot, into the mud. Gypsies rushed over from their vardos with pitchers and pots of water. Anton hurled himself at the band of boys. His stomach tightened at the memory.

"Soon they will come," Karioki whispered, interrupting Anton's thoughts. Anton nodded. They continued to wait in silence.

Suddenly an unbidden thought came to him. What would Gwenn Llewelyn think, Anton wondered, if she could see him now, lying naked with Karioki on the sand under the rocks, painted head to toe with dung and waiting for the elephant? The idea stirred him.

This time Anton heard the elephant before he saw them. His ear against the ground, he caught the sound of stones shuffling when they advanced. He heard a loud breathing above him just as the grey tower of a wrinkled leg swung past the rock-framed aperture in front of him. He saw the front rim of four wide toenails meet the ground when the ankle flexed. The leg straightened and the immense weight spread flat the softer pad that followed, like heavy batter spreading in a hot pan. Over his own encrusted smell Anton inhaled the rich musk-sweet odor of elephant.

Two animals walked into the murky water. They parted it with their trunks, swishing it gently about, snorting bubbles across the dark surface. Neither elephant drank. The male stepped two yards to one side. Scraping with his right front foot, the bull dug a trench in the packed sandy ground. The pit filled slowly with clear water, filtered through the intervening sand. Side by side, the animals drank, like a couple at dinner, drawing up the water with their trunks and funnelling it into their beak-like mouths.

The female waited by the side of the pool. Her trunk waved gently towards the ground while the bull approached. He stiffened his ears, flapping them once when he stepped to her. He slipped the pointed tip of his trunk into the corner of the cow's mouth, holding it there. The two animals stood motionless. The bull removed his trunk and swung it below her belly, arcing its tip upward and sliding it slowly along the moist open edge of her vulva. Thick dark fluid trickled down the male's cheeks. Perhaps a yard taller, nearly twelve feet at the shoulder, he firmed his trunk and pressed it along the swayed back of the female.

Anton saw the male's curved four-foot penis dripping as it swung stiff below him, strangely pink and unprotected. With a deliberate balanced movement the bull mounted her. His forelegs braced on her flanks. His entire weight shifted onto his thinner rear legs. He laid his trunk along her back and curled it. He raised his penis and entered her.

The cow cried out once like a child when the bull pressed several tons of weight against her rear. There was silence as the animals were one. Then the female eased forward and the bull lowered himself onto his front legs. She stroked his penis with her trunk. The dripping penis shrank into its sheath. The male raised his trunk and touched the ridge of bone above her eyes. The two elephant drank once more and passed from view.

Where was Anton? Karioki cursed two days later. Where was that big white boy when he needed him?

Karioki was running well now, breathing evenly as he swiftly picked his route through the Loita foothills. But the Maasai were still with him, trotting lightly in pursuit with their dreaded all-day gait. Without turning his head, Karioki knew how they would look.

One beast ran first, the other four in a knot behind. All were lean and naked but for streaming black ostrich plumes. Their long-muscled bodies were stained red with ochre and gleamed with sweat and the rancid butter they rubbed into their skins. The open loops of their earlobes swung low, stretched with beads and vials of snuff. Habituated to herding, fighting and lion-killing, alternately passive and ferocious, the Maasai *moran,* the young warriors, would be running with their heads thrown slightly back, without exertion, their greased hair flowing behind in tight braids, their eyes wide and trancelike.

In his right hand, carried low, each moran held a devilish spear. Too heavy to throw far, the weapons were built to receive the charge of a lion. One iron end was heavy, squared off and blunt, used for jamming into the ground while the kneeling warrior prepared to guide the tip into the chest of the hurtling beast. The central wooden hand hold was butter-polished and smooth. At the top, the two-foot blade, slender but for a thick spine, was shaped for deep penetration, ready to be forced home by the weight of the butt. If a spear struck him, Karioki knew, he would see its tip burst out through his chest or stomach. Before a moran threw one he would vibrate the weapon in his palm until it hummed, the better to control its flight. The last thing Karioki would hear before it split his back would be the singing of the flying spear.

Already they had run far. Karioki sought to lead the moran in an enormous arc with Anton and his rifle at its end. Anton was to be back in camp when the sun was at its height, and it was almost there. But could he depend on Tlaga to be there? Would this *m'zungu* know when to kill a man?

Karioki remembered the morning the Germans had attacked at Namacurra. The South Africans were forced back on one side. The Portuguese disappeared on the other. The German askaris and *ruga-ruga,* their wild irregulars, mostly pig-smelling Wasukuma, worse than Maasai, had got in among the fugitives and butchered them like women. Only the King's African Rifles and the Fusiliers held, and not for long. The white K.A.R. officers had been angry and ashamed, though his own lieutenant had fought like a lion. Would Tlaga be strong when the blood flowed?

Karioki glanced up at the sun. He turned his head to check the pursuing pack. One moran was starting to close on him.

Running on, Karioki thought of his grandfather's stories of the Maasai. For generations they had raided his people, slaughtering men and seizing girls and cattle. But today the white men kept the Maasai on their own vast lands, land too good and large, and partly once Kikuyu. Now he was on the land of the southern Maasai, the most wild of them all, and they had found him among their herds.

Karioki was heavier and stronger than any Maasai he had seen, and proud of his fleetness, but he knew these savages were good at this. They ran men down like a pack of long-eared wild dogs hunting an antelope. First one dog would sprint, then another and another, until no prey could shake them all. In time, one dog would rip a bite from the buck's belly while it ran, leaving its trailing guts to slow it as the death-smelling pack speeded its pace.

Already one Maasai had chased Karioki fast until the moran dropped, leaving the others to finish the weakened Kikuyu. Finally they would kill him as they killed a lion. While he fought the first, they would close in a circle of trembling spears, maddened in a hunting frenzy while they did together what none could do alone.

As he trotted, Karioki considered stopping to fight, using his strength before exhaustion took him, but they were still too many. Perhaps he could run until they were only two, or three.

On a leather strap over his shoulder Karioki carried his father's *simi,* the double-edged blade longer than an English bayonet, used often like a panga or short sword. His spear, bartered far from home after the war, was not the proper weapon of his tribe. Now it slowed his pace.

Slipping when he splashed across an unexpected stream, Karioki looked back to see the leader start to sprint, leaving his companions trotting behind. Karioki's lungs ached. He pushed himself and dashed up the next hill, hoping to see camp ahead and give Anton a warning whistle on the cartridge he held in his left hand. But the speeding man was gaining on him. As he reached the top, Karioki stopped suddenly and turned. His chest heaving, he hurled the spear. The Maasai ducked it and stumbled while Karioki burst down the far side.

Gasping, angry with disappointment, he found the camp empty. Just like the war. How could you depend on a m'zungu?

Karioki veered away past the camp and caught his right foot in the hooked corner of a root. On his knees, his ankle twisted, he tried to rise as the Maasai fell on him.

Three moran beat him down while he fought and screamed. He struggled in their grip, amazed they did not kill him. One drew Karioki's simi and cut shallow cicatrices on the Kikuyu's stomach, long double lines with dots pricked out between them. The marks, Karioki knew, that the Maasai used to brand captured women in former days. Not death for him, but a shameful insult to carry home. He resisted more violently and the leader slammed Karioki across the neck with the edge of his spear butt. Karioki lay nearly still while the other Maasai continued their work. If a Kikuyu brother were with him, instead of Tlaga, this never would have happened. The carver raised the blade to Karioki's forehead. The Kikuyu glared with hatred into the eyes of the slender Maasai leader. The man stood calmly on one foot, the other braced against the inside of his knee, his arm leaning on his planted spear.

While Karioki stared, there was an explosion and the spear jumped from the man's hand. In an instant Anton was among them, giving one moran a stunning blow with his rifle as Karioki grabbed the carver by the throat and seized back his simi. Karioki leapt at the Maasai leader and smashed him to the ground. Violently he cut two deep lines across the man's forehead, feeling his blade edge chisel the bone. The others began to run.

"Shoot them, Tlaga!" Karioki yelled. "Kill them!"

"No, my friend. And let that one go too," Anton said. "We have far to walk and there are many more of them. Are you all right?"

Anton offered his hand to help the remaining Maasai to his feet. The man ignored the gesture and raised himself to a crouch. Two bleeding stripes crossed his brow. Blood ran into his eyes. Holding the Merkel in one hand, Anton gave the man back his spear. Anton raised the rifle and aimed at a thorn tree eighty yards off. He squeezed the trigger and the trunk split in two. Before he could look down, the Maasai was running.

"You must learn when to kill, Tlaga," Karioki said with anger. "A man must always kill Maasai when he can." But at least the boy had fought. Karioki rubbed his stomach with smoldering ashes from the campfire, seeking to obscure the pattern of the cuts. What decent girl would want him now, disgraced with Maasai scars?

Anton lifted their packs and walked to the west through low sandy bush. Soon Karioki, favoring one ankle, fell in beside him and took his own pack. After a time, walking more slowly, Anton took back the second pack.

Hours later, as the sun dropped, they came to a line of low cloud hanging above a far-stretching ledge of layered rock. Anton pointed with his rifle at a cluster of trees set among a nest of boulders. "There should be water."

One boulder moved in the twilight.

"Eland!" whispered Karioki. He watched in surprise when Anton lay flat to catch the moving profile against the darkening skyline. Where had a white boy learned this trick?

It was indeed the giant antelope. The crest of its short ridged horns stood seven feet in the air as it browsed on the leaves of the trees. A breeze ruffled towards the animal. The eland raised its head, sniffed and stepped away. Anton knelt and fired one barrel at its shoulder. The massive antelope stumbled forward and collapsed among the rocks, groaning like an old man. It kicked its legs in the air. Karioki rushed forward and slashed its throat.

"This time, Karioki, we'll bring the fire to the animal." Eager for approval, Anton was pleased to see Karioki nod at the idea, even if he hadn't thanked Anton for his help with the Maasai. At least this time he'd intervened, although a little late, Anton admitted to himself, remembering Lenares and the foresters.

Soon flames glittered among the rocks on the long splintered ledge. Puffed clouds lay to the side like a wall of cotton wool. Anton approached the eland with his knife. He remarked the hump on its bluish-grey shoulders, the weight of its floppy bearded dewlap, and the blaze of its white-striped flanks. Only the head seemed out of proportion, too small for the animal's majesty. Its brown eyes were open, strangely appealing, almost alive. Anton closed them with his hand. Although famished, he hesitated before using his knife.

Karioki slit open the eland's belly. He wiped the Maasai bloodstain from his simi against the damp grass in the animal's stomach. He cut open the eland's chest and carved out the thick brisket.

"Eland, Tlaga, is the best meat. Even the blood-drinking, dung-filled Maasai, who are not men enough to eat meat, sometimes taste it. They call eland 'the cattle of God.' This is the only truth they speak."

Karioki and Anton cast the huge beast's innards far away to avoid luring hyena and lion to the camp. Not a concern at home, Anton thought, where gypsy mongrels kept the camp clean. Karioki and he cut up the carcass. He felt Karioki watch him as he worked with his knife. Together they hung the heavy quarters in the limbs of a tree.

Karioki saw Anton go through their provisions with unusual care. At least the boy was good with a knife, and one day he might un-

derstand the bush. Already he was better than any white Karioki had
ever seen. But he would never be a man until he had killed, Karioki
thought, scowling at the memory of the afternoon.

Anton put the last of their sugar thick in the bottom of the two
tin cups. Squatting on his heels, he heated water for coffee, staring
into the fire while the flames flared sideways in the rising wind. When
the water boiled, Anton emptied in the precious coffee and set the
pan aside. He watched the dark grains tumble past each other through
the simmering water. He stirred in a whirlpool with a stick. The rich
smell mixed with the odors of the broiling meat. He remembered
the scents of other fires, rabbit and venison and spiced English cider.
After the grounds settled, he filled Karioki's cup and his own.

"Today is the day I was born, Karioki." Anton handed Karioki his
cup. "Nineteen years ago."

"Oh, Tlaga! Tlaga! Tonight you must eat for the next nineteen
years! We must kill another eland!" Karioki smiled and put his hand
on Anton's shoulder.

Globs of dripping fat sparkled and jumped as the rich meat sizzled
on sticks over the fire. Anton thought of friends he might never see
again. The gypsies, Stone, the ship's doctor, Gwenn, Ernst. Would
his whole life be like that?

Anton reopened his pack. He undid the neat double-knotted string
of von Decken's parcel. Wrapped by a German, he thought. He
folded back the wax paper to discover a package and an envelope.
He opened the first and found four perfect sisal bulbils, the jewels
of German Africa, unlawful to send from the country. From these a
man might build a fortune. On the envelope he read the gothic script
of Hugo von Decken.

*May the bulbs make you rich, my young Englishman, and may the seeds
make you happy.*

Anton opened the brown envelope. It was bursting with the apple
seeds of Gepard Farm. With them was a note instructing Anton how
the seeds should be planted.

"Look, Tlaga!"

Anton raised his moist eyes and looked into the night. His heart
stopped. The wind cleared the thinning clouds from the blue-black
sky. The inverted crescent of the southern moon lit up the rest of
the world. At their side, the ledge dropped away, perhaps three

thousand feet, and became a bottomless cliff. Below them, forever, beneath a sea of stars, stretched an immense wide valley, sometimes flat or rolling, then ridged with rocky waves, expanding endlessly, on and on into the night, the boundless openness that he had always sought, free as the sky.

— 16 —

Why must you ask that hopelessly unamusing couple to dine with us?" Sissy said irritably. "They're so dreadfully Welsh. And the husband looks as though he'll never make it back upstairs."

"He did his share," Penfold said, immediately regretting the words of response. Never argue with a woman, his father had advised. He'd hate to think how Sissy would look after a few months in Mesopotamia.

Penfold raised his chin. He knotted his black tie without looking in the glass. His wife stepped into her oldest long dress. She lifted her thin legs high like a horse picking its way across a shallow river. He stood by the door and waited, tapping a fag on the side of his silver cigarette case before lighting it. The voice pursued him.

"And why the smarmy Portuguese with that endless round forehead, and that tarty sister? They probably sleep together. If they had their own table, at least we could charge them for dinner," she pointed out with rare concern, reminding her husband of the Himalaya of unopened bills.

Sissy waited for Penfold to open the door. They left their bungalow and walked in silence to the hotel. Before they entered the dining room, Sissy took her husband's arm.

Adam Penfold was not dining with the merry children and devoted wife who, in his young man's dreams, he had assumed would adorn his table. The wife was indeed there, in the flesh at least, but instead of children and devotion, she offered complaints and her styptic cool. The lovely whippets were the last pleasure they had shared, and now only brave Lancelot was left. Even his regiment she had resented. As some men come slowly to resemble their dogs, so Sissy was replicating her hunter, ever longer in the nose and jaw, too much bone in the limbs. Where would it end? he wondered. At least Anunciata, when the whim took her, made him feel young. He finished his gin while his damned leg began to throb and the hock was poured at last.

Raising his glass, Penfold smiled gamely. He looked around the table in the dim light of the hippo-tallow candles: Anunciata, Fonseca, Sissy and the Llewelyns. An improbably crew, his old tutor would have said.

"Every now and again," the black-gowned beak had warned him over sherry, "every gent feels like Ovid among the Scythians. Not alone, but with no one with whom to speak." Now Penfold understood.

This young couple was going to have it hard, Penfold feared, and Llewelyn was no Trojan. There was no spark in the young man's eye, only a sense of inadequacy that Penfold recognized too well. And already that sly Portuguese was sniffing after Gwenn. Worse, the crafty bounder was up to some scheme to assemble land that should be going to young soldier families, the sort that would build the country and look after the Africans and the animals. In Mozambique, where Fonseca belonged, it was all neo-slavery and Latin decadence. And now the Kikuyu were rumoring that the man was breaking the game laws when he hunted ivory north of Nanyuki. Nothing was sacred to his sort. If Europeans didn't play the game, what could one expect of the poor Africans?

"To my friends of the trail," Penfold said, lifting a glass, "Gwenn and Alan, and a jolly fine start on the new farm. And to the land we live in!"

He saw Sissy wince as he finished, her unvarying reaction whenever he offered a toast.

"Farming up-country, are you? On the Ewaso Ngiro?" Fonseca asked Gwenn in a friendly voice.

How the devil did he know that? Penfold wondered. Perhaps Spongey had told him.

"Yes, we're just on our way. Do you know the region?" Gwenn said.

"Actually I'm getting together some property up there." Fonseca smiled at her with full wide lips. "Perhaps we'll see each other."

Avocados, crated from Mombasa and shipped in straw like precious eggs, were served, their empty pit holes filled with peppered oil. Penfold spooned in some Marmite and stirred it about, spilling the darkened oil over the black edge of the fruit's shell. He ignored his wife's disgust.

"May I ask what you are adding there, Adam?" Fonseca said, calling attention to the sight.

"Just a dash of England, my dear Fonseca, just a dash of old England," said Penfold cheerfully, enjoying the Portuguese's condescension. He applied more of the sticky brown paste, splashing it about in the oil. Unlike his schoolmates, Penfold particularly favored the hard crusty bits of Marmite that congealed at the top of the pot if the lid was left off for a bit, one detail on which Olivio and the kitchen boys rarely obliged him. "Would anyone care for some?"

"I should doubt it, Treasure," said Sissy. Alan Llewelyn reached for the jar.

"Those of us who dined on bush-rat pie and fried monkey's brains during the war learned to pray for Marmite," Penfold said without sarcasm.

Yearning for the touch, he suddenly felt Anunciata's fingernails move along his leg. Penfold knew her interest was cooling, but with luck Sissy would drive her back to him, like an unwitting ferret chasing a plump rabbit into the jaws of a badger. Whenever Anunciata appeared, Penfold sensed Sissy arching stiffly with cat-like hostility, not that he could blame her. There must be something to this female-instinct business after all.

Penfold looked up and saw Fonseca busying himself with Gwenn, switching on that confounded oily smile, gazing into her sparkling green eyes as if they were the moon itself. Too bad things seemed a bit cool between Gwenn and her husband. The poor chap looked so sad.

Would there be mashed potatoes with the Tommy chops? Penfold frowned. He had told Olivio to be certain about the sprouts, but what about the spuds? Some days it seemed that brussels sprouts were his only physical pleasure. And one couldn't have a proper din-din without spuds. How typical, he thought, looking to his wife's right as the chatter rose, for this Fonseca fellow to get his dinner jacket wrong. Like all these jumped-up Latins, dressing carefully but not well. If he had to wear a full-length white jacket, at least the round collar should be double-breasted, more full, buttoned over at the bottom, not hanging open, too thin and narrow, like an embalmer's smock. But what could one expect? Far smarter was Llewelyn, diffident in his honest Welsh tweed.

And there was loyal old Olivio Alavedo, a man of values. Standing in his corner under the stuffed warthog's head, minding his business, a shiny round-headed doll, supervising the staff, neat and correct in his scarlet evening sash, black trousers and short white dinner jacket. At least the dwarf was properly turned out. And so were the two table boys, he thought, admiring their crisp white kanzu tunics and their sashes and low fezzes in matching scarlet. Actually, one boy had it just wrong, Penfold noticed with despair. The fellow had his sash the wrong way, with the pleats opening down, instead of upwards so they could catch the crumbs. He hoped Olivio wouldn't notice and give the poor chap hell.

Emptying his glass again, Penfold recalled the passage in Gibbon that described Olivio far better than the little man's own mother could have done.

"A large round head, a swarthy complexion," the historian had written, describing Attila the Hun, "with small, deep-seated eyes, a flat nose, a few hairs in place of a beard, broad shoulders, and a short square body, of a nervous strength, though of a disproportioned form."

Upstairs a few minutes later, Olivio turned the key to Number 4. The safest time, he had learned, was while they were at table, when Penfolds, guests and staff were all occupied. After the Thomson gazelle chops were served and the lord had his claret, the dwarf had slipped soundlessly upstairs. Once inside Number 4, he closed the door and locked it, risking embarrassment but not surprise.

He found the letter from Lisbon pinned under an open jar of Erasmus Wilson's Hair Pomade. The edge of the envelope extended over the top of the tall chest. Olivio brought over a chair and climbed up. Annoyed by the disorder, the dwarf screwed the black lid onto the jar of hair dressing, careful to get none of the clear grease on his fingers. He opened the envelope. He drew out the two sheets of heavy paper and began to read the Lisbon notary's formal Portuguese.

The writer's distinguished client, Senhora de Castanheda y Fonseca, had recently died, he read, in her seventy-seventh year, at home on the quinta Santo António near Oporto. She had no husband and no children. Her heirs would be the male children or grandchildren of her two late brothers.

Olivio, standing on his toes on the chair, raised his eyes to the photograph that now rested against the looking glass. He studied the two men again: the round heads, the small eyes. He admired the forceful expression of the shorter man in the clerical collar. His own grandfather? The dwarf set his face firmly and turned his head to a similar angle. He examined his reflection in the mirror. Yes, it must be! He and Vasco Fonseca were cousins! Their grandfathers were brothers! Breathless, feeling himself perspire, he resumed reading.

Senhora de Castanheda's elder brother, his late eminence Dom Tiago de Castanheda y Fonseca, the distinguished Archbishop of Goa, of course had no children, being a prince of the Church. Accordingly, the undivided estate of Senhora de Castanheda would pass to the sons or grandsons of the cleric's deceased younger brother, João. The writer's records and those of the family indicated that João's only son had perished of malaria on his plantations in Portuguese East Africa, leaving one son, João's grandson, and now his heir: Senhor Vasco de Castanheda y Fonseca.

So they did not know that the archbishop, too, had sired a son, and the son a grandson! Olivio Fonseca Alavedo himself!

The second page listed a preliminary inventory of Senhora de Castanheda's estate, including her collections of lace and silver, the decaying *palacio* outside Lisbon in Estoril, the fazendas in Brazil and Africa, her accounts in the Banco Espirito Santo, the cork forest in the Costa Verde, and one of the two finest port houses in the world, the Quinta Castanheda y Fonseca on the banks of the River Douro.

One half of this belonged to him!

In the absence of a will, the notary explained, the transfer of such property took time to arrange in Portugal, but if Senhor Fonseca would certify his identity and reply to the writer, this important work could begin. Of course there would be expenses.

Olivio searched the drawers for a pencil and a scrap of paper, desperate to transcribe the notary's name and address. He opened the top drawer, pulling it tight against his chest while he stood on tiptoe on the chair. He heard steps approach the door. The drawer jammed when he sought to close it. Typical African workmanship, Olivio thought as he lost his balance. He fell backward onto the bed. The chair crashed down. The dwarf heard the door handle rattle and Fonseca curse in Portuguese.

In a trice Olivio was at the window, the chair back in its place. Hanging outside from the sill by the fingers of his right hand, Olivio struggled to close the window with his left. He caught the window and pulled it down, but the dwarf's short fingers lost their grip and he fell into the white rosebush below. He extricated himself from the thorns, brushed himself off, and looked up to see Kina herself watching him from the Kikuyu village. He paused and recovered his dignity, even in his haste unable not to admire her overwhelming figure. He hurried into the kitchen and wiped drops of blood from his face. Calmly he entered the dining room with an unopened bottle of claret. Passing through to fetch a corkscrew from the bar, he saw that Fonseca had not yet come down.

"Must be having trouble finding his cigars," Penfold said when Olivio moved behind his lordship. In the hallway Olivio put the key to Number 4 on a hook before getting the corkscrew. He reentered the dining room and heard Fonseca on the stair. Olivio held Fonseca's chair and the Portuguese resumed his seat. The dwarf pulled the cork.

"Couldn't find my key." Fonseca looked at the nursery custard and declined to serve himself. "And I heard someone in my room."

"Most unlikely," said Lady Penfold, observing her husband speak quietly to Anunciata.

Olivio stepped into the hallway and returned with a key.

"Here is your key, senhor," the dwarf said to Vasco Fonseca. "It was on the hook for Number Three."

— 17 —

Anton imagined himself tucking in the spines of his wings, folding his clean perfect feathers tight to his sides, and screaming down eyes first, two thousand, three thousand feet, then breaking his flight, talons forward, wings strained wide against the fall, and snatching a snake or baby rock rabbit at the very instant he rose again, flapping heavily, without ever touching the earth.

In England, he had looked up to see the hawks, then lost them when they plunged. But here on his cliff by the Rift Valley, he gazed down with the birds of prey. He watched each winged hunter alter, stiffening from its relaxed broad-scanning surveillance to a narrow death-focused concentration. He tried to search for prey as the hawks did, living so neatly off the wild, selecting only what they needed.

Until the crescent moon rose again, Anton and Karioki lived at eland camp on the cliff by the Rift. Anton explored on his own while Karioki's ankle mended and they feasted on the eland. He learned to descend the great wall like a klipspringer, the small rock antelope that bounded along the escarpment. In the warm afternoons he would lie under a thorn tree on a narrow ledge and watch the plain below come to life as long shadows cooled the valley.

At first he saw little. His eyes were not trained to the animals and the landscape. But gradually he discerned more of the life displayed before him. As the shadows moved, he noticed spots shifting on what had seemed a tree trunk. A giraffe took form, then two or more. When some branches waved with the wind and others did not, he learned to isolate the spiralling horns of a stationary kudu among the twisted thorn trees. Or, if the air was still, he remembered old advice. Instead of looking for an animal, he would watch for movement while he glassed the valley.

How Lenares would have loved this land, Anton thought. A snake eagle sailed on the wind directly before him, so close that he saw its feathery brown wingtips riffling in the air as the bird scanned for prey worthy of its godlike dive. Anton lowered his eyes and compared the bird to his own tattoo.

When Karioki was fit again, Anton and the Kikuyu hunted together, exchanging lessons, though the African had more to teach. Anton knew he saw as far and as well as Karioki, yet he could not spot all the game the Kikuyu made out. He had never expected to find a man closer to nature than his *sikhdzjeno,* his gypsy tutor. But instead of studying the land, like Lenares, Karioki was part of it. Anton wanted to be the same. He also wanted to please Karioki and not lose him as he had all the others.

The precious Uttendoerfer bullets were too heavy for light game, and the spear too difficult, so the two hunters designed traps, gypsy trip snares and African pits, combining the lore of the bush with the tricks of the Romany. Karioki taught Anton the relationships of the animals. The cruelest enemies, Anton learned, always lived together. Leopard and baboon, serpents and mongoose, lion and buffalo shared forever their intimate mortal theatres.

In the evenings Anton taught Karioki the stars and constellations. Then the African would look into the fire and recite the tales of the old Kikuyu storytellers. How the Hippo Lost His Horn. Why the Rhino Has Small Eyes. They bartered the myths of Scorpius and Sagittarius for the tale of The Bongo That Forgot to Hide.

"Remember these stories, Tlaga," said Karioki one evening after repeating Anton's favorite, The Blind Boy Who Swam with Crocodiles. "My people live inside them. When a tale is told, everyone who ever heard that story is alive again, the old people and the little ones, listening in the shadows by the fire."

Anton thought of how the gypsies, too, repeated unwritten tribal legends by their campfires, tales also of chiefs and elders and witches, of herbs and spells, and of animals and magic trees. Sometimes Lenares seemed to be beside him, whispering advice.

Anton realized he and Karioki were developing a peculiar language of their own, mixing Swahili, Kikuyu and English. He felt his relationship with Kariokii lose its testy edge as the African gradually accepted him.

Anton remembered his friendship with Stone, how easy things were in the woods, how awkward elsewhere. In the forest or the bush, men were equals and you learned whom to trust. Perhaps he himself had treated Stone the way Karioki was at first with him, too prickly, overly aware of what separated one from the other when they were away from nature. Maybe the person who felt the disadvantage was the one who made the problem. In any case, he had found a friend.

"You are teaching me too much, Karioki," Anton said one evening while he sat on the ground by the fire and carved stiff pieces of eland hide to fit inside his worn-through boots. He opened his pack. "Now I am going to teach you to read, and you must teach me your language." He drew out his battered volume and smiled when he saw the bookplate: *Ex Libris Rugby School.* He showed Karioki an illustration of a young white boy in short pants and a wide round collar that spread toward his shoulders.

"This boy's name is David, and he will teach you the alphabet. Take this stick and do in the sand what I do with my knife."

"What is an alphabet?"

"It is something like your stories, Karioki." Anton hesitated. "An alphabet makes the words that keep a people together."

In the mornings they chanted the alphabet while they walked. They spelled words in the dust when they paused to rest or eat. In the evening they chose words from the book. Anton explained them while Karioki copied each one on the ground. Then Anton would read aloud from *The Personal History, Experience and Observation of David Copperfield the Younger of Blunderstone Rookery, Which He Never Meant To Be Published On Any Account.* Anton thought of England as he heard the familiar words carry into the night. He wondered what they meant to Karioki.

"Why is this Uriah Heep like a snake to David?" Karioki asked one morning. "First he crawls, then he bites." Karioki sucked on the sun-dried eland flesh that Anton whittled from a long strip while they walked. The ground was open and Anton carried his boots around his neck, saving their soles and hardening his feet.

"Because he is cowardly and jealous, Karioki, a schemer. And I think the girl and money are part of the trouble."

"But Uriah is clever. He should have many goats and cows to buy his own wives."

Anton laughed out loud and clapped Karioki on the back.

"How many goats would a girl pay for you, Karioki?"

"There are not goats enough, Tlaga."

The land was changing. The freshening air cooled them after they left the great escarpment at their backs and walked east towards Karioki's home. Anton discerned a long dark strip of green rising from the distant bush towards a range of flat-topped clouded hills.

"There, Tlaga, on the edge of the sky, are the mountains of the Aberdares. Beyond them the sacred mountain, Lenana, Mount Kenya, the home of god, Ngai himself. One day soon you will see the village of my fathers. But first you must hunt in the mountains like Karioki did when a boy. You are very old to learn, but I will teach you. Then, after you have killed the most difficult animal, Karioki will take you home."

"What animal is that?"

"Bongo. Sometimes, at a stream or by a salt rock at the edge of the forest, a man will see a female or a baby. But for many years you can be in the forest for the long rains, and in the time of the mist, and in the days of the sun, and never see one male bongo. He is a strong buck, almost red, with white stripes. His horns are black as the skin of a beautiful girl. And he is shy, shy as a shadow, like David when a small boy."

"Perhaps you will never take me home, Karioki, for I may never shoot one. Is that your wish?"

"No, Tlaga. I wish to see my father's fire, and my sister, Kina."

"Who is the enemy you said is waiting for you?"

"Chura Nyakundu, the Yellow Frog. He is powerful, and cunning like Uriah. Before I went to the war, one day I could not find Kina. I searched the village. Then I heard her sobbing from the house of this man. I ran to his door and found her. She stood before him without her apron. Her cheeks were wet. The small man was rubbing her with scented coconut oil, like meat before the roasting, and touching her where a woman likes to be touched. But my sister was very young, not yet circumcised. I pushed him down and took her. He made an oath to destroy me, Tlaga."

"Tell me about your sister." The thorny brush grew thicker and Anton sat to pull on his boots.

"She is a well-formed girl, but she cannot speak. Her tongue is silent as a gerenuk. Because of this, my father has kept her by herself. Among my people, the young men leave the villages and live in camps in the bush before they become warriors. The young girls, before they are able to have children, before they are circumcised, go to the men in the camps, bringing them food and njohi and playing with them all night. Only then do our women enjoy a man, for their bodies are still whole. This is the happy time for our girls. When they return home, soon they are circumcised, to make them good wives. Then they are married, they carry babies, they go to the fields. But my father did not let Kina go to the camps, for the elders and the *mundo mugo* said she was a special child. So she has not tasted these free pleasures like the other girls. She must be sad. She must be ready for a man. By now it is her time for circumcision."

"How old are the girls when they visit the camps, Karioki?"

"Ten years to twelve, Tlaga. They are so beautiful."

"Ten years old?"

"Of course, Tlaga. How old was your first woman?"

"I, well, you see ten would be a bit young in my country," said Anton, eager to change the subject. How could he tell Karioki he had never had a woman? "When will we come to your mountains?"

As they went on, Anton remembered stories of gypsy child weddings, the couples pledged at eight and married at ten. Of course, there was no sex until a second ceremony took place at puberty, and many marriages were dissolved. But others lasted for seventy years, the couples having shared more than any gaujos could. Even today, old gypsy ladies said these ways were best. Anton wiped his face with his red bandanna and thought of another custom, the *kitanepen*. The first time they made love, each lover would wear a diklo, afterwards using it to wipe each other's genitals. Then the two diklos were wound together and knotted at the ends and kept forever by

the Romany woman among her linen. Did Karioki's people do anything like this?

The flat crests of the Aberdares retreated with the horizon while
they walked. Finally the mountains rose abruptly. Anton stepped out
faster when they approached a belt of tall green forest. Not since
home had he sensed such cool shelter.

They entered the forest, a high sweet-smelling canopy of chestnut,
cedar and camphor, and underfoot the spongy damp mulch of fallen
leaves and evergreen needles, occasionally bumpy with black chestnut seeds. Karioki led him into the silent wood.

Anton heard a rush of water and thought of the forests of England.
Karioki crouched when they approached a clearing by a stream. Just
across the water stood a heavy-set reddish-brown antelope with white
markings and large ears. Without dropping his pack, Anton shouldered the Merkel and fired. The shot took the animal in the heart
and knocked it back as it fell.

"Bongo?" said Anton.

"No, no, Tlaga," said Karioki with derision. "Bushbuck. My poor
Tlaga is not ready to leave the forest. A good bongo has three times
the meat. You will know him if you see him."

In the night Anton woke and felt a light rain dripping through the
branches. Karioki slept on, curled under the hide of the bushbuck.
Anton rose and struggled to keep the fire alight. Finally he gave up
and crouched shivering under his wet blanket.

The darkness softened into the first grey light of predawn. He
heard rapid staccato cries in the trees above him, flitting about like
the call of a darting songbird. He made out a patch of white swinging
in the branches, and another and another: monkeys. The shifting
cries came again and again while one troop after another took the
refrain. Anton saw shadows move at the edge of the stream: four or
five men, short and slender. He heard the twang of a bow. An arrow
whistled and a single cry came from the sky. The forest went silent.

"Jambo!" Anton called out in a cheerful voice. "Good morning!"
The figures disappeared and Karioki leapt up.

"Tlaga?"

Anton pointed to the stream bank. Karioki walked over and peered
down as the morning brightened through the drizzle.

"Dorobo," Karioki said. "Forest hunters. Most are friendly, unless you frighten them. They are men of bows and honey and poisoned arrows."

Anton knelt and examined the long-tailed colobus monkey. A feathered arrow was set in its heavy chest. The monkey's hands gripped the shaft with thin tight fingers. Black, with a white mantle, it had the face of a small old man in death, hoary with snowy whiskers and a pure white beard. Anton was disturbed by the creature's humanity.

"When will the rain stop?" Anton said, thinking of England.

"After many days. Now we move camp."

They walked all morning, climbing steadily. The deciduous trees thinned and gave way to the pointed shoots of young bamboo. The slippery-wet forest floor was blanketed by the narrow spear-shaped leaves of tubular stalks that reached higher and higher above them, fifty or sixty feet tall. A mysterious twilight filtered through the yellowish green and brown bamboo. Young shoots rose thickly from the decaying remains of fallen giants. The ground was cleaner under the high canopy of the older trees, reminding Anton of the dominant oaks of the forests at home. Razor-edged leaves cut at their faces while they climbed. Lofty bamboo waved and brushed each other in the wind, sighing and conversing as raindrops and leaves floated down.

The leaves would make tracking difficult, Anton thought, while he struggled to keep pace with Karioki. With the rifle rolled in his blanket and tied across his pack, he grabbed bamboo poles for handholds. Once he slipped and clutched a thick bamboo. Slick and soft in his grip, the rotten tree crashed down with him when Anton rolled backwards, cutting his face on the sharp-leaved shoots.

At last they came to a ravine that sliced through the ridge. A pool appeared before them in the rain. To their right a thin waterfall dropped thirty feet from the rocks.

"This is my place, where Karioki came as a boy," the Kikuyu said, making a gift of the confession. "This is where Karioki hunts when his eyes are closed."

Karioki slashed twice with his simi, cutting gashes high in two strong bamboos. From these cuts he hung their packs well above the ground.

"Cane rats," Karioki said. He cut the tops off two more, leaving five-foot stumps. He carved a notch in each and slung one of the severed tops horizontally across both notches. He rested smaller bamboo diagonally against the horizontal pole. Anton cut creeping vines and they tied the poles in place. They roofed the lean-to with feathery branches that flowered fern-like from the tall bamboos. With the heel of his boot Anton dug a trench around the shelter to lead off the water.

Karioki gathered splinters of long-dead poles in the opening of the lean-to, facing the waterfall. He wiped them one by one on the inside of the bushbuck hide. He steepled the kindling into a small tower and took the waxed matches from Anton.

"Bamboo burns even in rain." Karioki struck a match. "A hunter needs only one match." The bamboo smoldered and the match drowned.

"Perhaps David can help." Anton opened his pack in the shelter and searched for a blank page in his Dickens.

While he built the fire and roasted slabs of bushbuck, Anton thought of an English Sunday breakfast. Eggs, bacon, fried bread, thick blood sausages, strong tea. Tea! How he missed his tea.

Karioki returned to the lean-to dragging handfuls of the long sting- ing nettles that had plagued Anton's bare legs during the ascent. "*Thabai,*" said Karioki. He broke off the leaves and boiled water in the pan. They feasted on bushbuck and boiled nettles. Rather like spinach, Anton thought, good enough if you're hungry. It wasn't tea, but Anton sipped the nettle broth for warmth.

Early that evening, lying prone in the shelter nibbling cold bush- buck, Anton looked through the rain to the misty pool. There, twice the size of a prime Suffolk sow, was an immense black hog, almost six feet long and four feet at the shoulder. Anton tapped Karioki's arm. Ten, twenty, thirty animals emerged at the water from tunnels worn in the bamboo forest. Anton lay still and tried not to scratch his nettle rash. The younger hogs, more grey than the black-bristled sows, snorted and rooted in the bank of the pool. Anton saw no full- grown boars. He eased the Merkel to his shoulder and fired one barrel. A huge sow fell. Rich breakfasts passed before his eyes. Sau- sages, pork chops, bacon.

"Do you have giant chickens in your forest, Karioki?" Anton jumped up and grabbed the simi.

Keen to hunt for bongo, Anton became impatient as Karioki settled easily into the camp, seeming to take no notice while the days passed. Each night Anton hunched in the shelter and listened to the coughing growl of a leopard echo through the dripping forest like the sound of sawn timber. He shivered in the frosty dawns and heard mournful winds moan through the bamboo. He thought back to the killing damp of Northumberland as if it were the brightest sunshine. Anton missed England. The villages, the gentle green hills, the flickering shadows of trout in the streams.

"When we have our cloaks," Karioki said one evening as he worked on the skins that were piled near the fire, "then we will hunt your bongo."

Patched together like a gypsy shawl, the pelts of otters and white-tailed mongoose were married to those of the bushbuck and the colobus monkey. Already the two hunters wore the softer skins of smaller animals as jerkins or vests, the hair side turned in to hold the warmth. Anton observed that Karioki's favorite cloth was the grey-brown skin of the tree hyrax, small, but soft and easy to work.

These rabbit-sized furry beasts, fat and short-legged, generously betrayed themselves by their nocturnal screeching. Alert to the shrill cries each night, Karioki hunted out their tree holes at dawn. He would take a bamboo pole, the end split into a fork, and force it into the hyrax hole until it met the moving softness of the animal's coat. Stabbing forward, but carefully, lest he pierce the pelt, he twisted the pole. The hyrax remained strangely silent in its torment while the hunter hooked its skin with the sharp bamboo before drawing the creature out.

Hunting one morning while Karioki softened and stitched the leather cloaks, Anton followed one of the tunnelled game trails that pierced the tangled twenty-foot-high thickets of collapsed bamboo. He concentrated on the spoor of a red duiker and crawled forward into the narrowing tunnel, his senses alert for the small antelope. A brief high sound caught his ear. He recognized the Dorobo hunting signal. After a moment, two more high whistles, with the urgent pitch of warning.

A man screamed. Anton knelt in the tunnel with his rifle off safety.

He heard the splintering crash of heavy bamboo poles snapping like matchsticks. In an instant the shadowy wet passage before him was choked with a fury of rushing black.

A Cape buffalo charged down on him like a cannonball in a barrel. Its shoulders and horns forced apart the bamboo like the prow of a ship. Anton fired both barrels and flung himself sideways into the cutting bamboo. His last sight before the bull struck him was its crazed red eyes, the white drool hanging from its nostrils and a cluster of broken arrows bristling from the beast's neck and shoulder.

He awoke as two Dorobo laid him down by the pool. Pain tore his chest. He heard himself groan. Karioki rushed to him.

"Banda was right, Tlaga." Karioki examined Anton's wounds. "This m'zungu is a child. I must not let my white boy hunt without me."

Moving his own hands slowly over his chest, Anton knew three ribs were broken. His left shoulder was brutally scraped and bruised. A long fine cut crossed his stomach. The muscles surrounding it were numb. Two small Dorobo bent over him, smelling of the forest. They ignored the ribs and shoulder wounds but gesticulated and argued over the cut.

"You were cut by a Dorobo arrow from the buffalo's shoulder. They say it was dipped in their finest poison, Tlaga, fresh *acocanthera*," said Karioki.

"How bad is it?" Anton dreaded what he saw in Karioki's eyes.

"If it stays in you, Tlaga must die. With this, they kill elephant."

One Dorobo took a bamboo shoot and dipped the tip in mud. Karioki held Anton down. The other Dorobo spread the cut wide while his companion scraped deeply through the length of the wound. Three times the man applied fresh mud and reamed out the wound while Anton bit on a scrap of bushbuck hide. The cut widened and the skin reddened around it while the pain grew hot. The man sluiced out the wound with water from the pool. The other Dorobo bent over Anton and sucked hard along the cut. Repeatedly he spat and washed his mouth. From a small gourd wedged in a hole in the lobe of his ear, the first man took crystals of rock salt. He pressed these into the wound, moistening each with saliva, drawing the poison.

Karioki watched Anton clench and unclench his fists and was surprised he did not scream.

After a few minutes one Dorobo flushed out the salt while his companion gathered a fungus that grew around some bamboo poles. "*Kirangi*," he explained to Anton. The Dorobo pressed the filmy fungus into the cut. The man heated a knife in the coals until the blade glowed red. He seared the wound closed with the fungus inside.

"Have they done it, Karioki? Is all the poison out?" Anton whispered. Even as he asked, he felt a pulsing pain spreading in his belly.

"Now we must wait, Tlaga, and see if you will die."

— 18 —

The mules and Alan looked more fit after three days at the White Rhino, Gwenn noticed as she attempted to evade Fonseca. The eager Portuguese, his broad-brimmed planter's hat in one hand, followed her to the wagon. He wiped his gleaming forehead with a handkerchief. He took Gwenn's elbow and helped her up to the bench. She smelled the after-odor of cigars over the sweet cologne.

Everyone had been so helpful, she thought. Penfold's men had worked on the wagon and strengthened the frame. Adam himself had checked the feet and teeth of all four mules and taught Alan how to watch for fever and foot rot. Even that curious little barman kept urging them to call upon him in the future if they needed help. Soon, he said, an Indian shop, or *duka,* would open on the road north past Nanyuki, and he himself would see that there the Llewelyns always found credit.

Penfold limped down from the verandah carrying a wicker hamper. "Lancelot asked me to prepare you a picnic for the road," he said, adding with a smile to Alan, "and there's something special in there from one old soldier to another."

But where was Mulwa? Gwenn looked around and saw him near the side of the hotel, speaking to a handsome African girl. Gwenn waited, wishing him well. Then she called his name, and Mulwa ran over and led the mules down the drive. Gwenn glanced back at the White Rhino. She saw the dwarf, his eyes fixed intently over the rail of the verandah, watching the young girl wave to Mulwa.

Soon they were on the road. The dusty track led the wagon higher, sometimes through gently rolling wild bush, occasionally past cultivation. From time to time they passed abandoned farmland, long rows of barren coffee trees, or broken fences and fields reverting to bush, and, once, what appeared to be deserted farm buildings surrounded by lines of tea trees. The low plants were sparse-leaved and withered.

At the end of the day they made camp in the shadow of a steep fast-rising hill, a great hump-shaped rock, an island in the bush. The drill was now familiar. Alan freed the mules, Mulwa raised the tent, and Arthur gathered wood and prepared for dinner. Gwenn took the rifle to the edge of camp, understanding that in Africa she must learn to hunt. She knelt and fired four practice shots, missing the hard-shelled grey fruit hanging from the high branches of a lonely baobab.

They had made a good twelve or fourteen miles, Gwenn reckoned, when she studied the government survey map. Tomorrow, or the next day, should bring them at last to the Ewaso Ngiro. "Muddy Water" was the river's discouraging name in Maasai, but Penfold promised it guaranteed fine grazing and plenty of hippos and crocodile. They were far luckier than most settlers, he said, and should find their plot staked out with numbered posts by the government surveyors. She hoped she could trust this good fortune.

Gwenn smiled at Alan after he brushed her hand. He almost flinched. Why did he never touch her? It was as if he did not know her. Would he get stronger? Would they at last be able to build their farm, and a family?

Tonight the hamper spared them cooking. In it they found enough for four, although Mulwa and Arthur declined the sandwiches. Both men seemed surprised they were invited to share the food. In the basket Gwenn discovered two roast guinea fowl, tomato and cucumber sandwiches on thick home-baked bread, roasted morsels of impala and Thomson's gazelle, and, for her soldier, a jar of Marmite.

As they fell asleep in the tent, their hands barely touching above the rifle that rested between the cots, Gwenn heard it for the first time. The far-off coughing grunt, then the thunder rolling and echoing low along the earth, heavier and heavier. A distant lion roared. She thought of Anna Gault. Gwenn slipped from her cot and knelt to say her prayers.

"The animals always know first, memsaab," Mulwa said, walking beside Gwenn two days later. For once the mules strained forward. "The river is near."

Gwenn looked up at Alan on the bench of the wagon. For him, she knew, their river could not come too soon. Her husband's eyes were almost closed. He leaned forward. His hands clenched the bouncing seat. She wondered what he must be thinking. Was Alan dreading their life in Africa?

They were climbing a rise that became a steep bank. Below, the Ewaso Ngiro curved around them. Perhaps thirty yards apart, its winding shores alternated between polished stone pools and sandy slopes. Mulwa helped Alan down from the wagon.

Gwenn put her arm around her husband's waist. Together they looked without speaking at the plain that rolled on green across the river, finally rising into distant hills. Here and there lightly timbered slopes ran down to stretches of clear downs, tufted and lush with fresh herbage, occasionally pitted with depressions crowded with green thorn trees, a sign of underground water. On their backs they felt a light wind freshening down from Mount Kenya, carrying their scent to the oryx and zebra and Grant's gazelle that grazed before them, moving dots on the landscape. Gwenn stopped breathing.

"We'll leave the wagon up here for now," Alan said quietly, "and camp down by the stream." He turned away from Gwenn and helped unharness the mules. Gwenn lingered, gazing across the land.

"Watch for crocodiles in the pools, bwana," Mulwa said when Alan led the mules to the water. Arthur carried down two camp chairs, the kettle and his panga. He started a fire.

Gwenn unpacked her brown Rockingham teapot for the first time. She cradled its plump familiar shape between her hands and remembered the comfort it had given her in the cold of Wales. She rinsed the pot in the Ewaso Ngiro before handing it to Arthur. Then she washed her face and hands and feet in a shallow pool and sat down to tea with her boots off. She waited for Alan to come and sit beside her. Busying himself around the wagon, he joined her as the tea grew cold. Gwenn pulled on her socks.

The mules grazed behind them, tied loosely to a rope stretched between two acacias. A troop of baboons chattered near a stand of flat-topped fever trees. The smaller monkeys rushed up and down the trunks and leapt from limb to limb, playing with the yellowish-brown pods and pink-tinged flowers. One thick-set male baboon lounged against a tree, picking at his bright pink gums and long yellow canines. Nearby, young males did sentry duty, shifting weight from foot to foot and rocking forward on long arms.

Gwenn heard the sentinel baboons break into shrill cries. They danced about wildly. Ruffs of hair rose on their necks. They bounded back to the trees. The four mules screamed in panic. Rearing like unbroken stallions, they snapped their leads and galloped through the river, bursting up the far bank and disappearing into the bush.

Mulwa dashed after them, struggling through the waist-high water. At once Gwenn moved to follow.

"Wait here, Alan," she said when her husband got to his feet. Gwenn saw a shadow of humiliation pass over his face when she turned to leave him. She touched his arm and ran into the river. Slipping and stumbling, surprised by the current and occasional deep pools, she emerged soaked and gasping on the far bank. She waved once to Alan and went after Mulwa.

Without the mules, she knew, there would be no farm. And if they chased after the mules, the animals would bolt for home. Best, she thought, to circle away from the river and drive them back towards camp. Gwenn was in her stocking feet. She tried to walk on the patches of reddish earth and wild grasses that separated the trees and thornbushes.

At last she saw the familiar hindquarters walking away from her. Dusty black, with a thin tail flicking. She entered the bush to one side and ran in a wide arc to cut off the mules. Climbing an anthill, she saw them in the failing light, moving off perhaps two hundred yards away. Where was Mulwa? She continued to run along a line that would take her beyond the mules.

Losing them again, panting and exhausted, slightly nauseous, Gwenn sank onto a rock, resting for a moment with her head between her hands. She examined her torn socks and the thorn cuts on her feet. Then she stood up, for the first time aware of the pain of the small wounds, and a cramp in her stomach. She looked in different directions. She was lost.

If she could just find the Ewaso Ngiro, Gwenn thought. Then she smelled the heavy odor of dead meat and spotted dried blood and drag marks on the ground before her.

A lion kill? From the hoofprints, probably a zebra. Not a mule, for the smell of spoiling flesh was already thick in the air. Suddenly she saw them in the dust: the unmistakable round pug marks of a lion.

Gwenn remembered the wounds of Anna Gault. Fresh sweat moistened her body. Dear God, she thought, please let the bush be kinder to me than to that girl. She turned and started to run, praying for the river.

At last she heard them calling her name. She stood exhausted in the twilight and saw Alan walk slowly into view with Mulwa and Arthur fifty yards to either side. Mulwa carried the rifle. Arthur led the mules. She waved and sat down and watched Alan do his best to hurry to her.

"Leopard," Mulwa said. "We found his marks near the trees where the baboons screamed. The mules must have smelled him."

Lion, leopard, she thought. She looked about the land, for a moment overwhelmed by the wildness of the prospect, missing the reassuring hedgerows and fences and stone walls that contained the farm country at home.

Back at camp, Alan opened their bottle of brandy while Gwenn bathed her feet. They ate and fell asleep under canvas.

For once Alan was up first in the morning. Returning to the tent, a new energy in his voice, he woke Gwenn. Surprised, she sat up and rubbed her eyes and looked at him. This was more the Welsh lad she remembered.

"I've found the first stake, Gwennie, Number Eighty-eight! It's ours, just along the river, three hundred yards upstream. The other stake must be downstream."

For five days Gwenn and Alan walked their land. They were cut by its thorns, refreshed by its streams, painted with its dust. They breathed its changing scents while each day passed from damp to warm to cool. They rubbed varied soils between their fingers, feeling it sometimes gritty from disintegrated rock, sometimes soft and earthy with red loam. At nearly six thousand feet, the days were still warm, even hot in the strong high sun, but each breeze and gust blew fresh. The evening air carried the cool of distant hills.

At the northern edge of their land, where a stream disappeared into a small papyrus swamp, they found the collapsing bomas of an abandoned kraal. Each rounded hut was fading slowly into the earth. The varied shades were melting into a single dusty grey as the thorn fence lost its form and the mud and dung walls crumbled from their spines of *lileshwa* branches, decaying flesh falling from a skeleton.

"Samburu," said Mulwa. "Worse than their cousins, the foul Maasai. One day they will come back with their spears and hungry goats."

"Will they bother us?" Alan asked.

"No, bwana, not you and memsaab, only perhaps your cows and animals."

They woke each morning to the aroma of fresh bread baking in a square tin box set in the coals. They washed in their river and breakfasted on strong tea, cold meat and warm bread dripping with dark wild honey. Then they left Arthur in camp with the mules and the shotgun. Gwenn or Mulwa carried the rifle, and sometimes a shovel, and Alan walked with his notebook. Occasionally Gwenn helped Mulwa dig holes to test the depth of the arable soil.

She and Alan would pause and sit side by side on a rock while he wrote notes or unfolded the government map. Resting a hand on her husband's shoulder while he spread the paper flat with his hands, Gwenn would try not to notice that even his fingers seemed thin and weak, no flesh or muscle under the tight skin between the bones of his joints.

To the east and south flowed the Ewaso Ngiro, with the Loldaika Hills across the river farther east. To the north, the map showed rising hills that joined the Lerogi Plateau. Beyond their vision to the west the Ewaso Narok and other rivers divided the bush before hills rose again, running on to the open grasslands of Laikipia.

Surprised, Gwenn found that hunting was becoming a pleasure. Obliged to learn their ways and chose among them, she was drawn strangely closer to the very animals she sought to kill.

"Soon memsaab good hunter," said Mulwa one afternoon, looking up at her with a hungry grin as he cleaned a Grant she had just brought down. Smiling proudly, without thinking, Gwenn reloaded the Enfield with sun-browned hands.

While she hunted in the late afternoons, Alan would rest and sketch in his notebook detailed maps of each section of the land: streams, waterholes, slopes, rocks, trees, red earth, dry bush, game trails. He kept a journal at the back.

Gwenn could not remember when she had felt so young. In the mornings she rose eagerly like a girl running off on her first picnic. The damp of Wales, the carnage of France, the horror of the *Garth Castle* were no longer in her world.

She had never relished food as on those first evenings back in camp. Each roasted guinea fowl and Grant gazelle tasted finer than a Christmas lamb in Denbigh. Walking home in the dusk, tired and thinking of dinner, their own land all about them, she would hear the mules bray a welcome. Arthur's cook fire beckoned through the thorn trees. Over a cup of tea by the fire she and Alan studied his maps and talked of where to build their first house. Even to speak of it was an unimaginable tingling luxury.

They chose their homesite halfway up the highest hill, to extend their view without spoiling the setting. The slope rose gently on the peninsula of an oxbow bend in the Ewaso Ngiro. Alan set four river stones to mark the corners. A wide fever tree spread its umbrella to one side. Behind the house a small level field was protected by a craggy kopje and the rising hillside. A spring emerged at the base of the boulders and worked its way down to join the river. Perfect for a garden, Gwenn thought. Beyond, in the clear of midmorning, they could see the white crowns of Mount Kenya.

That evening they sat long by the fire. They gazed up at the wide-sparkling night and spoke about a bungalow and crops and the future. For the first time in Africa, they kissed almost like lovers.

"There's something I've been wanting to tell you, Gwennie." Alan let go her hand and bent forward, looking into the fire. Gwenn felt fear rise cold in her stomach.

"I'm not sure we're going to be able to have children," he said. "I certainly can't try for quite a time, they told me."

Gwenn sat without speaking. She felt the evening chill descend through her and knew the worst was true. She stared up at the sky, blinking, and leaned her head back to keep the tears from leaving her eyes.

"It's time for bed." She rose and kissed her husband's cheek.

Gwenn lay awake in the tent, not hearing the cicadas and tree frogs that led the night sounds through the canvas walls. Reaching between their cots, she felt Alan's hand thin and cool as death in hers. For a week she had been counting the passing days with horror. Already, Gwenn realized, she was late this month. She remembered Anton Rider's words. "First you will suffer."

— *19* —

Anton lay almost still in the shelter. A charred dark scab covered the poisoned cut of the Dorobo arrow. For two nights he had raved while a sick pain swelled his midsection. By the sixth day only the pain of the burn lingered, and if he moved sharply the ache of his ribs swept that aside.

In the days that followed he read his favorite chapters, aloud or to himself: *Chapter IX, I Have a Memorable Birthday; Chapter XI, I Begin Life on My Own Account, and Don't Like It.*

Sometimes he exchanged lessons with Karioki. Or he daydreamed. He listened to the rain and the waterfall and thought of England and the gypsies, of the lifeboat girl and Gwenn Llewelyn, and of the free life he had found in Africa. What would Kenya hold? Would he see Gwenn again? He was glad he'd kissed her. He thought of her eyes and tossing hair and the perfect smooth skin of her shoulder when he touched her in the cabin. And her hand in his as he studied her palm. Did she ever think of him?

The two Dorobo came with food every day. The first evening, they had brought a tube of bamboo filled with the blood of the buffalo. Karioki heated it in the pan with salt crystals.

"Drink this quickly, Tlaga, and you will take the strength of the black bull." Karioki held the tasty dark broth to his friend's lips. Anton had never known such care.

The Dorobo brought honey, berries and fresh meat. To speed his healing, they made Anton eat thick honeycomb with the logy bees still inside it, spooning the sticky living mass between his lips on a splinter of bamboo.

Alone one afternoon, listening to the rain drip from the lofty bamboo leaves, Anton put his book aside and did what every fortune teller had urged him never to do.

He cupped his own right hand and studied the lines and creases he understood too well. If he were the client, what would he tell himself out of all that he read in the broad hard palm? A strong lifeline, he would say, but not yet well formed. Travel, and women, he would add as he flexed the stranger's hand. Two marriages, and two children, and a chance for great fortune. But always the jagged broken line of one unwelcome companion: violence.

Often Karioki sat beside him at the mouth of the shelter, keeping the fire, covering Anton against the cold. Early one morning Karioki disappeared with his spear, leaving the rifle within Anton's reach. He returned in the fading light with a parcel wrapped in bamboo leaves and held together by *muondwe,* the forest string that grew in long thin vines. Anton opened the package and found blobs of soft glutinous animal fat.

"Ant-bear fat, from a giant anteater, Tlaga." Karioki wondered why white men always healed so slowly. In the war he had watched young white officers die from wounds that would not keep a Kikuyu down for a day. But at least this m'zungu was a good walker when he was well and did not cry like a woman when he was hurt.

"In my village the old men use this fat for the stiffness that eats their arms and legs. With ant-bear fat we will save you, before those Dorobo witches finish you. When you are strong again, we will learn if Tlaga is a hunter, or just a white boy lost in the forest. We will see if you can kill a bongo."

In the mornings Karioki rubbed Anton's shoulder and chest and stomach with the ant-bear fat. In the evenings he would put his hand on Anton's shoulder, whispering and laughing and raising his voice with excitement, his eyes wide as he told tales of young Copperfield hunting on Mount Kenya.

"Have I told you, Tlaga, the story of The Night David Danced with the Wild Pigs?"

Disgusted by the shelter's foul smell, realizing it was his own, Anton rose one morning and walked stiffly to the pool. He removed his skin cloak. A light rain was falling. He entered the pool in his filthy shirt and shorts, jolted by the cold freshness that overwhelmed him. He took off all his clothes, wrung them out and flung them on the bank. He swam to the waterfall, the stiffness working out of his body while his muscles stretched in the clear water.

On its final descent into the pool, the water sluiced down from a rocky grey ledge. Anton lifted himself onto the shelf where the water dashed in his face. There he found a marble-smooth bowl, worn round as a teacup, two feet deep. He lay in it, naked on his back, drugged by the sparkling shower that drenched him.

Finally he rose, gasping from cold, and dove back into the pool. At the foot of the waterfall was a deep basin. Anton disappeared under the surface and opened his eyes, exploring its sandy bottom and the shelving rock that edged its depth. Bursting up, he floated quietly and looked about. Level with his eyes, a steamy fog hung over the surface of the water. He remembered swimming across the lake near Rugby, with the herons' blue eggs in his teeth, and seeing Stone standing on the shore with his toes in the water.

A cathedral of lofty trees surrounded him. The rain fell on his head. Through the cloud at the pool's end Anton saw a miniature short-horned antelope step to the water. Its chestnut coat glistened redly. Perhaps this was the duiker he had lost when the buffalo struck him.

Could this place, too, be Africa?

Anton climbed out by the waterfall, numb, but clean and whole at last. He brushed the water from his body with both hands. He touched the dark line across his belly and felt the ropy scar of the old burn on the inside of his right arm. He ran his fingers over his chest and felt the lumpy ridge where three ribs were knitting almost painlessly. He pinched the bump on the bridge of his nose.

"Now you stand like a man, Tlaga," said Karioki with pride the next day. He admired Anton in his stained grey shorts, ragged bush shirt, hyrax vest and monkey-skin cloak. "But when I close my eyes, the stink of a white boy fills my nose. Worse than a waterbuck. Before you hunt bongo, we must clean your smell. Now we move camp."

They carried their packs around the pool and walked through the bamboo towards the rising sun. Instead of the dense unyielding wall

of soaking vegetation that had resisted him at first, Anton now recognized it as a welcoming forest garden, an abundant familiar park
of secret paths and artful wiry hunters, of honey and birdsong and
flying squirrels and bats and badgers and creatures for which he knew
no name, and some he had not seen.

"Soon Tlaga will look upon the home of Ngai." Karioki dropped
his cloak and pack at the edge of the bamboo belt. "For this we have
waited until the end of the rains."

The ravine opened below them. A cloud of mist evaporated as the
sun crested a ridge. The rising light reached deeper and deeper into
the immense bowl of moorland. Lush and green, cut by streams,
dappled by stands of wild banana trees, with a collar of montane
forest waiting on the farther side, the valley sent up the scents of
heather and an early alpine spring. Two black rhinoceros, a long-
horned female and her calf, browsed at the edge of the forest below.

Anton opened his pack and passed his friend a handful of charred
pork chops. They ate and watched the sky burn clean. Two distant
peaks broke the blue horizon. Light glinted from the icy mirror of
twin summits. Anton recognized the peaks of Mount Kenya.

Taking up a handful of earth, Karioki rose. He moved his lips
without speaking and cast the soil before him towards the mountain.
He unrolled a strip of hide and offered Anton the honeycomb he
had protected from the forest insects. Before eating, Karioki spilled
thick drops of honey on the earth.

"For Ngai," he said, noting Anton's surprise. "I must teach you
about god.

"There man began, Tlaga, on Ngai's mountain," Karioki said as
they walked towards a stream. "First Ngai made Gikuyu, tall and
strong. Then Mumbi, Gikuyu's head wife, the mother of nine fat
daughters." Anton knelt and drank from his hands. Never had he
tasted water so clear and fresh.

"From their thighs came the nine clans of my people," Karioki
said. "After that, when he was rested, Ngai made the animals, and
finally the Maasai and the white man."

When they returned for their packs, welcoming coveys of small white
butterflies rose from the honey and clouded about them.

The tufted moor was swampy beneath their feet, oozing and sucking at Anton's boots when Karioki led him in a direct line across the valley into the lower forest. More dry than their old camp, the montane woodland varied as they walked. Islands of bamboo extended into the forest like fingers reaching from the moorland. Sometimes thick with dense *magomboki* shrubs and tree ferns, the forest opened into sudden green clearings. The glades were patchy with sunlight and rich with wild grasses and long-petaled purplish-pink flowers. They made camp against a rocky shoulder in the lower woods, under the dark branches of a wild fig tree. The heavy grey limbs of the tree hung almost to the ground.

"For good fortune, Tlaga, we will sleep under this *mugumu*, a sacred tree of my people."

Anton heard branches move high above them. He looked up and saw small monkeys dining on handfuls of tiny short-stalked figs. Karioki pushed aside the hanging creepers and pressed his forehead against the tree's smooth bark. "Tonight, we make no fire. You will not shoot again until you find the father of all bongo."

Karioki woke Anton before first light. "Take off all your clothes, Tlaga, and rub this *kiraiku* into your stinking skin."

"What are you going to use for your skin, Karioki?" Anton rubbed himself with the flaky native tobacco.

"Even in the dark, Tlaga, your skin is sickly white, like the belly of an old crocodile. Look at mine. Black as the horns of a bongo, perfect except where your German patched me like an old blind woman trying to mend a basket. But at last you smell like the forest. Dress and bring only your rifle and the meat. We will not speak again today. A white man's voice is still worse than his smell, and the bongo has wide ears to catch your noise." He looked at Anton and tried not to smile.

Until early evening, Karioki led Anton through the forest. Ignoring all other game, he moved from stream to stream and from salt lick to waterhole, searching for the large split-hoofed prints of the bongo. Everything else they found. Giant forest hog, rhinoceros, duiker, porcupine. Late in the day, they came on the round impressions of elephant. Anton walked in the clear prints to lessen the sound of his steps.

"If you do that, Tlaga, we will never find the bongo. Everyone knows it is bad luck to walk in the tracks of an elephant."

On the fourth day, the fresh meat finished, they subsisted on berries and chewy strips of smoke-dried bushbuck. They came to a thicker hilly section of the rain forest, darkly shaded, with damp heavy in the air. They crouched low under the cover of fallen bamboo. Karioki stepped into a narrow rocky stream that came to his knees. The moving water covered their sound and their tracks while he led Anton into the thickest forest.

The ground finally levelled, and the stream opened into a pool. Anton's legs were numb when he stepped from the water. Karioki squatted on his heels and studied old prints in the soft bank. He held up two fingers, then one finger, with the other palm held low above the ground: a mother and calf. Anton studied the two inward-curving oval prints of each hoof that almost met at either end. Karioki pointed to torn, partly eaten leaves. Anton pinched the remnants of severed shoots, estimating the time of feeding by the length of their dry withered ends.

Karioki nodded when Anton took ashes from his shirt pocket and tested the breeze. The two hunters reentered the water and walked thirty yards upstream. They settled into the undergrowth on their stomachs, keeping the pool in sight. Anton prayed a male bongo would come to drink or feed. The breeze shifted and eddied.

All night they lay in their cloaks, the skins stiff with night frost. From time to time Anton heard a bushbuck bark in the night and, far in the distance, the trumpeting of elephant. The next morning birds woke the forest. Reddish-backed monkeys, elegant in white ruffs, chattered in the trees. Anton dug a hole in the forest loam beside him. He rolled on his side and relieved himself. Karioki awoke and lay still for another hour, watching. At length he rose without speaking and the two men walked in the water's edge, following the river upstream.

After a time they came on fresh droppings of the two bongo. Hoping to find patches of favored plants where males might also feed, they took the spoor for an hour until the tracks vanished among new-fallen bamboo leaves. The two hunters cast through the forest. Each walked in widening circles until they found the track. The trail disappeared once more at a streambed. There Anton and Karioki burrowed into the forest floor, resting under their cloaks at the waterside while the rain fell.

Anton froze in alarm. Lying on his stomach in the dark, he was suddenly awake. He felt some creature move slowly along his left leg under the monkey-skin cloak. The hair on his legs prickled. The movement stopped. He fought the urge to jump up. Along his side he sensed something against him like a large moist log. Rhythmically, it swelled and contracted. It barely touched him when it expanded. Then it withdrew immeasurably, just beyond the limit of his active sensation. His mind raced while his body remained still. He realized what it must be. An immense snake, wet from moving across the forest floor.

Anton knew that Karioki lay no more than two or three feet to his left, for the cloaks of the hunters overlapped like the plates of an armadillo.

The creature moved again, probably drawn by the warmth of the men. It advanced in the darkness until Anton felt it glide slowly past his bent left elbow and along his forearm near his face. Still he felt it sliding by his ankle.

Almost certainly, he thought, a snake so thick and long must be a giant python. He recalled the picture in von Decken's library. Eight Africans walked in line. Each carried over his shoulder a two-foot cut section of a python, like thick logs borne to a fire. On the ground behind the men remained the monstrous head and perhaps five feet of the snake's length. The constrictor's jaws were open, stretched wide like a huge rubber collar around the protruding neck and shoulders of a young bushbuck. One head emerged from the other. Four dead eyes stared. Only the victim's horns prevented its total disappearance, the legs and trunk already broken and swallowed. Stabbed into the bushbuck's neck in the death agony of the python were two long rows of the snake's backward-pointing teeth. The accompanying text reported that, although tetanic, the bite of the python was not itself mortal.

When the serpent again lay still, Anton estimated the head of the python must be about level with his own under the cloaks. The head itself, he remembered, with its elastic hingeless jaw, was the size of a small donkey's.

Anton fought off panic. Nothing moved. He heard rain drum more heavily on the cloaks. He sensed the serpent's slight movements and thought of their three heads lying in a row beneath the stitched animal skins. Were the other two awake?

He knew his rifle was useless. With infinite slowness, consciously disengaging his right arm from the rest of his body to prevent his other muscles from moving with it, he slipped the knife from its sheath with his right hand. Then he lay still.

Forever, it seemed, there was no movement. Could a snake, Anton wondered, sense fear as other animals did? Did it sense heat when it hunted? Were the rain and the dead skins confusing its senses?

Violence exploded beside him. Anton leapt up, unable to see, afraid to stab out in the dark for fear of striking his friend.

"Tlaga!" Karioki screamed in a choking voice. Turmoil raged at the edge of the stream. Man and python struggled together in the mud and dead leaves. Realizing he could only help by engaging the animal on equal terms, Anton flung himself on the heaving mass.

Embracing the two opponents, he felt the python already wrapped twice about Karioki's torso. One of Karioki's arms was pinned to his side. The other, near the shoulder, was gripped in the python's jaws, giving the snake purchase while it bound its victim. Anton ran his left hand along the snake. His thumb and fingers did not reach half around it. He felt the snake advance its coils under his hand, corkscrewing up to Karioki's neck. Karioki kicked violently and all three crashed into the stream. Locked together in the darkness, they rolled and thrashed in the streambed like a single creature. Anton's head was under water. He felt the snake encircle his legs. It wrapped his ankles together, squeezing until he could not feel his feet.

Anton held his breath and sawed his blade against the python where it crossed Karioki's back. Solid muscle, thick as a tree, the snake went into spasm when Anton cut through its core. The python arched up over the water with the tension of a giant crossbow wound to its full. It pulled Anton from the water while he clung to it with one arm and sawed with the other. Anton feared Karioki's spine would snap when he felt his friend's hard back bound against his arm as if by ever-tightening screws.

The knife sliced through the python, cutting Karioki's back. One strand of skin and muscle held the snake together. Wrenching furiously, the python ripped itself in two. The bottom section thrashed and died. The tail loosened around Anton's ankles.

Anton dragged himself against the stream bank by his arms, freeing himself from the heavy coils. As he rose, Karioki and the living python crashed onto him. Groping for the snake's neck in the darkness, Anton felt the hard flatness of its head. He began to work with the knife through the rubbery skin behind the head. The jaw opened and snapped again and again, releasing Karioki's arm when Anton sliced deeper. He cut through the creature's neck and heard an agonized cry from Karioki.

Anton felt the severed head slide down against his naked chest. For one long moment the body lived on, ten feet of it binding and twisting, relaxing and tightening around Karioki. Anton slashed through it, freeing Karioki's arm. At last the scene was still.

The two men collapsed on the bank in the rain, gasping and shaking while the shock of struggle left them in the light of early morning. Anton's shirt was in rags. Pink slime stuck to his chest. They washed in the river and Anton studied the spectacle. Torn up as if by a plow, the bank was a flattened tangle of broken branches, animal skins and bloody fragments of the python, olive-toned and iridescent, two, five, ten feet long. The evil head lay half out of the water. Flaps of skin and slashed flesh hung from it like a gory collar.

Anton was unhurt, although his ribs ached again. But Karioki groaned and covered his face in pain. Tearing wildly in its final throe, the python had scraped the surface of his left eye. Anton took Karioki's head between his hands and spread apart the eyelids with his thumbs. He remembered holding Karioki's head while Ernst stitched him up at Gepard Farm.

Anton studied Karioki's eye. The pupil was still round, but the lower cornea appeared scratched and clouded.

Karioki bathed his eyes in the stream. Anton ripped one sleeve from the remains of his shirt. He soaked it clean and bound it over Karioki's head, covering the left eye.

"Follow Tlaga back to camp, Karioki." Anton collected the spear, the rifle and the scraps of the cloaks. "Tomorrow we'll start for your father's village and leave the bongo for another hunt. This forest is too dangerous for my black friend."

Back at camp Karioki lay by the stream with his face in the water. Rising, his eye swollen shut, he turned to Anton and tried to smile.

"You are always a little late to help, Tlaga, but your knife is sharp," Karioki said. Anton could not tell if he was joking. "Now you must find kirangi, for my eye. The fungus lives only on the old bamboo. While you are away, I will make a fire."

The afternoon was darkening by the time Anton came to the tallest island of bamboo he had seen when they approached the forest one week before. Moving with instinctive silence, he bent under broken poles and balanced easily while he tight-roped along slippery fallen trunks. Without thinking, he avoided resting his weight on the rotten wood. His head bobbed like a woodpecker to duck the cutting shoots that awaited his face. On the edge of a glade he saw a stand of lofty bamboo, some held upright in death by vines and creepers that bound them to their living neighbors. He remembered Karioki's instructions and searched for the oldest trees.

He found the fungus near the base of the tallest bamboo, first in delicate lacelike patterns, then in thick cakes where the old trees met. He rested the Merkel against a fallen pole and unsheathed his knife.

As he prepared to scrape the fungus onto the hyrax skin he had carried tucked into the back of his shorts, Anton heard a branch snap across the clearing. He looked up through the bamboo with one hand on his rifle. Nothing.

Then, six feet above the forest floor, he saw them. Anton froze. Two amber horn tips shone in the falling light. Thick horns emerged, three feet of smooth spiralled black. Two large oval ears twitched, scanning for what no man could hear.

The bull bongo stepped into the clearing.

Far heavier than Anton had imagined, the bongo had massive hunched shoulders, a powerful neck and heavy hindquarters. Twelve vertical white bands striped its flaming chestnut flanks. The muzzle, belly and neck were blackish. The animal turned and faced the bamboo. Anton saw two large white spots on each cheek and a single white chevron centered between the eyes. Painted by God, he thought.

The bongo turned lightly on white and black legs and browsed on a tall shrub. The knotted pale red stalks of the plant rose over ten feet and bent when the antelope took their nettle-shaped leaves. Anton remembered another animal browsing on leaves, the old jack hare at Windsor Park in England, the creature that had led him to Africa.

The bull bongo settled to eat and Anton sheathed his knife. Timing his movements to the snapping of the stalks and leaves, he raised his rifle. The bull advanced its lordly head deeper into the shrubs. Anton slipped off the safety on the Merkel. Hugo von Decken would be pleased. A perfect shoulder shot, perhaps forty yards. In his concentration Anton saw the ivory bead of his forward gunsight white and large as a cueball against the russet shoulder. The bongo turned its head in profile and shook its heavy horns from side to side. A shaft of late light sparked the amber tips.

It was too beautiful to kill. Anton stared without breathing and lowered his rifle.

BOOK II

1920

— *20* —

Allan Quatermain himself! And Umslopogaas, too, or I'll be damned!" said Penfold to Sissy and the Fonsecas. They sat on the verandah with drinks and samosas stuffed with spiced peas and onions. They watched two large wild figures stride up the drive.

Penfold's painting table stood at his side. Bottles of enamel colors were arrayed behind five lead figures. Four were Persian archers and slingers, the fifth an Athenian hoplite. The Greek's studded round shield was almost dry. Soon he would be ready for battle.

"Who's Allan Quatermain?" said Anunciata. Her eyes followed the advancing figure of the ragged European. "Does he have arms and shoulders like this one?"

"Quatermain's a rather dashing hero of old African tales, my dear," said Sissy. *"King Solomon's Mines* and all that. The sort of adventure rubbish that brings our silly English boys to Africa. The type of nonsense Adam favors. That or those dreary old Greeks and Romans, isn't it, Treasure?"

"Just as you say, my dear." Penfold glanced past his wife at Anunciata. He pinched the bronze paint out of his impala-hair brush before rising and taking up his cane.

"Umslopogaas was Quatermain's naked kaffir servant," Sissy said.

"Actually Umslopogaas was a prince, and Quatermain's friend to the death. A gentleman of the bush," Penfold corrected reluctantly, knowing it was hopeless. He looked at the two approaching men. "I've seen the black chap somewhere before."

The heavily muscled African, a leather patch over one eye, left the drive and hurried around the hotel towards the village.

"How do you tell which one's the savage?" Vasco Fonseca brushed a long cigar ash from his rumpled white jacket. "Even the white one's nearly barefoot. My horse has better shoes."

"Why don't you find out, dear brother, by asking the tall one?" Anunciata watched the young man step to the rail of the verandah carrying a battered grey pack and a spotless double rifle.

"Good day!" Anton removed his brown terai with a dusty smile.

"Good afternoon to you, sir." Anunciata sat up straight and ran one hand over her shining dark hair. "I'm Anunciata Fonseca. My brother, Vasco here, wishes to know if you're a savage?"

"Probably, but I'll let him decide that, ma'am, after he asks me," said Anton, enjoying the greeting after so long in the bush. His eyes remained on Anunciata. "My name's Anton Rider."

"Welcome to the White Rhino. I'm Adam Penfold," said the proprietor. Although uneasy, feeling a change in Anunciata, Penfold extended his hand with a friendly expression. "Looks like you could stand a few drinks. Olivio! Olivio!"

"Won't you sit here?" Sissy offered Anton the wicker stool beside her. "And please do lunch with us. I'm sure it'll be dreadful."

"Thank you, ma'am." Anton set down his pack and hung a ragged monkey-skin cloak over the railing. He sat down on the step. "If I could rent a room and wash up, I'd be most happy to join you."

"Why did you get that sticky paint all over your hands?" Sissy asked her husband. "Now you'll mess up everything."

Anton thought of Zebraman as he watched Penfold tighten the caps on the small bottles without replying.

In truth, all women are shameless, Olivio thought when he posted himself under the warthog head with a towel over his arm. He whispered instructions to the table boys, noting the trim of their daytime colors. Each man's sash and fez, set off by the immutable white kanzu, was a bright saffron. He watched the lady and Anunciata vie for the young Englishman like two she-goats after a fresh weed. Already prepared for lunch when the boy arrived, they too had gone to their rooms to improve themselves. Only one had been successful.

Lady Penfold's new rouge served instead to emphasize the alarming unity of her face and skull. But Anunciata, the dwarf saw as he breathed deeply, was opening the gates of hell. Her creamy silk shirt rose from her waist like waves pressing up against the heavy rounded prow of a ship. Her collar was open one button more than usual. If she were a bottle of champagne, Olivio thought, the slightest touch and the cork would hit the ceiling.

"Where in England are you from?" Sissy Penfold squinted into the young man's eyes with her most inviting look. She found it a bit tricky placing this one's accent. Usually that was the easiest part in assessing any Englishman.

"Here and there, really, ma'am."

What could the hag be thinking? Olivio wondered. He filled the lord's glass and wiped the lip of the bottle. Just because she had been fortunate to procure his own attentions, could this dry-boned scarecrow hope to seduce such a boy?

"Do call me Sissy," Lady Penfold said to Anton, drawing her face tighter with a smile. She remembered one reason why she preferred younger men: their bodies smelt better. Like honey. One couldn't stop sniffing them. "Do you ride?"

"Yes, I do."

"How nice," said Sissy, noticing the young man's long well-shaped fingers, curious about the correlation. "Hunting or showing?"

"Country fairs, mostly." Anton thought of the gypsy bareback displays and horse coping. He felt out of place but smiled to himself at the attention being shown him.

"Oh, I see—" Sissy began.

"Riding with our hostess is a rare adventure," Anunciata interrupted, arching her shoulders slightly towards the tall stranger. "Would you teach me to shoot your beautiful rifle, perhaps early this evening when it's cool?"

"Of course, ma'am." Anton turned his eyes to the bread pudding and stewed mangoes that a servant was placing on the sideboard.

Sissy was silent. She tightened her lips, resenting the creature's proposition, but weighing against this an attendant advantage: the woman's inevitable loss of interest in Adam.

Scandalous! They were all after this boy, Olivio realized. Here was a youth who could fish without bait.

"I think our young Mr. Rider's going to be rather overbooked, wouldn't you say, Fonseca? He'd best eat up," Penfold said, dismayed by Anunciata's interest in the younger man.

Better step back, Penfold reminded himself. If he wanted her back one day, he must not reveal his jealousy. "The best fence is no fence," an old love once told him.

"Getting awfully busy hereabouts," Penfold continued. "Everyone seems to be coming north. I wonder how the Llewelyns are getting on up there. Marmite, young man?"

"If you please, sir." Anton's heart jumped at Gwenn's name. "Did, did you say the Llewelyns, sir?" He felt Anunciata watching him as he hesitated with the question.

"A ripe little flower called Gwenn, dragging a withered British husband into the wilderness," muttered Fonseca. He pushed back his chair, scraping the floor, and rose. He took an envelope from his pocket and handed it to Olivio without acknowledging the dwarf. "Time for a siesta. Post this for me."

"Of course, senhor." Olivio bowed.

After coffee the dwarf stood in the rear doorway of the kitchen behind a barrel of the lord's favorite dark olives. He carried Fonseca's letter to Lisbon in his sash. He rolled his palms together and crushed a fistful of spiny dried leaves into a fine green powder. Olivio's eyes narrowed still more as he looked across the splintered top of the barrel and watched the hated figure of Karioki run to the chief's hut. More trouble. Was there no end to his enemies?

Olivio recalled the afternoon Karioki had knocked him down while he was playing innocently with young Kina. Besides this savage, only two men had ever turned their hand against the dwarf. Olivio's palms ground harder when he recalled the cruel indignities. On each occasion, just when his cunning was building his life, the insulting violence had confirmed his unnatural physical weakness. The first two tormentors, the leader of a gang of Indian street urchins and the British officer who discovered him spying, had paid already.

Lancelot whined from a mat in the corner of the kitchen. Reminded by the unpleasant sound, Olivio added a pinch of brown sugar to the poisonous green dust in his palm. Patiently, he watched Kitenji's hut and considered how best to settle his account with the brute. He knew the answer: Kina.

The dwarf turned and glared at the whining whippet. At last it was even thinner than Lady Penfold. He bent and smelled the unmoving beast. Always acute, Olivio's nostrils found what they sought, the rotting odor of approaching death. He sprinkled the sugared green powder into the animal's bowl.

The strongest emotion, the dwarf reflected as he washed his hands, and the only one peculiar to man, was revenge. He had seen what some called "love" rise and set faster than the winter sun. But revenge, revenge endured for generations, sometimes for centuries. He stared at the hut and savored again his first taste of this passion.

For two years young Ramchan had ridiculed Olivio, his stunted size, his mongrel race, even his round face. While other boys learned to beg and steal and hunt in the alleyways and markets of Goa, Olivio was left out. Slower and weaker, he could not play or fight or run. But one day he suggested a new scheme, for stealing more with less risk, for shifting blame to other boys of the bazaar. Soon even his size became an advantage.

One evening Olivio hid under a table in a coppermonger's shop when the store closed for the day. Later he drew the bolt and admitted Ramchan and the others. As his mates fled with lamps and plates and pots, one boy stumbled, raising the alarm. Only Olivio was caught. Given the choice of a beating or a reward, the fifteen-year-old dwarf identified Ramchan. A week later the enraged young villain found him.

Still bruised from his own beating, Ramchan forced Olivio into a hemp sack and closed it with a rope. He dragged the bag to the docks, scraping it over the rough dung-covered streets until the sack frayed through and Olivio's body was open with raw cuts and filthy abrasions. The young dwarf never forgot what awaited him when the bag arrived at the end of the crumbling stone pier.

First he heard the excited clamor of the other boys. He felt them lift the bag and dip it into a thick liquid that soaked through the torn sacking. He caught his breath and smelled it. Olive oil. But foul and tainted, not the rich clean scent of the pressed fruit he adored.

The youths dropped the greasy sack on the stones and cut it open. They grabbed Olivio as he scurried away. They held his face to the edge of an open barrel. A dead rat floated on the surface, its belly slit open, the swollen organs trailing and moving slightly in the oil.

Inches from his eyes, the young dwarf saw the rodent's whiskers resting lightly on the greasy liquid like the legs of a graceful water spider.

The boys ripped off the dwarf's clothes and lowered him into the barrel head first. For hours the gang tortured him, compelling him to play with the rat, ridiculing his name, forcing him to drink the oil and eat handful after handful of olives, green and black, always with the pits. Finally they covered Olivio's torn and slippery body in stinging red curry powder and released him in the bazaar of the harlots.

Fortunately vengeance was cheap in India. It took Olivio only six months of work as a curiosity and masseur in a brothel to hoard the money required. There, too, he acquired the art of intimate massage. He became an artist with kohl and vermilion, darkening a woman's eyelids with the silvery powdered lead and painting her lips and the areolae of her breasts with the red pigment of cinnabar. He learned how to employ his thick tongue when forced nightly to toil over the hanging flesh of an aging Hindi madam until even she came magically alive, throbbing and gasping like a schoolgirl's fantasy.

Unlike Africa, he thought, where no person did anything well, in India and Goa every need was satisfied by a profession with generations of obsessive expertise. Each subcaste lived by its special art. Criminal violence, too, had its code and its disciples.

One morning Ramchan sat cross-legged on his folded robe in the thieves' market, bartering bolts of stolen cotton. A man bent over and offered the youth a large jar of lamp oil. An accomplice led past a bullock cart, the wagon of a travelling smithy. Suspended by chains at the back of the heavy cart was the blacksmith's portable furnace, laden with glowing coals and hot irons.

One wagon wheel rolled over Ramchan's right foot, splintering the thin bones of his arch. The boy screamed. Lamp oil spilled over him in the confusion of the accident. A hook slipped free. The furnace fell open on top of him. Molten coals covered Ramchan's body. The oil ignited with a flash. The last image Olivio preserved when he walked off down a nearby alley was of the flaming figure staggering up on one leg, its arms extended like a burning cross. Not unlike the Portuguese fleet's celebration of its patron saint's day, he

remembered, when a heavenly blazing cross shone over the harbor
of Goa by night.

The faint smile of recollection left Olivio's face as he spied across
the barrel and saw Chief Kitenji and Karioki emerge from the squalid
hut. Supporting himself on his son instead of with his usual staff, the
old scoundrel gathered his villagers about him. Unable to hear the
distant words, Olivio watched with distaste while the savages welcomed Karioki home.

Then Kina ran up to the gathering, her high breasts barely shaking
despite their weight. A tribute to her youth, Olivio reflected with
anticipation. He moistened his lips. Karioki pushed all others aside
and took Kina in his arms. How could the girl let her own brother
embrace her so shamelessly? Disgusting! It was time to save her from
these dogs.

"Am I holding it the way you want me to?" said Anunciata. She
regarded Anton with wide brown eyes. She was kneeling beside him
in the sand of the dry riverbed. The donga's banks rose above them.
The rim of the gully was edged in grey thornbush and low yellow
flowers with purple centers.

Anunciata's left elbow rested on one knee. She held the heavy
Merkel against her right shoulder. "Could you show me how to
hold it?"

Anton crouched behind her and sighted along the trembling barrels
to the target, acutely aware of the closeness of her body. He reached
his left hand forward until it covered hers under the walnut grip. He
felt the warmth of her fingers inside his palm. He sensed his pulse
quicken and hoped his hand would not shake.

"Just slide your left hand forward to balance the weight," he said.
Her hair touched his cheek. He caught his breath and inhaled her
fragrance. "Press the rifle tight into your shoulder like this."

Anunciata fell backward against him, rolling into Anton's arms as
she turned. The rifle dropped to the ground.

On his back in the warm sand, Anton looked up into Anunciata's
laughing eyes. He felt her breasts against his chest.

"What bright blue eyes you have." She licked her tongue along his lips. Anton tried to move, knowing he should lift his rifle from the sand. "Keep still."

She sat up, straddling his stomach between her thighs. Anton saw the acacia leaves and clear sky through her hair. His breath came faster, but the nervousness was now only a pleasant buzzing in his ears.

Anunciata leaned forward and moved her hips until she felt him.

"Brush the sand off my shirt," she said. Anton hesitated. "Outdoors is always best," she added, as if speaking to herself.

Anunciata took his left hand. He felt the point of her tongue when she kissed his fingertips with wet lips. She stroked his fingers down across her bosom. "Like this," she said. "Now the other one. That's better, Blue Eyes."

She unbuttoned her cuffs without hurrying. Anton dusted her with uncertain hands. He was surprised she wore nothing beneath her blouse. He felt her nipples stiffen against the creamy linen. Anunciata put her head back. She breathed deeply and closed her eyes, tossing her hair from side to side.

When he stopped touching her, Anunciata opened the front buttons of his shirt and pulled it from his khaki shorts. Her fingernails moved over his stomach and up his chest. He felt his muscles tighten. His nipples tickled and firmed as her nails glanced across them.

"How did you get these delicious bumps on your chest?" She bent to kiss the ridges of his healed ribs.

"I had a fight with a buffalo." Anton thought his voice sounded strange.

Anunciata unbuttoned her shirt and enjoyed his admiration. She shifted her weight, stirring Anton further as she carefully resettled her thighs across his hips. Her tan pleated skirt covered his lower body like a tablecloth.

"Will I be your first woman?"

"I hope so." He felt himself against her.

"My brother was right." Anunciata smiled. "You are a young savage. It's time you went to school."

She lifted his hands to her breasts and encouraged him to clasp them firmly. Anton felt himself stop breathing.

"We don't want to wrinkle my skirt." Anunciata unfastened the silver buckle at the side of the garment. She unwrapped the skirt and folded it inside out before laying it on the sand.

Amazed, Anton stared up at Anunciata. Her silk underwear was a pale ivory against the olive of her slightly rounded belly. She rested one hand on his tight stomach and moved her body from side to side while she looked down at him. He longed to be inside her.

Awkwardly at first, then eagerly, Anton explored her with both hands. He squeezed and caressed her breasts. He stroked her neck and shoulders and waist until Anunciata rolled her eyes upwards and cast back her head. Then she leaned forward and put one hand behind his head, lifting him until his mouth found her breasts.

Overwhelmed by her honey-skinned warmth, Anton closed his eyes and lost himself as his body exploded. Anunciata fell off to one side when he twitched violently and kicked out.

In a few moments he became aware of her casually watching him. He lay on his back with his eyelids fluttering and his heart pounding. She had cast her underwear aside.

Embarrassed, thinking it was over, Anton groaned and tried to collect himself, certain he had made himself a fool. This was not the way it should have been.

Anunciata pulled off his messy shorts and leant over him. Like a cat she groomed him with her tongue.

"I must teach you not to be so selfish." Anunciata bent over him again. "To get a woman, Blue Eyes, it is useful to look like an Englishman, but to keep her, you cannot make love like one."

Unable to concentrate on her words, growing still more sensitive to her touch, Anton found himself stirring again. Arching her back, Anunciata raised her head and sat erect above him. Without using her hands she lowered herself onto him.

She gazed down at him, rising and settling, occasionally reaching behind her back to stroke him with her nails, maintaining the equilibrium of his arousal. Anton blinked again and again. The sky sparkled and spun above him.

At last he was inside a woman. He had never felt so alive.

Anunciata lifted a dry thorn branch from the sand and scraped it across Anton's stomach. He suppressed a wince and for an instant recalled the pain of his tattoo. Anunciata continued to raise and lower herself as she watched two lines of blood fill the long wounds.

"Do I have your attention?" she asked, dragging the thorns more firmly along the cuts.

Anton gasped and stared at her without answering. He felt her tighten. He wondered what Anunciata was going to do. She tossed the branch aside and rubbed his stomach with her palm.

"Now I will show you the way to hold every woman's heart."

She lifted herself from Anton, sighing as they parted. She lay on her side beside him, her lap near his face. She took his head between her hands and drew his face towards her. Confused, Anton smelled her sex and pulled back his head. He recognized the odor he had inhaled in the cabin of the *Garth Castle.* For an instant he saw a different naked woman.

Anunciata touched herself with two fingers and slipped the moist fingers deep between his lips. Anton thought of the two elephants by the pool. He was surprised by the strange sweet taste that smeared his tongue.

"You must kiss me, Blue Eyes."

Obedient, Anton found himself kneeling over Anunciata in the sand. His shirt lay beneath her. She raised her knees and slipped one of his thumbs inside her, leaving his other fingers free. Anunciata guided his middle finger between her cheeks and into her. Anton, astonished, moved his thumb and finger together, pinching and massaging the rubbery membrane that separated them. Anunciata moaned and made the sound of a kiss with her lips. She worked her hands through his hair and encouraged him while he learned to kiss and lick her, his head moving gently between her legs. From time to time she reached to fondle him, distracting Anton while she kept him ready.

"*Puta! Puta!*" a man's voice roared from the edge of the donga above them.

Anton leapt up, naked save for his boots, his cheeks shiny wet, his eyes staring. He tried to cover himself with his hands. Vasco Fonseca glared down at them. Dark and trembling with rage, a shotgun clenched in one fist, the man screamed at his sister in Portuguese. Feeling vulnerable, Anton took a step towards his rifle, but Anunciata, unmoved, not covering herself, calmly placed one hand on the Merkel.

"*Deixa-me em paz!*" she said to her brother.

Fonseca spat into the donga. He cursed once more and stalked away. Stunned, speechless, Anton pulled on his shorts with unsteady hands. He looked out over the top of the gully until Fonseca disappeared into the bush.

Anunciata reached up and drew Anton down to her. They lay in the sand and hugged. Anton's thoughts tumbled.

"Now you will never forget me, Blue Eyes," she murmured in his ear.

Anton sat up and smiled. He looked at Anunciata with new eyes. He noticed grains of sand sparkling on her damp breasts. Feeling in charge, he unbuttoned his shorts and slowly ran one hand between her thighs.

21

Olivio hurried to the small thatched cottage that was his home. Fonseca's letter was tucked into his sash. He held a steaming kettle in one hand.

"Bush Tudor," Lord Penfold mysteriously called the cottage, apparently pleased with the square-hewn cedar logs that framed its corners, eaves and windowsills. Originally the dwelling of the Penfolds while the White Rhino was going up, the house now affirmed the status the dwarf deserved. But what were these Tudors?

Olivio set his sandals by the open door and entered the front room. Layers of tan Indian mats, the fine, splinter-free Bengalis on top, covered the wooden floor. Embroidered cushions and plump spangled bolsters lay along each wall, sparkling richly with many-colored beads. Some faced a low copper table. A framed photograph rested on the table.

The dwarf looked into the back room, briefly admiring the traditional Portuguese bed that nearly filled it. He had shipped the bed from Goa. Carved of sandalwood from the Abu forest, it was the spacious high bed of a man of worth. He had declined to shorten its legs. The round stool of a Matabele chief stood near its head. A crucifix lay on one pillow beside a neatly folded copy of the *Anglo Lusitano,* the Goan newspaper published in Bombay. Where else could he follow the dispute with the Portuguese consul regarding the selection of the Goan representative to the Mombasa District

Committee? Or the cricket match between the Uganda Railway Staff and the Goan Institute? Or the outrageous proposal to replace one thousand Goans in the Kenya civil service, the scheme only defeated because Europeans would be more costly!

Hung low on the bedroom walls were a mirror and a bright painting of three mounted conquistadors leading a caravan of ivory and slaves shackled neck to neck with heavy wooden yokes. The first cavalier carried a long dark cross over one shoulder. His up-arching peaked helmet glinted in the sunlight.

The dwarf seated himself on a round cushion in the front room. The familiar photograph attracted his eye when he set the kettle before him on the table. Its uncertain sepia tones were faded like the memory of an old dream. The picture showed the sixteenth-century facade and worn limestone steps of the College of St. Paul, Goa's home for orphans. There Olivio had passed the few happy days of his youth. Posed stiffly, young scholars and teachers in cassocks lined the steps. In the front row, one child, round-headed, stood far shorter than the rest. His face held no expression. His small deep-set eyes stared down the camera. Olivio recalled the instant the shrouded photographer had squeezed the bulb and called out *"Ora!"* His heels braced high against the step behind him, the young dwarf had stood on discreet tiptoes, gaining one inch.

Soon Olivio must send the College of St. Paul another bank draft to assist the orphans of mixed race. In time the name OLIVIO FONSECA ALAVEDO would be chiselled forever into the tablet of benefactors.

The dwarf held a corner of the envelope to the kettle's steaming spout. One edge of the flap curled back, and he advanced the envelope across the thinning column of steam.

As he drew out the letter a shadow crossed the doorway. Olivio sniffed the air without turning his head. Chief Kitenji, that stinking Kikuyu thief.

"What do you want at my house?" The dwarf stared around with hard eyes.

"I come to invite you, revered Baba, to honor me by attending the *ngoma* for my son, Karioki. Tomorrow my village celebrates his return from the English war."

"What! Do you come to me again with empty hands? Did I give

permission for a disturbance in your rat-filled village? Are the lord's guests to be troubled? Before you speak like this, I have words to tell you."

"Our lord is back, dear Baba. It is he who gave permission." Chief Kitenji lowered himself and squatted awkwardly in the doorway.

"The master does not yet know the evils you did while he was away, nor the untold crimes of the whelp you call Karioki. Until today, I have protected your family, old man. But now you will give what you owe. When the sun rises tomorrow your daughter, Kina, begins to work as my house servant. For her there will be no ngoma. She will sleep here, on this fine mat. If not, your son will pay."

"My son has done no crimes, good Baba. And you know my daughter cannot speak."

"The child has many charms." The dwarf squeezed the lobe of one ear with rapid movements of his fingers. "I have waited too long. She is twelve. What other man would have such patience? Now at last you will provide her to me or I will grind your only son like corn between two stones."

"I see you open a letter," said the chief after a long pause.

"Be careful what you see, old man. If I think I see things stolen from the hotel in your son's hut, you will see him far away in an English jail. Get out. Go, tell Kina of her great fortune. Let the girl prepare herself."

Having dismissed the old wretch, Olivio opened Vasco Fonseca's letter to the Lisbon notary. The writer confirmed that he was indeed the only great-nephew of the late Dona Castanheda. He naturally expected, Fonseca wrote, that Senhor Gama should be rewarded for the complicated work of settling the estate of his distinguished aunt. In the meantime he required that the notary forward a substantial advance to the Standard Bank of South Africa in Nairobi, for Fonseca was investing in a land venture, assembling a great *propriedade* in British East Africa, and the opportunity to buy at bottom prices was at hand.

Olivio resealed the letter with tiny drops of clear melted resin. He copied down the address and returned to the White Rhino to direct the dinner service.

The dwarf entered the dining hall soundlessly and stood beneath the warthog. He looked about the room.

Familiar with her unmentionable needs, the dwarf understood at once that Lady Penfold was taut with sexual desperation. The spindles of her pale shoulders were bare in her turquoise dress. When she stood, her body would hang from these bones like a silk dress on a clothes hanger. Under the dinner table he saw her fists twist and clench in her lap. How could he transfer Lady Penfold's longing to a different woman? What was hideous in Lady Penfold would be a fountain of intoxication in another.

"Why can't these useless Kukes ever do one thing properly?" said Sissy with exasperation. "They don't even heat this revolting gravy. It's all thick and gummy on top."

" 'Ain't no bad soldiers,' " Penfold said to himself.

"What was that?" Sissy said.

"Just an old expression from the regiment, dear," said Penfold. " 'There are no bad soldiers, only bad officers.' "

"You were not listening to what I said," Sissy answered, terminating the discussion. She looked down at the wrinkles and faint brown spots on her hand. Why was age becoming such a beastly horror?

"I thought you might be able to use a pair of my old boots, Rider," said Penfold, transferring his attention. Now he'd lost Anunciata again, Penfold thought with resignation, but one couldn't blame young Rider. The lad might as well have his boots, as well as his mistress. Penfold gestured to a pair of dark-gleaming brown Wellingtons that stood against the wall like sentries.

"They're older than you are, my boy, but they'll last forever if you look after 'em. Old Box knew how to build a bit of leather. Just make certain you bone 'em now and again. I can't get the useless things on this leg anymore."

"That would be awfully kind, sir," Anton said, trying to be attentive. He felt Anunciata's toes climb his leg and hoped the dwarf wasn't watching from his low point of vantage. Anton remembered Anunciata's body settling over his. He couldn't wait to touch her again. He saw his host serve himself to the lumpy mashed potatoes. Anton wondered what Gwenn would be like. Penfold formed a deep hole in the center of the potatoes with the serving spoon before lowering a butterball into the middle of the cavity.

"Do tell us about the shooting lesson," Penfold said to Anunciata, glancing up from his plate. Concentrating again, Penfold filled the hole with gravy. He pierced its rim and admired the delicious dark flood that poured down the valleys. Rather like a volcano, he always thought.

"I'm afraid I was a bit wild." Anunciata looked at Anton with open chocolate-brown eyes. "But I'm sure our young hunter will teach me to do it the way he likes, won't you, Mr. Rider?"

"I shall do my best, ma'am." Anton tried to keep his eyes from Anunciata's breasts as she moved her shoulders. There was something he wanted to try with her. Perhaps he could go to her room tonight.

Expressionless, Olivio observed the scene.

Did he detect cold suspicion in Lady Penfold's eye? Could she be right? Had these two been up to some dirty mischief in the bush? Very likely, he calculated. No awareness was more tuned and heightened than that of a jealous older woman. The dwarf pursued her instinct.

Yes, the boy was even more distracted than at lunch. He even pretended not to notice this hot beauty. And Anunciata herself was still more confident than before. She gave out that pleased mixture of excitement and serenity that with her type often lingers after sex. But what of the shocking difference in their ages? The Portuguese goddess must be ten or twelve years older!

The dwarf glided from the dining room. Without making a sound he unlocked the gun closet in the hallway. There, in the camphorwood rack beside his lordship's guns and rifles, he found the boy's German weapon. Olivio pressed his wide nostrils against the breech. He sniffed. How well his nose always served him! He sniffed again. Not a trace of explosive! Neither the rotten-egg stink of the old black powder nor the sharp smell of cordite. Nothing here but the oily odor of a well-kept rifle. It had not been fired! More lies! What was an honest man to do in this nest of thieves and liars?

After dinner the bar boy served coffee and brandy on the verandah. Sissy wound the long handle of the Brunswick portable gramophone. Her husband stood on the top step with a cigar, looking out at the evening, swinging his bad leg. Anunciata stepped to his side.

"I hope you can forgive me, Adam," Anunciata said quietly, touching his arm for an instant, "but after all, you're married."

"I quite understand." Penfold swallowed his sadness. "And I must

say he seems a very nice young fellow." Penfold felt his age return.
"Brandy, my dear?"

"Close the door, my wild blossom, and stand on this mat by me,"
Olivio said in a smooth low voice when Kina entered his bungalow.
She stood with her head down and stared at the floor. Her hands
were clenched at her sides.

"Here in my household, you will dress as in the village, in your
apron. Take off that ugly English dress. That is for the hotel, or
churchie."

Trembling, the twelve-year-old girl lifted the shapeless cotton
frock over her head. A worn leather skirt hung about her waist from
a cord. The dwarf moved close to her. His mouth was at the level
of her navel. Olivio looked up and tried to smile. He walked around
her. He admired her strong arms and muscular tapered back, her
long neck and impossible breasts. Even from behind, looking up he
could see the high globes swelling past her sides under her arms.
Twice he put his face against her skin and inhaled deeply. Kina
flinched when he touched her. Olivio sniffed again.

"Clean for a Kikuyu," he said with approval. He reached up and
pressed the palm of one hand against the small round of her belly.
He felt her muscles tense flat under his fingers. There was no fat!
Like a wild animal's, her young lean muscles were tight against the
skin. The dwarf went behind her. He put both hands under the short
leather skirt and cupped one hard buttock. How long he had waited.

"Kneel here and be still," he said, annoyed by the sudden burst
of commotion filtering through his rattan window screens. The village
was preparing to celebrate the ngoma for her brother. Now Olivio's
face was nearly on a level with hers. His torso, proportionately, was
somewhat longer than his legs, but Olivio calculated that, if he stood
on the stool, she would be able to give him a French roll. Her breasts
were perfect for it.

The dwarf raised her chin with one hand so she could not avoid
the domination of his look. A wooden drum began to echo. He saw
a spark enter Kina's black eyes. For an instant their dark depth
distracted him, drawing him into her.

"Do not listen to that noise. Here with me, you have a different life. With Olivio Fonseca Alavedo you will not suffer the hot knife of the circumcision ceremony when they cut away your bleeding woman's flesh, forever emptying you of pleasure as they throw your clitoris to the jackals. You will not lie in a stinking smoke-filled hut, hated by the older women, the third wife of a man you despise. You will not grow old in five years with the hanging udders of a Maasai cow, bearing a calf every season. You will not be bent and ugly from toiling in the maize fields while the men drink njohi. No. Here you will learn from Olivio Fonseca Alavedo, and you will be a queen."

The dwarf snatched a set of thin-nosed pliers from the table. He severed the strings of ochre-red beads that encircled her wrists, upper arms, ankles and throat, each bead made from the shell of an ostrich egg, or from dried berries and fig seeds neatly drilled by the women of her tribe. Kina's eyes blinked and moistened as the ornaments fell to the mat. He gripped her left ear in his hand. He cut the copper loop with a twisting snap and drew it out through the hole in her lobe, careful to minimize the pain.

Olivio tilted the side of her head towards him and took the swollen lobe between his lips. He sucked it into his mouth, savoring a suggestion of blood. He ignored the tears that filled Kina's eyes. He did the same to her right ear. At last she was free of the barbarous hangings of her tribe!

Outside the cottage, the beat of drums grew louder. Not yet the remorseless repetition that led to frenzy, but a slow-building insistence. He sensed her body react. To the music, or to him, to Olivio Alavedo? The dwarf knew this must be the moment to make Kina his woman. If she bolted now, he would never control her.

Olivio reached into a fold in his sash and drew out a green silk kerchief. He spread its corners one by one under Kina's gaze, unveiling two antique silver and ivory earrings, dangling Arab bangles he had taken in barter for an unpaid bar bill at the White Rhino.

"When we are here together, little one, you will wear these precious jewels," he said. He held the earrings before her in one open palm. He wiped her eyes and cheeks with the silk. He placed the ornaments in her hands and returned his lips to her ears, addressing each as if it were a complete woman, to be approached and moistened slowly, the arousal suspended before entering. When his tongue could do no more, he insinuated the silver hooks through her lobes.

The ivory and silver danced against the black of her skin.

"Rest your knees on this." He placed an embroidered cushion under her. The window shades darkened and the music rose outside. He knew the savages would be dancing, the way they had before strangers came to Africa. The buttocks of the men would be bare, their bodies and legs painted with stripes, their feathered headdresses bobbing as they stamped in line.

Olivio lit an oil lamp and hung a small gourd above the flame. From his bedroom he brought two sugared toffees and fed them to the girl. He took the gourd and poured warm palm oil into his hand, recalling with affection his boyhood training in the Goan brothel.

Starting at the nape of her neck, he began to massage, working slowly to the cleft between her buttocks. Beneath his fingers her skin pulsed with the rising beat of the wild noises that invaded his house. How fortunate he had captured Kina before the savages circumcised the child. The hand of God.

Her eyes closed. Her head fell back. She moaned deep in her throat. Olivio came around to her front and inserted one finger between her lips. He could feel her come helplessly to life. Kina sucked his finger and he felt the ridges that lined the roof of her mouth. She gripped the dwarf's shoulder with a strong hand. Her nails cut his flesh. He freed himself and dimmed the lamp. He oiled her deep navel with circular movements of his thumb and began working upwards from her belly. She swayed on her knees. He stepped back and she steadied.

The throbbing din of chants and drums filled the bungalow when Olivio returned with thick warm oil for her breasts. Even before the dwarf pinched them between his moistened fingers, he saw the dense dark brown of her nipples shining and erect. One was marred by a nearby hair. He would deal with that later. His mouth was dry as a thorn branch.

As he touched her anew and felt his own arousal, Kina lifted the dwarf in both hands like a doll and hurled him violently against the cushions.

"A Tusker, please, Mr. Olivio," said Anton from the corner stool at the end of the bar. He admired the professional dance-like movements of the dwarf when the barman wiped the bottle with his towel and turned neatly on the narrow shelf to take a glass from the wall behind him. But why was the small man's face so bruised? And his eyes looked more sunken and tired than ever.

Anton thought of the fun he was having with Anunciata and felt sad at how much of life the dwarf must miss.

While Olivio served him, Anton remembered the wandering dwarfs who attached themselves to the gypsy camps and caravans, anxious to join the fairs and village entertainments. He had sat by their fires and shared their meals. Always they were either wildly merry or deeply gloomy. Always, he was told, they died young. Once, when his mother was away again and Lenares was travelling alone, Anton had passed two months with a wagon of the little people. He worked with them in the mornings while they practiced tumbling. Without success he tried to imitate the startling swiftness of their movements and the energetic perfection of their teamwork.

"If you could use each inch and pound like us," their leader had encouraged Anton one day, "there would be no better man in England."

"Thank you," Anton said in Romany when Olivio set down the beer.

"What?" said Olivio, standing still on the shelf. "Do you too speak Hindi?"

"Excuse me. I wasn't thinking." Anton sensed comradeship in the question. "That was Romany, for 'thank you.' "

"What is Romany?" The dwarf clasped his hands together on the bar.

"The language of the gypsies. Long ago it came from India, from Hindi."

"Then perhaps we share a past." Light came into Olivio's hidden grey eyes.

Anton stared at the small man and recalled Romany tales of the ancient connections to India, how the occupations of the gypsies were derived from the Hindu castes, the despised trades of animal trainers and gamblers, dancers and fortunetellers.

"Barman! Two double whiskies!" an English voice called. "Pesi pesi!"

Wondering where Anunciata could be, Anton turned to watch the game of cards. He saw Fonseca still playing poker with four farmers, and winning again.

"Don't worry if you're short of sterling," Fonseca said when one man threw down his hand. "Just scribble a note for an acre or two."

Anton and Olivio looked on as the cards passed. Coins and bills and notes collected before the Portuguese, a bit too steadily, Anton noticed, and always more when he had the deal. A blackleg? Anton stopped watching the cards and studied the man's hands. He remembered the man's reaction whenever Fonseca saw his sister with Anton. At least his fury had now diminished to annoyance.

"Damned luck's worse than a drought!" One farmer stood and dropped his cards. "Even whisky's cheaper."

Anton listened carefully while Fonseca dealt. He heard it again. Not the crisp lifting of a card dealt from the top of the deck, but a slick slipping sound as one card was pulled out from between two others. The man was dealing seconds. Holding one card in place on top, probably an ace, while he dealt the second card instead. Then he would deal the top card to himself.

Anton stepped from his stool.

"May I join you?" Anton said with a hint of awkwardness. He put a hand on the empty chair to Fonseca's right. That position would give him not only an advantage, as the last to bet, but also the best view of the dealer's hands when the Portuguese dealt himself a card.

"If you have any money, boy." Vasco Fonseca shuffled without looking at the cards. "Care for a real cigar, a Crema de las Antilles?"

"Thank you. Straight poker?" Anton asked. He thought of the scene in the donga with Anunciata and determined not to let it give Fonseca an advantage. "Could we have a fresh deck please, Mr. Olivio?"

One farmer cut the new pack. Anton played slowly, as if uncertain, aware that Olivio's deep-set eyes followed every card. The luck began to even out. In time the winnings gathered before Anton. Another farmer, whose stake had dwindled to a few coins, bet it all on another poor hand, lost, and left the table.

Penfold entered the bar with a plate of steaming goat samosas dripping with Pan Yan sauce. He passed them to the men and sat down with a groan and a long gin, his back to the bar. He bought drinks for the losers. He noticed his gold half hunter resting open on the table next to Fonseca. Penfold recalled how the man had played with the prisoners during the Kaiser's war.

Now it was the turn of the Portuguese to deal. Fonseca looked around the table, staring briefly at Anton. As usual Fonseca called Five Card Stud. He dealt one down card to each player.

Anton studied Fonseca's thumbs, always the digits of misfortune. The man's left thumb, short and thick, was held flat against the center of the deck. Anton noted the unusually broad devil's saddle, the curving space between Fonseca's thumb and index finger.

"Excuse me, please, Mr. Fonseca," Anton said, "but that was not the right card."

"What?" said Fonseca in a severe voice, his hands frozen above the table. He glanced to the side when his sister entered the bar. Anunciata approached the table and touched Anton's neck with one hand.

"Would you mind redealing?" said Anton. "I believe you dealt a second."

"The devil I did!"

"You misdealt," Anton said. "Please deal again. What harm can it do, since none of us has seen any cards? What do you think, Mr. Ambrose?"

Surprised at this sophistication, Olivio admired the boy's technique: making a new enemy for his enemy.

"If he dealt wrong," said Ambrose, pushing back his chair roughly, "I'm damn well going to want more than new cards. He's already got half my farm."

"Do you accuse me of cheating, boy?" Fonseca's skin darkened and he banged both hands on the table.

"I said, sir, that you dealt a second," Anton stated evenly. He looked the older man in the eye and felt his cheeks tighten. "Perhaps it was an accident."

"Steady on, Fonseca, be a good chap. It's only a game," said Penfold in a helpful tone. "Why don't you just deal again?"

"It's a matter of honor," said the Portuguese, indignation high in his voice. His brow shone.

"If it's honor you want," said Anton, rising, "I'll help you look for it outside. But if you prefer, I'll make you a sporting proposal. If your hole card is an ace, give me your stake. If it isn't, I'll give you mine. Otherwise, why don't we just divide all the money on the table into four equal piles and play a game of darts?"

Fonseca glared menacingly but did not move or speak.

"Good idea," said Ambrose while the other farmer nodded. "We'll split it all evenly." He apportioned the money and moved to the dart board. The Portuguese remained still, his expression frozen.

"I say, Fonseca, do you know what the Samburu do when they catch a fellow pinching honey?" said Penfold from the bar.

Fonseca looked at Penfold and did not reply.

"They bend his limbs at the joints and tie them up with hyrax gut, nice and tight, rather like a lobster in a Paris fish market, you know. By the time the gut rots away, the thief can never again straighten his legs and arms. I saw one of the poor sods once up north, scrabbling about in the underbrush on his knees and elbows, scrounging for roots and berries."

Anton offered three darts to Fonseca. "Like to go first?"

"A game of peasants," the Portuguese said to the room.

Fonseca collected his share of the divided money and turned to leave. Then he stepped back and put his face so close that Anton smelled old tobacco on his breath when the man spoke through scarcely open lips.

"All of this I will have back from you, boy. In flesh and bone."

22

Gwenn lay on her side between two clusters of sharp-leaved sansevieria and waited for the Grant gazelle to emerge from the bushes and give her a clean shot.

She was tired. It had been a hard five months since she waded ashore in Mombasa on Christmas Day. She could feel her body changing, growing leaner and more fit as she worked with every fibre in her frame. Yet it was more womanly, her breasts and slender figure fuller while her body made a new life within her.

At first, horrified she was pregnant, she thought of Reilly's child as a monster. Revolted, aghast that the connection would never end, she wished the baby would die inside her. She wanted to clean herself of both Reilly and this creature, to start over, to kill father and child if she must. But after a time she grew confused. She knew how many women prayed for children, how many had suffered sons and husbands killed. The fear that Alan might never be a father worked on her. Now she was resigned, sometimes dismayed, other days secretly delighted. Occasionally she felt a sense of maternity stealing up on her. She wondered how the child would look, praying it might have nothing of its father.

Gwenn had taken to wearing loose clothes, typically old army bush shirts, but sometimes she was surprised, almost annoyed, that Alan did not detect the change. It seemed as if her body no longer lived in her husband's world. Each day his coldness cut her. Even if they could not make love, they should need each other's warmth. Often they did not touch for days. Were other marriages like this?

She tried not to lean on her stomach and wondered how much longer she could wait before she told him. Day after day she put it off and contained her secret, thankful her pregnancy was so unapparent. She refused to spoil this precious time, knowing it must be different afterwards. The child would never be Alan's, or even truly hers. But this might be her only chance to have a baby. Would Alan be able to live with it, or would he hide deeper in his stony Welsh fortress? Would he ever touch her again?

At the base of the abandoned anthill a few feet in front of her, Gwenn saw a shadow cross one of the airholes that once ventilated the dense underground fortress for the swarms of termites that had toiled below. A furry grey muzzle appeared at the hole, then two tiny sharp eyes on a flat head little wider than its neck. Small ears, each a perfect half circle, barely broke the slender profile. The animal emerged slowly from the hole, upright, but slim and tubular like a snake. A mongoose? Wary, watchful as a sentinel, it looked left and right with rapid movements of its head. She saw it bend low and freeze. Pointed like an arrow, its body advanced so slowly she could discern no movement. Then she detected an imperceptible bunching of its hindquarters.

Without breathing or moving, Gwenn rolled her eyes to find the object of the creature's concentration. Invisible before, she saw it now. A mottled lizard, patched with reddish grey, indistinguishable from the dust and rocks, with a triangular head and broad belly. Was it asleep, or was it hunting too? While she admired the lizard, the furry arrow struck, pinning the reptile's body with its foreclaws and punching sharp canines into the victim's soft neck.

After a brief scuffle the mongoose dragged the twitching lizard under some rocks. Proud, it stood on its hind legs and gave a shrill twittering cry. Its snout was moist and shiny red. Nine or ten mongoose emerged from different holes and hurried to join the feast.

While she waited for the Grant gazelle, she knew what Alan would be doing. Early one evening, nauseous and exhausted, she had sat with her back against a tamarind tree and watched her husband.

Putting aside pain and fatigue, Alan took the shotgun and walked to the edge of their land. Like a Druid, he gathered stones, a few

from the river but most from the ground itself. Some were small
rocks strewn at the feet of collapsing kopjes. Others were wedged
between the roots of acacias or scattered in the dust like lost marbles.
He lifted each one and brushed it clean with his hands, then dropped
it or carried it back to his pile. He washed a few in the river. Carefully
he built a foundation, the base of a rounded pyramid. He added
ascending layers, fitting and matching rock after rock with an energy
she rarely found in him. Finally, four feet tall, there rose a perfect
cone-shaped cairn. Sweeping his long dark hair from his eyes, Alan
circled around it, replacing stones, checking for strength and balance.
When it was finished, he picked up the extra rocks and gave them
back to the river. He marked each new cairn on the map in his
notebook.

When they had picnicked as young lovers before the war, she
remembered, they always added a single stone to the cairns that
marked the old pastures and marches of the Welsh hills. Generations
before, during the border wars, men had died for the right to build
a cairn. Calling them *carns,* in the old Welsh way, Alan said they
were man's only monument that did not diminish the land.

"My Druid," she used to call him. Now his job was nearly done.
One more cairn and the farm would be bordered with Alan's rocky
necklace.

They had accomplished much in three and a half months, Gwenn
reflected, but it was a bare beginning. Their bungalow, in truth a
hut, was a one-room rectangle of mud and wattle walls. The roof,
temporary, she hoped, was fashioned from branches and the straw
of wild grasses. The rough thatching was secured by belts of zebra
hide. The floor was a gift of the white ants. Made from the ground
red dust of a termite mound, it contained millions of masticated
secretions with which the tiny workers had cemented their city.
Mulwa had worked the material into a paste with water. Packed hard
and smooth, it was easy to clean and cool in the day.

Arthur cooked outside at the back, on flat river stones he had
taken days to select. Each one was the gift of Ngai, he said, washed
down the Ewaso Ngiro from the icy streams of Mount Kenya. Too
thick, he explained, and the stones were slow to warm. Too thin,
and they would hold no heat. If one cracked, bad luck was certain,
and the kitchen must be moved.

Gwenn's vegetables, each precious packet of Sutton's Seeds the gift of her Gran, were in the ground, irrigated by narrow trenches channelled from the spring. The day they chose their house site, she had knelt on the hillside and opened the hard ground with a pick and a shovel and a trowel. She turned the red-brown soil over and over and sifted it between her fingers while she picked out stones and thorn twigs. Then she raked in handfuls of mule dung. Gwenn could hardly wait for her own leeks and turnips, potatoes and cabbage and beans. Tomatoes and rhubarb, garlic and herbs would come later. When she had time, she would plant strawberries in rows under fruit trees, two and a half feet apart, with lime sprinkled between them.

On the far side of their oxbow hill they had planted small experimental plots of tea, coffee and flax to test the farm's blend of altitude, soil and weather. The roof of the bungalow extended to make an earthen-floored verandah by the fever tree. In the evenings she sat there with Alan, talking over the day's work and planning for tomorrow while night sounds rose and the fire softened to coals.

If only they had help, so much more could be done before the heavy rains of October and November. But they were alone, which was part of the heaven of it, as if on a lost island. Four of them could not do it all, and Arthur resisted anything that smacked of farming, grumbling that he should return to Nanyuki and go about his business. "For women, or Wakamba," the Kikuyu said, shaking his head, whenever Gwenn asked him to help her dig or plant. Soon the rains would come, and a year would be gone.

Gwenn saw the silver leaves tremble in the high brush where the Grant was grazing. A covey of guinea fowl scuttled out towards her. She raised the rifle. The branches parted and a horse stepped into the clearing. A shortish hardy-looking animal, bearing a tall rider in a wide-brimmed felt bush hat.

"Don't shoot!" the man said, a smile in his voice.

"It's you!" Gwenn caught her breath as she stood and faced the horseman.

The man sat easily, the feet of his dark boots wet and his sleeves rolled up over strong arms. He rested a double rifle and a handful of lavender flowers on the low pommel of his cavalry saddle.

"The boy from the boat! Excuse me, you aren't a boy—"

"Anton Rider, Mrs. Llewelyn. How are you?"

For a moment Anton stared at her. She seemed different: healthier and younger. Her face was tan under a floppy straw hat. Her hands and wrists were sun-browned, her tawny hair cropped short, her breasts more evident under the khaki shirt. She held the rifle easily in one hand. She seemed strong and at home. The apple-green eyes smiled at him while he dismounted and removed his hat.

Gwenn looked at him without answering. He was so much bigger and more confident. Only the bump on his nose and those dangerous blue eyes were still the same.

"Thank you," she said when he gave her the flowers, just touching her hand.

Anton had assumed, after Anunciata, that he would never again feel awkward with a woman, but now he felt his old shyness returning.

"Jambo," he said, turning a bit too eagerly to greet Mulwa. *"Habari n'gani?"* He turned his eyes back to Gwenn, his confidence recovered. "Your friend Adam Penfold is following in the wagon. He's down by the river looking for a crossing. Jump up and we'll go help him."

Gwenn handed the Enfield to Mulwa and climbed up. Anton mounted behind her.

"What's your horse called? I think I've seen him before."

"Rafiki. Means 'friend' in Swahili. He's half Abyssinian, so he should be safer from tsetse flies." He hoped she appreciated his knowledge.

Anton moved Rafiki to a brief rocking canter. She felt him place one hand firmly on the side of her waist. At the Ewaso Ngiro they found Penfold struggling on the far bank to force the wagon mules across a shallow passage. Penfold backed into the stream on foot, trying to lead the resisting animals by the head. Both mules resisted. One reared up and lifted the Englishman partly out of the water, wrenching its halter from his grasp. Penfold slipped on his weak leg and fell into the stream.

Anton urged Rafiki into the river. Determined to act confidently, he gripped Gwenn about the waist with one arm. She was pressed against him. Together they splashed across.

Gwenn, comforted by his touch, felt the wet shirt cling to her breasts and stomach when they dismounted by the wagon. For a moment she sensed Anton's eyes on her.

"The mules're scared of crocs. May have smelled them on the bank," Penfold said. "I've popped my shoulder out again. Just trying to fix it." He winced and manipulated his right shoulder. "Let's get this lot across. They'll follow Rafiki if you ride him over first, Gwenn. Rider and I'll flog 'em on from behind."

For the first time in her life, Kina lay in a bed. She sucked the chocolate from her thumb and tilted her head in the candlelight while she followed the dancing silver of her earrings in the looking glass. She inhaled the sweet Punjabi incense. From time to time she moaned or gave a soft grunt. Her coal-black face, perspiring lightly, shone against the cream linen of Olivio's pillowcases. The bedding of a gentleman, he hoped she realized, as he toiled beneath the sheet.

Even her rounded shoulders now excited him, their ebony contour framed by the spotless cloth. The fifty-nine beads of his rosary hung about her neck. The ivory crucifix dangled low on the paradise of her bosom. Her breasts, he knew, were resting over the folded edge of the sheet, two ripe dark melons on a white porcelain platter.

Kina licked her fingers and reached under the sheet. She rubbed the dwarf's round head while it bobbed and nodded between her thighs. He enjoyed the appreciative caress of her strong fingers. For an instant he spoiled Kina too soon with her favorite attention.

Then he felt it. The disgusting stickiness of her hand when she pinched his ear. Was it possible? Could the young savage be fouling his bed with chocolate?

Olivio's round face emerged at the top of the bed, flushed and damp, his mouth open, his thick tongue extended over his lower lip as he gulped a breath. His uneven shoulders were naked.

"Pig! Pig! You dare soil my bed!" He seized her left wrist in both hands and glared at her filthy fingers. Enraged, he pushed the side of her hand into his mouth and bit hard into the soft flesh along its outer edge. He tasted blood and chocolate on his tongue and bit deeper.

Kina screamed and reached her right hand into the box of soft chocolates on the bedside table. Olivio hung on to her bleeding hand like a terrier. She mashed a handful of chocolates onto his head, smearing the mass of cream fillings and brown fragments through

the few strands of his hair and down his wrinkled body. Olivio gasped
and lost his grip. She seized both his ears and forced his head beneath
the covers.

"Flax is the thing, Llewelyn, flax. Bung those seeds in fast as you
can," Penfold urged after dinner, gesturing with his good arm towards
the sacks piled in the wagon. "With the war over, they can't get
enough of the stuff at home. It's already three hundred quid a ton
delivered, and going higher."

"What do they use it for?" Gwenn thought of the eleven hundred
pounds they owed Raji da Souza in Nairobi.

"Everything," said Penfold. "Sails and shirtfronts, damask linens
for my dear wife, and nappies for the little princes back in England.
When I die, make sure they wrap me in it. It's smoother than cotton
and twice the strength. Just plant away. Try sisal too, if you can get
any bulbs."

"We have only three or four of us to do the planting," Alan Llewelyn said.

"Perhaps young Rider will give you a hand." Penfold squinted at
Anton's feet. "After he puts a bit of polish on his boots."

Gwenn glanced at Anton in the firelight.

" 'Fraid not, sir. There's no farmer in me." Anton laughed, immediately aware of Gwenn's disappointment. "Though I could help
till Karioki gets here. Then we're off for a little hunting and chasing
the next hill." He felt guilty for not taking better care of the boots.
Penfold had brought him a second pair, the same smart hardy Wellingtons in gleaming black.

What would Gwenn be like if she were free? Anton wondered
hopelessly. Would she think he was too young and rootless?

Confused, he thought of Anunciata, naked, enjoying the risk of
it, stealing across the hall of the White Rhino to his room. She had
come like a dream, standing by his bed, touching her own breast
with one hand and sipping from a bottle of champagne, wearing only
his terai as she watched him waken. The moonlight shone through
the window on her buttocks while she aroused him. Then Anunciata
turned her back and leant over with her arms on the windowsill and

her head low. Was she the same with other men? He wondered how long she would be his.

"Your friend Karioki was a bit sulky about his sister when we left, but for now I reckon he favors village life over soldiering or bush-bashing with you." Penfold looked at Anton and dipped the end of a cigar in his brandy. How nice it would have been to have a son like Anton. "Maize beer and wenching, you understand, Rider, in-stead of hunger and fighting to the death with Huns and pythons. Chap has a point."

"What about his sister?" Gwenn said.

"Kina's working for my little rascal, Olivio, and she seems to be taking a fancy to him. Mad about him, really. Curious, but one never knows about these things." Penfold gazed across the fire with lonely eyes.

"And the Fonsecas?" Gwenn asked.

"Anunciata's still stirring up the bar. Seems a trifle restless." Pen-fold paused. "And her brother's sharping all the land he can find title to, some of it just along the river from here. His Irish minions say they're going to make things rather nasty for our friend Rider."

Penfold saw distress in Gwenn's look and changed the subject. "I say, Alan, when are you and Gwenn expecting the baby?"

Half awake on her cot, her face to the wall, Gwenn heard Alan rise. Her mind raced through the horror of a few hours before.

"September," she had answered Penfold, feeling her husband's shock. Alan shrank farther into the shadows across the fire. After a time, he rose and walked to the bungalow. Later, finding him in his cot, she sat on the floor and hugged him, whispering into the darkness the story of her rape on the *Garth Castle*. She felt the lean body stiffen and withdraw inside itself as she spoke. When she finished, Alan was silent. Gwenn cried and sobbed. Alan put one arm around her woodenly and at last they wept together. Gwenn yearned for him to hold her tight, like a man who still wanted her. She considered slipping into his cot. Then she stood and went to bed.

"Why didn't you tell me, Gwennie?" Alan's voice had asked later in the night.

"Because I love you, my Druid boy," she said, trying to revive a note of intimacy. "I wanted us to start over with a new clean life. I couldn't bear to spoil it."

Like every morning, she heard Alan draw on his boots and step out the doorway when the first shards of light pierced the unfinished walls. Gwenn turned onto her back and stared at the grass thatching of the roof. She held her belly in both hands and thought of the life they still could share.

A chill swept her. Was this her time to suffer? She sat up and looked around the bungalow. Alan's notebook and shotgun were missing. She put one hand to her mouth and jumped up. Frantically, she dressed.

Gwenn hurried past the tent where Penfold and Anton slept and walked to the sloping bank that edged the river. She followed the line of finished cairns. She had just stepped clear of a thick patch of thorn trees when she heard a single gunshot a short distance ahead. She was too late.

She ran to a jumble of loose stones that were gathered on the bank and stared down to the river. Alan lay on his face in a shallow pool, the shotgun in one hand. Red circles swirled into the water from his head. She stumbled down the bank and knelt in the water beside him. A patch of dark hair and fragments of his face floated about him.

Sobbing hysterically, Gwenn flung herself down in the pink water and pressed her cheek to her husband's shoulder. She closed her eyes and gripped his thin sides with her arms. It would always be her fault. "Oh, Alan, my Alan," she said while she rocked him.

Suddenly she was aware of a commotion in the water nearby. First a swishing, then a scraping sound interrupted her despair. She raised her eyes and saw them.

Awake in his tent, Anton listened to Gwenn hurry past along the path to the Ewaso Ngiro. Then he heard the blast of a shotgun. He jumped up, pulled on his shorts and ran to the river with his rifle.

Anton stepped to the bank and looked down. Two crocodiles were advancing towards Gwenn. Their thick bodies switched rapidly from left to right as they scuttled forward. The first was already erect on its extended legs. Its wide belly was off the ground, its long jaw slightly open while it raced towards the bleeding figure. Anton noticed the puffy pale sack of its hanging jowl and the outward-pointing angles of its uneven jagged teeth. The second crocodile burst from the river with a slap of its spiny-plated tail on the water. It rushed forward and slid into the shallow bloody pool.

Gwenn rose, her hair wet, her feet still in the water. Anton fired his right barrel. The first crocodile collapsed on its stomach. Its jaw thrashed. Its tail flailed violently. With Gwenn in his line, Anton hesitated to fire again. The second beast seized Alan's body by one shoulder. Gwenn screamed and bent to lift a rock. Anton fired again, hitting the crocodile in the base of the neck. His rifle empty, he jumped down the bank while the animal dragged the body towards deeper water.

Anton grabbed Alan's shotgun and ran after the crocodile. The animal's snout entered the river, holding the corpse across it like a fish in the beak of a heron. Anton pressed the gun against the beast's head behind its eyes and pulled both triggers. The loaded barrel fired. The dying crocodile slipped into the current. Alan's body floated free.

For a moment Anton stood in the shallow moving water with the body in his arms. He was surprised by its lightness, like the remains of a child. Gwenn stared at him from the pool, her hands wound together. Her shirtfront and sleeves were wet and red. Once again, Anton realized, he was too late. The next time, he must protect her.

— 23 —

Soon you'll have the whole damned farm." Ambrose rubbed his red weathered face with both hands. He ordered a gin and turned over the ivory backgammon cube to accept the doubled bet. "Fortunately, it's never been any use anyway. Either baking or drowning, and seventy miles from the blasted railway."

"At least it's not money." Vasco Fonseca rolled the dice. He took his last two pieces off the board and prepared another I.O.U. for his opponent. He looked up and addressed the American hunter lounging at the bar. "Care for a game?"

"Reckon it looks a little slick for me." Rack Slider chewed on a wooden match. "I'm just waitin' for some clients to come downstairs. Safari's ready to roll."

"Don't they play backgammon in Texas?"

"The Sliders come from Oklahoma." The American turned his back and slid his empty shot glass towards Olivio before stepping from the room.

Distracted while he devised ways to recover control of his young mistress, Olivio polished the bar. From time to time he looked up and watched his cousin, as he now thought of the hated Portuguese. Before long Fonseca would ruin this hopeless English farmer.

Olivio recalled the morning after the end of the war. He thought of the two tired backgammon players, and the I.O.U. he himself had received for "ten well-watered acres" of the Ambrose farm. Fonseca, Olivio discerned, shared the dwarf's view that it was not necessary to cheat Ambrose. The man's weaknesses, drink and inattention, would provide his own defeat.

At the same time, this game held interest for the dwarf. The Ambrose farm, Lord Penfold said, was across the Ewaso Ngiro from the Llewelyn plot. Soon other soldier settlers would be moving in all around. Some single men had banded together to share bigger farms. One large property belonged to forty disabled veterans, each contributing what money and work he could. Only the English, Olivio thought, would waste valuable stolen land on hopeless cripples.

As the soldier settlers drifted through Nanyuki and paused at the White Rhino on the way north to their farms, the dwarf watched Penfold and Fonseca greet them, Penfold with advice and friendship, Fonseca with drinks and cards. Already the Portuguese had amassed debts from nearby farmers, men for whom starting a farm in virgin bush would be challenge enough.

Olivio considered his own interest: maintaining the Llewelyn farm. The dwarf drew from his sash the slip of paper Raji da Souza had sent him and laid it on the bar. He read the name: Dr. Gonçalo Barreto, a Lisbon advocate, said to be among the most distinguished, close to the mother Church, and no doubt more costly than sapphires. Yet if this lawyer would advance Olivio Fonseca Alavedo's claim to the Fonseca estate, what was he not worth? But could Olivio trust this distant Portuguese? How might he bind such a man to the task? How to harness the intrigues of Lisbon and become their master, not their victim?

Before he found an answer, Olivio's mind returned to the twelve-year-old girl waiting in his cottage, lounging among his sparkling cushions like a fat kitten among silks. Was she now preparing her breasts with clove-scented palm oil, as he ordered her to do each day, or was the idle child hunting for the hidden chocolates? The dwarf considered his next scheme and heard his master's limp on the verandah.

"I say, Olivio, fetch me a beer and some samosas, if you would. Perhaps a dash of lime chutney. It's been a dusty ride." Penfold nodded wearily to Ambrose and Fonseca and adjusted the sling on his right arm. "There's trouble at the Llewelyns, and I'm off back up there tomorrow with some help."

"What happened, Adam?" said Fonseca.

"Llewelyn got himself killed in a shooting accident, and if Gwenn doesn't get some seed in the ground before the rains, she'll lose the place," Penfold said. "If these new farmers don't make it, this country's never going to work."

"I am afraid, lord, that at the White Rhino we have also suffered cruel news," Olivio said, his grey eyes wide.

"What's that, Olivio?"

"Brave Lancelot has died." The dwarf thought of the beast's black tongue as it lapped up the sugared poison for the last time. "The dog's agony was beyond tears. He licked my hand and his spirit left us." But, Olivio thought, the hyenas got the body.

Anton forced the shovel into the dirt piled near the hole by his head. He dropped on his knees to wrench out a last stone. Naked to his shorts, he was painted with the reddish earth that clung to his sweat. The cords of his arms strained. The bones of his fingers stood out like claws while he struggled to shift the stone. It remained unmoving as if fixed to the center of the earth.

Scraping with his hands, Anton found a root binding the stone in place. He reached up for the short-handled axe and saw Gwenn sitting against a grey-barked tamarind tree with a notebook in her hands. He wondered what she was reading and tried not to stare. The dense-leaved branches drooped around her from the rounded crown of the tree. Anton dared not think about her.

Gwenn looked up. She tried to smile at the young man and twisted a seed pod in one hand while she regarded him. How strong and natural he looked. How thin and wasted her poor Alan had been. Feeling guilty at drawing the comparison, she lowered her eyes to the notebook. Gwenn had found it waiting beside the uncompleted cairn after Alan's death. She pressed between two pages one of the tamarind's scarlet-veined yellow blossoms. Gwenn rose and straightened her shoulders and walked back to the bungalow, feeling the tightness in her belly. What would she tell the child? Had she loved Alan enough?

At last the stone was free. Anton heaved it up to join the assembled rocks gathered by Alan Llewelyn. The ends of the severed olive root were clean and near-white at their core, still defiant and alive. On his knees again, Anton smoothed the floor of the six-foot hole with his hands. He angled the corners with the army shovel and cleaned up the debris.

Sweat dripped from his chin while he stood exhausted in the pit. He heard a voice carry from the river. Rising on his toes, he looked down to the Ewaso Ngiro and saw a wagon in midstream, a man and woman on the bench. For an instant he thought he saw the woman's hand resting on the driver's leg. Karioki led the mules through the water, talking loudly and slapping the stream with the handle of his spear.

Anton climbed out and ran down to the river to help, hollering a greeting. He entered the water. Penfold and Anunciata waved from the wagon. Anton saw a coffin strapped in the back beside a mound of canvas-topped supplies. On the far bank five Kikuyu women watched the crossing.

"Tlaga!" Karioki cried and the two friends embraced in midstream.

Anton grinned and took a step back in the water to look at Karioki. "I see you've brought your women."

"A few, and soon Tlaga and Karioki will be hunting again!"

"Right, Karioki," Anton said, thrilled at the prospect. Then he thought of Gwenn and his concern at leaving her alone. "But first, I'm afraid, we have to help around the farm a bit."

Gwenn sat on the hard-packed floor with Alan's notebook on her knees. Her back rested against one of the three chests that supported his body. It lay straight and stiff, tightly bound with heavy stitches into two layers of army tent canvas.

Lying in the bungalow at night with his body near her, Gwenn had asked herself what she should do next. Should she sell the land for less than her debt and return to Denbigh, pregnant and homeless, without a man? Perhaps she could have the baby at Gran's and leave it there while she found work.

For the past two days, she had thought again and again of Wales and her parents. Her thoughts had roamed from moments of early childhood to the last day before she had departed for Africa. Especially she remembered holding the door ajar and looking up as her Dada came home from the mine for his evening meal, always, he told her, too dirty to kiss.

Gwenn let the memory carry her until she could see her father standing in the doorway. A man of the tunnels, he was each day a bit less human and alive. Too tired to speak, he would undress in the small front parlor, dropping his grimy clothes on a newspaper in the corner before seating himself in the womb-like tin bath. Fresh clothes, darned and folded, waited on the table by the tub. Closing the door to the kitchen after her, Gwenn's mother carried in to him earthenware jugs of hot water and poured them slowly over her man's shoulders.

After a half hour of scrubbing, he would enter the kitchen with a nod to the children. Too hungry not to eat at once, he sat erect at the corner of the table. The top button of his collarless shirt was buttoned under the black knob of his Adam's apple. The wrinkles of his neck and forehead were pale lines against the grime that was still part of him. In the tomb-like darkness under his eyes, dirt and exhaustion were one. Below his rolled sleeves, the grey of his forearms was blotched with thicker stains of dull black. Had he ever been young and handsome like her mother said? While he ate, his white knuckles stood out against the coal dust that gloved his hands. Gwenn's mother sat by his side, turned towards her husband with her hands clasped in her lap. She watched his plate, knowing it was not enough.

Or, Gwenn pondered, instead of going home, should she stay on in Africa? Should she struggle alone on the unmade farm and raise her baby in the bush? With all its hard beauty, she couldn't help wondering if any of them could ever really belong out here. Perhaps a few, like Anton Rider. But the Gaults were right to go home.

The first night she had wept, felt her stretching rounded stomach with both hands, and dreamt of the life Alan and she might have shared. In the morning she waited for her husband to rise and grope for the boots at the bottom of his cot.

Light crept through the walls. She was beckoned by the unavoidable day, her first truly alone. She heard the boubous chatter in the trees and smelled the smoke and bread of the morning fire.

Gwenn had passed hours lost in Alan's notebook, needing to cling
to his memory. For the first time since he had gone to war, the
notebook made her know again the Alan she had loved at home.
Drawn in pencil, shaded, finely lined, the river, the bush, the distant
hills were there. Campfires and folding chairs, Mulwa and Arthur,
birds and antelope, rocks and plants and anthills, and, over and over,
her own face and hands. The bungalow itself was drawn in each stage
as it was raised, always with the fever tree reaching wide beside it
like a friendly neighboring spirit. The maps became less tentative as
she turned the pages, each one more precise, more neatly drawn.
She came to the center sheet and cried again.

A drawing of what he dreamt: the bungalow, extended now with
two wide wings, one of stone, sat above the flowing oxbow, with a
garden and the fever tree beside it. Behind, rolling to the shadow
of the hills, were rows of crops, some low and flowering, others neat
and tall as soldiers drilling. Flax, corn, tea? Sheep and cattle clustered
in broad free pastures. By the fire before the bungalow were three
small figures. Under the drawing were the two Welsh words Alan
had carved on the fever tree, *Carn Tref*.

She remembered the steep narrow streets of Wales, the row houses
with their tall brick chimneys, and the besieging mountains of black
slag looming at the edge of town.

Gwenn wiped her eyes and closed the book. She saw Arthur hurry
past the doorway to meet Lord Penfold and the Kikuyu women.

She stepped into the sunlight and said with a warm smile, "Welcome to Cairn Farm."

Early in the evening they stood on the bank by the grave. Adam
Penfold led the service, his hat tucked in his sling, a shabby Book
of Common Prayer held closed in his left hand. Earlier Gwenn had
walked ahead of the others to the grave, followed by the women.
Karioki and Anton, Penfold, Mulwa and Arthur carried the cedar
coffin.

Anunciata, her hair in a scarf, prayed softly in Latin. The eight
Africans stood in silence while three English voices carried the 121st
Psalm into the early evening.

"I will lift up mine eyes unto the hills," they said together, and
Gwenn could not help but do so.

Wavy lavender lines melted upwards from the ridged horizon to meet the immense soft orange of the sun while it hovered briefly on the edge of the land. How could it still be like this?

Gwenn bent and lifted one of the large stones that Alan had gathered for the final cairn. She set it at his head over the fresh earth. Anton paused and watched her. He lifted a stone and placed it with care beside hers. Penfold and Mulwa did the same, and so the twelve of them continued until the cairn was complete. It was not, she thought, as well formed as the others, but it stood where her husband had wanted it.

"Time for a drink, my dear." Penfold took Gwenn by the arm and led her back towards the fire. "We've brought cold roast eland and a case of claret to see us through. Tomorrow we'll all get cracking on the farming."

"Thank you. I was surprised you knew the service by heart."

"I wish I didn't. The Germans taught me."

Gwenn freed her arm and stepped to the side and looked back. Her friends walked past on to the fire, leaving her alone. Her body trembled and shook. She gave way and cried.

"Untie me at once! Or I will feed your stinking grandmother to the hyenas, as your evil father would have done himself before these English came!"

On her hands and knees, Kina crawled around the copper table, giggling as she checked each rawhide bond. With a flat cushion under his naked back to protect him from the cold hardness of the metal, Olivio was trussed to the tabletop, one limb to each copper leg. The crown of his head extended past the table's edge.

"Do as I say, swiftly, my wild blossom, and your love will slip sweet candy between your lips."

The girl crawled into the bedroom and was still.

With time to reflect, Olivio pondered again what he must write to Dr. Gonçalo Barreto if he were to procure a trusted champion. For a fee, Raji da Souza had obtained the Lisbon lawyer's name from the treasurer of the Goan Institute of Nairobi, himself an experienced realistic man who dwelt on the threads of the Portuguese empire like a fat-bodied spider.

But how was Olivio to secure this distant advocate, to make him a man whose interest would be bound to his? There was always one way. Of course: the iron law of self-interest!

Kina returned with a pot of honey and a saucer of curry powder. She knelt by Olivio's head. His sunken eyes looked up between the round cliffs of her breasts. Could there be such another pair of nipples?

She dipped one thumb in the honey and touched it to his lips.

"I bought that for you, my sweet, for your pleasure," he snarled between clenched teeth. "You know I detest it."

Kina grabbed his wide nose in one hand. The dwarf closed his mouth. Smiling playfully, her eyes alight, she pinched the hairy nostrils together. At length Olivio gasped and parted his lips. She forced in her thumb, too far, and he gagged when she smeared honey across the roof of his mouth. She sprinkled curry powder on the tip of his tongue and along his lips, leaving his mouth gummy with a spicy paste.

She turned with her back to him, still on her knees, with the backs of her strong thighs against his head. Olivio looked up, his eyes staring from side to side. She separated her legs and raised her soft leather apron so that it settled like a shroud over the face and shoulders of the dwarf when she lowered herself over his sticky mouth.

Buried under her beauty at last, Olivio inhaled the heavenly odors above him. He thought of Dr. Gonçalo Barreto. So, a Lisbon lawyer. Close to the Church. Clearly an evil man possessed of rare greed and skill. What must be his price?

Losing his concentration when he thought of Portugal, Olivio got ahead of himself. The girl began to rock and moan and tighten her muscular thighs about his ears. Used as he was to tight places, the dwarf found it impossible to find air. He bit into the soft wet flesh, tasting the juice of the woman mixed with the honey and spice. Kina reared up with a scream. Turning instantly, her eyes popping as if they had no lids, she slapped him hard, first across one cheek, then the other. The dwarf gasped painfully as she knocked his face left and right. Again Kina lowered herself over his head. She groaned when he rewarded her.

That was it! Whatever the advocate secured, one fourth to go to the mother Church and one fourth to the lawyer himself! Or perhaps a trifle less, one fifth and one fifth? If that wouldn't buy him allies to the death, nothing would! Olivio worked his tongue and inhaled her smells. How proud his grandfather would be! The blessed Archbishop of Goa, after all, was not a man to tolerate the vice of greed in others.

If that demon Vasco Fonseca craves a life of misery, Olivio thought, moving his teeth in excitement, let him fight the princes of the Church! They were accustomed to devouring fatter vipers than this one.

He felt the sweat of Kina's thighs moisten his smarting cheeks. She moaned, lowering her weight and pressing the back of Olivio's round head against the sharp edge of the copper table. Better still, his mind flashed while the pain cut him and he bit again, he would offer the palace in Estoril as a retreat for the cardinals! His teeth closed. What foulness could they not do there!

With a cry of ecstatic pain, the girl collapsed onto Olivio's head. Overweighted, the table flipped on its end and overturned, banging the dwarf's face against the floor as his feet shot up and struck Kina in the back.

— 24 —

There he is again!" Gwenn said to Anton. For nearly a week, on and off, they had spotted the Samburu moran watching from a distance, usually standing stiff-legged on an anthill with his weapons, the sunlight glinting on his metal collar. Anton was glad he and Karioki were at the farm.

He was beginning to feel at ease with Gwenn. Slowly, one fragment at a time, while they walked or worked or sat by the fire, they had talked about their lives at home. Miners and gypsies, cave-ins and horse fairs, the forests and the hills. Surprised to hear himself, Anton had revealed more than he intended. One evening Gwenn, standing embarrassed like a schoolgirl with her clasped hands behind her, had sung for him the old hymns of the Welsh choirs.

Anton wondered if Gwenn could ever behave like Anunciata.

For nearly three months Karioki and he had alternated farming with hunting and exploring to the north and west. But however far they safaried, westwards along the streambed of the Ewaso Narok, or north into the kudu thickets of the Karisia hills, the journeys were never complete. Each sunset seemed to pull Anton farther west, to the elephant country celebrated by the tales of Karamojo Bell, or beyond, to the source of the Albert Nile. Every northerly breeze carried the sharp air of the dry bush to the north and made Anton dream of the Sudan and Abyssinia.

Nevertheless, back at Cairn Farm, Anton and Karioki always did more than either man intended. Anton dreaded the tilling and planting that lay ahead, determined not to share in that final commitment to the land. But clearing the ground, repairing equipment, hunting for meat and tending the animals were chores they both accepted. Anton sought to recall the Romany medicines and treatments when he cared for the weary mules. After they strained against the chains and dragged resisting stumps from the earth, he would lead the exhausted animals to the river and wash them down at the end of the day. He salved their sores and cleaned their hooves.

In the evening Karioki often joined the women at their meal while Anton sat with Gwenn by the fire between the cottage and his tent. Sometimes they shared a comfortable silence. Then Anton would speak of his safaris. Following his interest, grateful for his help, Gwenn learned to ask about the game and the bush before mentioning the problems of her farm.

Now they both studied the tall still figure, posed like a sentinel, or, Anton thought, like a dik-dik on a ledge by the Rift.

"When you see one Samburu," Karioki had warned, "others will follow, just like the whites and the filthy Maasai, the cousins of these goat people. If the tips of their spears are naked, Tlaga, they have come to fight."

Anton and Gwenn rested their rifle and shotgun against a baobab. Anton led her forward to meet the Samburu moran. A breeze gusted up from the plain to the north, the air pervaded with the sweet scent of the off-white and pale yellow blossoms of acacia bushes.

More heavily built than the Maasai of Anton's experience, his gleaming brown skin only slightly tinted with red, the long-legged moran stood serenely with a throwing club under one arm and two six-foot spears held lightly in his hand. One weapon, slender and wooden-shafted, carried a thin leaf-shaped blade. The other, with a far larger blade, bore the heavy metal butt of a Maasai spear. Both blades were edged with sheaths of antelope hide that protected each point with a conical leather crown. One was topped with a black pompom of goat hair, the other with a tuft of ostrich feathers.

An antelope skin, rubbed smooth with clay and grease, hung about the Samburu's waist. His hair was plaited in fine red lines, parallel and neat, long at the back and in a short bang on his brow. The man's left arm bore two shiny-skinned scars. Yellowed ivory disks hung in the lobes of his ears. Colored beads and copper wire circled his neck.

He regarded Gwenn and Anton calmly over high cheekbones. Anton felt Gwenn's fingers touch his arm and tighten.

"Jambo! Habari n'gani?" Anton held up one hand. He carried a sack of maize meal in the other hand. Anton looked at Gwenn and nodded reassuringly. Now was the time, he judged, to help her befriend these occasional neighbors. He could not stay with her forever, and she might need their friendship and protection.

The moran did not speak, but studied Anton and Gwenn. After a moment he smiled and his dark eyes flashed.

Anton put down the sack and opened its drawstring. Not looking at the gift, the moran whistled between his teeth. Two young women appeared, then three boys with a goat. The women walked around Gwenn, examining her boots and long tan skirt. They drew close and touched her fair hair with the palms of their hands. Open-mouthed, chattering, they pointed at her green eyes. Gwenn smiled at Anton. She nodded at the African women and touched the sack. The women ran their hands through the ground maize, sifting it between their fingers and smelling it before lifting the bag and carrying it off.

The moran gestured for Anton and Gwenn to follow. Anton took Gwenn's arm and guided her forward. The Samburu led them to a dry streambed. There another, younger Samburu worked a long stick that was plunged into the dry floor of the sand river. Two spears were planted like stalks in the sand, their varied blades flowering six feet above the ground. Raising the stick, the man pushed it into the golden pink-tinged sand, angling and twisting it while he forced it deeper. The first Samburu crouched on his heels, watching.

"I'll go back for the guns," Anton said. Gwenn rested on a quartz-sparkling rock that protruded from the sandy floor.

The working man looked up and grinned. Gwenn admired his body: erect, smooth, devoid of softness, yet full and long-muscled. Her gaze drifted to Anton as he walked towards her with the firearms. She noticed the form of his body as she had not done before. Lacking the graceful posture and cat-like tension of the Samburu, Anton was more solid in the shoulders, with heavier arms, yet relaxed and rangy in his movements. Only that funny broken nose spoiled his look. She wished Anton were not quite so young. What could he know of making love?

The moran spun the wooden rod faster between his hands and rocked it from side to side, expanding the hole that its point carved beneath the surface. Slowly he drew up the pole. Five inches of it glistened dark and wet. Drops of water hung from it and sparkled in the light.

The Samburu offered the stick to Gwenn, and she touched it with her lips. The water was cool and sweet. When she handed back the pole a large woman appeared and offered her a calabash. Gwenn pulled the bark stopper from the gourd and inhaled the strong smell. Goat's milk. She drank and passed it back, but the woman declined, wagging her head from side to side and pointing to Gwenn's extended belly.

"She's quite right," Anton said. "You drink that up."

Gwenn took his arm. Together they walked home through the bush and the fields as the light fell. Anton enjoyed the warmth of her arm in his. He breathed in the smell of her hair as they strode through the cool evening.

What were these swine saying?

His infant-like feet bare and cold, Olivio stood on a pillow in the closet of guest room Number 3 and waited for his pupils to enlarge in the darkness. It was a moment for care. No one knew better than he that the White Rhino was more celebrated for creaking floors and thin walls than for moist omelets and smooth linens.

He drew the towel from his sash and polished the last of Lady Penfold's crystal fingerbowls. Most had been casualties of the hard trip to Nanyuki, smashed at the train station or broken on the road. The survivors, he recalled with amusement, had been shattered by clumsy Kikuyu servants, usually while Lady Penfold yelled at them. This one he had put aside for a higher purpose than rinsing the lady's bony fingers.

The crystal at last impeccable, he ran one forefinger around its lip until the cut glass began to vibrate. He stilled it with a touch and held it to the wall adjoining Number 4. He pressed one ear against the bottom of the bowl.

The voices came to him as through a trumpet. Amateurs, he knew, sometimes set a drinking glass to a wall to gather and magnify sound, but who besides Olivio Fonseca Alavedo had employed a fingerbowl?

"It's my money and my notes," a man said with severity, "and we'll do it my way."

Fonseca!

"We are not in Macao or Portuguese West, Mr. Fonsici," said a languid English voice. This must be that swine-fat government man, Hartshorne! His lordship had wondered what brought this city creature back to Nanyuki. "Without the approval of a representative of His Majesty's Colonial Office, more specifically a land officer, such as myself, no land changes hands. Am I clear, Mr. Fonsici?"

"F-O-N-S-E-C-A, Hartshorne, Fonseca. Your job is to help me assemble, at the lowest cost, the biggest piece of the best land. That needs my money, your government stamps, and, shall we say, the work on the ground of this Mr. Reilly here."

"Without me and my brother, you blokes can't own nothin' up there," said a loud Irish voice. "This land's been nicked from the niggers to give to us old soldiers. You don't look like any Limey soldier I've seen, Fonseca, and you ain't a proper nigger, neither, though some of you Portagees are dark enough to lose at night."

"Senhor Fonseca and I are proud to be in partnership with two Irish gentlemen," Spongey Hartshorne interrupted. "Now let's have a look at the map."

The dwarf wiggled his toes and moved his good eye to a knothole he had long ago punched open. All he could see were three figures bending over the bed.

"Main thing's the water." Hartshorne tapped the map with his nails. "Water. One year in three there's no rain. If you're on the Ewaso Ngiro, though, you can make it through. But the river's tricky too. The blasted bed shifts about like a Somali tart in a miner's camp. One week of hard showers, and the water jumps her banks and settles into all the old dongas."

"Already," said Fonseca as he drew on the map, "we've got Reilly's own bit here; then, just nearby, most of Ambrose's old farm that runs along the river here; and then scattered pieces there and there, where I've got notes from some of these hopeless old soldiers."

"Some of them hopeless ones pushed von Lettow and his Krauts out of your stinkin' Mozambique, Fonseca. Where were you?" said Reilly.

"Let's try to bowl for the same wicket, gentlemen," Hartshorne said with impatience. "The two pieces we need next are this one and the Llewelyn farm here, right in the middle. Then the big bite'll be the disabled soldiers' section."

Olivio, trying not to shift his weight and scrape the bowl on the rough wall, thought of the substantial loan he and Raji da Souza had made to the Llewelyns. Every seed, each shovel, even the farm itself was partly his! Once again, this devil Fonseca was after what belonged to him! But the dog did not know that Olivio owned ten acres of the Ambrose farm, just next door, on the river itself. When the time came, the cur would learn.

"With the husband dead and no money," Fonseca said, "the Llewelyn place should be easy. We'll be doing that little beauty a favor."

"It's about the only farm with its own water, apart from the river," Hartshorne said. "Springs and waterholes, along here. They're on our new survey reports but don't show on the maps yet. That's why I watched who won it in the raffle."

"Money ain't the only way to get it, neither," Reilly said. "That girl's needin' a new man, and I know her well enough from the boat."

"Maybe you two should ride up there and see what's to be done." Hartshorne looked at his nails. "We've got to get that land together before word gets out where the new rail line is headed."

"I can stop by," said Reilly, "and teach her a little Irish poetry."

— 25 —

Haven't seen the old place this lively since the Bachelors' Ball in '13." Adam Penfold straightened his bad leg and pushed a glass across the bar to Olivio. He studied the platter of chopped mutton samosas and chose the one most heavily sprinkled with flaky red pepper. "Where did you get that fearful bruise on your forehead?"

"Something fell on me." The dwarf thought of Kina's firm damp thighs. He poured a double whisky and surveyed the dim crowded scene from his perch on the shelf. "Business is good, my lord, if chits are money."

The dart board held the noisy attention of a party of up-country planters, tired men from the steep hillsides of the Aberdares.

"Spent all week feeding arsenic to the red spiders and pink mites that're gobbling my tea trees," said one, chasing his whisky with an ale. "Now it's time I poisoned meself."

"The buff are stomping my irrigation pipes, the stinging caterpillars are eating the coffee beans, and the Kuke squatters are scoffing more maize than the locusts," said his opponent. The man leaned forward on his front foot and threw a dart into the eye of Vladimir Lenin.

A photograph of the Bolshevik leader haranguing workers at a tank factory had replaced the picture of the Kaiser on the dart board. Olivio had read in the *Anglo Lusitano* that the Royal Marines, with little else to do, were ashore in Russia, fighting to oust this bearded troublemaker. These British, the dwarf conceded, were not so stupid as they seemed, at least not all of them. Still at war, Russia was unable to export her flax, thus creating an opportunity for Kenya's fibre growers.

"What we need is a jolly Sunday-lunch farm picnic," said one drinker, "like the old days. Start early and shoot anything."

Behind the dart players, a knot of men encircled the backgammon table, generously advising the loser. Vasco Fonseca, across the table, smiled through the thick cigar smoke. He offered drinks and doubled the cube.

Down the bar, four men rolled poker dice near the corner where the rifles of the drinkers hung on pegs and revolver belts dangled from duiker horns.

Two men arm-wrestled at the square table in the center of the room. Their fists were locked together, trembling over the line of the equator. Their arms were steepled above the trench that Adam Penfold had cut in the dark wood many years before.

The two wrestlers hunched in concentration over their joined right hands, grunting while they strained, teeth clenched, elbows pressing into the tabletop, their bare forearms swollen hard. Each man's left hand gripped the under thigh of his left leg as he levered to get his body behind the struggle. To either side a candle flickered low on the table. One flame would be crunched out when the loser's hand was forced down to extinguish it. Both men were tall and heavy shouldered, the older one grey and missing his right leg below the knee. The younger man, even larger, wore curly reddish-black hair over the low forehead of his broad sweating face.

"Any more bets against Paddy? Anyone for Captain Jos?" the younger man's companion called out in slow Irish tones from behind his wrestler's chair. "It ain't too late to wager a florin, two bob to call which candle sizzles!"

"I'll take it, on Jos." Another spectator tossed his silver onto the edge of the table.

Behind the competitors, a group of old Tommies began to sing:

> *She was young, and she was tender,*
> *Wictim of a willage crime.*
> *'Twas the squire's 'orrid passion*
> *Wot robbed 'er of 'er honest nime.*

Recognizing the tune from the *Garth Castle,* Anton turned and leaned his back against the bar. After four months of farming and bush-bashing, it was a nice change to be back at the White Rhino. He squinted through the smoke of the tobacco and the oil lamps while his eyes searched the dark room. He studied the curly-haired man. He looked at the contorted face and clenched right fist, then at the left hand grasping the heavy leg. Raising his eyes, Anton saw it. His old knife, stuffed into an outsize sheath on the man's belt. His choori, stolen on the ship. It seemed that years had passed, though it was not yet one. He felt the gold earring of Lenares hanging beneath his shirt.

Anton stiffened. His eyes hardened when he saw the other Irish-man standing behind the chair. Mick Reilly. He thought of Gwenn and of Reilly's hand crushing her bare breasts when Anton burst in, the smells of sweat and sex heavy in the cabin. Anton's nails dug into his palm. He felt the tense anger rising in him. Slowly, he cautioned himself, remembering his lessons. Slowly. He forced his jaw to relax.

Anton set down his lager and lifted his hat from the bar. A cheer rose as the older soldier's hand crashed down into a flame. The man scraped hot wax off the back of his hand against the edge of the table. He nodded at Paddy before taking his crutch and moving to the bar.

"Too bloody bad, Cap'n Jos," one bettor said to the loser. "If you hadn't stepped on that mine, you would've hauled that Irish bugger over the table. He's got shoulders like a buffalo."

"Anyone for a try?" Mick Reilly hollered, searching through the throng. "Any bet you call!"

Anton, the terai low over his eyes, his hair reaching to his collar, seated himself in the empty chair.

"What's your stake?" Paddy said.

"No money." Anton rested his German knife in the trench in the center of the table. "Let's wager our knives. Two falls out of three."

Paddy lifted the knife and tested its edge against a torn thumbnail. He turned the blade, holding it close to his face in the meager light while he read the mark. "Solingen, eh? Hard steel. The Hun's best. Right, let's 'ave a go."

The big Irishman drew the gypsy knife and placed both weapons

across the wooden trench before him. He stood and stretched. He
flexed his shoulders and raised both arms over his head until his
hands touched the beam that crossed the room. He sat down, spreading and stretching his fingers.

"Barman! Barman!" Mick Reilly yelled. "A candle!"

"No need to raise your voice so, young man," said Penfold. The
backgammon game stopped. Fonseca and other drinkers gathered
about the center table.

"And who the blazes are you?" Reilly said.

"Adam Penfold."

"Easy Mickey, have a drink," said Paddy. "One thing at a time.
Any bets?"

"This ain't the bleedin' House of Lords," Reilly muttered. "We
came out here to get away from all that pigwash."

How true, Penfold acknowledged to himself.

Olivio stepped along the shelf and selected the squat stump of a
candle from a mug that hung off the back of the bar.

"May I wager tonight, my lord?" the dwarf asked when he handed
the candle to Penfold. His employer nodded and took the candle.

Penfold lit the wick from the cigar taper that burned on the bar
during busy evenings. He limped to the center table and tilted the
candle, forming a pool of hot drops on the waxy mess already there.
He set the candle in the bed of soft wax. He looked Anton in the
eye. A smile creased Penfold's craggy face.

"Keep that one burning, my boy," he said.

But in the eye of his young friend, Penfold was surprised to detect
no sparkle of excitement. Instead, he recognized the dead-calm
enamelled hardness he had seen in some men before they kill.

"Any more takers?" Mick Reilly stood in the smoke-thick bar with
one hand on the back of his brother's chair. Noisy and jolly, a gang
of friends hung about him. Reilly's other hand held a sheaf of ten-
rupee and ten-shilling notes. "Come on, lads, step up for it, two-to-
one says Paddy burns another man, two falls out of three!"

Like the circled mob at a cockfight, the watching men closed tight
around the wrestlers. Fonseca lounged at the edge of the crowd and
placed bets on the bigger man. Without looking up, Anton felt the
excitement of the room surge into him. He kept his hands before
him on the table, trying to keep his long brown fingers relaxed while

his body hardened with tension. In front of him, across the trench in the table where the two knives lay, Paddy's beefy forearm covered the wood. It rested huge and white like a skinned ham, speckled with uneven pale freckles and coarse red hairs. Anton looked at the gypsy knife.

"Patience," Lenares whispered. "Husband your skill. Work the other man's strength and violence against him." Waiting for the match to begin, Anton listened to his teacher's voice and kept his eyes down to avoid recognition.

Paddy, Anton reckoned, might be the stronger, but he could not be as fit. If Anton could stretch out each fall, make him struggle, he might beat the larger man. But Anton's true advantage, he knew, was that only he realized what the contest was about. He remembered another lesson of his boyhood, one that might have spared him a thrashing at the Needham Market fair: never reveal your hand.

Paddy lifted his right hand above the line of the equator, his elbow on the table. Anton did the same, and the bigger man lowered his arm to join palms. An antelope-tallow candle burned on either side.

"Ready, go!" Reilly said quickly. The two men locked grips.

Instantly Paddy had the advantage. Taking an edge on the start, the man's broad hand seized Anton's a shade too high, getting a grip on the side of the fingers instead of on the square of the palm. Anton hardened his hand just in time and felt the Irishman begin to squeeze together the knuckles of his hand.

With his grip set but the first advantage lost, Anton stared down at the table in a fury of concentration. Knowing he could not push down his enemy's hand, he forged his body into a rigid cast from his feet to his fingertips. He felt his toes curled tight in his polished brown boots. The broad muscles of his thighs became stone arches as he strained. Like an oarsman's, the armorlike ridges of his stomach delivered to the upper body the leverage of his legs.

Smoking, drinking, laying bets, the crowd encouraged the wrestlers. Some hung over the combatants. Others touched the table. But to Anton they were distant as Mombasa. Only one face penetrated the wall of his concentration. Its grey eyes gazed up at Anton in the smoky gloom. Just over the tabletop to Anton's left, round and pale above the dark wood, Olivio's visage was suspended like a hazy full moon floating on the line of the horizon.

Soon Anton's arm was no longer part of him. Like a boulder blocking the mouth of a cave from the entry of an enemy, his hand and arm existed on their own. All he did was keep the stone in place.

Already, he knew, it had taken longer than Paddy had imagined. Still the hands were gripped and nearly balanced, although Anton judged that his own leaned a trifle down. He felt the other man's hand begin to sweat.

Paddy twitched his hand from side to side, effecting minute changes in his grip. Anton's elbow, covered by his shirt sleeve, shifted slightly on the table. Anton felt the moisture from the man's palm and fingers spread to his own. Bit by bit, Paddy's grip slipped lower on Anton's fingers. Too late, Anton realized the cost.

Drawing himself up to his full height in his seat, the Irishman suddenly leaned down on Anton's bending wrist with all the weight of his body.

Anton's hand flattened the candle with a crash. His upper arm and shoulder still locked in position, he was lifted from his seat by the force of the movement.

Cheers and curses filled the room while the two wrestlers stood to stretch.

Back on the bar shelf, Olivio served fresh drinks. Rarely had business been so good. Tonight some cash, even tips, crossed the bar.

"A beer and the two quid you owe me, you little blighter," Reilly said to the dwarf.

Olivio paid the man his wager. Little does the ape know, Olivio thought, that I myself stand across his path. Before these Irishmen and Fonseca and the idiot Hartshorne steal my farm, they must defeat not just Mrs. Llewelyn, but Olivio Alavedo and the moneymen of Goa. He looked across the room to see Fonseca counting his winnings. With satisfaction, the dwarf reflected on the letter now en route to the lawyer in Lisbon. What would Fonseca do then?

"Here is your beer, sir," Olivio said to Reilly. He observed young Rider speaking to the lord, rubbing his right hand with his left.

Never, except in himself and long ago, had Olivio seen the concentration he found in the boy's face when he wrestled. It took more than a sport or a knife, Olivio knew, to strip a man so bare. Even these English did not take games this seriously. Had he seen in those narrowed ice-blue eyes the fire of hate, perhaps even the rich energy of revenge?

"Will you take another bet, sir?" the dwarf said to Reilly.

"I'm givin' three-to-one on Paddy. How much do you want?"

Olivio held up a thumb and four short thick fingers. He reached into his sash with his other hand. He unfolded two white five-pound notes and passed one to Reilly.

"Would you care to hold the bet, sir?" Olivio said when Reilly grabbed the money.

The two wrestlers were seated again. Penfold set a fresh candle stub to Anton's right. Anton wiped his hands on his red diklo and tied it about his neck.

"Care to try this one with our left hands?" Anton asked in an easy voice.

Paddy grinned up at his brother, who nodded.

"Why not?" Paddy rolled up his left sleeve and put his elbow on the table. Anton did the same.

"Hold on," Fonseca called from the edge of the crowd. "Then my bets are off."

"Shame!" cried several men, shouting Fonseca down. "It's to Paddy's advantage! He's already gone twice with his right."

"Flippin' Portagees never understand sport," muttered one old soldier.

"Excuse me, Lord Penfold," Anton said as he met Paddy's left palm with his. "Would you mind calling the start, please?"

"Go!" said Penfold.

Anton closed his hand and caught the edge of the Irishman's fingers. Paddy cursed and struggled to recover the advantage. His face flushed when Anton pressed him. A thick white froth of beer beaded the big man's lips.

Anton stared into the table. His right hand pressed upward against his right thigh. His will fought to bring his two hands together. His mind reached back to the rusted lower deck of the *Garth Castle*, leading down the echoing metal corridor to the donkey engine room.

Again he struggled to join his two hands. At first imperceptibly, then slowly, the Irishman's wrist began to arch. Anton remembered the smell of his own flesh when the molten pipe had burned through his skin. He felt the cords of his neck harden like cables. His hands grew closer together. For the first time the binding force of Anton's shoulders added compression to the vice of his arms. He felt the burning scar inside his right elbow.

With irresistible violence Anton slammed Paddy's hand into the candle.

His face dripping, the big man stared at Anton. Cheers and yells rose around them. Olivio gazed down from his shelf without expression.

The back of Paddy's left hand rested in the hot wax where he held the young man's hand in a loose grip. He released Anton and stepped to the bar with Reilly.

"Double or nothing, my little bugger?" Reilly said to Olivio, holding the barman's winnings in his fist.

"If you please, sir," Olivio said. "But if you don't mind, I'll take my fifteen pounds now."

Anton kept his eyes low when Paddy sat down heavily before him. The older man leaned back and cracked his knuckles while he licked the beer from his lips. Concerned lest his own elbow slip, Anton raised his hands from the table and rolled up the sleeve of his right arm, exposing the goshawk tattoo in the gloom.

The wrestlers set their elbows and raised their right forearms. The crowd tightened. Leaning on a cane, Penfold took his place by the side of the table. He raised his hand.

"No more of that fancy calling, your grace," Reilly said. "We'll start it together. Are you set, boys?"

"Ready, go!" Penfold and Reilly said together.

Dead even, the two hands clenched in the air, trembling with exertion above the line of the equator.

Without relaxing, Anton looked up to see a new man enter the bar. Big, robust, he wore a frayed leather jacket and a battered grey bush hat. He took two bottles of beer from the bar in one hand and stood behind Reilly and his friends, facing Anton.

"Good fortune, Engländer!" the man called out loudly. The German accent knifed through the din of the crowd while he raised a bottle to Anton with a hard face.

Ernst! Anton realized, distracted for a second. He felt his hand edge down a fraction.

At once Anton gathered himself, staring at the table while he squeezed with both hands. By now he knew the body of his enemy, the sour smell of his sweat and the meaty hardness that underlay the soft flesh of his broad hand. He could feel through the man's fingers the brutish undisciplined strength, and now a new tension.

Anton looked up. He was conscious of Reilly staring at him as he had not done before. Had he at last recognized Anton? Reilly whispered in Paddy's ear. Anton caught Paddy's look. His mouth slightly open, his eyes fixed, the big man stared at the tattoo and the thick mottled scar on the inside of Anton's elbow. His small eyes met Anton's.

Anton exerted himself. He fought to bring his hands together, seeking the first advantage. The long muscle of his forearm, dimpled in where it ran along the bone, was raised and swollen with strain. The scar rose from it, pink and smooth-surfaced. Above it, Anton's biceps filled the rolled shirt sleeve. He felt the taut breadth of his shoulders straining as if he were lifting the earth itself. He gave a steady extra pressure.

A fine line opened along the edge of Anton's scar. Misty drops of blood, barely pink at first, sweated out along the rim of the old wound.

Anton sensed the uncertainty in Paddy's hand as the Irishman poured sweat. Anton kept his own hand bonded to his enemy's. If a hand were to slip, the loss would not be his.

Trancelike, with only Reilly comprehending their silent drama, the two men were a single statue. Paddy sat taller in his seat and began to work his wrist. Twisting slightly, first one way, then the other, he sought an angle of advantage. With each movement, Anton tried to pick up any slack and bear down a degree or two to build an edge. Finally he could feel it. Paddy's hand was now defending, trying to recover the center. Anton held the place, not seeking more. He knew it was more tiring to be pressing upward than for him to be leaning down. Drops of blood filmed down over his old scar.

Gradually Anton felt Paddy lose the steady energy that gave him strength. He noted the shortening spurts of exertion that the man threw into his effort. For Anton it was a time for patience. Avoiding the temptation to press hard in the man's moments of weakness, Anton reduced his own strain, just maintaining his edge with enough strength to keep the Irishman fighting to recover.

Testing, Anton relaxed a trifle. Paddy fought back to the center, grunting with relief. Anton strained again, forcing the man back to where he was before. Five times Anton did this. Each time, drops of blood slid down from the scar across the black hawk of his tattoo and dropped to the table. He too was tiring, but not, he knew, like Paddy.

Although still strong, and occasionally struggling with the angry uneven exertions of a wounded buffalo, Paddy was no longer in the match. One or two watchers, perhaps Reilly, Anton thought, saw the contest as it now was. Fonseca leaned against the wall, chewing an unlit cigar, his arms folded across his chest.

Anton glanced up through the smoke to the bar. There, on a stool, her ankles crossed and long legs swinging, he saw Anunciata, the only woman in the room. She moved her lips in a kiss. He knew every man in the room desired her.

Above Anunciata, the lamplight playing up over his face with haunted shadows, the dwarf gazed down like a stone Buddha. His head cast the dark figure of a huge globe onto the wall and ceiling above him. Anton tried to look into the deep-set shaded eyes. Did he understand?

Although Paddy's bursts of effort obscured the fact, Anton, when he pressed, could move the large man's hand almost at his will. Three times more he alternately relaxed and strained, drawing out the final energy of the man facing him.

Hearing Paddy grunt, Anton looked up across the table. There, inches away, he found the staring red-lined eyes he once had seen on a cornered badger, wounded in a trap, waiting angrily while a gamekeeper moved to finish the snarling animal with a shovel. Eyes that blazed the creature's pure emotions: hate and fear inseparably mixed.

Do you remember the boy in the donkey engine room, Anton asked silently. He looked through the smoke into Paddy's eyes. *Is he cooked?* your brother asked you.

Anton forced the man's hand steadily down, until it hung three inches over the flaming candle. There he held it, no longer pressing down.

"Not quite done," Anton said aloud, staring Paddy in the eye.

He smelled the ugly odor of charring hair. The thick red fibers shrivelled and burned away on the back of Paddy's hand. The man thrashed with new strength. He jerked his hand upwards against Anton's pressure. Again and again Anton forced him back and forth above the flame, tiring Paddy with the man's own exertions, until the grip of the sweaty fingers weakened once more. Anton's arm dripped blood. He lowered the large pale hand over the flame, preparing to reverse his strength if the Irishman sought to collapse.

"Come on, Paddy," Reilly yelled, "fight for it, man! Frig 'im! It's the bastard from the boat!" Around him, their money at hazard, Reilly's friends began to shift and mutter.

Anton ignored the angry mood and forced the hand toward the candle, four inches, three inches over the flame. There he suspended it. He felt the heat blaze through his nails. The tips of his own fingers blistered in the fire. He recognized the smell of burning skin and flesh. He held fast and looked up. Paddy's neck was swollen like a rotten fruit about to burst. His red face dripped sweat. His lips trembled. His mouth opened. Spittle ran to his chin.

Mick Reilly cursed. He lifted a broken whisky bottle from the floor.

"*Nein,* my friend, let them finish their little game," Ernst roared. He dropped his beers. Reilly raised the broken bottle. Ernst grabbed Reilly's arm in both hands and swung him violently around into his companions.

"Done, I think," said Anton. He lowered Paddy's hand slowly into the flame. As his own fingertips touched the wick Anton released his grip. He snatched up a knife in each hand, the thin blade in his right. Paddy kicked back his chair and came for him. Blundering into Penfold's cane, Paddy stumbled. He crashed onto the square table, breaking it in two when he fell.

Instantly the bar was a battlefield. Only Fonseca stood against the wall, watching with unconcerned eyes while the other men pitched in. Ernst, after delivering a few slamming blows, was down under a pile of Tommies.

Olivio jerked the trigger. The short elephant gun fired with a deafening crash and a .450 slug exploded through the ceiling.

Every man froze and looked to the bar. Knocked off the shelf by the recoil, the dwarf was scrambling back up the ladder with the old Rigby in his hand. Centered again on his shelf, breathing hard, Olivio stood with the opened rifle. He put the spent brass cartridge against his lower lip and whistled fiercely. His face shone in the lamplight under a halo of rising smoke.

"One of the White Rhino's sportier parties," Penfold said to Anunciata as he poured a whisky.

"I hope," she said, "no one was trying to sleep upstairs."

26

One more furrow and it would be enough for the day. Before Gwenn, five feet long, weighted with the ballast of the mahogany moldboard that topped it, the heavy blade of the Deere breaking plow fought to open the earth. The narrow prow, designed to slip past stones and stumps, broke the surface and churned up the virgin earth of Africa. The rear of the blade cut deeper, nine inches, to expose the subsoil to the light and let the land breathe. Like a new child, Gwenn thought, bending with a groan to pick up a stone.

Ten oxen, six too few for the work, hauled against the trek chains. The prow bucked and jammed hard. The back of the blade shimmied to one side.

"*Pole pole*," Karioki urged. "Slowly." He let the reins loosen around his shoulders. He smiled back at Gwenn and held up both hands. At least Karioki was still here, Gwenn thought, missing Anton. Understanding his restlessness, yet annoyed at his absence, she wondered what he could still be doing at the White Rhino.

Two months ago, Gwenn would have urged Karioki to flog the animals on, straining man and beast and probably snapping a chain from its anchor plate. Today Gwenn and the oxen knew to stop.

She walked to the side of the field for a pickaxe. Karioki stepped to the front of the plow. Gwenn bent to lift the axe and felt blood flood her head. Dizzy, almost losing her sight as images swirled before her, she settled on a rock the mules had dragged to the edge of the field.

Gwenn closed her eyes and felt the life move in her belly. She wondered again what the baby would be like. Only three or four more weeks. In a fortnight she would accept the Penfolds' invitation and ride to Nanyuki to have the baby at the White Rhino. What luxury, she thought. But if she were away for a month, she worried what might happen to Cairn Farm. Anton had said he might come back and look after it, if he were still about. But she knew he would do it from affection, as a favor, not from love of farming. Failing that, Penfold would recommend one of the drifting soldiers who had not found a farm.

Her head cleared and Gwenn felt a light wind floating off the river behind her. She opened her eyes and gazed southeast, across the plain and beyond the Loldaika Hills to Mount Kenya. Already it was August. With the long rains finished, the crystal sky brought the mountain near. On its shoulders, dark belts of cedar and bamboo gave way to the snowy mantle that kept her Ewaso Ngiro fresh.

Sometime soon, Adam had told her, she might expect the elephants. Drifting down from the mountain forests, traversing streams stocked with rainbow trout, they would cross the European plantations and the patches of *shambas*, or native farms, and make their way to the plain. Usually they would journey in small groups or clans, but sometimes hundreds would pass in a few days.

Wandering northwest across the Laikipia Plateau, the elephants would pause at the Ewaso Ngiro, as a man might, for a drink and a bath. Quick learners, she was told, they usually avoided damaging the crops, knowing death might follow. But sometimes, if hungry or angry, they would destroy acres of maize in a single night. She hoped she would be here to see them.

Gwenn looked at the broad field beside her. The wide-horned brown oxen, bred from sturdy South African stock, stood motionless with Afrikaaner patience. Adam Penfold had sent them up to help open Cairn Farm. Already the oxen had taught Gwenn more than she had taught them. Each morning she helped adjust the yokes and chains and harnesses to ensure a straight even ox-pull. A faulty hitch, and the furrows would not be true. She looked at her hands and reminded herself to wear gloves.

Desperate to make the land hers, in the initial weeks without Alan she had risen before first light, rousted out the Kikuyu and staked out the day's plowing. Pressing all day, she saw harnesses snap and the oxen grow thinner. Karioki and the women grumbled that even working for Chura Nyakundu, the evil dwarf, would be better than this. At least the Yellow Frog never pursued them into the fields.

In time she had learned that the African day had a rhythm of its own. No matter how hard she pushed, or how late the start, at the end of the day the pace was always the same: one acre of heavy plowing before the shadows lengthened. If her attitude was unsympathetic, everything resisted: the Kikuyu, the oxen, even the land itself.

Karioki waited for her, patient as an old tree. The five Kikuyu women, assigned to clearing the turned earth of weeds and stones and branches, stood chatting a few yards back. Only she herself, Gwenn realized, was in a hurry. Fortunately, Kikuyu men were willing to help with the plowing itself, for even in the dignity of their traditional idleness, cattle had been their duty.

She stood and carried the pick to Karioki. In two days, she thought as he worked to free the blade, they could begin the cross-plowing. Some new farmers did not bother with this heavy chore, one of the mistakes Adam had made. Without it, the seeds would take, but the land would never be as aerated, as rich and healthy. Next, before the rolling, must come repeated disk harrowing, first six, then three inches deep, dragging angled rows of concave steel plates through the soil to break up the great blocks of earth thrown up by the breaking plow. Flax, she knew, required a fine tilth.

Late next month, or in early October, the first thirty acres would be ready to welcome the seed, twenty acres of the best land for flax, and ten for maize and beans and wheat. The flax seeds would have to be drilled in, not broadcast. The wheat would need less rain. Most of the year, the sheep and oxen could graze on wild grass. But in the dry seasons, they would need silage, stored green fodder, either lucerne grass or young mealie corn or, in time, fresh feed from an irrigated patch. Each cow or ox would need ten acres to support it. Each sheep, three.

She would require more seeds and tools, more animals and machinery. Raji da Souza had offered further credit through his friend Olivio Alavedo. "Anything to help with Cairn Farm," the kind barman said.

Most of all, however, Gwenn needed a farmer, a man who knew flax and the diseases of cattle and sheep. She knew this would never be Anton. She wondered what he would be like when he was older. Would he settle down? How would he make his living?

As the plow worked forward, Gwenn followed, making certain the furrow stayed true, wary lest Karioki ease the work by raising the blade. If the furrows were shallow or uneven, the precious rains of October and November would be trapped in shallow pans below the surface and the subsoil would never be rich. To reduce evaporation, she would have to till once more after a big rain.

At the end of the last line, Karioki turned for home, pausing by the river to water the oxen. Gwenn saw him wave to the women as they strolled back towards the farmhouse. The youngest girl lingered behind to wait for him. Gwenn walked slowly over the day's work, line by line, stooping and tossing away the odd branch or stone. Forty-two furrows, each six feet apart. None as perfect as Alan's cairns, but the best she could do this year.

Despite herself, she tasted the bitter anger that was in her. How could Alan abandon her and leave the struggle of life all to her? She caught herself, feeling a sense of guilt. She did not miss Alan as she should. And she worried too much about Anton, concerned to save him from the vengeance of Mick Reilly. Sometimes, though it made her angry with herself, she wanted Anton to be there just to feel his touch as they walked about the farm.

Gwenn stooped once more and felt a pain twist sharply through her. She gasped and fell to her knees. She dropped the stone and crawled to a patch of grass under the tamarind at the side of the field. There she collapsed beneath the tree and closed her eyes. A wave of pain seized her. For an hour or more she lay on her side, holding herself, knowing it was too soon, but feeling the urgent pain, followed by a calm as if her body was gathering itself. Then it was upon her.

She was losing her water. The baby. She rolled onto her back, knees raised, feet spread, toes pointing out. The pain left her. Cool sweat covered her. She drew calm long breaths, trying to remember what her Gran had done when her cousin had the baby without a midwife.

Waves of cramps seized her. Every muscle drew in to her center.

She felt the cords and tissues of her body act as if they were not her, some tightening like bonds, others stretching with magic elasticity. Beneath her the moisture soaked her skirt. She loosed the line about her waist and rolled from side to side to unwrap the skirt, spreading it beneath her like a sheet. She lay on her back and felt the bumps of the tamarind's pods and fruit through the cloth. Currents of pain folded over her, then receded and returned. Leaves and sunlight spun above her while she looked up through the pale grey branches and bright rounded leaves.

Suddenly she heard a rustling in the bush behind her. She panicked when she heard the branches part. Oh, God, I must reach the rifle.

Gwenn knew it was too late. The rifle was beyond her reach. She was barely sitting up, her head clearing, when she heard the snap of a branch and turned her upper body to face the danger.

"Gwenn-saab!" the Samburu woman said to her.

"Oh, Victoria, thank God it's you! Please help me to the house."

Victoria dropped an empty maize sack and knelt at Gwenn's feet. She gestured for Gwenn to lie back. She pulled off Gwenn's coarse petticoat and spread her legs apart. She touched Gwenn's belly with her hands and looked between her legs.

"No housie." Victoria shook her head. For an hour she sat by Gwenn and held her hand. Gwenn closed her eyes and felt bursts of pressure rising in her body like a pump. Dear God, it's coming.

Victoria knelt at Gwenn's feet and took one of Gwenn's hands in each of hers. Leaning back, the heavy woman pulled hard, forcing Gwenn to a sitting posture. Victoria stood and dragged Gwenn up until she squatted, her feet apart, her weight evenly balanced on heels and toes. She placed Gwenn's elbows on her knees and helped Gwenn clasp her hands before her. Then Victoria stood behind her, bracing her own legs against Gwenn's arching back. Gwenn closed her eyes and leaned against her friend.

Her mind swung between distant memories and sharp details of the scene around her. Gwenn thought of Queen Victoria. Unable at first to remember every Samburu name, Gwenn had named this new friend for her remarkable resemblance to Her Majesty. The same straightforward open eyes above puffy cheeks, the comfortable shape of the full round face, even the dignified carry of the solid body. And equally dependable.

Finally it came. Her body trembled and strained. The pain was forced aside by the vitality within her. Victoria gripped her shoulders. Gwenn pushed down with all her force. She pushed again and felt her body unhinge. Her hips spread. A tight smooth movement overwhelmed her.

Gwenn collapsed on her side as Vicky knelt and lifted the baby. Bending, the woman severed the cord with her teeth. She carried the child down to a shallow pool, slapped it twice, and bathed it in the failing sunlight.

A sturdy wail brought Gwenn back to consciousness. Vicky sat beside her and gave her the baby, swaddled in the rough maize sack. Gwenn's eyes were too full to see its gender, but she stroked its head and felt the curly hair.

"Big man," said Vicky when she hugged Gwenn's shoulder. "Very very bestie."

"I got worried when you didn't come to the White Rhino to have the baby," Anton said two weeks later as he unsaddled Rafiki near the shed. He regretted he had missed the birth. "So I thought I'd ride over and see how you were getting on, but I guess I'm a little late."

He knelt and rubbed the baby's tummy. Lying naked on an impala skin in the late-afternoon sun, the infant kicked his feet and opened his mouth. Anton noticed the red curls and green eyes.

"He's so beautiful," Anton said. "I'm sorry I wasn't here to help."

"That's all right. What could you have done?" Gwenn said lightly, careful not to show her delight at his return. "Vicky helped me."

Gwenn's hands were white to the wrists. Specks of curds dotted her hair. I must look hideous, she thought. She glanced at Anton and wondered if he'd been staying with Anunciata at the White Rhino.

"Do you like cream cheese?" Gwenn asked, businesslike, proud of her work. "It's not as easy to make as it looks. But it may be better to ship and sell than butter. The old farmers say butter should 'cut like soap and break like iron,' but ours is always too sour and hopelessly pale."

"Can I help?" Anton said, groaning to himself. He looked with dismay at the messy worktable. A pile of gummy white cloths covered one edge of the rough boards. Empty tin molds waited at the far end. If he wasn't careful, she'd turn him into a milkmaid. He sniffed the tall milk can. "Isn't this cream awfully sour?"

"It's meant to be a week old before you make the cheese," Gwenn said with annoyance. "Then you drain all but the last spoonful through a fine cloth that's folded over three times and let it stand another day before you add salt."

"What's wrong with the last spoonful?" Anton started to smile.

"The bottom's nothing but hard curds, of course. Spoils the cheese. Would you mind opening that cloth there? Just scrape everything into the middle."

"What's the baby called?" Anton rolled up his sleeves. He opened the sticky white rag and gingerly gathered the soft raw curds into the middle with the edge of his left hand.

"Wellington, because of his big nose. Not like that, Anton. Don't be a sissy. You have to get your hands into it." Gwenn noticed his arms. She cupped her hands around his and scraped the mess into the center. He let her hands guide him. For a moment their fingers joined in the sticky moist curds.

"Then you move it onto a clean cloth like this," she said, leaving his touch, "and fold the corners up tight and put a ten-pound weight on it. After it's been pressed for twelve hours you've got a lovely block of white curd. Would you mind going back to the river and getting a few ten-pound stones?"

"Wellington isn't a very good name for a farmer." Anton licked his thumb. "This needs a lot more salt."

Gwenn stopped working and brushed back her hair with white hands. Her lips tightened. More salt? She looked up at Anton with sparkling eyes.

"Maybe he'll be a big brave soldier." She put her hands on her hips. "Or perhaps, Anton Rider, a mighty hunter on horseback who wanders about by himself killing animals." She was certain he would leave again, and damned if she would press him to stay. "When are you going on safari?"

"I'd better get your ten-pound stones." Anton grinned and remembered Lord Penfold's advice: Never argue with a woman. He went to the river and rinsed his hands.

Why did she have to say that? Gwenn asked herself as she went over to pick up Wellie. If she acted like such an angry old shrew, he would never want to stay.

Anton walked back towards the shed carrying three shiny river stones. He paused a few yards away. Gwenn's blouse was open. Her full left breast was exposed, the nipple rosy and beaded with milk. Wellington mashed his face down into it, then set the curled fingers of his hands on either side and resumed drinking. Anton turned slightly aside.

"Oh, thank you." Gwenn smiled, aware that his eyes were on her. "Would you mind setting a stone on top of the cloth there?"

Anton passed her quickly as she continued.

"You might open up the first one, under that bag of nails there, and see if it's done. If the curd looks all right, just cut it into quarter-pound bits and stuff them into that tin mold."

Wellington raised his face and gurgled. Anton moved the nails and uncovered the block of raw curd. He took out his knife and gripped the spongy coagulated mass with one hand. If I knew my old choori was going to be used for this, he thought, I would've let that pig keep it.

"No, no, Anton, never cut cream cheese with a knife! Use that wooden paddle there."

"I promise I'll never do it again." Anton was unable not to grin. "I'd better get back to the hotel and see if I can help in the kitchen."

"If you make me laugh," Gwenn said, opening the right side of her blouse and shifting Wellington to her other breast, "he'll bite me."

"Gold!" Ernst von Decken closed his eyes and leaned back his head. "Gold."

The German's boots rested on his saddlebags. He passed the empty bottle of Gepard Farm schnapps to Anton.

"Gold's the answer," Ernst said, wiping his mouth on the back of his hand. "We could both use some. Farming's hopeless, even worse than you think. But for gold I need a Britisher partner, like you. Otherwise they won't let me dig my share here in Kenya."

"Gold?" said Anton, thrilled at the possibility. He looked across the hotel verandah to the brightening sky.

He had nothing to offer a woman now. Gold could be the way to make his fortune and still be free. Then perhaps one day he could be with Gwenn without living like a farm slave. But she'd been so infernally cool and prickly when he'd seen her last week. She hardly seemed to need him. Maybe, after the rape and Alan's death, she wanted some time without a man. Anton thought of her love for Cairn Farm, and the hellish drudgery that went with it. The grunt of snores rumbled from the bar behind him.

"Gold?" he asked Ernst.

"First they found gold in Matabeleland in 1867, so you Brits stole that from the kaffirs and made it Rhodesia," Ernst said with a snort. "Then, in '86, they found more in the Transvaal, so you stole that from the Boers and called it South Africa. Finally, before the war, we find the stuff in German East Africa. So now, with the League of Nations, you pinch that, including our own Gepard Farm, and call it Tanganyika. Today they're even finding gold in this wretched country."

"That's hard news about the farm. I hope your father's all right."

"It nearly killed him, but he's tougher than an old rhino. He's gone to Cairo. Says he'll try cotton," Ernst said. "The Englishmen have just emptied our farms. Sending us all home. But one day we Germans will be back. You'll see. Trouble is, Gepard Farm is home. They're selling off every German farm and business from Dar to Kilimanjaro, holding auctions at the old Kaiserhof Hotel. 'Enemy Property,' your British governor says. So let's run down to your Kenya goldfields, boy, and grab our share. Then we can buy back the old place in your name."

"You never told me there was gold. Where is it?"

"They've found new deposits, easier to work, on both sides of the border, near Lake Victoria. On our side, down by the Lupa River. On yours, over by Lolgorien. They say the gold's just lying about by the side of the streams. All you do is bend down with a pan and scoop it up, or make some barefoot Wanyamwesi bend down for you."

"Let's go! I'll come with you, but first you must come up-country with me while I help look after a friend's farm for a few weeks. You can do the shooting. There's good oryx and Grant and Tommy." Anton hesitated, hoping Ernst did not notice his confusion. "Have you fed your horse?"

"My horse doesn't eat."

"Does it drink?"

"Of course. Benzine. She's a *piki-piki,* an Excelsior motorcycle. Six and a quarter horsepower, twin cylinders, sidecar, three speeds, lamp, pump, tools, Dunlop studded treads, the whole parade. Ready to fly. When you grow up, you should get one."

"Arf, arf," Olivio said.

Moving slowly on his hands and knees, the dwarf rubbed his right shoulder against Kina's ebony leg. She reached down and took his short neck between her fingers, pinching hard and kneading the twisted muscles where they emerged from Lancelot's old leather dog collar. He recalled the hated whippet. "Arf, arf."

Olivio lowered his round head. Admiring the steep vaulted curves of her arches, he licked her feet, not tentatively with the tip of his tongue, but in the wide-tongued slavering manner of a drooling puppy. Even after the footbath, he thought, and months of the privilege of his most intimate attentions, this child of the bush could not lose the dusty scents of Africa. He pressed his mouth hard against the top of her foot and felt the firm lattice of young bones under her skin, and the soft elastic rise of the veins. He perspired as he considered the treasures that awaited him above. "Arf, arf."

What more could he do? Olivio asked himself, thinking of his enemies while his thick tongue lapped over the glistening skin. Beneath the moisture his eyes detected the tiny scratches of a thousand barefoot steps across the rocks and thorn branches of the village. He remembered the old Goan legend of the rock balanced above the gorge. With one touch from an honest man, the great stone would start to rock at the top of the hill before breaking loose and beginning to roll. Gathering speed, jarring and bouncing, it would crash down with the din of a rockfall, crushing his enemies like broken ants.

Already, the dwarf reflected, he had dislodged the stone. His letter to the lawyer was on the sea. Soon the steamship would tie up in the mouth of the Tagus at one of Lisbon's busy docks. The glorious Vasco da Gama himself had sailed for Goa from that very harbor!

The mail sack would be cast ashore and carried to the great city, with his letter burning inside it. The next morning his epistle would be on the desk of the lawyer, Dr. Gonçalo Barreto. Olivio's commitment to share the spoils with Barreto and the Church was contained therein, duly witnessed and notarized in Nairobi. Inside it, too, was the reference to the late archbishop's confessional diaries, safely stored in the sacred archives of Sé Cathedral in Lisbon. There the holy men should find the confirmation of his ancestry.

Satisfied that at least the tops of Kina's toes were licked clean, Olivio pressed the side of his face against the prickly mat. He took one big toe in his mouth. The large toes were the only ones he was able to take into his mouth when she stood, for their tips turned up slightly. All the others curled down against the floor. He sucked and bit hard just above the nail. Kina jerked violently on Lancelot's old leash. She screamed and lifted Olivio's upper body off the ground as the collar bit into his Adam's apple. The dwarf gave a choking cry and his face turned red.

27

These are the bones of my farm." Adam Penfold pointed his
thorn stick at a thicket of abandoned tools and machinery in a gully
near the White Rhino. "Some days I think I would've done better
planting raspberries over the ruins of Carthage, salt and all. Maybe
we don't belong in Africa." Penfold wondered when he might see
England again.

He led Anton and Ernst to a rusting cultivator.

"This cemetery is the harvest of fifteen years of experimental farming out here, trying to make friends with these dear highlands."
Penfold gestured with his staff. "Each scrap of metal cost me a few
more acres of Wiltshire. But most of it was my own silly mistakes,
and who could leave? Every time Sissy asks me to pack up, I close
my eyes and smell the air. Then duty calls, and it's back to the bar
for a double."

"Your English friends didn't mind pushing my father off his farm."
Ernst grunted.

"What's this?" Anton poked about, examining the coffee pulpers
and hullers, the Dingo Cream Separator, the Rutherford Disc
Weeder and the Kirstin Stump Puller.

"That's one of my favorites, a genuine Alfa Laval Coffee Sheller,"
Penfold said. "But after the cutworms ate the beans, we tried to
make it do everything except what it was built for. Finally, the boys

bent all the blades and here she is. On a good day that old Dingo there used to skim fifteen gallons an hour."

"Couldn't some of this be used again?" Anton asked. "Perhaps we could take something useful up to Gwenn." He was keen to see her.

"There's no room in my sidecar for this rubbish," Ernst said.

"We might send her the Speedo Flax Scutcher and my Myers Pump. That's a nice piece," Penfold said. "And I'm giving the disabled lads whatever they want. Some of them passed by this morning in old trek wagons. What a sight. The march of the damned. Be a proper miracle if they make it. They carted off my best machine, the Defiance Windmill, missing a blade or two, of course."

"Time to go, my boy." Ernst gripped Anton's shoulder. "I hate the smell of a dying farm, and I'm too old for a night in the bush without a tent and a cook and a couple of young women."

The three men walked back to the hotel. Ernst checked over the Excelsior. The front mudguard gone, but otherwise complete and gleaming, the machine had Ernst's pack and saddlebags lashed behind his seat above the spare spoked wheel.

Anton was daydreaming about Gwenn, seeing her looking cross, with her shirt open and curds in her hair. He was startled when Anunciata stepped down from the verandah and met him by the side of the hotel. He knew she realized where he was going. Still drawn to her, he stiffened when she rubbed one hand along his chest and kissed him on the lips, holding her body against his.

"*Vai com Deus,* Blue Eyes, my strong boy." Anunciata stood back and looked into his eyes uncertainly.

Ernst swung a leg over the bike and kicked the engine to life. Anton squeezed into the sidecar beside the two German rifles. Penfold handed him his pack. The machine growled and spat exhaust.

"With no mudguard up front," Ernst said loudly to Anton while he drew on his leather-rimmed aviator goggles, "you'll wish you had a pair of fine German lenses. No more blue eyes for you, my young Engländer."

Olivio approached from the hotel with quick small steps. Behind him came a kitchen boy carrying a sack that trembled and jumped on his shoulder.

"Hens!" Olivio said breathlessly. "Four living chickens for dear

Mrs. Llewelyn. Tell her, Mr. Anton, that whatever she requires, perhaps we can provide. Give her this note, for credit at the Indian *duka*. The store is so very miserable, but they have some things to use."

Olivio tied the noisy bag onto the sidecar behind Anton.

Ernst lowered his boot on the accelerator bar. The Excelsior rolled. The kitchen boy clapped. Guests raised glasses and waved from the verandah.

"Tell Gwenn she's welcome whenever she likes, baby and all. The old crib is waiting," Adam Penfold called after them. "It's never been used," he added in a lower voice.

"If these chicks make it," said Ernst, "I'll pretend I'm a Britisher and rooster them myself." The bike moved down the dusty trail.

"*Guter Gott!* The English cripples!" Ernst screamed several hours later into the roar of the engine. The Excelsior skidded fast around a bend. A broad riverbed opened before them, its high bank only yards away. Anton squinted into the dust. He saw murky water and damp sand cluttered with a chaos of broken-down wagons, unhitched ox teams and struggling men.

The sidecar bounced on the arching root of a fig tree. Ernst braked and downshifted. Wheels spinning, the bike slid sideways off the crumbling riverbank. Anton was flung from his seat as the prow of the sidecar flipped over and the Excelsior crashed upside down into the water.

Stunned, Anton sat in the mud-like sand and saw the sack of chickens float downstream. Its passengers thrashed violently while the filthy bag settled into the river. A man reached after it and hurled the bag onto a patch of sand.

"Looks like you needed a bath, son," said a one-legged soldier. He extended a hand to help Anton stand in the shallow water. The man's crutch sank deeper into the sandy bottom as he helped Anton up. "The lads call me Captain Jos. I saw you at the White Rhino."

Beside them half a dozen men were flipping the Excelsior back onto its wheels. Ernst spat and groaned when Anton bent over him.

"You've done it. Damn thing's kaput." Ernst ran his fingers along his right collarbone. "The swine English have got me at last. Four years of hellish campaigning, and every handsome bone still together.

BARTLE BULL 289

Now I break my neck trying not to crash into their wandering hospital."

Anton helped Ernst up the far bank. There the syndicate's doctor sat waiting in his Scotch cart. A grimy white cross was painted on its side. Drawn by four mules, the light wagon must have crossed the ford before the first overloaded vehicle bogged down.

Beside the doctor, Anton saw a stout green and orange parrot, its cage bound to the seat. Pecking with a curved yellow beak, fluttering short wings against the sides of its prison, the bird cleaned the underside of its feathers. Behind the parrot a man lay on a padded stretcher that was trussed to the medical chests on either side of him. Long-legged and lean as a gibbet, the doctor stepped down from the cart.

"It seems our sick parade is never closed." The doctor sighed, introducing himself to his new patient. "I'm Fitzgibbons. Medical Officer, Second Lanc's."

"Captain von Decken, Third Field Company, Schutztruppe." Ernst clicked his heels feebly and ducked his chin while he kept his good arm around Anton's shoulder.

"My friend's broken his collarbone," Anton said.

"Unless you are a trained surgeon, young fellow, Dr. Fitzgibbons shall perform the diagnosis himself," the doctor whispered. He lifted the knife from Anton's belt and with one stroke slit the German's shirt through the collar and down his back. "Unload these chests. Cover them with a blanket, and lay this idiot motor racer on his big belly."

Anton obeyed and dashed down to the river to recover the rifles from the water. All around him men and animals toiled in the stream. He made certain the Excelsior was safely up the bank and then returned to the doctor. He thought of Gwenn and wondered how long this would delay them.

"Can I help?" Anton observed Ernst's pointed bone pricking into the skin of his shoulder like toes under a blanket.

"You look better suited to working with the four-legged oxen." Fitzgibbons returned Anton's knife and trembled as a cough echoed in his thin chest. He sat on the metal step of the cart and put both hands across his mouth. Coughing tore the doctor uncontrollably.

"Excuse me," Fitzgibbons said after it passed. He wiped his face on his sleeve and glanced down at his German patient. "Your mustard gas. 'The breeze of Passchendaele,' we used to call it. Now, boy, hop down to the river and ask Bevis to give me a hand. He's the only one-armed chap who still looks clean. Even though your fat friend's a Hun, we'll do our best to mend him."

"Halt the Hun! Halt the Hun!" the parrot cried.

"Never mind Kaiser," the doctor said. "He only has two speeches."

"How dare you name your filthy bird after the Emperor!" Ernst lifted his head. His eyes stared while Fitzgibbons pressed a chloroform pad over his mouth and nose.

"Better have Bevis bring along one of the stronger chaps, too," the doctor said. "I'm going to stretch your friend a bit, and he may not like it, but it's better than cutting him open and making a worse mess. He's untidy enough as it is."

"Cut it off! Cut it off!" cried Kaiser.

All afternoon, while the doctor attended to Ernst and his other patients, Anton helped the disabled soldier settlers empty seven heavy trek wagons and double-team the fittest of the oxen. With thirty-two animals and a dozen men straining into the pull, the wagons were hauled from the swampy riverbed like stones to the pyramids.

The reloaded wagons were drawn up in two neat lines. The Transport Officer checked each one and made certain the animals were fed. Anton watched him work down the picket line in the shading light, examining yoke galls and harness sores, often bending to run his hand down an animal's legs. Already the tents were up, the lanterns lit, the rifles pitched like tepee poles. From time to time Anton saw men make their way to the doctor's cart.

Anton sat on the ground beside Ernst, cleaning the two hunting rifles. Wrapped in a blanket, the German rested in a camp chair. His left arm was in a sling belted across his stomach. His head was braced back against a tree. His mouth was open. Occasionally he gave a choking grunt.

"Quartermaster!" Jocelyn said. "Good news. We've a mule with a broken leg. Cut him up and pitch him in the stew. Make sure you save the hide."

"Right, Cap'n Jos," the cook said. A single shot echoed across the camp. "Do we use the brains and tripe?"

"We've swallowed worse'n that, matey." A Tommy looked up from a game of cards. The man's black eyepatch glinted in the firelight while he passed around a bottle of Navy rum.

"Chuck in the chicks," another man said.

"Sorry, sir," Anton said. "They're a present for a friend. I'll shoot some meat tomorrow."

Hungry, Anton smelled the odor of beans and meat and onions blending with the wood smoke. The men spooned thick stew and wild spinach into dented tin soup plates. The chatter of spoons scraping dishes carried across the camp. Reluctant to take more than his share, Anton looked up at the night sky. The cough of a distant leopard reminded him of the Aberdares and Karioki.

He rose and brought a plate of food for Ernst. He touched his friend's arm. The German woke with a snort.

"Ach! What has your English butcher done to me." Ernst groaned. "Find me a drink, boy, while I eat this mess."

"If I were a butcher, Captain," a voice sighed from the shadows, "you'd be in the pot."

"Where the Kraut belongs. Then we'd have plenty to eat," the man with the eyepatch said, passing the rum to Ernst.

The one-eyed man walked to a tent and returned with an accordion.

"I found this in one of your trenches," he said to Ernst with a slight smile. "It was the only thing that didn't stink. Join us, or give us a song yourself. What'll it be, lads?"

" 'Waltzing Matilda,' " voices answered, and the men began to sing.

Anton thought of gypsy guitars and Lenares and the old songs and tales of distant fires. His eyes glistened in the fire sparkle. He felt Ernst watching him and winked at his friend.

"Your turn to sing for your supper," the man with the eyepatch said to Ernst.

"I know only one song." Ernst buttoned his dirty collar with his right hand.

Anton was surprised to hear melancholy in the German's voice. Ernst gripped Anton's shoulder and pulled himself to his feet with a groan. He stepped back from the fire and passed one hand over the stubble on his scalp.

" 'Haya Safari,' General von Lettow's marching song of the Schutztruppe," Ernst announced. He raised his chin.

Silence took the camp. The British soldiers looked at each other. Fitzgibbons suppressed a cough. Anton listened for the leopard but heard only the shuffling of oxen and the whistling screams of a tree hyrax. Tomorrow he would see Gwenn.

"*Tunakwenda, tunashinda,*" Ernst began in a hearty singsong.

> *Tunakwenda, tunashinda,*
> *Askari wanaendesha,*
> *Tunakwenda, tunashinda . . .*

"Gives more milkee, Gwenn-saab, if hands are warm." Vicky bathed her hands in the stream of urine that steamed from the cow in the cool morning air.

Gwenn copied her when the other bony Samburu cow relieved itself in sympathy. Holding gourds in their left hands, the two women massaged the teats and began to milk.

Thirty yards behind them, where the Samburu moran had found water, a well was set in a hole eight feet deep, surrounded by a wall of thorn branches. The young moran stood in the well, water to his waist, passing up leather buckets to two boys who emptied them into a hollow-log trough outside the fence. Cattle and donkeys and goats jostled and waited to drink. Two camels sat patiently, chewing with expressions of condescension. Ropes were bound around their knees and forelegs to prevent them rising.

"One day, Victoria, we'll have good cows on Cairn Farm," Gwenn said. "Friesians. If we're lucky, they'll have a dash of Jersey to make the butter yellow. The cream'll be rich enough to bend your spoon, as my Gran used to say, and we'll turn Wellie into a butterball."

Swaddled in an old army blanket, braced against a locust tree, Wellington Llewelyn kept his green eyes on the two women. He ignored the distant spectacle of the mist clearing from Mount Kenya. Two months old, he sported curly red hair and two deep dimples. His prominent nose twitched when he smelled the fresh warm milk. He swung two chubby arms and called for attention.

Late in the afternoon, with the gourd in one hand and a heavy hoe in the other, Gwenn walked home to find Anton and Wellington.

Anton had been back at the farm for a week, but sometimes he seemed more interested in Wellie than in her.

Gwenn paused to scrape the mud from her boots with the hoe. Anton's clear voice, slowly reading *David Copperfield*, reached her through the thornbushes. She stopped to listen, forgetting her fatigue. Her face softened.

> *The warriors of poetry and history march on in stately hosts that seem to have no end. . . . bring to my mind the boy I was myself, when I first came there. That little fellow seems to be no part of me; I remember him as something left behind upon the road of life—as something I have passed, rather than have actually been—and almost think of him as of some one else.*

He read as if he knew each word.

Gwenn went forward until she saw them. Karioki lay on his side, his eyes closed, a shotgun beside him. Anton's foot touched Karioki's shoulder. Anton sat with his other leg crossed under him and his back against the tamarind tree. Wellington Llewelyn lay asleep on Anton's lap, his curls a mess, the Dickens resting on his stomach, a brittle seed pod broken open in his hands. Blue morning glories grew on thin creepers in the bushes behind them.

Why can't it always be like this? Gwenn thought.

> *And the little girl I saw on that first day . . . where is she? Gone also.*

Gwenn stepped into the clearing with her forefinger to her lips. Anton grinned and continued to read.

> *Am I in love again? I am. I worship the eldest Miss Larkins.*

What an unusual young man, Gwenn thought, noticing, as she did every day, the startling blue eyes against his sun-browned skin. Cairn Farm seemed alive when he was here. Soon he would be gone and she would be alone again, for the November rains were nearly over and Ernst was fit to travel. If only the three men would stay, she

The White Rhino Hotel

might really have a farm. Was that the only reason she wanted them to remain?

Thanks to Penfold's help and Goan money, Karioki had brought merino sheep and Friesian cattle from Nanyuki, though recently he was spending more time with Victoria's friend Alberta than with the animals. Even Ernst was helping. With one hand he had planted Anton's precious sisal bulbs in the experimental plot behind the bungalow, grouching and complaining while he worked. Each day before the rains came, Ernst directed the field work in a loud voice. At first the Africans resented him, as Gwenn might have, but now they took him as he was.

When the days were clear, Anton helped Gwenn and the Kikuyu women plant the flax. When it rained he cut and trimmed posts for the dairy shed. But at the end of one long day she was saddened to overhear his words to Ernst.

"I'll never be a farmer," Anton had said.

Today was the first day without rain in three weeks, but Gwenn could see deep clouds darkening Mount Kenya.

Anton closed his Dickens, pressing between its pages an orange flower with a black center. Immediately the baby complained.

"Soon Wellie won't go to sleep unless you're reading *David Copperfield*," Gwenn said. She heard the first thunder grumble over the mountain.

"Soon I'll be teaching him duck-on-a-rock," Anton said.

"Teatime." Gwenn picked up her son and pressed her nose into his tummy. Wellie giggled and kicked when she kissed him. She loved his unresisting affection, the smell of his new skin and the comfort of snuggling with him. But sometimes she craved a different touch.

They walked along the Ewaso Ngiro towards the bungalow, passing the cairns and watching the torrent that reached near the top of the riverbank. They approached the house and found Ernst, rifle in hand, staring across the river. Gwenn came up to him with her son. The German pointed across the water.

Downstream, she saw them. An open motorcar, three horsemen and four Africans on foot. Gwenn felt herself grow cold.

"It's your degenerate allies," Ernst said to Anton. "That oily Portuguese cardsharp and his pack of Irishmen. Must be out figuring whose land to steal. Let's pray they try to cross. If the crocs don't chew on them, they'll wash up in Somaliland."

"I'm not worried about them," Gwenn said, determined to save Anton from more trouble with the Reillys. She felt her hatred return. "They've no business with me." Gwenn wondered if she would be alone when they returned.

In a few moments the party passed from sight. Would she be able to cope with them on her own?

Gwenn served tea to her friends. Their camp chairs rested on the earthen floor under the thick thatched roof of the verandah. A surrounding trench drained off the rains. Gwenn saw Mount Kenya disappear in the distance as grey curtains of water stabbed down from the black sky. She remembered Reilly at the camp in Nairobi, threatening to see her often when he came north.

"As soon as the rains break," Anton said without looking at Gwenn, but thinking he must get her some protection, "I'll ride over to the disabled chaps' farm and find someone to help look after things here." He glanced at her. "Perhaps you'll join me?"

Gwenn lay in bed and swung Wellie's hammock by pulling on a cord. She heard Ernst and Anton talking by the fire.

"Gold . . . Lake Vic . . . Lolgorien . . . Excelsior . . . Anunciata" were words that reached her. Anunciata? Could Anton really like this woman? Anunciata must be even older than I am, Gwenn thought, annoyed by her own jealousy. Gwenn listened to the sky rage above the mountain. Still Cairn Farm was dry.

Why was Anton always so shy with her? Perhaps he thought she was too old and serious.

"Tlaga," she heard Karioki say with alarm, "the water is coming. Is everything on tall ground?"

Gwenn pulled on her boots and drew a long shirt over her nightdress. She found the three men standing by the riverbank in the darkness. Ernst held a burning stick aloft. The river rushed past near their feet. The debris of the bush littered its surface.

They heard a gathering sound in the distance upstream, like the growing roar of an advancing locomotive. It became steadily louder until it filled the night.

Suddenly it was upon them. A wall of water raged along the riverbank like the blade of a giant plow. Anton grabbed Gwenn from behind and pulled her to higher ground. The floodwater flashed past them, two, three feet above the river's surface, sliding on top of it like an independent force, tumbling stumps and tree trunks on its crest.

The rainstorm burst. Ernst's torch went out. The four figures, speechless, listened to the water. Aware of him, her clothes and body wet, Gwenn felt Anton's arms still around her, pressing her breasts. She leaned against him. His rain-soaked body stuck to hers as if they were one. She put her hand over his and shut her eyes, for a moment forgetting the farm.

"Tlaga, behind the house!"

Gwenn heard another roar of water behind them. Anton released her and they stumbled back to the bungalow. Ernst seized a fresh brand from the smoking fire. They stepped behind the building. There, climbing the slope towards them, Gwenn saw the river.

"We're on an island!" Ernst said. "The river's broken its bank and filled the old donga!"

Calmer, shortcutting the oxbow, the divided river flowed steadily and swiftly against its new banks, leaving the bungalow and the campfire like a raft floating in its center.

"Time for a coffee?" Gwenn asked, forcing a smile, feeling the rain cool on her face.

"Time for Gepard Farm schnapps." Ernst settled down by the smoldering fire with the last bottle from his pack. "On our plantation, in German Africa, we never put up with this sort of nonsense."

— 28 —

Work for women, Tlaga." Karioki shook his head. "Even a white boy must not work on his knees." He stood and watched Anton labor with his hands and a trowel in the high ground behind Gwenn's bungalow.

"For this, I, Karioki Kitenji, son of a chief, have taught you to hunt?"

"Soon it'll be your turn, my friend." Anton glanced up with a sweaty face. "After I leave, I want my brother Karioki to stay and look after Mrs. Llewelyn."

"For you, Tlaga, I may do this, but my hands will not touch the earth."

"Just make sure she and Wellie are safe."

"Yes, you have my blood on that. That white boy needs a man to teach him, or he will be helpless in the bush, like you, and will work on his knees with the women. And it is true, there are many *bibis* here who need Karioki." He shook a finger at a passing Kikuyu woman. The young lady raised her chin and ignored the attention.

"Thankfully none of them is ten years old."

"Have no fear, Tlaga, the little bibis, too, will come with gifts when they learn Karioki is here."

"Boys' talk?" Gwenn came up behind Anton with a picnic and the twelve-gauge as Karioki walked away grinning. "What are you planting?"

"A surprise for my hostess. Apple trees from Germany. A present

from Ernst's father. They're still a bit young, but I wanted them in
before I left for the goldfields." Anton felt her silence. "One day
you must plant pears, and garlic.

"When you and I get back from the disabled soldiers' farm, Ernst
and I are off," he continued, regretting the words as he heard himself
say them. He felt as if he had already left. Would Gwenn be safe?
Or perhaps it was because he didn't want to leave her. Was he stupidly
walking away from what he wanted?

Gwenn knelt beside him without replying, determined not to urge
Anton to stay, hoping he would do so on his own. She watched him
work.

Anton scooped out another small, perfectly square basin in the
moist earth. He eased a seedling out of the wooden box and settled
it in place before patting in more soil. Eighteen young plants sat in
neat rows, each nestled with straw and surrounded by a small circle
of raised earth. All were protected by a chicken-wire perimeter. One
wall of the fence was the chicken run itself. Olivio's handsome red
hens, fatter and more quarrelsome since the arrival of Adam, the
leghorn rooster, were guarded from small predators by a cage of
doubled wire set into the ground.

"Why are you making the holes square?" she asked, annoyed by
her own bossiness. "They should be round."

"These are Mr. von Decken's instructions," Anton said, careful
not to argue directly. He took a crumpled note from his shirt pocket
and handed it to Gwenn with dirty fingers.

"*Be certain to make each hole square*," she read aloud, admiring the
formal lettering of Hugo von Decken's German hand. "*If the holes
are round, the roots will grow inside them in circles. If square, the roots
will reach into the corners and then work their way out into the earth
and grow strong. Do this well, my young English hunter, even if you are
not yet a farmer, and my apple trees will see your grandchildren.*" Gwenn
felt herself blush.

"Time to go," Anton said abruptly, standing and stretching his
back. He picked up his Merkel, wrapped in gazelle hide, and led
Gwenn across the crude bridge that now connected the bungalow
to the rest of Cairn Farm. The trunks of two tall fever trees spanned
the river. A walkway of branches was nailed into their yellow bark.

Anton had examined the river again that morning. On the other side of the bungalow, the old bed of the Ewaso Ngiro was drying and silting up. For the present, until it disappeared, a small oxbow lake separated the house from the land to the east. He saw a family of weavers at work near the water. They hovered frantically with twigs in their beaks while they built a hanging nest suspended from the limb of a fig tree. What fine farmers these tireless birds would make.

Gwenn folded back the canvas cover of the Excelsior while Anton checked the petrol and tires. She fastened a fresh impala carcass to the pillion, a present for the disabled settlers. Then she tied a scarf over her hair and pulled on Ernst's goggles before climbing into the sidecar.

They rode north across the ocean-like plain. Seeing new country, Anton felt alive with the wind and the engine's roar. The distant rim of the Lerogi Plateau brightened in the crisp light of morning.

A troop of baboons was feeding in the red oak grassland to their right. Seated as at a tea party, they ate with careful fingers, leisurely devouring the pink and white flowers that rose fresh after the rain.

Even at low speeds the Excelsior bounced and bucked while Anton avoided the worst stones and brush. The life of the bush parted before them like fish before the prow of a ship. Coveys of francolin darted away close to the ground. Zebras cantered off, raising dust, then turned to watch. Hares and duiker leapt aside. White-bellied bustard, gooselike, honked twice and rose heavily into the air. Farther away, Anton saw the heads of three giraffe peering towards them in curiosity. He slowed and pointed. Gwenn nodded and smiled up at him. Gaining speed close alongside a patch of acacias, ducking to miss the thorny branches, Anton grinned and held up one thumb when the heads of the giraffe rocked on their long mottled stalks.

Anton saw two kori bustard, several feet from beak to tail, dashing away in an elegant fury of grey and black feathers. Laboriously, like overloaded aircraft, the birds flapped along in the path of the bike and accelerated into a long takeoff, leaving the ground when Anton and Gwenn came to them.

In an hour they approached a layered stone hillside. Its edge rose above the thickening bush like a stack of grey plates. Anton braked and turned to Gwenn. Both her cheeks were bleeding just below the goggles. Fragments of wait-a-bit thorn branch clung to her face, a few hooks caught in the skin. Anton knelt by the sidecar as Gwenn removed the goggles.

"Sorry," he said. "It's my fault."

Gwenn smiled and looked at him and shook her head.

He drew the curved thorns from her skin one by one. Fresh beads of bright blood rose in the line of wounds. Anton remembered the thorn cuts on his own stomach. "Outdoors is best," Anunciata had told him.

He tore off his shirttail and wiped Gwenn's face with water from the canteen. His face close when he touched her cheek and found her blood on his hands, Anton was distracted by the open look in her green eyes.

"Thank you." Gwenn leaned in the seat and kissed him on his dusty cheek, pressing her lips firmly against him.

Anton flushed, eager to embrace her, but Gwenn climbed out with the picnic. Together they climbed the grey and tan rocks. The wind was rising while the day warmed.

Gwenn shook out her hair in the breeze. Anton watched her, remembering her hair blowing when the surfboat crashed in to the beach at Kilindini. He filled his lungs and recognized the dusty-clean scent he had first caught one night in the crow's nest over the Indian Ocean. Turning slowly, shielding his eyes with both hands, he gazed across the land.

"I wonder what's behind those hills."

That was the trouble, she thought, looking at Anton and understanding where his wandering eyes led him. She knew he wanted to be with her, even if he didn't know it, but he didn't want a farm. He wanted Africa.

They sat and picnicked in a smooth sandy depression near the crown of the rock, smelling the pungent yellow flowers that grew out of sand-filled fissures in its surface. They laughed and spoke of Wellie and Karioki, Olivio and Adam Penfold, but not of Anton's departure or the problems of the farm. As they talked, Anton kept thinking of Gwenn's kiss, uncertain what she felt, but determined not to lose the moment.

He had to touch her.

Anton set his hand against her cheek and felt the line of small wounds against his palm. He moved his hand to the back of her neck and slipped his fingers upwards through her hair. Gwenn closed her eyes at the touch. She arched her neck and put her head back to feel his fingers harder on her scalp.

Suddenly they heard an agitated movement near the rock below them. Anton and Gwenn crawled to the edge and looked down.

Almost human, a family of six long-legged red monkeys was gathered together protectively. The two adults stood on hind legs, using their stiffened tails for support. They peered through the bush from their full height. The female, perhaps half the size of the male, clutched a small lizard in one hand. The male ascended into an acacia. His ruff stiffened with alarm. He stared forth like a lookout in a crow's nest. His small rounded ears flattened against his head. His close-set eyes glared out from under long black brows. He bared his canines and jumped down with a shrill scream. The female led the young monkeys off while the father drove his family before him.

"Could be a leopard," Anton whispered. Too late, Hugo von Decken's first rule flashed through his mind: always carry a rifle or shotgun in the bush.

Wary, Anton led Gwenn down to the base of the rock. They jumped onto the sandy ground and heard a vicious snarling from the location of the motorbike.

With one hand on his knife and the other holding a stone, Anton stole forward, keeping Gwenn behind him. At first, fixing on the massive heads, he thought they were hyena. Then he saw the large round ears and long slender legs. Wild dogs.

Five of the wolf-like animals, perhaps two and a half feet at the shoulder and sixty pounds, snapped and snarled around the bike. Anton's rifle had been pulled from the sidecar. Its gazelle-skin wrapping was in shreds. Three dogs, lean-bodied, with short coarse coats, wrenched and tore while they fought to devour the hide. Two others ripped into the canvas covering of the impala carcass that was lashed to the pillion. Anton saw bits of meat and blood on their black lips. Frenzied and upwind, they had not yet smelled Gwenn and Anton.

Finding her at his side, Anton took four shotgun shells from Gwenn's pocket. He gave her his knife. Hollering loudly, hitting one dog with his stone, Anton ran in among the animals. He leapt into the sidecar and stood on the seat while he loaded the shotgun. The startled dogs gave a rolling muffled bark and backed away, their

heads bobbing slightly while they examined the intruders. They
rushed in and Anton fired both barrels. Two dogs fell. The survivors
fled into the bush.

Anton loaded the Merkel while Gwenn climbed into the sidecar.
The dogs, now ten or twelve strong, hung at the edges of the clearing,
snarling and repeating a soft howling call, rallying the pack. Several
dashed forward close to the bike when Anton started the engine.

At first intimidated, the animals kept back when the Excelsior
began to move. Anton pushed the bike hard, hoping to pull away
and discourage the pack. He passed his diklo and the two shells to
Gwenn. She reloaded the shotgun and tied the kerchief across her
face.

The ground was torn by gullies and projections of low shelf-like
rock. Wherever there was soil, it nourished low thorn scrub and
stunted acacias. Anton slowed, fearing speed would disable or flip
the bike.

In a few moments Anton heard the dogs above the engine. Yipping
in excitement, not yet in sight, the pack hunted them through the
bush. Anton looked back and saw the wild dogs, strangely beautiful,
streaking splotches of brown and yellow and black, forty or fifty of
them, streaming through the bush on a broad front. Heads low,
tongues out, they ran on long thin legs. Bushy white-tipped tails
flowed after them.

The motorbike emerged into more open country. Anton accelerated to twenty-five or thirty miles an hour. The dogs stretched
behind in an extended line, keeping pace fifty or sixty yards back.
In the fore, a few animals strained, working to exhaust their prey.
Anton glanced back, remembering stories of wild dogs pulling down
lion, becoming their only enemy once the great cats grew aged or
infirm. Gwenn turned around in the wildly bouncing sidecar. She
held on with one hand and leaned far back over the pillion to cut
the impala free with Anton's knife. The carcass fell behind them,
bouncing and rolling from the canvas just as the first dogs
reached it.

For a moment their lead extended. The first ten or fifteen dogs
paused in a roiling knot and devoured the antelope. A few tore at
the meat-scented canvas. The others ran on.

Anton looked ahead, seeking to avoid the rough ground. He drove

in a long curve, aiming for a gap between two kopjes. Under him
he felt the old bike complain. Like a tiring horse, he thought. A
grating chatter joined the steady roar of the engine. He saw Gwenn's
sidecar wobble and vibrate as if it sought to pull away and go on a
journey of its own. Running on the worst tire, it took a jarring beating
with every bump and stone. The main connecting strut, rewelded
twice and damaged again by the river crash, was straining at the joint,
the metal shell of the sidecar slightly torn where it met the body of
the motorbike. Anton feared it might pull loose.

He looked over his shoulder and saw the feeding dogs rejoin the
others. From the back of the pack a dozen broke away, cutting across
country for the narrow gap between the rocks. Gwenn checked her
gun and took off the safety.

Forced to slow by a field of rocks, Anton knew the dogs were
gaining. The leaders were thirty or forty yards back. He saw the
flanking pack dash on to his right to cut them off. The bike roared
up to the kopjes. There was no clear ground between the two piles
of boulders. He slowed. The flanking pack was soon beside them.
The lead dog galloped abreast of Gwenn. Its legs pumped like pis-
tons. Its tongue hung out. With every stride the bones of its shoulders
rose sharp against its mottled coat. Used to tearing open the belly
of its running prey, the beast came in close, its eyes staring and its
long mouth open.

Anton slowed. The motorbike smashed the dog aside when it
skidded across the flat stone platform that connected the two kopjes.
Anton struggled to recover control and keep the bike moving. Three
dogs, tangled together like one creature as they attacked, threw
themselves against the sidecar. Gwenn fired the shotgun.

The head of one dog was blown from its neck. The stump fell
away. Gwenn pulled the second trigger. The two other animals fell
in the path of their followers. The sidecar trembled while the Excelsior accelerated and emerged into a field of coarse wild grass.

Two Europeans mounted on mules stood in the center of the field.
Behind them flowed the Ewaso Ngiro. Tents and roughly thatched
buildings rose two hundred yards to the left.

Anton braked and jumped off with the rifle. The slavering animals
hesitated and hung back. He fired twice. Two dogs fell. The pack
scattered into the bush.

"Did you have a nice ride over?" Captain Jos looked down from his mule. Dr. Fitzgibbons was mounted beside him. A handkerchief held to his mouth, the surgeon nodded a greeting, coughing painfully while Jos continued. "You're pretty sharp with that rifle. I used to be an instructor, but I was never that quick."

"It was lovely country," Anton said, "but the impala we brought you got eaten on the way. And the piki-piki took a beating."

"We all take a beating in Africa, my boy, but maybe it's worth it." Jos looked at Gwenn as she removed her goggles and bandanna. Her shining eyes were set in an oval of clear skin surrounded by layered red dust.

Gwenn breathed deeply and steadied herself before she rose, annoyed by the trembling of her hands. She couldn't believe how much Africa took out of you, how hard it all was. She wiped her face with the inside of the cloth, feeling the crusty scabs, and remembered Anna on the train drawing patterns on her sister's dusty face.

Gwenn glanced at Anton. Already at ease, he seemed happy and excited like a boy stepping from a cricket pitch between innings. With some help, she thought, she might just take care of the farming, but how could she ever deal with all these physical horrors by herself, without a man? It was a life, she realized, that neither a man nor a woman could manage on their own. She must think about Wellie and their future, and how to build something better than they could have had at home.

"Afternoon, ma'am," Jos said, touching his hat. He dismounted and offered Gwenn his hand as she stepped from the sidecar. "We're all terribly sorry about your husband's accident. Let us know how we can help."

"Thank you. I was hoping to find someone to help with the farm."

"Maybe I can find a man for you. As it is, we've too many officers here giving each other orders, and no rankers to carry 'em out. Right now they're all busy chasing down an ant bear. We'll have to cook him tonight instead of your impala."

"What's an ant bear?" Gwenn asked.

"An aardvark, an enormous anteater that's been tearing up our fields. We've had eight boys digging out his burrow since dawn. They've dug a twenty-foot furrow, some of it ten feet deep, but so far all we've seen is a ruddy great tail pitching dirt in our faces. Would've saved a few backs if we'd had him digging trenches in Flanders."

Soldiers and Africans were gathered in a noisy circle near the camp. A few women and children, white and black, were scattered among them. Anton took Gwenn's arm. They joined the throng and saw two men digging feverishly with shovels at the end of the furrow. A cheer rose and children screamed when a massive tail and two clawed feet were exposed, hurling earth behind them. A man seized the tail and two others grabbed the first man's legs. The animal scrambled deeper, pulling the men after it. The first man was soon in the burrow up to his waist. Choking and coughing, he let go. Two fresh men took the shovels. Again the hind legs appeared. Two men rushed forward and tied a rope to each leg. With ten men hauling, the ant bear was drawn out like a fishing net from the sea.

"Here he comes!" a man yelled when the animal whirled about at the tunnel entrance. For an instant the ant bear, a heavy creature five or six feet long, seemed dazzled by the light of day. Anton noticed its kangaroo-like tail and high humped back, nearly three feet tall. Its tongue, glistening with sticky mucus, hung from the flat end of a long pig-like snout. Each toe mounted a huge straight claw. Turning on its tormentors, the ant bear sat erect and struck out with its foreclaws. It lunged violently and snapped one rope as the men scattered. A soldier fired a shotgun and the animal dashed away. Pellets struck it in the neck without effect.

Chasing it down, a gang of soldiers and Africans grabbed the trailing rope. One African clubbed the ant bear across the forehead with a heavy mattock. The implement splintered. Bleating, the animal reared on its hind legs and broke the rope, somersaulted, and dashed across the field with men streaming after it. Quickly it went to ground in another burrow. Again the men dug and earth flew. Man after man emerged spitting sand and clay. In time fresh ropes were secured to its legs and the animal was dragged forth, clawing and lunging.

"Isn't that enough, Captain?" Anton said. Jos nodded and Anton fired.

"Even my lads won't eat that greasy ant bear, but the boys'll scoff it up," Jos said. "They say the hide makes fine strapping."

"Everything's good for something out here." Anton thought of his recuperation in the Aberdares. "Dr. Fitzgibbons will find that ant bear grease pretty handy for dressing wounds."

"Still trying to teach me my trade, are you, young man?" The doctor sighed. "I was cutting and stitching men before you had your first shoes, if you had any."

"Cut it off! Cut it off!" called the parrot from a branch in the shadows.

"At least Kaiser's got the right idea," whispered Fitzgibbons. He kicked the glowing ends of sticks deeper into the fire.

"What are you doing with those flax seeds, Tony?" Anton watched Bevis pick seeds from different gunnysacks and sprinkle them into a large pan set on the coals. "Even the mules can't eat that stuff."

"The seeds that go *bang* and hop out of the pan are still alive, you see. We can plant 'em. Like from that sack there. They've no smell, no green seeds, and they jump about like madmen. Those are the ones that'll make us rich. The ones that shrivel up in the heat, mind you, like these little Dutch buggers at the edge of the pan, these're hopeless," Bevis informed him. "Even the sack smells damp and musty."

"Damned seeds are like the rest of us out here," moaned Fitzgibbons. "Only one in ten'll ever make it."

"Healthy seeds or no, flax'll be grim work," Jos said. "Clearing, planting, tending, pulling, scutching, retting, drying, milling, grading, sacking. There's no end to it with flax. Then we'll need sheds and wagons to haul it to the railway. And who knows about next year's markets in Glasgow and Odessa? Maybe we're better off with wheat or tobacco. If we weren't all such a broken mess, we should do what this boy's doing, and wander down to Lake Vic and find ourselves some gold."

Troubled by the mention, Anton looked through the firelight and caught sadness in Gwenn's eye.

In the morning two veterans of the Royal Signals worked on the bike while Gwenn and Anton breakfasted by the Ewaso Ngiro with Captain Jos and the Bevises. Finally they prepared to set off, equipped with a fresh picnic and encouraged by the promise of help for Cairn Farm.

"Do you know how to drive?" Anton offered Gwenn the driver's seat.

"Yes, Anton, I do." Gwenn remembered the ambulance school near Dover, and how for a few days it seemed a lark, before the first shattered drivers returned from France. Sunken-eyed, seeming twice their age, the veterans told their sister drivers about the Marne. Acres of wounded were waiting in the fields when their ambulances drove up. Cries and moans merged together like the murmur of the sea as one approaches water, one woman said, trying to prepare her listeners and discourage those who could not cope. Gwenn shivered and took the driver's seat.

She drove slowly to spare the motorbike. They did not see the wild dogs while they crossed the familiar bush.

After a time they came to the tall shelved rock and she stopped the bike. Anton stepped out with the picnic. They climbed hand in hand without speaking.

At the top they found the sandy depression and short-stemmed yellow flowers. For a moment they sat quietly and let the place come back to them.

"Where was I?" Anton said.

He put his hands on Gwenn's cheeks. She closed her eyes and they kissed. She lay on her side and looked up at him. He dropped down beside her and pressed her neck with kisses while their bodies met.

Finally they lay naked on their stomachs in the warm sand and looked out over the land, their perspiration drying in the easy breeze, their bodies touching from shoulder to hip, chins resting on forearms. Anton's diklo lay knotted with her scarf. His left arm rested along Gwenn's back, his hand about her neck.

Below them dust devils spiralled away, light-hearted waltzers pirouetting among the thorn trees.

BOOK III

1921

— 29 —

'll roll you for another shot, young fella. You can't always be that lucky." The lanky American dropped the poker dice onto the bar from his right hand. "Right. Two pair."

"Three Queens. A lager, if you please, Mr. Slider." Anton noticed Slider's hand as the Queen of Spades settled near the American's fingers. Then Anton's eyes searched through the smoke down the long bar of Nairobi's New Stanley Hotel.

"I told you to call me Rack, Tony. I'm not one of your poncy gin-sippers with shiny shoes and a filthy mind, like that bunch of flowers in the corner."

"I'm certain you're not, Rack."

"Speakin' of dirty minds, by the time the Black Tulips get done with that Kraut buddy of yours, we'll have to scrape him off the wall like a squashed June bug. He hopped upstairs randy as a jackrabbit. But after what the Tulips went through with them Irish pigs, he'll seem smooth as your Duke of Wales."

"Which Irishmen?"

"Pair of jailbirds from your boat. One of 'em, Paddy, he's bigger'n a longhorn and twice as ugly. Seems he tried some nasty stuff even the Tulips couldn't handle. They ran for it and the two Micks beat 'em bloody. Poor gals couldn't work for a week. Made some of these farmers late getting home."

"I think I know the men you mean." Anton rubbed the scar on

the inside of his arm and thought about his knife with a flash of hatred.

"I reckon you do. I hear they're looking for a young wise guy that gave them a hard time on the boat."

"Let me see your right hand," said Anton, changing the subject. "I'll read your palm if you like."

"OK, but it better be good news." Slider opened his hand. "This ain't my line."

Anton pinched together the American's fingers and studied the scarred knuckles and deep lines.

"Am I goin' to die with my boots on?"

Anton looked his new friend in the eye. "Yes, I'm afraid you are, but not today."

"That'll do." Slider snatched his hand away and knocked back his whisky. "Why don't you leave your fat kraut here and come hunting up north?"

"Thanks for the offer, but it's time I made my fortune. Yesterday I opened a bank account and paid our gold mining license, twenty-two shillings. Now that we've sold the bike and bought a lorry and all the gear, tomorrow we're off for Lolgorien and the Migori River."

"When you crawl back from the Migori flats, boy, bone broke and dripping with fever, you'll be darn glad to help old Rack take out a few safaris. It's cash money, and the clients' wives like a young buck along. You'll find a broad's legs look best between you and a fire, especially the rich ones. If you weren't such a pup, I'd make you tackle the Tulips yourself just to learn what it's all about. Probably time you had your first gal.

"Now here comes one fit for a Yank. My God. Just think what's waitin' inside that shirt." Rack Slider stepped from the bar stool and tipped the brim of his cowboy hat with a smile. "Can I buy you a drink, ma'am?"

"Good afternoon, Blue Eyes." Anunciata ignored the American as she curled one hand around the back of Anton's neck and kissed him on the mouth. "I've missed you. Can you join me upstairs for a glass of champagne?"

"This is my friend, Mr. Rack Slider," Anton said to Anunciata.

"He's a rustler, and he loves to buy champagne." Anton wanted to go upstairs himself, but he knew it would not be the same.

"Now I'm going to close my eyes for a minute and dream about Hansel and Gretel." Ernst lowered his hat over his eyes and rested his head against the cracked cover of the seat. "Just keep her pointed on this track northwest and kick me when you need help."

Proud to be at the wheel for the third time, Anton drove the old Studebaker with care. Originally a roadster, she had been stripped down after a rhino accident and converted into a short truck with an open wooden box body behind the cab. Wide running boards extended along each side. Tool chests and cans of petrol and oil were lashed to the boards. Prospecting pans and pickaxes, salt and sugar barrels, ammunition boxes and tents crowded the back. Just loading the lorry had excited Anton.

He reached out the window and rapped his knuckles on the wooden panel of the driver's door, touching his own crude painting of a cheetah. A poor copy, Anton thought, of Hugo von Decken's old symbol of Gepard Farm.

Ernst's mouth gaped wide. His snoring was steadier than the clatter of six cylinders as the Studebaker worked to climb the edge of the Ngong Hills that ran to their left. Here and there Anton saw neat rows of coffee trees patching the green slopes, trying to bring order to the wild hills. Higher still, drifting in and out among clusters of acacia, he spotted the massive blackness of the feeding buffalo.

Anton stopped the lorry and killed the engine. He stepped down and scanned the hillside through Ernst's battered field glasses. First three or four, then fifteen, twenty, twenty-five buffalo traversed the bright circle of the Zeiss lenses. The animals seemed so close he was surprised he could not hear them move. Where there were buffalo, there must be lion.

Anton climbed a small rise. He was up to his knees in wild flowers and waving grass. He wiped his face with the new bandanna Gwenn had made for him before he left.

"A new diklo for my tinker," she told him as she said goodbye. He tied the red kerchief about his neck.

To one side the hills rolled on like the knuckles of a giant green hand. To Anton's right, and before him, Africa fell away to endless open horizons. He could smell the freedom of it. He remembered his dreams when his eyes fell shut in the grimy rooming house in Portsmouth, Baldwin's *African Hunting and Adventure* lying open under his hand, Gordon Cumming's *The Lion Hunter* waiting at his elbow. Anton smiled, threw his hat in the air, and yelled as loudly as he could, "Hurrah! Hurrah!"

"Blast you, boy, are you mad?" Ernst hollered from the Studebaker.

Motoring northwest from the town of Naivasha early the next morning, the truck heavier with four crates of beer, they came to the Melawa River, broad but easily crossed at a shallow ford. Ernst stopped and gave Anton the wheel.

"I'll say this for your empire," Ernst said, the promise of generosity in his tone. "Not only is it swollen wide like a Belgian sow, but there are two things you Britishers do well in these stinking filthy countries: brew beer and train the tarts. Ours lie there like dead cows in a slaughterhouse, waiting to give up their soft meat. As usual, we Germans have to do all the work." Ernst belched thoughtfully and emptied a second Tusker. "But your whores move like angry bees. Just take those Tulips. Lean and smooth, silver bells tinkling, driving a man mad, probably because you English don't have the energy yourselves."

"You should talk to Rack Slider about it."

"Slider? If there's one thing Americans don't understand, it's women. They're always trying to please them, a hopeless campaign. Useless. You can excite them, anger them, chew them, but never please them."

Not interested in Ernst's philosophy, Anton thought he would turn to something more useful.

"What do you know about gold mining, Ernst?"

"One thing von Lettow taught me, boy, when I watched him carve his sandals from a scrap of kongoni hide. In Africa, as soon as you do something yourself, you're an expert. Do you think von Lettow was a cobbler?"

"What do you know about gold mining?" Anton asked as the Studebaker braked unsteadily on the first downhill curve.

"What does a starving man know about beefsteak?"

"Are these brakes all right?" Anton said a few moments later when the Studebaker struggled to crest the rim of the Mau Escarpment. Before them the twisting track dove thousands of feet down the wall of the Great Rift.

"I myself have checked her. She'll go down anything."

"No doubt she will." The gears grated when Anton shifted down to second. He heard the motor take the strain from the brakes.

Anton thought of Karioki and eland camp and his birthday on the valley's edge. He wondered how Karioki was getting on at Cairn Farm with Victoria and the oxen and his reading lessons.

Anton's *Copperfield* had finally broken in two, almost in half, just where David, after the picnic, confesses his love to Dora. Anton had left the first half at the farm, and Gwenn had promised to read with Karioki every day. He remembered cleaning the blood from Gwenn's face and drowning in her green eyes when she kissed him. She always seemed so self-sufficient and fresh, so cool-skinned and proud. But when he touched her, she trembled like a piano wire. He missed her and wondered if he had been right to leave.

"Watch out!" Ernst yelled.

The sandy edge of the road fell away towards the valley floor three thousand feet below. Anton took the Studebaker into a tight turn. He felt it drift sideways and heard the pop of small stones when the sliding front tires forced them over the side.

"Saved by the beer," Ernst said when the heavily laden rear wheels bit and drove the truck around the bend. The vehicle recovered and Anton concentrated on his job.

An angry grinding sound cut through Ernst's snores as they neared the valley floor. Anton felt second gear begin to slip. The transmission popped into neutral. The Studebaker gathered speed, surviving another tight bend. Anton pulled on the hand brake to slow the lorry for a final narrow turn. The vehicle skidded around the corner. A burning smell filled the cabin. They freewheeled down. A gentle curve met them at the bottom, but the truck continued its straight plunge, ignoring Anton's attempt to keep the bucking Studebaker on track. The wheels left the ground. The lorry turned sideways in mid air and jolted onto one side, finally bouncing back onto its wheels and tearing straight on into the bush. They crashed through thornbushes and jarred to a stop against an anthill with the radiator steaming and the left fender forced into its front tire.

"What a smell," Ernst said. "It's time my Englishman took a bath."

Somewhat disgusted, Karioki watched Wellington crawl towards the stuffed calf. How could any child be so unnaturally white? Even worse than the grown ones, the m'zungus who were taking over the land. Almost colorless, save for a faint pink hue that seemed to glow beneath the skin, the small boy resembled the fatty membrane that covered the sweetest meat of the eland. But unlike the great antelope, this baby was crowned with thick red curls. At least he was properly fat, Karioki noted with relief, and had knees and elbows that dimpled when he moved. Except for his knees, the child was smooth as a river stone. Roughened by falling and crawling, the knees were perpetually cut and filthy, like those of any healthy toto. One day he and Tlaga would teach this boy to hunt.

Wellie stood erect and clutched the neck of the calf. Together the child and the stuffed skin fell to the ground. Straw burst through the rough stitches that held together the remains of the animal.

Distracted by the commotion, Victoria and the hump-shouldered Borana milk cow turned their heads to look. The dead calf had done its duty, keeping its mother in full milk so Vicky could extend its yield. Killed by a leopard at the edge of the boma after six days of life, the calf had been skinned by the Samburu. With its hide stuffed with straw, it lived on, tied upright against a dead thorn tree like a sacrificial goat. Anxious to feed its offspring, the mother stayed in milk.

Although these Samburu were practically animals, Karioki reminded himself, at times as wild and menacing as any striped hyena, they had certain skills. Trained by crafty elders, the Samburu understood the tricks of nature. They planned for survival, not for riches. Perhaps he should explain this way of living to memsaab Gwenn, though already she was learning from the women.

White farmers, Karioki had observed, tried to wring too much from the earth. They cleared the forests and killed the game, then failed with one crop or animal after another, until either they found one that worked or they abandoned the weakened land they had stolen. And now they wanted the Kikuyu to do all their work, forcing them to labor for a time each year by levying hut taxes in every village. Yet when his people planted their own coffee, the police came and ripped it up, claiming it was spreading pests and disease.

Gwenn walked back to the Samburu village to collect her son. Twisting a dry stalk in her hands, she considered all there was to do. Would she ever have time for herself? While she was trying to cure the leghorns of eye roup, other women were having fun in the Ladies Motor Trials, or working with the East African Women's League on the new women's franchise.

She approached the boma and watched Victoria and Karioki playing with Wellie. What a difference Anton's friend was making to the farm.

Wellington lifted his arms and staggered forward to meet his mother. Karioki watched. Gwenn lifted her son and kissed him, tickling his dimples with her nose until he squealed and his feet wagged like a puppy's tail. She felt the earth and the prickly straw that clung to him and smelled fresh milk on his breath.

"Please, Vicky, never give him milk until it's boiled." Gwenn checked her son's curls and scalp for red pepper ticks. "You're very naughty."

"It was only a few drops, to make him strong, like a Samburu moran."

"Or sick, like a Welshman in Africa." Gwenn laughed. "Come on, Karioki, let's get Wellie home. How's David Copperfield getting along? Have you gone over what we read last night?"

"David is so lonely, memsaab, so lonely." Karioki frowned and shook his head. He stepped closer with the shotgun in one hand and the wrinkled pages in the other. He poked Wellie in the stomach with the corner of the book. "For David I think the days are very difficult. And this Uriah slowly hunts him, most patient, like a jackal waiting his turn at the body. I hope every day is more easy for our friend Tlaga."

"Oh, I hope so too." Gwenn lifted Wellington on one hip and took a gourd of milk in her free hand. While they walked home, she stopped often to check the fields, stepping between the rows of flax, anxious about the inconsistency of the struggling plants. A few were straight and healthy. But the stems of many, only four inches tall,

were starting to blacken, swell and crack. Probably flax wilt, Gwenn
feared, dreading that the deadly fungus would invade the plant below
the ground and obstruct the water-conducting tissue.

She approached the bridge that led to the house and paused to
visit the six merino sheep, the latest gift of Adam Penfold. How
could she ever repay him? Imported from Australia, these fine-
woolled Spaniards flourished on the low star grass near the Ewaso
Ngiro. Wellie reached down and grabbed his favorite by its woolly
brown coat while she checked the unresisting animal for parasites in
the corners of its eyes.

"Memsaab! Come quickly, memsaab!" she heard Mulwa holler
while he ran to her across the fenced pasture. "Men are in the house!"

Gwenn handed Wellington to Mulwa and hurried forward. She
crossed the bridge and saw three horses tied to the rail before the
house. A heavy-set man slouched by the fire in Alan's favorite camp
chair, a bottle of beer in one hand. The heels of his army boots were
dug into the cold grey ashes at the fire's edge.

A dark shadow filled the doorway to the cottage.

"Welcome home, dearie," Mick Reilly called to Gwenn with a grin
as he stepped into the light. She recognized his curly reddish hair
with horror.

"Get off my land," Gwenn said angrily, seizing the shotgun from
Karioki. "And take your brother with you. I warned you, Michael
Reilly. I told you I'd go to the police if you bothered me again."

Then she recognized what Reilly carried in his hand: Alan's notebook of Cairn Farm.

"How dare you! Give me that!" Gwenn grabbed for the book.

The Irishman grinned and held the notebook behind him. To her
disgust, Gwenn nearly touched the man when she reached out. Reilly
snatched away the shotgun and put the book in his pocket.

Karioki stepped forward to help her.

Paddy stood and tossed his bottle into the fire. A pistol on his hip,
he backhanded Karioki across the face. The African staggered but
stayed on his feet. Gwenn saw Karioki's body harden and crouch.
The scars on his chest stood out when his muscles tightened. Karioki
glared at Paddy with unblinking cat's eyes. Paddy put one hand on
his revolver.

"This could be fun." Reilly gripped Gwenn by one shoulder. She tried to pull away. He grabbed her more securely by the upper arm.

Karioki reached into the fire and snatched out a flaming branch. He took another step forward.

"Stay back, nigger." Paddy drew his pistol. "This ain't your business."

"Go from here!" Karioki yelled at the two white men. "Do not touch Mrs. Llewelyn!" He advanced towards Paddy with the burning limb in his hand, ignoring the flames that enveloped his fingers.

At that moment a third man appeared from behind the house. The others hesitated.

"Excuse my friends, won't you, Mrs. Llewelyn. They're rather rough." Vasco Fonseca doffed his hat. He wiped his forehead with his sleeve. He removed a long unlit cigar from his teeth and smiled with heavy lips. "Perhaps you'll offer me a coffee. Then you and I can speak of business while my partners examine our property."

"We have nothing to talk about." Gwenn tried to shake loose from Reilly's hand. "Get off my farm, all of you."

"We have to discuss your future, Mrs. Llewelyn," Fonseca said. "You have built your house on my land, on the wrong side of the river. You must leave."

"Prove that to the Land Office." Gwenn struggled to free herself. Karioki took a step towards her. Paddy fired.

"No!" Gwenn screamed.

The African dropped the branch. He staggered backwards. He clutched his stomach with dripping hands and gasped loudly. His eyes stared hate like a leopard.

"Not a handsome shot," Fonseca said calmly. He took a small double-barrelled pistol from a side pocket of his jacket.

"What are you doing?" Gwenn yelled. "You can't—"

Paddy fired a second time. Wounded again in the stomach, Karioki collapsed on his side at the edge of the fire. His lower body and forearms were shiny black with blood. He tried to move his legs.

Gwenn kicked Reilly, fighting and striking the man with her fists. She elbowed him and squirmed violently, trying to run to Karioki.

The African struggled to stand but could only get onto one knee.

Fonseca stepped to Karioki.

Shaking, his legs bloody, Karioki braced himself on the fingers of both hands. His mouth opened and he looked up with enormous blazing eyes. Gwenn saw them weeping as he fought to rise. Fonseca put the small weapon to the side of Karioki's head.

Gwenn screamed.

Fonseca pulled the trigger. Karioki collapsed on his face, his feet in the coals.

Gwenn bit Reilly's wrist, drawing blood as she broke free. She rushed to Karioki and seized him by the ankles. With bloody hands she dragged his body from the fire. She lifted the torn book from the back pocket of his shorts. Gwenn rested one hand on his shoulder and glared up with shining eyes and tight narrow lips when the Portuguese spoke.

"You saw what happened, Mrs. Llewelyn," Fonseca said without emotion. He removed the empty cartridge from the upper barrel of the ivory-handled pistol. "Even in this country, it is a crime for a negro to attack a white man."

"You killed him!" Gwenn cried. "He was only trying to protect me. You're worse than animals!"

— *30* —

Ever since you destroyed second gear," Ernst said, "she moves like an old French whore, either too fast or too slow."

"*Jawohl, Kapitän.*" Anton turned his head at the familiar complaint and gazed out the glass-less passenger window. To disagree with the German was to quarrel with the tide.

"I'm surprised you lost the war, Ernst."

"In Africa we didn't. And without your English perfidy, we would have won here despite everything."

"How was that?" Anton saw his friend's hands tighten on the wheel.

"For four years we were cut off without supplies from Germany, hunted in the bush like wild animals. One chance the Schutztruppe had. In 1917 a great airship, a dirigible, sailed from Bulgaria to resupply us. Seven hundred feet long, the blimp was packed with machine guns and medicines and built of German genius. Her canvas skin was designed to become tents, her gas sacks would be our sleeping bags, her muslin lining would bandage our wounds. Her steps and catwalks were lined with boot leather. Her wire frame would become radio antennae. Her picked crew would replace our dead comrades. With this ship, von Lettow would have conquered Africa."

Ernst stopped speaking and wiped his hardened face with one hand. He and Anton exchanged a glance before the German continued.

"Like a great eagle, she sailed higher than your winged planes could find her. She flew over Greece and Turkey, over Egypt and the Sudan. Her wireless was damaged, but over Khartoum she received a message in German: *General von Lettow has surrendered, you must turn for home.* Von Lettow surrender! It was a British message, a trick. The airship's captain, a seaman, turned about, back to Bulgaria, the longest dirigible voyage in history, all destroyed by British lies."

Anton did not reply.

A palisade of green acacias rose on the horizon before them. An hour later they were among the fresh-leaved thorn trees, approaching the banks of a wide river.

"Jump down, boy, and find us a ford," Ernst said, his voice again relaxed. "Could be the Migori. Don't be afraid to get your feet wet. A swim bath would do you good."

Ernst stopped the Studebaker. Anton searched the bank for a shallow solid crossing. He saw several Africans watching from across the river. Twice Anton walked into the water and stepped back when his feet sank into the muddy bottom.

"Right there, it's perfect," Ernst called while Anton continued upstream, trying to ignore the loud voice. "All we have to do is keep our speed up when we hit the bad bits."

Anton shook his head and pointed upriver. Ernst ignored him and reversed thirty yards to the crest of the sloping bank. Gunning the engine, he lunged forward in first with Anton's door flapping open. The lorry strained at the top of the gear and plunged into the river, splashing up arcs of water on either side. Almost halfway across, the wheels spun and the tires cut into the soft mud.

The Studebaker lowered itself into the water, the engine still driving the wheels. Cursing, Ernst switched off the motor and opened his door. The river flowed through the cab and out the passenger door. On the far bank a growing band of natives, chatting and gesticulating, observed the Studebaker settle into the streambed.

Anton waded out to the truck and removed a rope from the back. He reached under the water and secured the rope around the mounts of the damaged front fender. He walked through the water towards the waiting Africans.

"Jambo!" Anton saluted them. He placed the rope on his shoulder and started to strain. Half a dozen men and boys moved to help, the

adults putting aside their spears and buffalo-hide shields. Ernst stood
on the running board, pointing and yelling instructions.

The Studebaker remained in place. Water lapped against the spotted round head of the cheetah on the driver's door.

The Africans, Nandi, Anton guessed, were darker than the tribes
he had seen to the east but had the lean hardness of the Maasai.
They stopped pulling as soon as they realized the task was beyond
them. Anton and the Africans unloaded the lorry while two boys ran
to the village for help. Ernst sat on a packing chest in the back of
the vehicle, beer in hand, bawling orders and groaning whenever he
helped balance a sack or chest on a man's head.

At length a shaven-headed elder appeared. His wrinkled face was
mounted on the hard erect body of a young man. He had long oval
holes in his swinging ears and a knobbed staff in one hand. A clam-
oring host of eighty or ninety men walked at his side and behind
him, most with plaited hair and carrying heavy stabbing spears. Clusters of excited boys swarmed about them.

"I am the *laibon,* the chief. These are my sons," the leader said in
Swahili while he gestured with long gnarled fingers towards his
followers.

"The water is deep," the laibon said in the loud controlled tones
of a man educating imbeciles. "This lorry is not the first to stop in
the Kipsonoi River. Some smaller, some larger. All white men need
help. But none have sunk so far and needed so much."

The laibon walked to the pile of unloaded supplies. He lifted a
panga and felt its edge before tossing it to one side with contempt.
He built a pile of goods beside it. A metal bucket. Tobacco. Sugar.
Two shovels. A bolt of patterned cotton from the coast. He gestured
again at the truck and spoke slowly to the older European.

"You are so deep. Many Nandi must pull with their hearts."

"Greedy bugger. You can see it in his eyes," Ernst said to Anton
while he watched the laibon and his shaven-headed elders organize
the men into two lines. "If you hadn't ruined second gear, my idiot
friend, I'd have made it through without these munts."

"You lose again, Paddy," said a loud Irish voice. "Grab us a couple
of beers from the midget."

Paddy rose heavily and shuffled across the quiet room. The .38 on his belt bumped the side of the bar. He slapped two dirty hands palm down on the gleaming leadwood counter. He opened his mouth to speak and looked towards Olivio. The dwarf's eyes met his and Paddy hesitated. Not wishing to reveal his scorn, Olivio looked down as if unaware of the demand for drink. He noted the predictably filthy broken nails on the thick-knuckled fingers. One nail was missing altogether, leaving a raised horny callus in its place. The dwarf prepared to clean the bar again. From the corner of one eye, he saw the American hunter carelessly tossing darts.

"Pair o' Tuskers," Paddy said at last. "Cold."

Olivio took two beers from the locker. He remembered Lord Penfold's unusual instructions following the death of that dog Karioki: no credit for Fonseca or the Irishmen. The dwarf thought of their participation in the scheme against the Llewelyn farm. Olivio paused and ran his fingers through the few greasy strands at the back of his scalp. He drew two mugs from a wooden peg, letting his fingers soil their lips.

"Four shillings, sir." The dwarf's hands held the throats of the bottles.

"They're but one shilling apiece," Paddy said harshly. "That's two bob."

"The other gentleman hasn't paid for the first two, sir."

"Put 'em on me bill, me account," Mick Reilly called from his seat.

"You have no account at the White Rhino Hotel, sir."

"Says who?"

"The lord. Four shillings, if you please."

"What do you think you are, you shrunken greaser?" yelled Reilly, standing up. "You run accounts for every Limey fag an' toff that stumbles in." He reached a hand across the bar and seized Olivio's sleeve in his fist. "Or ain't we as good as them?"

"Maybe, maybe not." Rack Slider stepped towards the end of the bar. These must be the Micks who beat up the Tulips and were after young Tony. Slider lifted his hat and resettled it on his head.

Reilly wrenched at Olivio's sleeve. The dwarf's eyes narrowed to glass beads. Olivio went rigid as he felt himself pulled from the shelf. Without turning his head, he remembered that the American's gunbelt hung on an antelope horn nearby.

"I don't think Shorty likes that, mister. Perhaps you'd like to let the little fella loose." Slider dropped his dart on the bar. "We don't want to mess up a nice saloon."

"Keep out of it, Yank." Reilly hauled Olivio towards him. "When I drop this slimy midget, it'll be on this side of the bar." Helpless, the dwarf felt the old rage burning in him while the man dragged him across the wooden counter.

Slider reached for his gunbelt.

Paddy, the dart centered in his immense clenched hand, slammed his fist down on Slider's left hand, nailing it to the bar.

Slider roared and tore his bleeding hand straight up from the bar. The dart still pierced through between the thin bones on the top of his hand. He swung completely around and belted Reilly open-handed across the face.

"Me eye!" Reilly screamed, both hands covering his face. Blood seeped between his fingers.

Released, Olivio crashed head first down the front of the bar. He looked up to see the American covering the two men with a revolver.

"Unless you bastards are better at the gunplay," Slider said in a hard drawl, "you best walk out of here before I teach you how we finish this kind of thing in Elk City."

Slider placed his trembling left hand on the bar. The dart was still set in its center. He kept his gun steady while Paddy led his brother from the room. Unable to see high enough, Olivio wondered if Slider's blood was spreading across the bar.

"This ain't over, Yank!" Paddy yelled back when the two men neared the doorway to the verandah.

"When you're back on your pins, Shorty, climb up here and pull this out for me," Slider said through closed teeth, his eyes on the door and his pistol still in hand. "Then splash your best whisky over it and give me the rest of the bottle."

— *31* —

Keep walking, laddie. This stream's spoken for," the prospector called sternly to Anton.

White-bearded, with wavy grey hair touching his shoulders, the man leaned on a long-handled shovel. Its blade was buried in thick vegetation and moist dark earth. Wide leather braces held up his heavy brown trousers. Spectacles and a leather tube hung from his neck on two cords. A shotgun with a worn stock rested on a pack nearby.

Anton raised one hand and slogged on through the tangled vines and branches that ensnared his boots and cut his legs below his khaki shorts. His other hand held the barrel of the .450 which rested empty, breech closed, across his shoulder.

"But if it's a billy of tea you're after, instead of gold dust," the man said in a friendlier tone, "that you can have."

"I could use both, sir." Anton lifted his hat. "But I'd love some tea first."

"I'm called Graham, Shotover Graham." The man bent forward stiffly while he led Anton up the slope to his camp.

A wide green tent, patched and faded, stood among a clump of wild fig trees, their bark a pale yellow. The tent flaps were tied open to either side. The canvas floor was spotless. A handsome woman was reading a book in front of the tent. She sat with dignity on a folding stool by a fire. Dark, but not African, she had strong cheekbones and clear brown eyes under a broad forehead. Perhaps fifty, square-shouldered and slender, she wore a shirt and trousers and braces like Graham's.

"This is my wife, Jezebel Graham."

"How do you do, Mrs. Graham." Anton looked about at the meticulous camp and speculated about his host's accent. The woman closed her book and poured Anton a cup of tea from the cylindrical tin billycan. "Are you from Australia, Mr. Graham?"

"Lord spare me, son. We can read. We can write. We're New Zealanders. I'm a sheep farmer, if I hadn't caught the gold bug. And what are you doing wandering about these diggings on your own with naught but a fancy rifle? There's no game here but snakes and flies."

"I'm looking for a place to camp and start panning. I've left my partner and our gear ten miles back until I find us a spot to start. Our lorry couldn't make it past the first swamp."

"Well, you're new here and you won't find it any easier than your lorry. I've worked streams from the Yukon to the Rand, and this one's a proper wench. A right teaser. For months a man digs and pans and sluices. You kill yourself, till you can't straighten your back when the sun's gone, and there's nothing. Then just before you quit and toss your pan into the stream, your heart stops. There she is. The devil's glint. That sparkle of the gods. Just a bit of the heavy dust. One magic sprinkle. A first kiss. So you flush out the sluices, check your claim, hire more boys, and set to, digging into the banks until the skin peels off your hands like gloves. But not one grain more. Not a point of gold. It's a business to make you old fast, or to keep you young forever."

"Better have a second cup, young man." Jezebel spoke without seeming to interrupt. She looked Anton up and down. "Mr. Graham likes to talk."

"Just three miles on," Graham said patiently while he sprinkled tobacco along a sheet of rolling paper, "they found fresh traces last month, less'n a dozen ounces all told. Now there's seventy or eighty camps scattered along sixty miles of river. Even the Africans are working, mostly for food, of course, helping the lads move earth and run the water.

"Settle down here for some supper, son. While the wife's stirring it up, I'll tell you a bit about this trade. In the morning you take some Kavirondo boys and go fetch your mate. The wife's a Maori, best bush cooks in the world. But don't ever ask what's in the pot, or your hair'll turn like mine."

"This is no work for a German officer," Ernst said two days later. He stood beside Anton and Shotover Graham and scowled at the feverish activity along the broken bank of the Migori River. The water flowed past them, eighty or a hundred feet wide, sluggish and thick from the work upstream.

Teams of men, white and black, tore away at the undergrowth and dug out the land. Clearing and scraping, they toiled to open new lines of trenches, artificial ribs leading to the spines of the natural waterways. Each inlet and feeder stream was the beginning of a dozen muddy canals. Higher on the banks and surrounding slopes men dug test holes, drove claim stakes and burrowed into the hillsides. Other men knelt and sloshed water from pans, gradually thinning the muddy silt in flat-bottomed tin basins while they tipped the water from side to side.

In the far distance, at more advanced diggings, Anton saw men move in their workings, like bees in the compartments of honeycombs. They pushed crude wheelbarrows and shouldered heavy baskets. Others built flumes and bent over long wooden sluice boxes, rough sloping troughs with grooves or slats across their bottoms to separate the treasure from the sand and mud and gravel.

"Time you lads set to work," Shotover said to Ernst and Anton. He squatted and unrolled the paper he drew from the frayed telescope case that swung from his neck. Like a chart of the ancients, all done in his own hand, it was more than a map. Decorated with crossed picks and tiny shovels, it was framed with sketches of the vines and leaves and bushes that covered the land. The ground and the diggings were done in pencil. Here and there, in blue ink, were coded markings where gold had been found.

"It's always a puzzle," Graham said. "The trick is to let the other lads drag the pieces about for you until they make a picture that you see before they do. I'm too old to move all the earth and water in Africa, but I can still shift a little, if it's the right bit. Somewhere near here the stuff is waiting for me. I can smell it. Not in irregular deposits, like the shoots of quartz we're all working now, but a proper lode, a band one thousand foot long. Even in Rhodesia, we only had three-hundred-footers.

"Meantime, if I was you boys, I'd dig here, or here." Graham tapped the map with a short blunt pencil. "If the gold they're finding was washed downstream, none of this is any use. But if it's local stuff, I reckon you've a good shot here. After you're set up, we'll find some Kavirondo or Watendi chaps to help."

"Shouldn't we find the schwarzes first?" Ernst said.

"Let's go." Anton grabbed his rifle, a panga and a shovel. "A little digging'll be good for your shoulder."

"First this boy is my idle guest on the finest plantation in German Africa," Ernst said to Shotover that evening. "Then I save his life in a bar fight with a gang of animals from a barbaric island in the North Sea. Now I work to make him rich. And what does he do? He hands me a shovel and enslaves me in this hellhole of lost Englishmen." The three men sat around the fire and waited for Jezebel's stew.

"Pass Mr. Graham the whisky." Anton sharpened Shotover's pencil with his knife. "Tomorrow we'll make an earlier start, Ernst."

"I'd add water," Shotover said, accepting the half-empty bottle of Long John scotch and pouring two tots into his tin mug, "but this filthy river's so stirred up, even our tea looks like mud." He took a sip and paused for breath.

"You'll never understand what it's really like," Shotover Graham said, reminding Anton of old man von Decken when the miner stood erect and his grey hair framed his crinkled face against the night sky. Anton noticed the fine broken veins on his cheeks and nose. "Except for a few old dogs like me, there ain't a miner on this river. The rest're farmers, broken-down soldiers, pommies mostly, or drifting idlers like the Hun here. Not a man jack of 'em can dig the skin off a rice pudding.

"In the old days, when I first left the sheep to look after themselves, the same men went from strike to strike, as easy as you'd cross that patch of bush. Australia, the Yukon, Mashonaland. Only the natives were different, and not much either. At each strike, one man in two hundred got rich, thirty or forty died, and the rest prayed for next time."

"Why are you helping us, Shotofer?" Ernst asked, keeping one eye on the cooking. Jezebel chopped the roots of a handful of ferns and sprinkled the diced fragments into the stew. The legs and feathers of small birds were scattered near the cooking pot.

"SHOT-O-VER, young man. I'm helping because we can use each other. Sometimes one old man just ain't enough. A man gets lonely for a chat with the lads, even with my lovely Jezzie here. And your young friend has a way about him, as my lady's been telling me. She wouldn't mind us leaving him back in camp one morning, would you, Jez? These Maori girls never tire out." He took his wife's hand.

"Do you have any other maps in there?" Anton tried to ignore Jezebel's wink and pointed to the leather tube with his choori.

"All of them. The Klondike. Hunter's Road. The old Shotover River herself."

"The Shotover River?" Anton smelled the stew.

"You see, lad, at first it's usually the water that finds the gold for you, not men. Then we learn its beds and veins and dig till we find the lode, or never find it. The river does in a big way what you do in a pan or sluice. She separates the gold from the sand. The faster the river, the farther the gold carries. But it always settles. And it's heavy, so it works down through the silt to the river bottom."

"When my husband was young, you should have seen him," Jezebel said, while Shotover rolled a perfect cigarette. She turned from the fireside towards the men, with the black iron lid in one hand and a stirring stick in the other.

Anton's mouth watered. He noticed the coals that burned near the pot. He threw a pinch of salt among the brighter embers.

"He was tall and strong like you and your friend, but without this one's belly." Jezebel slapped Ernst's stomach with her wet stick. The German growled and used a thumb to taste the sauce on his shirt.

Reading the fire, distracted, his eyes suddenly arrested, Anton knelt and studied the patterns among the coals. He wiped his face with his new diklo and stared. No longer flickering, no longer blue and red, for a dying moment one burning image glittered: a perfect golden coin.

"My boy took me up into the mountains in New Zealand where the men were mining in the snow," Jezebel said. "High up on the South Island, where my people do not live. For once the white men had to do all the work. They never found enough gold, and they were lazy. So they made the river do it for them. Deep in the mountains, the Shotover River washed through the goldfields. One man, smarter still than my Graham, thought if they could shift the Shotover from its bed, they would find a long beach of golden sand buried underneath. So the men came from all over, from California and New South Wales, with dynamite and shovels and dreams. And my handsome young boy took me there, and I called him 'Shotover.' "

"For two years it worked," Graham said. "We blasted a tunnel through a mountain, one mile of hellish dark and explosions till we burst out the far side. Some of the lads never made it out. Then we diverted the river through the tunnel. When the old riverbed dried out, we dug into her while the weaker chaps died around us, leaving their boots and picks and secret maps to their mates. Every now and again we'd find it: a small rocky basin, like a bathtub, but deep under the riverbed, where a patch of soft stone had washed away. One by one, for hundreds of years, grains of gold had settled in the bowl. When the river slowed in the winters, layers of sand settled over the gold. In the heavy rains, stones and boulders washed down and covered the sand. We moved it all. Every rock. Every grain. Always finding just enough to keep us going. It was high up, and no one to help. So we used the river again, feeding it into fire hoses, with four lads holding the bucking brass nozzle while we washed away the silt. A few men got rich, and a few of those made it out. They swaggered down like gods from the mountains, rich and strong as bulls. With their pokes, small leather bags, knotted inside their belts, hanging under their shirts and coats."

"We'd better get some sleep," Ernst said, emptying the bottle, "if my young friend is going to work like that tomorrow."

"Thank you ma'am, and a very good day to you." Anton finished stropping his razor on a boot and accepted a mug from Jezebel. She took the lid off the billy and poured the dark tea.

The steaming mug warmed his hands. He breathed in the sharp morning air, remembering they were camped at four thousand feet, only thirty miles from Lake Vic. His aching back reminded him of his first week on the Portsmouth docks. Missing his friends, he thought of cheerful breakfasts by another fire, with Gwenn and Wellie and Karioki.

Already Shotover was on his dawn walk, pausing frequently for breath, ambling a mile or two upstream. Studying the workings of other miners, each morning he chatted with the African helpers and swapped a plug of tobacco for a cup of tea when he stopped to speak to friends. Returning before breakfast, he would unroll his map, editing and adding notes. With his spectacles mounted on the tip of his nose, Shotover worked slowly with a pencil stub and an old gum eraser.

Anton sipped his tea and kicked the ends of burnt sticks deeper into the coals of last night's fire. He bent to blow up a flame and heard the grumbles of Ernst's snores.

"*Kapitän von Decken!*" Anton hollered. "*Achtung!*" He kicked his sleeping friend. "*Die Engländer kommen!*"

"You have crippled me with this work." The German groaned. "I may never again rise."

Anton squatted by the fire with his tea. He watched Shotover work his way back along the messy riverbank. In the distance the first curls of smoke rose from morning fires. Anton took a bit of grease from the suet pot and worked it into his boots with his fingers.

"More tea?" Jezebel said.

Anton glanced into the bottom of his mug. A pale muddy film clung to the inside walls of the battered tin vessel, reminding him of the river. In the bottom of the mug a few dark tea leaves spread like patches of seaweed over the sandy grains of river silt. Scattered among them, three or four sharp specks glittered in the early light.

"Gold!" Anton whispered.

"What are you reading, my dear?" Lord Penfold asked, astonished to see his wife with a book.

"*Five Years' Hell in a County Parish,* Treasure, by Reverend Synott, the rector of Rusper."

Relieved, Penfold passed his glass across the bar to Olivio. The dwarf handed him last week's *East African Standard* and a reading monocle in an old chammy case.

Penfold reluctantly began to work through the *Standard* from back to front. Advertisements for Dooma Dooma Safari Hats and a Bates Steel Mule caught his eye. A Steel Mule? Twenty-five horsepower, tall caterpillar treads in the rear, and made in Joliet, Illinois, no less. What fun it would be. If only he could afford one, perhaps a tractor like that could make the place work yet. But the prices. Four bob for a single pair of Four Wind Puttees.

He groaned and turned to the correspondence page. *Stop natives throwing their sick and dying out of their huts*, demanded one writer, detailing how the Kavirondo buried their dead to the neck and covered the head with a cook pot before lighting a fire all around it. *Who owns Kenya's gold, blacks, whites, or the King?* asked another correspondent.

"Now there's an idea!" Penfold exclaimed to his wife. "You know the way those wretched baboon keep messing about with the native maize?"

Sissy did not look up from her reading when Penfold continued.

"Chap from the Transvaal writes in to say they caught one baboon, shaved him, dyed him blue and turned him loose. Never saw another baboon 'round the place again. Scared 'em silly. What do you think of that?"

Penfold scanned the headlines: *Campaign Against the Mad Mullah in Somaliland. Township Rat Squads Use Break-Back Nipper Traps. Indians Steal Ostrich Eggs for Mosque. Select Committee on Sexual Assaults by Natives Upon Europeans Terminated Due to Lack of Incidents.*

Why was the Legislative Council in Nairobi having such trouble with the Native Witchcraft Bill? And all this bother over R.I., Rigorous Imprisonment, and using flogging and the cat for native crimes? At least things were even worse at home. Men out of work. Strikes in the mines. Ruddy socialists making mischief. Unrest in Ireland. And the Huns weren't paying their war reparations. Probably saving up for another go. No doubt they'd make even more mischief next time. They'd never change, he thought, remembering von Lettow chucking away his boots and marching barefoot through the bush for three weeks because many of his men had no boots themselves.

"I believe I'm coming down with Nairobi throat again," Sissy said to her husband's back. "They say everyone's got it. What a beastly country."

Penfold spotted an advertisement. Petogen Tonic for Jaded Nerves. Sounded about right, but she wouldn't like it. He noticed an alternative, Alkia Saltrates. *Clogged Intestines Breed Poison Like a Swamp Breeds Mosquitoes.* No, that probably wouldn't do either.

"Why not try some Beecham's Pills?" he proposed helpfully.

"You're not paying attention, Treasure," Sissy said with annoyance. "You know they're for constipation and liver trouble. It must be this hideous climate."

"Sorry, dear. Just pop down four of your quinine and cinnamon tablets, the big brown ones." Penfold checked last month's weather in London. He put aside the newspaper and remembered the numbing chills of Wiltshire. "Would you prefer supper on a tray?"

"Heavens, no."

"Dinner in one half hour, my lord?" Olivio said.

"Splendid. Impala shepherd's pie, I trust? Perhaps a few pickled mangoes on a separate plate for me, old boy, with a little Gentleman's Relish. Is anyone joining our table this evening?"

Being the keeper of a caravanserai had few advantages, Adam Penfold reflected, but one was that his wife and he rarely had to dine alone. Usually they could mess with the hotel guests. Tonight threatened to be an exception.

With the dogs dead, what was there to chat about? Would it be one of those mute dinners, when he could hear himself chew each brussels sprout and Sissy moved those thin lips only to complain about the servants? He remembered how sweet her mouth had looked the first time he noticed it when they were young.

"Still sorting the post, eh?" Penfold said to Olivio. He lifted an envelope to examine the three-masted carracks on its stamps. "From Lisbon. Must be for Fonseca. Handsome jobs, these Portagee stamps. Everyone's good at something. I'm sorry, Olivio, it's for you, actually. And here's another set of the same stamps, lateen sails and all. This one's for Fonseca. I'll give it to him myself when he comes through."

"Very well, my lord." The dwarf slipped his own mail between the folds of his sash. He descended the ladder, annoyed that the letter for Fonseca had lost its way.

Only one thing could distract him from what lay ahead, Olivio thought when he closed the door of the bungalow softly behind him. He leaned against the door and sniffed.

The first room was dark, but a hazy glow shone through the doorway from the bedroom. He smelled the incense, finding it a trifle
sweet and thick for a gentleman's taste. Kina was overdoing it again.
He undressed and took the leather dog collar from the low nail by
the door. He raised his chin and belted the collar about his neck.
At least she no longer made him wear Lancelot's leash.

Lighting a gas lamp, Olivio sat naked on a cushion. He scratched
himself and opened the letter from Lisbon.

My Dear Sr. Alavedo,

I am honored to undertake the mission you require,
and on the terms you propose of a one-fifth interest in
the estate, despite the difficulties that will attend it. At
first study, there seems merit to your claim. In the King-
dom of Portugal, and throughout its worldwide estates,
illegitimacy does not preclude inheritance. Our Church
and Sovereign recognize all infants born under their
protection.

I commissioned a few moments with the Secretary to
the Cardinal and have enjoyed an audience with him. He
salutes the shining faith of your gift to the Church of one
fifth of your inheritance. He will shortly certify your claim
as a descendant. But he requires that, prior to calculating
the respective interests, the estate restore to the Church
the gold plate that the late archbishop brought home
from the Convent of St. Monica in Goa.

The Secretary is a devout and practical man. For a token
spiritual remembrance, sufficient only to maintain a modest shrine on the road to his village, and perhaps to complete his family crypt, doubtless he will urge an honorable
arrangement.

Slow moans from the bedroom interrupted Olivio's concentration.
He adjusted the collar on his neck, scenting the whippet's odor with
revulsion as he freed the pinched skin above his Adam's apple. What
was the wicked child up to? Had he not ordered her never to indulge
herself without him, always to save for him the privilege of stirring
her young body? But perhaps she could not help herself when she
thought of him. Olivio forced his mind to return to the Church.

Difficulties arise, however, with your cousin, Vasco Fonseca. I have already raised the matter with Senhor Fonseca's lawyer, a typically disputatious councillor of the commercial class. Professing outrage, formerly unaware of your excellency's existence, he rejects my proposal of an equal division and has written to his client for instructions.

Have faith, Sir, that your claim is a righteous one and that, with the blessing of the Church herself, I labor to secure it justice.

With the compliments of your servant,

Dr. Gonçalo Barreto

So Fonseca would soon know of his cousin's claim! Olivio returned to the first page, but groans and gasps tore his mind from its duty. His hands trembled as he folded the sheets of paper back into the envelope and slipped it under a straw mat beneath a pile of brocaded cushions. Later he would place it in the strongbox under his bed. The dwarf tightened his wide leather collar, the way she liked it, and fell to all fours.

SENIOR SERVICE

H.M.S. DREADNOUGHT

SMOOTH VIRGINIA TOBACCO
GALLAHER TOBACCO LIMITED

— 32 —

No." Shotover restrained Anton and Ernst from rushing to the river. He held Anton's mug in one hand. Tiny specks of gold glinted among the tea leaves. "If we show excitement, there'll be a forest of claim stakes down there before we can dip a pan. You can only see a dozen from here, but there's four hundred white men digging on these Migori flats. First, Jezzie, exactly where did you get the water for the tea, lass?"

"About a week ago," Jezebel Graham said, pointing to the water cask, "I cleaned the barrel properly, scraping out all the muck and brown worms. Then I filled it again just past Croc Point, upriver where the water's still fresh. Each morning I walk along the bank with the washing and on the way home get a fresh bucketful to top her up."

Shotover laid out four pans by the barrel. He poured each half full, leaving the barrel almost empty. He stood and pinched Ernst's shirt between his fingers.

"Just right." Shotover patted the faded shoulder patch of the Schutztruppe and began to unbutton the filthy garment. "Give me your shirt."

"My shirt? It's my best one."

"I know, but maybe it'll make us rich. Besides, anything hanging on you deserves a second chance."

Anton slapped Ernst on the back.

Shotover draped the heavy grey cotton over another pan. Anton noticed the line of tight stitches that ran neatly up the back of the shirt where Gwenn had sewn it together after Dr. Fitzgibbons sliced it open.

Shotover poured out the remains of the barrel, filtering them through the cloth and spreading the sediment across the drooping surface of the shirt. Speechless, the others knelt about him.

Dark sand, small patches of clay-like mud, grains of gritty quartz, and tiny wiggling organisms lay before them.

"Only Britishers would drink that mess," Ernst said.

"Now we'll take a cup of tea while she dries." Shotover moved the shirt to the top of a wooden chest.

Anton felt his body perspire and tingle as if he had just survived a buffalo charge. He bit his lip and moved back to the fire.

"Remember the rules," Shotover said. "After we pick our spot, we get a Protection Notice from the District Commissioner. That's ten bob, and we've got to stake her out fast with four-inch poles. Then we've a fortnight to decide where to peg our claims inside that Protection Area. Each claim is a hundred foot by a hundred foot and costs us ten bob more, but we can have as many as we can pay for."

"Meantime we've got to pay for food, supplies and some diggers," Anton said, aware he was the only one with more than a few shillings. "We'll need more money."

"That's it, boy," said Shotover. "Money. And with the kaffirs flogging eggs at a shilling for fifty, not to mention those bananas and teeny pineapples, one good breakfast could cost us the right claim, especially if we have to fill this huge great belly your friend's hauling about. So your Hun better pull in his belt a couple of feet."

"Best be clear before we start," Ernst said, sniffing, seeming to enjoy his own smell. He stretched and scratched his white stomach. His sun-browned neck, Anton thought, rose above it like something from a different body. "We'll go equal thirds on the gold."

"Fourths," Shotover said. "Jezzie found it."

"Fourths," Anton said. Ernst turned away.

An hour later, only a small pile of sparkling quartz grains and bits of coal-like grit remained in the center of the shirt. Shotover wiped his spectacles and reset them on his nose. He bent over the material and blew across its surface. Quartz fragments flew to the side. The heavier black grit remained.

"Black iron dust, pyrites," Shotover grumbled. He looked up into the small group of silent faces. He drew a long breath and puffed harder. The dark grains rose and fluttered to the edge of the shirt. Left behind, nestled in the fibre of the cloth, golden specks sparkled.

Anton struggled to suppress his excitement while they all stood and hugged each other. Jezzie brought a Senior Service cigarette tin from her tent. She opened it and drew out a pair of tweezers. The men watched intently as she collected the gold in the tin and slipped the flat box into her pocket.

In the evening the three men sat by the campfire and waited for Jezebel to open the tin. Imprinted on its lid, the H.M.S. *Dreadnought* steamed through the whitecaps. Jezebel lifted the cover with careful fingers. No one spoke as they admired the small pile of gold dust settled in one corner. Jezebel shook the tin delicately, and the heavy uneven grains danced to the center.

"It's a start," said Shotover. Anton noticed exhaustion in his voice. " 'Course, what we're really after isn't all these bits that've been washed about by the water. It's a proper lode we need, the source of it all, buried fast somewhere in a line of quartz."

"How would we recognize it?" Anton said.

"You'll know. It's like seeing a beautiful woman for the first time. Suddenly you can't see anything but her. The quartz is like her clothes. Lets you see just enough. It takes work to strip it away, and many a lad suffers trying to do it. The promise of it makes you ache. But when finally she's yours, it's a breath of eternal life."

"Get your back into it, boy," Ernst said while Anton struggled with his shovel against the tangled overburden of decaying vegetation. "You'll never grow up as strong as these schwarzes unless you sweat more." Ernst gestured with a leg of roasted chicken towards the glistening Kavirondo laborers. "At your age I worked all day without looking up."

"This stuff's three feet deep, Ernst, before we get to the pay streak, and that's another foot thick. It'll go faster if you grab a pick and give us a hand. We've only five days left to peg our claim."

"No, no, not now. What we need is more kaffirs, and I've got work enough getting the ones we have to give us an honest day. Just look at them. Two shillings a week, and all the *posho* they can eat, and damned if the munts don't squat down every time you blink." Ernst sucked his fingers.

"More chickens means fewer diggers," Anton said. Two weeks had passed, and they had found no more gold.

Anton looked across the stream and saw Shotover bend stiffly to check the tip of a sounding pole. Beside him a Kavirondo digger, broad and muscular as Anton himself, held the six-foot pole higher to spare the older man. Two other diggers worked in line behind him. Each man punched his pole through the overburden at the edge of the stream, working it lower and lower until he felt the grind of paydirt, the gritty layer of quartz and mud and shingle that held the possibility of gold. Shotover would examine the pole tips to determine if it was worth tearing away the vegetation and digging out the holes.

Thirty yards down the bank, where their stream joined the sluggish water of the Migori River, Jezzie knelt down, crooning a Maori ballad and rocking a pan from side to side. She sloshed out the water while she hunted on her own. Early in the afternoon she abandoned her prospecting and walked back to prepare supper and get the camp in order.

"Welcome, gentlemen," said Shotover that evening. He removed his spectacles and looked up from his game of solitaire. "I already have the cards out."

Anton lifted his eyes from *David Copperfield* and saw three Afrikaaner miners step into the firelight. Soon, he knew, David's wife Dora would be dead and David would be alone again.

"Perhaps the boy or the German would like to join us for a few hands," said Shotover to his new guests. "This is Mrs. Graham."

The first Afrikaaner looked at the smiling dark woman without acknowledgment. From the thick soles of his low-heeled boots to the rounded crown of his hat, the South African, like his companions, was clothed entirely in black. The woollen garments were the heaviest Anton had seen in Africa. The man's cheeks were weather-cured and wrinkled like the tops of Anton's boots. Even in a land where many white men went unshaven, his beard and hair were startling. A true pure white, not smooth or silky but coarse and wide-spreading, his long beard seemed stiff with electricity. It covered his chest like a snowy apron and moved like a single thick sheet when he bent to lean a single-barrelled rifle against a packing case.

Anton thought of Hugo von Decken describing the last of the old Afrikaaner elephant hunters slogging through the bush with their large-bore roers.

"We are called Vegkop," the man said in guttural English. He looked down at the two decks of old cards, then nodded towards his companions. "My brother and his son. While we play, my nephew will study the Book by the fire and pray that we be forgiven. He is too young for this sin. Cards, like gold and young women, are the devil on earth."

"Of course, *mein Herr*." Ernst frowned. He set the camp stools around Shotover's wooden chest. He placed the oil lamp atop it and adjusted the height of the wick. "We are made to sin so that we may repent."

The Vegkop brothers nodded and sat down. Anton, Ernst and Shotover joined them while Jezebel bustled about the camp.

"Cup of soup?" Shotover asked many hands later while Jezebel filled tin mugs by the fire. She handed one to the dark-bearded young man who sat on a log in the firelight. The thick-paged Old Testament was spread across his knees.

The brothers accepted the soup and stared at their cards before exchanging glances and shaking their heads. Anton tried not to look at the pile of motley coins gathered on his side of the lamp. Every pocket was empty. Rupees and shillings, florins and guilders, even two Maria Theresa silver dollars and a Canadian gold piece, all had come easily to Anton. He glanced again at the brothers' hands. Never, not on a sailor or a miner or a farmer, had he seen the mark of such work. Short broad fingers, blunt, almost even in length, and flat square palms were armored as if with a single callus.

One brother, Anton recognized, wished to end the game, but the elder could not stop.

"If we have faith, brother, we must win," the older man said. Under the straight broad brim of his hat, the corrugations of his brow shone damply between the parted white hair that swept down to the sides of his face.

"We have no money," said the brother. "How are we to go on? Is this our punishment?"

"I have an idea, *meine Herren,*" said Ernst helpfully. He gathered all the money and handed it to Anton. "Money, my papa taught me, is the devil's curse. But work, work is virtue itself. Redemption. Let us put away this money. Instead of coins, let us play for days of honest work, in your diggings or in ours."

The old Afrikaaner looked at Ernst's stomach, then raised his eyes.

"A guilder is a guilder." In the lamplight the man's blue eyes shone hard as a gun barrel. "But if you lose, will you work as I work?"

"I suffer from a broken shoulder and will do what I can, may God watch me." Ernst met the cold gaze without blinking. "But my strong young friend here will toil for two, like a yoke of Cape oxen."

Back in the cottage in Denbigh, Gwenn shivered as she waited for it to grow cold enough to light the small coal fire. From October to March, each miner's family was allowed six buckets of free coal a week. The fires were Gwenn's first job. If she lit the fire too soon, it would not last through the evening. If she lit it too late, it took more of the soft coal to warm the room.

Trembling, her fingers stiff as she searched for a match, Gwenn woke suddenly from her dream when she felt something drop onto her cheek. It moved. She slapped one hand against her face and felt the smooth-arched back of a large beetle hard against her palm. Its struggling sharp-pointed feet pressed into the skin of her cheek. She pinched the creature between her fingers and flung it to the ground.

Gwenn shivered and reached for the bedclothes that lay on the floor. Then she noticed the sound.

Above her head a continuous rustling moved through the dry thatch of the roof. She heard the faint squeaking of agitated bats. Next came the louder noise of a hurried scurrying movement. An animal, squealing and desperate, fell to her pillow, another onto the blanket. Bush rats, grain eaters. Gwenn jumped up, trying not to scream lest she frighten Wellie. Safe in his hammock, the boy slept on, the zebra-hide ropes that suspended him tied to the posts of the bungalow.

The floor moved under her bare feet. She danced about as the rats, screeching and snarling, bolted for the doorway. Gwenn felt a hundred sharp stings cover her feet and ankles. She took a match and lit the lamp that hung from a beam. The hard-packed floor was covered by a sliding red carpet. Safari ants.

An army was marching through her house. Insects and mice dropped to the ground from the thatch above her. Each falling creature was covered by the gripping pincers of tiny jaws. She saw a scorpion at her feet, carried like a pasha on a litter of moving ants. Its hinged tail lashed fruitlessly, the poison wasted on enemies without number. A black carabid beetle dropped nearby, its legs nipped off by the red ants. Other ants worked at the joints of the thrashing lobster-like claws of the large carnivorous beetle. Gwenn leapt onto her bed. A long-limbed jumping spider fell on her shoulder. Red ants clung to its legs.

The ants were climbing the feet of her bedposts. The first scouts appeared on the bottom of the blanket, hesitating on the new terrain, advancing left and right, their feelers and pincers twitching and alert. The leaders disappeared into the folds of rough khaki wool. Other ants fell from the ceiling and joined them, wandering like lost soldiers until they found their comrades.

Gwenn crouched at the head of the bed with her bare knees against her chest. The room was moving around her. She heard Wellie cry out in a sharp voice. The rope at his feet had become a slithering red cable. The bottom of his blanket, itself alive, tossed violently as the boy kicked out, screaming.

Gwenn leapt up and tore off his blanket. Ants clung to her hands and climbed her wrists. Wellington yelled and kicked. His pale round belly was dark with ants. They were one moving creature, emerging and swarming out from the bowl of his navel. Others coursed along his legs and climbed his neck in thick dark lines. A few reached his mouth and nose. The boy clawed and scratched at his stomach and throat, cutting himself with his nails as he fought.

Gwenn grabbed her son and ran across the ants to the door. She screamed for Mulwa and Arthur. Just roused themselves, they joined her on the riverbank. Gwenn dipped Wellie in the dark water. She scraped the ants off his belly in the moonlight. A few hung on, their jaws buried in the child's soft skin and flesh.

"*Siafu*, memsaab! Soldier ants!" Mulwa called while he ran for a can of paraffin. In a moment he returned and rubbed the liquid over the boy. The last insects let go and were swept away by the stream.

Gwenn bathed Wellington again at the edge of the river. He shivered and kicked his feet.

Beside them in the shadows, ants moved in legions of thousands, crossing the bridge and invading what had been an island. Others fell through the chinks into the water. Gwenn stood in the river to her ankles with Wellie shivering in her arms. She directed Mulwa to build up the fire and spread the coals to both sides. Behind her, she heard Olivio's leghorns cackle hysterically while they flapped and scrambled, clinging to the screen walls of their cage.

Even for their animals, she thought, Africa was too much. She sat by the fire and dried her son. Always the land fought back as if it would never be theirs. Every living thing from home, each seed and creature, found cruel new enemies. Leeches and locusts. Hyenas that ripped the udders off cows. And now Fonseca and Reilly demanded her cottage. She remembered Llewelyn marking out the corners with rocks from the river, and his drawing of the completed house with one wing made of stone. She fought the tears that rose in her eyes.

But already Wellington seemed part of this strange world. Somehow it seemed too late to take him home to Wales.

She remembered sitting by the pit elevator on a Saturday waiting for her Dada to come up as the steel cable whined while it traversed the great elevated wheel that rose above the town like the tower of a village church. The cage climbed slowly from the mine shaft. Finally the steam whistle blew and the elevator clattered to the surface. Two miners, demon-like, faces pitted with coal dust, swung open the gate. She expected her father and his friends to step out, their pit lamps and empty lunch pails hanging from black hands.

But the cage held a different cargo, a pit pony. Dead, lying broken on its side, the creature was brought up before its stink poisoned the air. With both front legs smashed and splintered, but still heavy in the shoulder and haunches and thin in the flanks, the short horse, too, was black as death. Only the raw wounds of its harness sores, the galls hairless and red at the centers where the skin was always broken, seemed fresh and clean. At last the pony's eyes once again were open to the light.

Below-ground, she knew, other horses toiled in their hundreds, sheltered at night in vast underground stables. Each animal was brought to the surface once a year to rebuild itself on the rich summer grass of the hillsides. Every horse was washed down when it came up, but the natural color of each animal was hopelessly dimmed and penetrated by the dust of the pits. One summer's evening she had seen them in the hills. A herd of smoke-toned geldings running together along the edge of a lush valley pasture, scores of them, grey as the ghosts of old miners. Did they resist, she wondered, when the morning came to go back down?

Gwenn looked up from the fire and saw Mulwa staring at her with concern.

"How long will the ants keep coming, Mulwa?" Gwenn asked after a moment. She rocked Wellie in her arms and peered across the campfire at the bungalow.

"If it is one army, then one day, two days. If other columns come together, then four days, five days, Gwenn-saab. Once, in my grand-father's time, after a great fire in the forest, the siafu marched through his village for seven days. Always they come before the rains."

Mulwa drew two burning logs from the fire, adding them to the lines of glowing coals that protected their flanks. As far as Gwenn could make out, the ant regiments moved only on a narrow front, the dense column a foot wide where it flooded off the bridge like molten red metal pouring from the bucket of a foundry. They flowed on through the house, swarming through and down and under the walls, emerging at the far side, never hesitating as they regathered and marched on to the east, where the first light now welcomed them.

"Lend me your shoes, please, Mulwa," Gwenn said. She handed Wellie to Arthur. She pulled on the roughly patched boots and splashed paraffin over them and her lower legs. She ran into the cottage. A strong oily odor greeted her. For an instant she paused and heard only the steady rustling of the ants. Her bed was alive with them. Ants fell into her hair. She felt others crunch under her feet. She snatched up her boots, the shotgun and a handful of Wellie's clothes. For a moment she searched for Alan's notebook. Then she remembered that Reilly, with a laugh, had left with it in his pocket, threatening that soon he would be sleeping in her bed. She clenched her fists with hatred.

Gwenn handed everything to Mulwa and poured paraffin over her own boots. She ran through the ants to the garden behind the bungalow.

Within the wire enclosure Anton's apple seedlings were undisturbed, though groups of ants scouted between the circles of raised earth that surrounded each plant. Gwenn saw the remains of four hens nearby. Two were picked clean, recognizable only by small ruins of feathers, beaks and long-legged claws. The third, on its side, flapped weakly while the ants worked at its open breasts and stomach. Adam and one hen survived. In the far corner of the cage the rooster hung from the screen roof of the chicken run. One claw struggled feebly with the wire. The other, forced through the mesh in the bird's desperation, had saved it. Caught fast, the claw had suspended Adam during the long night. Another leghorn roosted in the branches of a thornbush. Methodically the chicken picked and ate ants from her legs and stomach.

Gwenn freed Adam and carried both birds back to the fire. She tethered them to a camp chair with Mulwa's bootlaces.

Later in the morning Gwenn took Wellie across the Ewaso Ngiro to the west bank. The corkscrew-horned merinos, tended by the Kikuyu women, were safe and fat. Even the crops, though hard pressed by other adversaries, were undamaged by the ants, which still marched past the edge of the flax towards the bridge. Occasionally she saw parties of flanking ants ranging among the plants, pausing to devour the fat yellow caterpillars and other pests that lived on the underside of the leaves. Useful, she thought.

Taking a panga from the toolshed, Gwenn slashed at a dead thornbush and gathered kindling. In an hour a mound of brush and logs was piled across the column where the siafu approached the bridge. Forming a rough funnel, intended to lead the insects to the river, not the bridge, the barricade extended several yards to either side. Undiverted, the safari ants moved forward. They held to their route, traversing the loose wooden barrier in a dancing red chain.

Gwenn glanced at her son.

Wellie sat happily on a khaki blanket to one side. He crawled to its edge and held his face near the ground. He studied a company of red ants while they explored the lips of the holes that led to a warren of large black stink ants. From time to time an inch-long black ant would emerge, battle with a few safari ants and then dart down another hole, occasionally gripping a single red ant in its jaws. If a band of red ants gained an advantage over a black ant, other stink ants sallied out to rescue it.

To Gwenn's young African, it was all a game.

Mulwa held a match to the dry grass piled at the edge of the brush. Flames raced along the dense barricade. Smoke gusted back along the ground, covering the army that marched relentlessly into the furnace. The ants crackled and sizzled like corn in a pan. Gwenn gasped and turned away as a thick smell, oily and putrid, fouled the air.

Maybe she should let the ants have the cottage, she thought, immediately dismayed by her own bitterness. She watched Wellie and neatened her short-cropped hair with both hands. It was time to get to work. Time to start building a new stone house on her own land.

— 33 —

I*mpossivel!*" Vasco Fonseca exclaimed aloud. "Twenty years I've worked out here, making my family rich, waiting for the old witch to die! Now that stunted mongrel claims half my inheritance? I'll have the bones from his flesh."

Standing on tiptoe on two pillows, Olivio peered through the knothole in the closet. He smiled when his cousin slumped onto the foot of the bed, his face twisted, the letter from Lisbon clenched in both hands.

A loud knocking drew Fonseca to his feet. Two men entered the room.

"What happened to your eye, Reilly?" asked the smooth voice of Spongey Hartshorne.

"That bleedin' Yank hunter stabbed me. Now she's infected. I may lose her, but I'll kill that bastard Slider."

Olivio twisted his head at a different angle against the wooden wall, hoping to enjoy a glimpse of the wounded man. Two splinters pierced the tender shallow flesh above the dwarf's cheekbone. He flinched and put Lady Penfold's fingerbowl to the wall. He felt the cool crystal against his ear.

"Down to business," said the irritated voice of Fonseca. "It's time we got that Llewelyn farm. We've given her enough time. Soon the government will announce the new rail line and land prices'll shoot up."

"What do we do next?" said Reilly.

"Now that the river's shifted," said Hartshorne, "Fonseca here must file his claim to the land her house is on, arguing that everything east of the river he bought from Ambrose. Then I'll have the Land Office pitch her out fast. Meanwhile Fonseca'll offer to buy the rest of her place and the Land Office will sell her another farm somewhere else."

"If she holds out on us," said Reilly, "we can always make a little trouble around the farm. I wouldn't mind paying 'er a few friendly visits meself. I know what she needs. She likes me a lot better'n she lets on."

"Another thing," Hartshorne said. "The railroad will bring money. Fonseca must speed up that creosote plant we talked about."

"Creosote?" Reilly asked.

"Of course, coal tar," Hartshorne said. "Every rail tie and telegraph pole needs creosoting to save it from termites and the rains. Your brother Paddy could manage that. It's simple enough, and he's too much of a bog peasant to be useful for anything el—"

"You friggin' Limey poofs want us Mickeys to do all your work," Reilly said before Fonseca cut him off. "It's lads like us as won the war. One day all you fancies will have to do your own work."

"Perhaps you English-speaking gentlemen can entertain each other later. I have a family matter to deal with."

His cousin must have some evil to attend to, Olivio surmised with concern.

A taut rope extended from each wooden leg across the coverlet and bound one of Olivio's limbs. Spent, he lay on his back in the center of the high bed. Trimmed with lace, the pleated white nursery bonnet of a well-born English baby covered his scalp. Its scalloped border rose in a neat arc across his round forehead. Looted from Lady Penfold's chest of unused baby clothes, the bonnet was secured by chin straps that met in a bow above the dwarf's knobby Adam's apple. Other baby clothes, torn and soiled, lay on the floor. He recalled the pleasure Kina had taken in dressing him, and wondered how jealous Lady Penfold would have been. Patches of moist bittersweet chocolate dappled parts of Olivio's naked body, forming a sticky paste where the powder of Cadbury's Bournville Cocoa, one of his lordship's favorites, mixed with sweat and coconut oil.

At the foot of the bed, Olivio's head was slightly lower than his feet. He resisted the dizzy sensation of the blood gathering behind his eyes.

He knew Kina, exhausted, was asleep in the front room, tumbled among the cushions like a puppy. Her loins and lovely sticky face would be smeared with chocolate, and a bottle of Lord Penfold's 1879 white port was probably empty at her side.

Olivio sniffed. He gathered in his wide nostrils the blended scents of incense, the dying paraffin lamp, perspiration and chocolate, and something else. A different smoke. The smell of burning straw. At first only a suggestion, soon a swirling cloud floated through the doorway and drifted over the bed.

Fire!

"Kina! Kina!" the dwarf cried. "Wake up! Kina!"

Olivio narrowed the palm of his tiny right hand. He extended and pressed his fingers together while he sought to slip the hand through the rope bond. He tried the left hand, slightly smaller than the other, narrowing it as if entering a woman. Hearing the first crackle of flame, he jerked sharply with both feet. But he had taught Kina too well. To be aroused by the sensation of helplessness, he had explained, a man must be securely bound.

The dwarf stared at the brightening wall above the headboard. He saw the beads of the hanging rosary fixed and dark against the dancing shadows projected through the doorway by the rising flames.

"Kina! Kina!" he screamed. "Kina!"

Could she be too drunk? Or unconscious from the smoke?

Olivio smelled burning oil above him and looked up. The thatched roof ignited with a single flash of fire. In the painting on the wall to his side, the mounted conquistadors rode proudly into the flames that shone from their helmets. The rattan of the adjacent window screen glowed hot, then blazed before the riders like the welcoming gates of hell.

Carrying a blanket and wearing a nightshirt, Adam Penfold rushed out of his bungalow in time to see Rack Slider kick in the door of Olivio's cottage. The flaming structure flared against the night sky like an immense sparkling torch. Clusters of Africans hung about in the shifting shadows, not moving to help, as if observing some distant event. Penfold passed one group and heard a man curse out the words, "Chura Nyakundu," the Yellow Frog.

Penfold dashed into the hotel kitchen and plunged the blanket into a basin of soapy water. He ran out limping and saw Slider stagger backwards out of the cottage. Choking and gasping, the back of his shirt on fire, the American dragged Kina after him by her feet.

"Where's Olivio?" Penfold yelled at Slider above the roar of the blaze when he threw the blanket across the man's back. He saw Kina's naked body, horribly burned, tremble when she coughed. Chief Kitenji lifted his daughter in his arms.

"Must be inside," Slider sputtered. He retched and wiped away the black mucus that hung from his nostrils.

Penfold wrapped the wet blanket around his head and shoulders and grabbed a panga from a watching man before entering the flaming doorway of his old house. The roof blazed above him. Oily smoke thickened densely above the line of his shoulders. Penfold dropped to the ground and crawled into the bedroom.

The edge of the mattress was smoldering. Unable to see, Penfold advanced to the head of the bed. He felt Olivio's naked legs with his hand. Trying to move the body, his hands found the ropes that bound the dwarf. Penfold slashed the cords. He stood and lifted Olivio. He held the dwarf like a child against his chest under the blanket. Short lengths of rope hung from Olivio's ankles and wrists. Penfold chopped through the weakened wall with the panga and staggered into the night.

"Is he all right, Adam?" Fonseca jostled several Africans aside as he rushed forward. "Can I help?"

Not replying, his hair and eyebrows singed, Penfold carried Olivio into his house. He laid the little man on his own bed. Olivio lay still, a dark charred doll against the white sheet. A blackened scrap of linen was stuck to the burns of his scalp. Penfold put his right ear to Olivio's chest. The dwarf's heart was beating. Adam Penfold felt the crisp tissue against his ear and smelled the burned flesh and hair. He was reminded of the war. How disturbing, Penfold thought again, that when a man burns he always smells like roasting pork.

"Please fetch some towels and water," Penfold said to Sissy, who stood watching from the doorway to her room. "And ask the kitchen for a pan of cold wet tea leaves. Someone started that fire with paraffin in the thatch."

He started to clean Olivio's body. The upper half of the dwarf seemed evenly scorched, as if grilled lightly in a stove. Through his tears, Penfold saw the small body continue to react. Raised blisters puffed out over Olivio's face and upper body where moisture and blood returned to the surface. Penfold began to pat with the cool wet towel. Between the blisters, pieces of flesh flaked away and adhered to the cloth.

"Cut it off! Cut it off!" the shrill voice of the parrot cackled through the throbbing furnace of Olivio's pain. Not able to see, the dwarf felt the damp towel that rested across his face. He scented the tea in which the compress had been soaked. Darjeeling! Parched from the opium, his mouth and throat dry as sand, he pressed his swollen tongue against the towel. He smelled the vile stink of Kaiser when the bird hopped closer on the head bar of his lordship's brass bed.

"What've you been giving him for the pain, Penfold?" he heard the doctor whisper. "There's nothing worse than burns."

"A Roman god's been doing the job: old Morpheus himself. I've been bunging morphine into him, Fitzgibbons. Had some left over from my leg. He's taking to it like a Chink in an opium den," Adam Penfold said. "We've been pouring water down him as well. The first two days he kept throwing it up, but now he's weeing away like an old vicar. At least his plumbing seems sound enough."

"After I examine his face, we'll puncture all these blebs, the big blisters, and give him a bath in lukewarm salt water. Then the job is to keep down infection while he tries to heal. Feed him a cup of sulphur and treacle every morning till his pee looks like orange juice. Where's the girl?"

"They're just bringing Kina in now. Her own people threw her out when they learned our little devil had made her preggers."

"Let's take a peek at the rest of him." Fitzgibbons lifted the sheet and whistled. "Look at that, will you! What a waste. Remarkable, really, for such a little chap."

Olivio felt a rush of pride and heard a commotion at the door.

Several men carried in a cot and set it against the foot of his bed. He heard Kina moan and complain just as the lingering shield of the narcotic left him. Pain raged through his chest and arms.

"She'll have some nasty scars." Fitzgibbons sighed. "But the baby should be all right. Now let's have a look at the little bugger's face and eyes. Better close the curtains."

Concentrating, gathering his mind, Olivio sought to distance himself from the agonized creature within him. He smelled again the oil blazing in the thatch above his bed. Oil! He thought of his enemies and the pain retreated. Could they believe he did not know who they were?

Olivio felt the towel rise from his cheeks. He sensed his eyes trying to blink. One lid seemed permanently closed, the other elusive and uncontrollable. Light poured into the open eye as if a lamp filled his head. It circled and spun inside him, carrying him with it in a brilliant dizzy spiral.

"Interesting. Ectropion, by God. Haven't seen this since the war," murmured Fitzgibbons.

"Ectropion?" Penfold said.

"Right. See how the eyelid's gone inside out, with the membrane showing, now that the outer lid's had it? We can play with that one, but the left eye's worse. Already got those corneal ulcers. He'll be damned cute with a patch, but most of this skin isn't going to be so pretty. No pigment left. Some'll be white and flat, and bits'll be pink and raised, 'proud flesh' we call it in the trade. And he won't be needing any manicures."

"How can I help?"

"Grab a rag and start scraping. Before we bathe him, we'll catch up on the debriding, stripping away all this dead tissue like the skin of a snake. Then we'll give him a plunge in your posh safari bath in the corner there." Fitzgibbons gestured towards the short enamel tub with an oak-grained exterior that rested against the wall in a fitted wicker basket. "Looks about the right size, and it'll be easy to take outside and clean."

The surgeon looked at Penfold.

"You'd best get the hang of it, my lord, 'cause the best part'll be in a week or two when his body decides which bits of flesh it wants to keep, and which don't suit it. Then you've got to slough off all the dead meat and give him another salt bath. Even opium won't hold your little bugger then."

"You'll be here, won't you, doctor?"

"Didn't our Lord give his lordship two hands? The boys are keeping me busy up at the farm." Fitzgibbons wheezed and his breath shortened. "Any schoolgirl can manage this one. I reckon you chaps had a pretty cushy war out here, eh? No proper Huns about to keep you sharp."

"Halt the Hun! Halt the Hun!" cried Kaiser.

May we come in, Mr. Alavedo?" Gwenn asked from the doorway, holding Wellington by the hand. Wellie stared silently at the two bandaged figures, one small and propped up in bed like a costumed doll, the other a big black lady seated in a chair by the bedside.

"Please do, dear Mrs. Llewelyn." Olivio turned his bandaged face away from Gwenn. Never had he conceived of such pain or such kindness as he had experienced in the last six weeks.

"This is my fiancée, Miss Kina Kitenji." Olivio tried to reduce the movement of his lips and face. Each word hurt him as he spoke it. "How is Cairn Farm?"

"How do you do, Kina. The sheep and cows are munching away, and the maize is happy, but the flax is about dead, and the tea and coffee aren't taking hold. Now they're telling me the tea seeds should've been packed in charcoal to increase the rate of germination. We'll try again. Mulwa and the Bevises are looking after what's left."

"Next year will be better, Mrs. Llewelyn. You'll see. What brings you to the White Rhino?"

"I'm leaving my son here for a few days while I see about some business in Nairobi. That man Fonseca is claiming the land our house is on, and in a fortnight there's a hearing at the Land Office. We could lose everything. I have to see your friend Mr. da Souza and organize money and a solicitor."

"I will provide you a letter to Senhor da Souza. You shall have all the money and all the solicitors and barristers in Nairobi." Olivio paused.

"I hope I'll have more luck with a lawyer than did David Copperfield." Gwenn tried to sound cheerful. She remembered the words of Uriah Heep: *Even though I am a lawyer, Master Copperfield, I mean, just at present, what I say.*

"I am not familiar with that person," said Olivio, trying to concentrate. "You and I have a long account with this Vasco Fonseca. Does he also own the old Ambrose farm next to yours?"

"Yes, and more land along the river. It's as though he knew where the railway was going."

"Few animals walk in a straight line, Mrs. Llewelyn. One thing I promise: under every stone Senhor Fonseca will find a scorpion. Is that you, my lord?"

"It is I, old boy, just bringing a little medicine." Penfold bent and handed Wellie a two-inch Black Watch bagpiper. "Anything I can do?"

"Today there is, my lord. Under my old bed there is a fine mat. Beneath this mat there is a hole with a metal lockbox inside. The key hangs under the hotel bar."

"Right you are," Penfold said.

"How is the bar, my lord? Does it shine?"

"I'm doing my best to look after it, but she's not the same without you. I'll dig up your box while Mrs. Llewelyn shows Kina how to change the dressings. Make sure Olivio laps up the morphine before you start in on him, Gwenn."

Still groggy after the women finished, Olivio felt over the box with his freshly bandaged hands. Each finger was separately wrapped, like fat cigarettes. Repeatedly the key fell between the dwarf's fingers.

"Please, my lord, could you? There is a paper on top. Would you help me?" Olivio asked with embarrassment.

"Here we are." Penfold took the small key and turned the lock. "Seems to be an I.O.U., dated 1918, transferring ten acres of land to you. Good lord! It's for part of Ambrose's old place! Fonseca's farm now. Your bit's smack in the middle, on the river. Perhaps you should sell this to Gwenn. That would give the Portagee rotter something to think about."

"No, my lord. Forgive me, but you do not understand." The dwarf gathered himself before continuing. How could a man like his lordship comprehend the need for a weak man to destroy his powerful enemies, not by fighting them himself, but by finding for them adversaries who were stronger still?

"Mrs. Llewelyn, sir, is already set against him. To give her this land would not do enough. I must make Fonseca a greater present: the gift of a new enemy. Someone who owns nothing else. A neighbor who will take these ten acres in a grip of iron: young Mr. Anton, I think. One day he may pay me a little gold. Now, my lord, if you do not mind, please hold my hand inside yours, with a pen, and I will sign over my land to Anton Rider. Then perhaps Mrs. Rider— I mean Mrs. Llewelyn, excuse me—will give the paper to a solicitor in Nairobi."

Gwenn blushed as Penfold took pen and ink from a shelf. Penfold sat on the bed and held the paper against the box. Under their gauze, the bones of the tiny fingers strained within Penfold's like the legs of a bird caught in one's grasp. Carefully their two hands worked over the paper.

Olivio paused and reflected, tired after the effort. He had not known the world held such friendship.

Wellie bumped his head under the bed and protested while he drilled the lead bagpiper on the floor. Penfold witnessed the signature as Gwenn spoke.

"Would you have an address, Adam, where I could write to Anton? I need his help with the police in Nairobi. Seems they won't listen to my case unless I have a witness."

"Post Office, Lolgorien. That's where all the miners hang about. What's the matter?"

"I need a sworn statement from Anton. I'm going to prosecute Michael Reilly for rape."

"Can you imagine it?" Sissy Penfold said to her husband while she wound the victrola. "That woman marching into High Court in the middle of Nairobi and claiming she was raped! The cheek of it! Raped, if you please! Raped!"

"Why don't you go for a ride, my dear?"

"It shows one the type they're letting into the country these days.

What will the Africans think of us? And what was she doing travelling without her poor husband? They say sometimes she doesn't even wear a wedding ring. Who ever heard of a lady being raped?"

"I wouldn't know any."

"By the way, Treasure. It's time you got that black hussy and your wretched little man out of the house. Such an odious smell, and those ghastly scabs. His dreary crying keeps me utterly sleepless. He rackets on all night till you blunder in and top him up with opium. And heaven knows what filthy things they do in there when they're alone."

So that was it, he realized at last. Sissy never had cared for sex.

Yet again Adam Penfold heard the Piccadilly Band open with "Dancing at the Savoy." He turned away and splashed a few drops of rifle oil onto the bar and began to wipe with his pocket handkerchief. The bar was clean enough, but the shine did not seem even. Rather like a poorly polished shoe, with the heel not properly done. Why couldn't he do this as well as old Olivio Alavedo?

In the Penfolds' bungalow the dwarf lay still in the brass bed. His mind cleared and floated apart from his body.

Olivio heard the banging of a hammer driving nails. Was he back in the quarter of the carpenters and masons in Goa, in the shadow of the Arch of the Viceroys? Or was it the alarm bells in the seaside towers of the ancient fort church? Did he smell again the ocean breeze gusting north from the Malabar Coast? Was he home?

No, the uncertain tempo of the hammering could only mean it was an African at work. Olivio opened his right eye under the loose gauze that covered his face. He detected light and moving shadows when he turned his head. The pain rejoined him when he stretched the contracted cracked skin and the fresh scars under his chin.

Yes, it must be his new cottage. Soon it would be ready, his lordship had assured him, larger and even more dignified than the first. With a small verandah, a nursery and a separate chamber to bathe in! One day Olivio would order the proper curved red roof tiles from Goa. What would they all think then?

"May I come in, Kina?" asked his lordship's voice. "Royal Mail, Olivio. A letter from Lisbon, from some grand barrister, by the look of it, and another from your fat chum da Souza in Nairobi. Damned sight more promising than the stuff that's been coming in for me.

Soon we'll have nothing left in Wiltshire but the old well, and she's been dry for three hundred years."

"My lord, could I trouble you to read them to me?"

"Of course, old boy. Just let me put Wellington down. We'll let him bother Kina."

Wellington ignored the suggestion. He toddled to the waiting safari bath and launched his empty walnut shells.

Later, drifting gently with the opium, Olivio felt the metal box resting against his leg. Everything was safely locked inside. The key was under his pillow. He considered his good fortune and all that his lordship and Gwenn had done for him. Soon he must dispatch more funds to the orphan school in Goa.

Kina was seated on the bed beside him. She held a long straw to his parched lips through a slit in the gauze. He felt the split end of the dry African stalk stab his tongue. Olivio sucked. The strained fresh pineapple juice cooled his mouth. He let the drink, wonderfully sweet, settle under his tongue, savoring the rum that strengthened it. For an instant it reminded him of the drink of his own people, *feni,* patiently brewed from the sap of Goan palms.

He sucked and wondered if he would ever again taste the finest of all drinks: cashew feni. He thought back to the private gardens in the courtyards of the rich. There the grand ladies of Goa lounged in the cool surrounding hallways. Flattering garden light filtered in to them through polished-thin oyster shells set into the latticework walls. The precious cashew trees grew nearby in the courtyard. Each was guarded more closely than a princely heir. In a proper Goan household, there was one garden boy, a low-caste Hindu, for every eight trees. The small red cashew apples grew just above the nuts. This fruit, he exulted, when crushed and distilled, and matured in darkness for eighteen years, yielded cashew feni, or *fontainhas.*

Olivio swallowed again. At last the White Rhino's miserable cook was almost doing something well, but could he trust the dog not to poison him? Must he have Kina taste everything first?

As before in his life, the dwarf realized, he was learning to accumulate small pleasures to replace those of other men. There were many ways to heal.

He felt a strong hand on his foot. The covers were pulled back.

The girl began to massage his toes and arches, using the medicinal petroleum jelly, rich, like the cold tea leaves, in soothing tannic acid. He felt her breasts rubbing up and down along his thigh. Was this possible? Could they be still larger and firmer than before?

So, Olivio reflected, patting the strongbox with his bandaged hand, the first battle was his. In Lisbon, citing the attestation of the cardinal's secretary, the Commissioner of Testaments himself had certified Olivio Fonseca Alavedo's claim as a natural descendant of his eminence, the late Archbishop of Goa. Now the mortal question was the division of the estate.

Alas, things were proceeding less well in Africa. Da Souza had received an ugly report from his spies in the Land Office. He had warned Olivio that the Llewelyn farm and their investment were in danger. Under Hartshorne's influence, the Land Office was about to award the entire farm to Fonseca. The Portuguese, astonishing as it seemed, were prepared to uphold the rights of an honest man, for a price, of course. But how could a gentleman trust these English?

From time to time Kina paused and kissed the dwarf with her tongue where she worked, sucking gently against his flesh. Was she trying to get his attention? At least she had not forgotten her lessons. The mark of a master teacher, he reflected. Slowly she advanced upwards, bringing life where his body was not burned.

"Time we checked those ugly Boers are giving us a fair day's work." Ernst grunted. He spooned more thick wild honey into his coffee.

"If you shovelled like the Vegkops, we'd have more treasure than the Kaiser." Anton threw a bucket and pick into the wooden barrow and lifted its handles. "As long as we don't ask them to do the same work as the black chaps, they'll do anything."

Anton wheeled the handcart down to the feeder stream in the center of the claim. This was the last day's work in the dry half of the partly dammed streambed. Tomorrow they would knock down the dam and let the stream flow through all of its old bed before damming the other side and working the floor.

Too stiff to bend, Shotover walked backwards along the dry channel with a crude rake. Four-inch nails protruded through its wooden spar. He dragged the tool through broken stretches of clay and silt,

checking one last time, searching for the glint of quartz. A tall Kavirondo followed with a basket.

"Trouble is," said Shotover, sensing Anton behind him, "the damn
stuff never settles in a straight line. It wanders about the streambed
like a she-goat. And the bed wanders as well. We still haven't found
the lode. But she's somewhere. Probably a quartz reef three foot
wide cutting into one of these hills, running on between shelves of
clay and shingle."

Occasionally Shotover paused and forced himself to crouch, bending his knees and keeping his back straight. He would work his hands
into the streambed and sift the material between his fingers. Once
or twice he nodded to the Kavirondo, who would fill the basket and
carry it to the nearest sluice.

Spread out along the bank, each slanting ten-foot sluice box was
managed by a Vegkop. As murky water washed through the box,
flushing out the lighter materials, Africans dumped in the silt and
ore. Under unblinking Afrikaaner eyes, three other blacks panned
the remains that settled between the slats. Altogether, three hundred
pans a day.

Casually but regularly, Jezebel passed by, collecting the occasional
grains of gold dust in a tobacco tin. At day's end, they sat by the fire
while Shotover heated the gold in a pan and blew off the black iron
dust. Each evening the Vegkops received a share. Shotover buried
the rest under his tent. So far, there were only two tins. Soon they
would run out of time and money.

Anton walked the wheelbarrow up to the hillside that was his. Six
Watendi joked and laughed while they tunnelled into the slope,
extending the earthwork that Shotover hoped might strike the lode.
Anton thought of the gold coin he had seen in the fire.

The Watendi leader made a sad face and pointed to an abandoned
pit six feet deep. Anton knelt and looked down. At the bottom their
mascots lay dead. The larger of two hissing sand snakes had consumed
its companion. The shorter snake had starved as the larger serpent
ate all the rodents and the skinks and other lizards that the Watendi
dropped into the pit. Finally the bigger reptile, unfed for a week,
wrapped itself about the smaller and devoured it, tail first.

But why, Anton wondered, squatting beside the pit, would the
well-nourished winner die so soon? Only two days ago, it lay in a

wide circle, still swollen, too stuffed to coil up. Anton slipped out his knife and jumped into the pit. Thinking of the python and Karioki, he held the snake behind the head and slit it open. The partially digested victim lay inside, its scales and vertebrae caught in its enemy's throat. Vengeance, Anton wondered?

"What's the matter?" Ernst stared down from the edge of the hole. "Are you hungry?"

"No," said Anton, "but I think the dinner choked the diner."

As he raised his eyes to meet Ernst's, the two snakes in his hand, Anton spotted a band of quartz sparkling along the wall of the pit. He stood still.

"Let's get Shotover!" Anton exclaimed without taking his eyes from the wall. He stroked the quartz with his fingers and brushed away the soil. "I think our snakes've made us rich."

Anton trotted towards the river and looked along the bank. In the distance he saw Shotover leaning on his rake. Anton ran towards him.

"We've found it!" Anton hollered as he approached. "A streak of gold!"

Shotover began to hurry towards Anton, stumbling while he made his way along the bank. As he left the river Shotover came faster, climbing the slope, for a moment almost moving like a boy.

Anton paused and cheered as his friend rushed towards him. Then Shotover slowed and his feet dragged. The old miner appeared to stiffen. His body rocked. He bent forward and the rake fell from his hands. Anton saw him try to straighten himself. As Anton ran to him, Shotover trembled like a tree in a storm. He staggered to his right and collapsed on the hillside.

Anton knelt and cradled Shotover's head. The old man's arms were limp and twitching. His eyes stared. He gurgled, and choking sounds came from his throat. His mouth drooled. Anton held him while his body calmed. He wiped Shotover's face with his diklo and lifted his friend in his arms.

Jezebel and Ernst hurried to meet them as Anton walked towards the camp. Shotover seemed to be asleep. His body was loose.

After a time Jezebel emerged from the tent. Her husband was sleeping on his cot.

"I think we found his lode," Anton said. "In the old pit by the hill." He set a chair for Jezebel by the fire and poured three cups of tea from the billy.

"At last," she said without sadness. "I knew it would be like this. My Shotover's too old for this life. He was bound to have a stroke."

They heard Shotover stir. Jezebel dipped a cloth in her tea and returned to the tent. She raised her husband's head and moistened his lips. Shotover's voice began to work, at first only a grumbling in his throat. He tried to sit up but fell back. He coughed and spat before he spoke.

"What am I doing in here? Take me outside. I want to see the sky."

Ernst and Anton carried the cot from the tent and set it beneath a fig tree. Dappled sunlight filtered through the leaves.

"That's better," Shotover said in a dreamy voice before he fell asleep.

The next morning Shotover made them carry his cot to the edge of the snake pit.

"Take a pick and jump in, laddie!" Shotover said, excited as a boy.

Anton handed up fragments of quartz to Ernst and the Watendi. Everyone waited in silence while Jezebel cleaned Shotover's spectacles. The miner examined each bit of rock as he turned it over with his left hand. The fingers of his right hand shook when he tried to use them.

"I must see for myself." Shotover's body fidgetted on the cot. "Take me into the pit."

Anton looked up at Jezebel. She nodded. Anton put down his pick. Ernst lifted Shotover and knelt by the side of the hole, passing him like a baby into Anton's arms.

Anton felt Shotover's body tremble as the miner craned his head to the side and examined the shelf of quartz through his spectacles. He lifted his left hand from his stomach and set it against the rock. He closed his eyes and moved his fingers back and forth along the wall of the pit. Then Shotover opened his eyes and began to scrape frantically with his hand, struggling in Anton's arms as he tried to expose more of the quartz.

"Shotover Graham!" Jezebel called down.

Shotover gasped. He placed his bleeding hand back on his stomach. He nodded and put his mouth close to Anton's ear.

"We've found it, laddie." Shotover settled peacefully in Anton's arms. "At last, it's our lode. It doesn't smell like a thousand-footer, but it's gold. Your snakes found it for us. Now we have to break out the quartz and start crushing it." Soon he was asleep.

The next morning Shotover planned the day's work. Propped up in his cot, he gave detailed instructions in a slow voice.

The following day Anton helped Shotover to a camp chair by the fire. The New Zealander struggled to master his right arm and leg. He clutched his map case in his good hand and gave directions for the work. Even Ernst listened with respect, nodding while he watched Anton shave the grizzled miner's cheeks with his straight razor.

"It's no good," Ernst said a day later, interrupting Shotover's lengthy instructions. "You can't run it from up here. It means too many mistakes, too much wasted work. We need you where the gold is." Ernst turned to Anton. "So, my Engländer, while you dig with the munts today, I'll make him a Selous chair. Then we can put him back to work."

In the evening it was ready. Ernst had nailed and lashed the sides of a folding camp chair to two poles extending fore and aft of the seat. The next morning two Watendi were assigned to Shotover. Holding the ends of the poles like stretcher handles, they carried the miner about the site.

"Now the lazy old devil has to earn his share," said Ernst.

"Happy birthday, my young man!" Jezebel smiled and rose on tiptoe to rub noses with Anton.

"Thank you, ma'am," he said, bending to do it again, looking forward to his morning tea. This was better than his birthdays in England. And today one of the miners should be returning from Lolgorien with the mail. Anton hoped he would hear from Gwenn.

"What about my nose?" grumbled Ernst.

"Rubbing noses is a custom of my people," the Maori woman said. "His is bigger, with a grand bump in it, and you've had too many birthdays."

"Time to get to work, lads," called Shotover from his chair. "The gold never waits."

My Darling Anton, the letter began. Anton lay on his bedroll and rubbed Lenares's gold earring between his fingers. He read Gwenn's letter by the failing light that entered at the head of his tent.

Wellie and David C. miss you. But what about Gwenn? Didn't she miss him? What else could those words mean?

I've terrible news for you. Karioki has been killed by Reilly's brother and Fonseca, and they're all saying it was self-defense. The truth is Karioki was just trying to protect me. Stunned, Anton sat up and put down the letter, unable to continue.

Karioki, his best friend. Dead. Gone, too, like Lenares. And it was Anton's fault. He himself should have stayed to look after Gwenn. He wiped his eyes. And once again, he thought with anger, the trouble came from Paddy and Reilly.

What should he do now? Did he have to leave the goldfields just when they'd found the lode and he had a chance to make his fortune? He had to decide.

I'm going to prosecute Reilly for rape, and I need your help. They don't like women bringing this sort of case, especially out here, and Reilly's already saying it wasn't rape. So she was going after that swine Reilly. High time, but Reilly and his mates were a rough bunch, and a rape trial would be a painful scandal for Gwenn. Most women made a secret of such horrors. He felt proud of her.

But what would all this do to Wellie? Who would he think his father was? Anton recalled his own boyhood. The loneliness, the lost friends, learning to wander. Who was his father? Why had his mother never told him? Maybe she didn't know herself. This was going to be hard on Wellington when he grew up, but maybe it wouldn't matter so much out here. And Gwenn, he knew, would never leave her son. Perhaps later he himself could look after Wellie the way Lenares had taken care of him.

Your friend Olivio has had a cruel accident, if accident it was. He thinks Fonseca tried to kill him by setting fire to his cottage. He says if you come right away and help me with the Reilly case, he has a present for you.

"Happy birthday to you!" voices suddenly sang into the night.

Anton put away Gwenn's letter and hurried through the fig trees to the fire.

There they all were: Ernst and the Afrikaaners, the Grahams and the Kavirondo, and his own team of Watendi, grinning and proud of their strike. And miners from the flats, dozens of them. Some carried fish spitted on long sticks. Others brought chickens ready for the fire. The Watendi offered a sand snake sliced up like French bread. Anton smelled Jezebel's stew and frying bananas and her fresh raisin cake baking in a tin, "Spotted Dick" she always called it.

He made an effort to smile when Ernst stepped forward and gave him a wet kiss on the cheek, and his last hoarded bottle of beer. Anton blinked and looked at the faces around the fire.

Once again, like David, Anton would have to leave his friends. He'd miss Ernst and Jezebel, and he hated to abandon Shotover and the gold.

Later, when the coals glowed dim and the camp was still, Anton lay on his back in his tent. He thought of his last birthday, with Karioki at the edge of the Rift, and tried not to feel sad. He saw his friend hunting in the mists of the Aberdares.

"Here, Tlaga," Karioki had told him, "my spirit will come to hunt."

Anton thought of Gwenn. He must go back and look after her. He remembered the morning she smiled into the wind while the boat swept her ashore. He recalled putting his hand under her shirt that afternoon on the rock, first along the firm impression of her spine, then up her smooth stomach to her breasts.

Anton lay awake. From time to time he peeked out at the vast sparkling sky. He stiffened when he heard something approach. The stars were obscured. Jezebel knelt at the head of his tent. She bent lower and rubbed her nose against Anton's.

"Mr. Graham wants me to give you a birthday present."

— 35 —

Drink up, Rafiki, it's all yours." Anton dismounted and felt the unsteadiness in his legs after a long morning in the saddle. The Abyssinian stroked the Ewaso Ngiro with one swinging hoof and blew through his nostrils across the water's surface. The horse avoided the silty moving water and drank from a clear sandy-bottomed pool in the streambed.

Anton knelt and splashed water over his face and neck. He climbed on a rock and turned to see the land to the east. Running gently down from the green highlands of Mount Kenya, the rocky bush levelled where it met the flatter reaches of savannah and thorn plain that spread to the north. Anton drew his map from a saddlebag. Travelling as fast as his legs and occasional transport allowed, it had been a hard fortnight's journey northeast from the goldfields to the White Rhino. Soon he would see Gwenn. First, only a few miles on, he would find his own land, ten acres, just purchased from Olivio for one Senior Service tin of gold dust. The land was his, with game and water and all the life of Africa.

Satisfied, Rafiki raised his head. Anton remounted. Rafiki shook himself and pawed the riverbank, a sure signal he was about to drop to his front knees and roll in the warm sand. Anton raised the reins and turned the horse's head away from the river. He rode on towards a cluster of acacias that waited beneath a spiral of planing vultures.

The wind shifted towards him. Rafiki pranced nervously when horse and rider caught the rank stench of a kill. Anton encouraged

Rafiki forward and took two .450s from the double row of cartridge loops on his shirtfront. He thought of Rack Slider when he drew the rifle from the American's open saddle holster. Designed for a quick draw rather than for protection of the weapon, the scabbard, like Rack, was looser than its British counterparts.

"Do you think I'll need it, Mr. Slider?" Anton had asked when the Oklahoman helped him saddle up at the White Rhino.

"Need it, sonny? What did the cowman say when the Boston gal asked him if you need to carry a handgun in Amarillo? 'You can be in the Panhandle one year, and you may be here two and never need it. But when you want it, you'll want it mighty bad.' "

Like decaying boulders, the broken carcasses of two young female elephants lay side by side in the dust. Snapped-off acacia branches, the pods uneaten, rested beside them like lost garlands. The wrinkled grey bodies seemed incredibly old, freckled with the white droppings of vultures and marabou storks.

The swollen bellies, ripped open near the hind legs, revealed the nocturnal visits of lion and hyena. As if chopped with a giant cleaver, their mutilated open faces welcomed the broad-billed storks that worked at the eye sockets and at the wounds that had held their small tusks. Inside the bellies of the elephants, the long speckled necks of feeding white-backed vultures twisted and stretched like serpents. Only the elephants' trunks, still entwined, looked as they had in life.

Scraps of flesh hung from the curved beaks of the vultures. Their white ruffs gory, some too bloated to rise, they flapped heavily about the bodies. Anton walked to the elephants. The vultures resentfully backed away in a noisy arc, hissing and cackling. The marabou, less cheeky, croaked hoarsely and flew off. Knowing the storks were the first defense against locusts, Anton admired their rising flight when the immense birds tucked long white legs against their stomachs and drew pink neck pouches into their shoulders.

He dismounted with his rifle and tied the nervous horse to a root. He leaned the Merkel against one elephant's leg and climbed on her shoulder to examine the bullet wounds. Five in all. Two in the head, one lung shot, and two clean hits in the upper shoulder near the heart. Anton took out his knife and sawed through the inch-thick skin to get at the lung shot. He pressed his fingers into the spongy tissue and recovered a bullet that had not been damaged by striking bone.

Anton studied the nickel-jacketed bullet: lighter than a .450. He put it in his pocket. He wiped his hands with dry earth and walked in careful circles about the scene. Seventy yards off, he knelt to study a set of tire tracks and found three rimless brass .404 cartridges but no nearby footprints.

For several miles Anton followed the tire tracks north, knowing the direction was roughly his own. The trail joined the new rail line that was advancing to its final stop.

He dismounted and examined the wooden ties that lay under the narrow-gauge rails, here laid directly on the ground in what he understood was sometimes the old style of the first line to Lake Vic. This final section was "light railway," intended only to serve the last outpost farms on this edge of the African empire.

Anton bent and rubbed a wooden tie with one hand. He smelled his fingers. A slight stickiness and the thick oily odor of coal tar clung to them. Creosote. He could almost smell Paddy and Reilly. As Olivio had warned him, Fonseca and the Irishmen were already at work on Anton's land. He remembered Karioki.

He mounted and cantered gently, rocking with Rafiki's long stride, thinking about the elephants and Gwenn and Lenares. How he would love to look up from a campfire, just once, and see his old gypsy teacher step lightly into the firelight, his dark eyes sparkling while he leaned his rifle against a tree. Then to have one evening of talk, telling tales, and hearing the African night sounds rise, and teaching his friend what each meant, and what a day in the bush might hold.

Anton rode on between the rails and the occasional marks of car tracks. His attention was drawn by stacks of telegraph poles, each saturated with the sticky dark preservative.

In two hours he came to a cluster of acacias and a signpost bearing the faded word AMBROSE. He breathed deeply and looked across his bit of Africa. In a moment Anton would ride on his own land. He dismounted and rubbed the gritty red earth between his hands. Below him, thick smoke drifted about the plant. Angered by the filthy sight, he slapped Rafiki's shoulder with the reins.

"Where the devil do you think you're going?" Reilly asked Anton a few moments later. The man's good eye squinted angrily when he looked up and tried to grab Rafiki's twitching bridle.

Behind Reilly bulked two long steel cylinders, each the length of a railway carriage. The lower one rested near a railroad siding one hundred yards from the main track. A large metal door, perhaps six feet tall, hung open on greased hinges at one end of this cylinder. A nauseating smell flushed out when the breeze gusted by. Two sweating Africans, bandannas bound over their mouths and noses, worked inside the tank, scraping out the residue of gluey dark-brown creosote. Piles of telegraph poles stood nearby, ready to take their turn inside the cylinder.

"You've been breaking the Game Ordinances, Reilly," said Anton. "Killing elephant off license, young females, and shooting from a vehicle."

"Not me. Must've been the greaser. The boss likes to shoot sitting down, especially at night, using the 'eadlamps. Now keep riding."

Reilly beckoned to a group of men working nearby under the second cylinder. Raised on tall crossed struts that suspended it over the rail siding, the pump tank hung in the air like the swollen body of a long-limbed poisonous spider waiting for a victim to settle beneath. It would pump heated creosote into the lower tank, building pressure to impregnate the timber. Mounted on each cylinder, Anton noticed two glass-faced gauges, one marked for pressure, the other for heat up to two hundred and twenty degrees. The men moved toward him. Anton saw a large figure carrying a greasy wrench in one hand. Paddy. Wearing a pistol.

Anton thought of Karioki and felt anger seize him. He cautioned himself. Slowly. Patience. This was not the time.

"Where'll I find Fonseca?" Anton asked Reilly, ignoring the men that gathered around him.

"He's down the way, moving into his new house, the old Llewelyn place. Don't you bother 'im." Reilly picked under his eyepatch. "He's probably up to a little wenching with me old girlfriend."

"Next time I see you, Reilly, you and I are going to work on your manners. It'll be hard work. In the meantime, you and this crew better start getting your rubbish together. You won't be staying long."

Paddy struck Rafiki with his wrench. The horse bolted.

Anton calmed Rafiki while the men jeered and laughed. At a hundred and fifty yards he turned Rafiki and stilled him. He saw the men staring after him. Anton took a moment to control his anger.

He drew and fired his Merkel in one motion. Sounding like a single shot, the two .450s slammed through the gauges of the lower tank.

"That'll give them warning," Anton said aloud. He ejected the empties and rode on.

Coming at last to the river, he checked the water for crocodiles and urged Rafiki across a shallow ford well downstream from Cairn Farm. He climbed the bank and began to canter, smelling the bush-scented wind while he circled back from the north across the endless thorn plain. Browsing in his path, first curious, then disturbed, five giraffe fled elegantly before him, rocking smoothly like giant dusty hobbyhorses. Anton raised his hat with a loud whoop and broke into a gallop. At last broadside, he sailed along among them, his head at the height of their stretching chests. Hearing nothing but the dinning hooves, he was intoxicated by the noise and the smell and the dust they threw up around him. He slowed and the giraffe left him.

Passing the Samburu bomas at a trot, he approached Cairn Farm. Anton looked for signs of change, remembering the plans and the unfinished work. He recalled that although the shifting river had cost Gwenn her cottage, the farmland itself should still be hers. He entered the first pasture through a break in the fence. He dismounted and reset the downed rails, noting the tracks of stampeding zebra. Riding on, he saw piles of rocks and brush at the side of the wheat field and thought of the work they had required. He continued past a field of withered flax. At its edge the tamarind tree stood by the river.

Anton came to the sheep field and reined in Rafiki. At the far end, near two tents and a canvas shelter, he saw five or six people setting stones, building the walls of a new house. A small figure played on the ground to one side.

For the first time in his life Anton felt he was coming home. He sat still on his horse. Then he stood in his stirrups and waved his hat. He saw a woman stand erect inside the new walls. Dropping a stone, she wiped her face and pushed back her hair. She gathered her skirt in both hands and stepped over the wall and began to run across the field.

As Gwenn reached him, breathless and smiling, Anton swept down with one arm and lifted her.

Kina knelt among the thorn branches. She gathered the shrivelled white blossoms with both hands. One basket was piled high. Slender lavender lilies and five-petalled yellow hibiscus rested on a bed of thyme and sage. When her hands were full, she cupped her palms together and pressed them to her face. The crisp pungency of the leaves mixed with the richness of the flowers.

Sitting on her leather skirt in the dust and resting the loaded basket on her lap, Kina arranged several longer grey-green leaves on the palm of her left hand. She pinched together the centers of flowers, loosening their seeds, and pressed the flowers into the leaves. She wrapped the leaves around the flowers and formed a small ball that she rolled between her palms, crushing the plants and extracting their scents. Kina smelled the ball and smiled and placed it in the empty basket. She pulled out the bitter yellow stamens from the core of each lily, then rolled the lilies into the centers of new balls.

When she finished, the floor of the second basket was covered with a layer of uneven green balls. She smelled the palms of her hands and scraped together the fragments of leaves and flowers that remained in the first basket, rubbing the crumpled flowers against her cheeks. Petals stuck to her face and fell on her chest. She looked down.

Why was her little man so fascinated with her breasts? Too large, the other girls told her, as if her silent tongue were not hardship enough. One day, they joked, after seven totos, her breasts would hang to her waist, tickling the dust when she bent to work in the fields. She touched one, feeling it larger and firmer than ever before, as it prepared to nourish her first baby. Now the girls spoke to her differently, for she had never gone with them to visit the young men in their camps in the bush. And when the girls came back, happy and sore and laughing with stories, she had not joined them when they prepared for the circumcision ceremonies. But at last she was tasting the pleasures the other girls had enjoyed so briefly. She touched herself absently, her fingers soon moist, and thought of the different life she would have, with the powerful man who loved her. She put her fingers against the scars on her face. How could she please him more? One day she must make him her father's friend.

Kina rose and walked down the hill, Mount Kenya immense and protective behind her in the clear light. She looked about for the things she needed.

She found a young *mukuruwe*. When it was mature, its dark green leaves and flat top would be set off by pink and white peacock flowers. Old women would come to take the tree's medicine. The bark would treat fever. The crushed pods would heal sick stomachs. But the tree was still young, with thin supple branches. For her it would serve a happier purpose.

Kina set down her baskets and tested several branches. She flexed them and bent them back and forth. She severed one at its base. She broke off each small branch that grew from it and drew it through her tight fist and stripped it clean. It whistled when she swung it. Perfect. Kina flicked it sharply against her leg and felt the pleasing sting of the small knobs where new branches had started to grow. Olivio would love it.

Kina picked up her baskets and rambled on, slapping her leg with the switch as she walked.

She came to her favorite tree. Twin-stemmed, with light brown bark veined by fine vertical fissures, the *muho* was bright with clustered yellow flowers. Awkward with her tight growing belly, she climbed up and sat in the fork of the tree, dangling her legs as she had done when she was little. The fruit of the muho hung around her in a canopy. She broke off one long spiralled capsule. Inside the brown shell were many seeds, each with two tiny transparent wings to help it carry on the wind. She collected the seeds in the palm of one hand. When they were clean and free of the fragments of the shell, she filled her cheeks and blew hard across her palm. Kina begged Ngai for a son. The seeds flew off.

"Time to visit your friend the poacher," Tony Bevis said to Anton. He passed his breakfast plate to Mulwa and stood up to leave the fire. Anton pinched Wellie's nose and handed the giggling boy to Gwenn.

Bevis and Anton walked down to the river. They splashed through the water and climbed out onto the east bank of the Ewaso Ngiro.

"Get off my land!" Vasco Fonseca shouted from the doorway of the old Llewelyn cottage.

Anton and Bevis ignored the Portuguese and walked to the Willys box body that was parked nearby. Reaching over the side slats and into the bed behind the driver's seat, Bevis pulled at two rolled zebra hides with his only hand. Anton helped lift out the skins.

"You're trespassing, gentlemen. Get away from my car," Fonseca called angrily as he hurried over. "The Land Office says this property belongs to me."

"This is Mr. Bevis, Mr. Fonseca. He's Deputy Game Ranger hereabouts." Anton unrolled the first skin and let two small tusks fall to the ground. "I remember you cheat at cards, but I didn't know you poach twenty-pounders from your motorcar."

"Let me see your rifle, Mr. Fonseca." Bevis rolled a rimless cartridge between his fingers. "Your four-oh-four Jeffery."

"I've already got the mortgage on your disabled soldiers' farm." Fonseca looked at Bevis's empty sleeve. "You're months late with my money already. Unless you mind your damn business, I'll have the whole crippled lot of you chucked out."

"The Game Department meets at Nanyuki the first of the month, Mr. Fonseca. I'll see you then. Be sure and bring your rifle. Meantime, I'll just hang on to these tusks and the cartridges."

"Get off my property."

Following Bevis back to the river, Anton paused and turned around, addressing the Portuguese.

"By the way, Mr. Fonseca, you've built your creosote plant on my land. On my section of the old Ambrose place. Please be out of there by the end of the week."

— 36 —

Have I lost you, Blue Eyes?" asked Anunciata, armed for Olivio's wedding in a clinging silk dress. "Has the beautiful farmer stolen your heart?"

Anton hesitated. Anunciata pressed two fingers against his lips. Only her brown eyes were sad. "Be careful, my handsome English boy. Weddings are contagious. No matter what they tell you, it is what every woman wants."

Anton saw Gwenn step onto the verandah of the White Rhino just as Anunciata rose on her toes and kissed him. The Portuguese woman slipped one hand into his trouser pocket and whispered, "Don't change."

Anunciata turned away and Anton removed the note from his pocket.

Be careful of Vasco, he read. *My brother is dangerous.*

Exhausted by the pain of dressing, his head pulsing, his cheeks and forehead bandaged, Olivio sat for the last time in the folding campaign chair in Lord Penfold's bedroom. Tonight Olivio and his bride would sleep in their own house. A Turkana with a spear would be on watch outside.

The dwarf's tan trousers, just too long, were on and belted. The new white shirt was tucked in, but still open over the glazed surface of his now hairless chest. Again he raised both hands to the top button. He compelled himself to ignore the sharpening pain when he bent his arms and stretched the drum-taut poreless skin of his wrists and elbows.

His fingers would not serve him. Some had no nails. Smooth and rounded like the tips of rubber gloves, a few still carried surviving nerves, their insulation destroyed, their alarms too sensitive and shrill. His unsweating poreless flesh acutely susceptible to heat and cold, largely denied the unthinking adjustments of other people's bodies, Olivio sensed the warmth of the day begin to rise.

The dwarf finally secured the collar button between the thumb and forefinger of his right hand. He concentrated and tried to seize the left collar in his other hand. Disobedient, refusing the authority of his will, the left hand would not help the right. Some nerves too numb to tell him when he touched the buttonhole, others too hysterical to let him grip the cloth, instead of being his servants, these antennae were now his master. He struggled once more. Even the hinges of his joints defied him.

Weeping, Olivio tried again. His mind was glitteringly alive. His heart, prepared for marriage, was torn with love and rage.

"May I come in, old boy?" asked a voice at the door, incurably crisp but warm.

"Please, my lord." The dwarf brushed his eyes with one unbuttoned sleeve. Hot with exhaustion, he felt only the back of his body moisten with perspiration.

Adam Penfold entered, two glasses in one hand, a bottle of champagne in the other, a white Wiltshire rose in his teeth. His creamy linen suit, pressed but baggy, fitted him like a comfortable friend. A stained striped tie, black and pale blue, swung free outside the buttoned jacket. He set down the drinks and the flower.

"If you wish to change your mind, Olivio, it's your last chance to make a dash for it. I've got Rafiki saddled out back."

Olivio sought to stretch his face into a smile, dreading the indignity of his condition being assessed.

"Better get our kit together," said Penfold without hesitation. He knelt with a groan and opened wide the dwarf's tiny white shoes, the confirmation footwear of a Catholic schoolboy. Penfold kneaded each stiff new shoe before easing them on and tying them. After pouring the champagne, he buttoned Olivio's shirt and knotted the

red and green tie of the Goan Institute of Nairobi, the seven castles
of Portugal detailed on its shield. Penfold tucked the long tie into
the top of Olivio's trousers.

Lord Penfold handed a glass to the dwarf. Olivio received it in
two hands and looked up. Penfold raised his glass and toasted. "Hap-
piness and wealth." The two men drank.

A pink-and-white party tent waited between the Penfolds' bungalow and the dwarf's new cottage. Its round crown and fluttering
forked roof pennant reminded Penfold of a mediaeval camp.

A fortnight before, Adam Penfold, acting as Olivio Alavedo's
father, had paid a call on Chief Kitenji to secure Kina's hand for the
dwarf. Limping over to the round hut, Penfold had carried two
buffalo-horn cups in one hand and a gourd of njohi in the other.
Behind Kitenji stood Kina. Penfold filled both cups and offered one
to the chief.

"Daughter," Kitenji had asked, turning to look at her, speaking
very slowly with loss in his eyes, "shall I drink this?"

Kina had nodded twice, keeping her eyes on the ground. Her
father and the Englishman drank from the cups. The two old friends
had agreed on a handsome bride price: nine heifers, a two-year-old
bullock, six wool blankets, Rhodesian tobacco and snuff wrapped in
banana leaves, and twenty gourds of njohi.

Penfold stood in the back of the tent by the Goan priest, waiting
with the ring to perform his duty as best man. At the other end, he
saw Anunciata smiling up at Rack Slider. For once the American
wasn't wearing that hat. Raji da Souza stood nearby with his hands
clasped behind his back. Turbanned and resplendent, the moneylender beamed and bowed whenever he managed to engage Lord
Penfold's eye.

Sissy, Penfold knew, would not be present. Out for a day-long
ride with a guest and her new wolfhounds, she had declared, with
surprising heat, that the ceremony was "absurd, a disgrace." But at
least the new dogs seemed to be enjoying themselves out here. A
useful mixture, these Irish hounds: Great Danes crossed with deer-
hounds, and just a drop of Borzoi blood to give them dash.

Gwenn waited near the entrance with flowers for the bride. Honey-
tan and straight, lovelier than Penfold could have imagined, her
freshness made him feel doubly old. Her hair seemed shorter and

lighter under the broad tilted brim of a pale straw hat. Her green eyes smiled across the tent.

Penfold saw Wellington maneuver a lead gun carriage and caisson of the Royal Horse Artillery across the hills and valleys of the canvas floor, among the feet of the dozen African men who stood whispering beside Gwenn. Some were dressed in the staff party uniform: white kanzu, sandals, and lime-green sash and fez. Others were barefoot, wrapped in cloaks. Carried in from the bar, the upright piano waited with Jill Bevis on the stool. Dr. Fitzgibbons stood behind her, watching Kaiser as the parrot hopped about on top of the piano. Wellie's pet mongoose, Nappy, scuttled along the wall of the tent, stalking a lizard. Rather a nice touch, one had to admit, naming Wellington's snake-eater after that frightful French tyrant.

How natural it all seemed out here, Penfold thought, looking about the tent, but how impossibly bizarre this would be anywhere else. Was that why he could never go home? Here even the Church of Rome was more accommodating, though Kina's efficient conversion, baptism and confirmation had cost him a few guineas. But the old priest had explained it. For four centuries, ever since they conquered Goa, always short of European women, the Portuguese had encouraged intermarriage. And why not?

Suddenly all was silent. Anton entered the tent carrying the campaign chair in his arms. His black boots gleamed. Olivio sat erect on the curved slats of the wooden seat with a white rose in his buttonhole. Anton set the chair down between the priest and Lord Penfold. Olivio pulled himself forward to the raised front of the seat. His left eye was flat and dull. But his right, dark and deep-set, glinted out like a miner's lamp beneath the bandage that crossed his brow.

A whispering commotion rose near the entrance when Chief Kitenji and Kina stepped inside. Kitenji paused. Expressionless, dressed in a monkey-skin cloak, he clenched his staff. Kina, one cheek wildly aflame with a wide pink and white scar, but womanly even in her white cotton Mother Hubbard, hesitated until Gwenn encouraged her forward.

Something recognizably like "A Mighty Fortress Is Our God" filled the tent as Jill Bevis banged away on the keys, a new wedding band bright on her finger.

"Sorry, padre," Penfold whispered to the priest, "she doesn't know any Holy Roman tunes."

Then Penfold nodded and held out a hand. The two women and Chief Kitenji marched stiffly towards him. Just look at Gwenn. If he were a day younger, damned if he himself wouldn't slip the ring on her finger instead. What was the matter with young Rider? Why didn't the idle youth get on with it? This girl, Penfold thought, was the very best: appreciative rather than spoiled, a woman who had suffered but remained somehow fresh and undefeated. And what a stunner.

Penfold extended his arm in front of Olivio, and the dwarf gripped it with two white-gloved hands. Trembling with exertion, the small man pulled himself to his feet. He rocked slightly in his new shoes.

"*In nomine Patris et Filii et Spiritus Sancti,*" the priest began.

Speaking swiftly, he led a shortened service. The Latin words, if not the Roman ritual, were congenial to Penfold's schoolboy ear. The priest turned to Kina, and she nodded her consent. Olivio whispered, and Penfold acted for him. He took Kina's dark hand in his and placed the ring on her finger.

It was done. Tinny but triumphant, the piano gave them "Jerusalem." Then "Greensleeves" welcomed all hands to Pimm's by the piano. Holding Kina's hand between both of his, Olivio sat in the campaign chair on a cushion. He nodded or spoke softly to each guest in turn, accepting their respects.

After a toast by Raji da Souza, Penfold led a roaring chorus of "For He's a Jolly Good Fellow." Then Anton lifted Olivio in his arms and carried the dwarf to the new cottage.

Naked at last, save for his head bandage and a fresh pair of soft gloves, Olivio sat up in bed and looked around with his mouth open. In time, he thought, mindful of Kina's pleasure, it might prove convenient that several of his fingers now bore no nails. Scraped of its charred surface and restained a darker brown, the carved sandalwood headboard braced the pillows behind him. Instead of the mirror, he now faced a magnificent scene, the wedding gift of the Institute.

Goa's majestic Palace of the Inquisition dominated the broad canvas. Its finely grained Indian limestone shone in the painting at his feet. Thinking back with pride to his lessons at the school for orphans,

Olivio recalled that the palace had been consecrated to its sacred use in 1560, at a time when Goa was a larger city than London, or Lisbon itself.

Squinting with his right eye to admire the detail, the dwarf brightened when he identified the occasion: the first day of the lavish ceremony of the auto-da-fé! The time of sentencing! Determined to exterminate the enemies and unbelievers who surrounded Goa, the Church was preparing for the splendid spectacle of the fiery executions the following day. Manacled Hindus and Moslems knelt before the ecclesiastical tribunal in the foreground. Behind them hooded priests directed the decorative arrangement of the stakes, the kindling and the wooden crosses.

What an inspiring example! Was Olivio Fonseca Alavedo to treat his own enemies by a lower standard than the Church of his fathers?

The dwarf recalled again, as he did in his prayers every morning and every night, his debt to Fonseca and to the man's Irish pawns. Such men understood greed and violence. But vengeance? In this they were infants. Primitives. In a curious way, even his suffering was a gift from these men, for what revenge could he not take now? Which of them had poured paraffin on the thatch of his roof, which of them had cast the match, these were details.

Olivio studied the painting. Had not the holy fathers themselves laid the fires even before the sentences were passed? Was he to do less than these men of God?

Beyond the fire itself, his enemies had committed still more sins that cried for justice. The thieving after his properties in Africa and Portugal. His humiliation by the Irishmen in the bar. The insult of Fonseca's arrogance. And the scars of his bride. Kina! Where was his wife?

Through the door he heard Gwenn take her leave. Was Kina ready?

All was silent save a faint rustling. Olivio's stubby toes touched one of the small balls of rolled herbs and wild flowers he had found scattered in the bed. He snared one between the horny soles of his feet and played with it, giggling quietly when it tickled him. He considered his marital duty, thankful he had prepared with morphine. Dry as an old olive pit, his lips and tongue, even his palate and throat, cried out for moisture.

A bottle of feni waited on the bedside table, the wedding gift of his banker, Raji da Souza. The dwarf lifted the heavy vessel with both hands. This was not the coarse drink fermented on the palm plantations of coastal Kenya, but the honey-smooth elixir of Goa itself.

With delight he heard the whistle of a switch cutting the air next door, then the satisfying crack as it struck a resisting object, followed by a whimper of pleasure. His black angel was teasing him with promise.

Olivio laid the round bottle on his stomach and struggled to draw the stopper with his front teeth. Frustrated, he turned his head painfully to the side. His cheek rested on the yellow blossoms that covered the pillow. He grimaced and gripped the short cork between his molars. Squeezing the end of the bottle between the palms of his gloved hands, he rolled it slightly to left and right across the scars of his belly.

With the cork still caught in his mouth, the bottle slipped free. The feni spilled onto him. Oily with its richness, he smelled the ambrosia that flooded over his body. It was not palm feni. No! It was the most treasured of all nectars, the drink of the gods: cashew feni! Olivio lost consciousness in the clouds of memory and scent that absorbed him.

The cork fell onto his tongue, rolling too far back to spit out, almost lodging in his throat. Olivio reached into his mouth with one hand. He coughed and his teeth cut painfully through the glove into his scarred fingers.

The door opened. Naked, her breasts incomparably huge and firm above her rounded belly, her ebony nipples erect, Kina slipped onto the bed with a slim branch in one hand. She covered Olivio's mouth with her lips and sucked out the cork, leaving a sticky taste on his tongue. Chocolate, Cadbury's bittersweet! Her warm body glistened with the thick confection. Would the disgusting child never learn? There was still so much to teach her! The rich odors of cashew feni and chocolate mingled, and his wife overwhelmed him.

— 37 —

Either a Senadore or a Crema de las Antillas, Olivio reckoned
as he sniffed the heady smoke that drifted before the man into the
darkened bar. At least he had not lost his sense of smell.

Vasco Fonseca tossed his panama onto a table and slouched down,
resting his tall-heeled boots on a chair. He turned his head and looked
up at the leadwood bar. He took the wet cigar from his lips and
stared.

For the first time totally unbandaged, the ghostly head of the dwarf
was suspended in the unlit room below the mounted animal skulls.
Like an egg or an embryo, it was an oval of purish white. Its pigment
mostly gone, the poreless skin alternately smoothly scarred, then
pitted and ridged in swirls of proud flesh where the underlying tissue
of cheeks and jaws had debrided away, the face of the dwarf con-
fronted him.

All softness lost to heat and pain, Olivio's face was reduced to its
surviving functional parts. His left ear, the central tissue gone, was
an empty loop on the side of his head, open like the handle of a
pitcher. Taut dry skin clung tightly over the beak-like bone of his
nose. Only the wide nostrils flared as before. He had no eyebrows.
A few long hairs on his crown and an occasional eyelash stood out
against the white of the little man's head.

"Greetings, cousin," said Olivio in Portuguese. He poured two
glasses of Fonseca Bin No. 27.

"You are no cousin to me." Fonseca ground his panatella under one heel.

"Our mother Church does not agree." Olivio brandished an envelope in one gloved hand. He looked at the mess on the floor.

"For your price, the cardinal would christen monkeys. Look at you. Disgusting."

"Every hectare, every carriage and pig, every olive tree and stable, each spoon and family portrait and pipe of wine is one half mine. In Oporto, in Estoril, in Mozambique, in Macao, in Amazonia."

"I'll share my bed with dogs before I divide one field with you."

"Unless you bargain with me, cousin, my children will dance in our aunt's palace. They will be small and dark and perfect and exquisitely dressed. All Lisbon will seek their favors."

"What do you want?"

"I will give you my half of our estates in Portugal in exchange for all the lands you claim in Africa. The rest we will divide. And one other thing you must do. Leave my friends in peace. Here is the document. You need only sign."

Fonseca stood and stepped to the bar. He glared at the dwarf from dark deep-set eyes. His domed forehead shone with sweat. He raised a glass of port and gulped from it. He snatched the paper from the bar and threw the wine and the glass in Olivio's face.

Fonseca picked up his hat and strode out. Fragments of glass lay on the bar shelf. The heavy red wine dripped from the dwarf's face like tears of blood.

"This'll be hard news for Gwenn." Anton passed the Land Office notification back to Lord Penfold. "I'm going to ride up there and see how I can help her, and I want to make sure they've shut down that stinking creosote plant."

"First it was the bungalow," Penfold said, accepting a weak morning whisky from Olivio. With a girl like that waiting up-country, he hoped this boy had something on his mind beside creosote. "Now she's lost the whole place. I did my best, but Hartshorne was right. It's Land Office policy to keep the original houses and farms together, so Fonseca's getting it all. They're offering her a new spot way over by Lake Baringo. Then only the elephants'll see her."

"Perhaps, my lord," said Olivio, "I too should safari to Cairn Farm. I have much to discuss with Miss Gwenn, and I wish to see this farm myself."

"Aren't you better off staying here?" Penfold tried not to seem aware of the dwarf's face. Olivio poured a shot for Rack Slider. "It's a rough ride in the wagon," Penfold said. Slider drained the small glass. Penfold wondered when this American would learn how to drink whisky.

"Four hundred years ago, my lord, raving with fever, Vasco da Gama sailed from Mombasa across the Indian Ocean. For twenty-two days he journeyed in a boat three times as long as this bar. Death lay with him in his bunk," Olivio said. Why didn't his friends want him along? He poured drops of Young's Rifle Oil onto the fingers of his impala-skin glove and rubbed the leadwood in a circular motion without looking down. "On the twenty-third day, Vasco da Gama found India."

"Tell you what, Shorty," said Slider, looking at his left fist and flexing his fingers. "You take that old buckboard and I'll ride shotgun. No telling what sort of sport you two might find up there, and we want to make sure the youngster here doesn't get in trouble."

"Why don't you shorten your stirrups, Mr. Slider? You'll fall off if you ride like that," Anton said, as he helped Olivio up to the cushioned bench of the wagon. Rafiki's saddle rested among the supplies in the bed of the cart.

"I was roping dogies from these stirrups before you were sucking milk, sonny. You Limes don't know what a man's saddle looks like. You just mind your mules and buckboard."

Roping dogs? What did the American mean? Olivio wondered.

Merlin, Lady Penfold's favorite wolfhound, dashed up and leaned upright on its hind legs. Two thin hairy paws scratched the end of the dwarf's seat. Olivio recoiled. Perhaps he could pay the American to rope and hang this doggie?

Merlin dropped down, opened his long mouth and relieved himself on a front wheel.

Anton slapped the reins on the backs of the mules and they were off, the beginning of Olivio's first trip north of the White Rhino

Hotel. The dwarf glanced back to see Lord Penfold and Kina waving. Olivio gripped the seat with both gloved hands and bobbed his head in reply. At last he was on a man's journey.

"Are we going too fast?" Anton asked after a time, his mind absent as he remembered long days wandering about England in the vardo. He recalled another departure, setting out from Tanganyika with Karioki, and all that his friend had taught him. This time Anton knew he had a harder job to do. He wondered if he would be able to kill when the time came.

"Perhaps we could stop for a moment." Olivio's arms were exhausted. His outsize straw hat scraped his forehead. He felt the heat building inside the closed oven of his body.

They paused under a thorn tree. Slider trotted on ahead, riding flat in the heavy western saddle while he led Rafiki through the bush. The dwarf licked his dry lips, and Anton handed him a tin canteen.

"What brought you to Africa, Mr. Anton, so very far from your home?"

"I had no home, Olivio. I came to be free and make my fortune."

"So did I. So did I. Have you found these things?"

"I'm not sure." Anton grinned. "I've one hundred and twenty pounds in the Dominion Bank in Nairobi and three cigarette tins stuffed with gold dust. But I don't know how long I'll be free." Anton thought of Gwenn. Now he was not certain what freedom meant.

"That's more money than his lordship can count, and he has no freedom. For a woman, you see, Mr. Anton, marriage is security, usually their word for money. For a man, of course, it is poverty. Would women want to marry so if it was the other way around?" Olivio looked at Anton with his mouth slightly open, almost smiling, and closed his good eye in what might have been a wink. Anton flushed. "Let us go on now," the dwarf said.

In the early evening, Anton and Slider made camp. Olivio served a cold supper prepared by the White Rhino's kitchen.

"Why do you have that big knob on the front of your saddle, Mr. Slider?" Olivio said later. He sat cross-legged on his cushion close by the dwindling fire.

"That's a pommel, Shorty. In the Panhandle, that's what we hog-tie the cows to while we're branding 'em."

"In America you tie hogs in a pan?"

"Pipe down, our pal here's only a baby and needs his shut-eye. Don't you never sleep?"

"I do not sleep out of the doors, Mr. Slider. You may rest, please. I shall keep watch and listen for the lions."

Riding on ahead in the crisp morning, Rafiki frisky and puffing steam under him, Anton thought of the dwarf. Earlier, lying half awake, huddled and chilled with dew on his face, Anton had seen Olivio take form while the light brightened.

First Anton saw only the small man's shadowed outline, erect across the glowing coals. Clear at last, the dwarf sat awake and perfectly still, a plaid blanket tight around him, propped like a teddy bear against Slider's saddle. One eye was dead as the button eye of a doll, the other more alive than the hottest coal. His different eyes, Anton realized with a slight chill, were rather like the dwarf himself: at times absent and inhuman, at other moments more alert and intense than any man should be.

Anton cantered up to the cluster of acacias. Dark smoke rose from the creosote plant. Only two figures moved around the tanks. Anton took his field glasses from a saddlebag. He felt the rush of excitement that seized him when a hunt began and his senses heightened. A few moments later Slider and Olivio joined him.

"Why don't you rest here, Olivio, while Rack and I ride down and see what they're up to."

Olivio watched the two horsemen trot down to the creosote plant. He sat perched on the bench of the wagon with the German field glasses propped on his knees. He dismissed the pain he knew would never leave him. The mules were still in harness. Tied to the low branch of an overhanging fever tree, they grazed on the tufty wild grass.

Without intending insult, his two friends had left him behind, Olivio reflected with bitterness. Just like his schoolmates in Goa, they considered him inadequate to the physical demands of a man's adventure. At least a few ladies knew better.

The dwarf scanned the scene with the glasses. He moistened his lips and studied the two long steel cylinders, stacks of waiting timbers and the dusty Willys motorcar belonging to his cousin. He saw Fonseca emerge from a work shed beside the trench-like saw pit with the cross spar of a telegraph pole in one hand. Two long doubled-handled saws rested on the ground near the hole, surrounded by soft mounds of sawdust. A third long-toothed saw was lodged vertically in a log that traversed one end of the pit. The two horsemen rode up.

"Poaching again, Mr. Fonseca?" Anton said when he dismounted and saw the rhino horns and leopard skins in the back of the Willys. "Do you still shoot from your car?"

"You English care only for animals," the Portuguese said. "How much do you want for this land?"

"Close this filthy plant now. It's time you left," Anton said. "You're ruining my land and driving off the game."

"Must've been a mighty cute little rhino." Rack Slider lifted a small curved horn from the rear of the box body. "Did you have one of your Micks strangle this one?"

"Just drop your gunbelt in the hole there, Yank." Paddy emerged from the shed holding a twelve-gauge shotgun like a toy. "And don't you give me no excuse to shoot this thing, Rider, 'cause I know right where I'm going to put it."

Anton felt himself grow taut. His sheathed knife seemed to move closer to his hand.

Up on the hill a small figure lashed two mules. The wagon careened downwards. One front wheel mounted an anthill. The cart crashed over on its side. The racing mules dragged the broken wagon through the bush.

"In case you're missing your friend Reilly," Fonseca said to Anton, "I've sent him over to visit his old sweetheart. Mrs. Llewelyn spends too much time alone."

Slider touched his belt buckle and grinned at Anton. Turning slowly towards the saw pit, the American threw the rhinoceros horn at Paddy and went for his revolver.

Anton's knife flashed and Paddy fired. Slider's chest burst inwards in a red splash. The blast knocked his body into the saw pit. The slim gypsy blade buried itself to the hilt in Paddy's stomach.

Anton lunged at Paddy. He grabbed the shotgun and the second barrel fired into the air. The huge man stared down with shocked eyes and pulled the knife from his stomach. Anton hurled the gun into the open doorway of the creosote tank and attacked the Irishman. Snarling, blood flooding his shirt and trousers, Paddy met Anton knife in hand. Locked together, the two men staggered at the edge of the pit. Paddy reeled backwards. He fell against the teeth of the saw. His back opened. He collapsed into the pit with Anton on top of him.

Rack Slider's still face gazed up at Anton from its sawdust pillow. His trousers soaked in Paddy's blood, Anton fought with the wounded giant at the other end of the trench. Paddy's stomach and back spurted blood with each exertion. Lying bent on his side in the narrow space, grunting and raging, Paddy held Anton's left arm in an unbreakable grip. He tried to drag Anton down and grab his enemy's throat with his free hand.

Anton clutched for his knife in the sawdust. Their faces close, Anton saw again the hatred in the pig-like eyes fixed on him during the arm-wrestling in the White Rhino. Paddy's hand caught his throat. Anton's vision blurred. His lungs grew hot. He remembered Karioki. "You must learn when to kill, Tlaga."

Anton jammed his knife back into the wound in Paddy's stomach. He cut upwards to the breastbone. Spilling open like a gutted fish, Paddy's body gave up. Only his eyes lived for a moment. Anton crawled from the pit, intent on galloping to Cairn Farm. On his knees, covered in blood and sawdust, Anton looked up. Fonseca clubbed him across the side of the head with the telegraph spar.

— 38 —

What would it be like if they had to move? Gwenn wondered, resting for a moment near the Ewaso Ngiro with her back against the tamarind tree. She tossed a stone towards Alan's cairn a few yards away and glanced over at Mount Kenya, shouldering through the clouds above the distant bush.

Gwenn took some hard red soil in her hand and smelled the land. She examined her short broken nails and the rough palms of her hands before raising her eyes and looking about her.

How could anything be as beautiful as this? Dear God, how could she leave this farm? It was more home than Wales would ever be. Under this tree Wellie was born. Beneath those rocks her husband was buried. Every furrow knew her struggle. Even moving from the bungalow to the new stone house had been a cutting sorrow. And a new farm would be still more isolated. It would mean starting again. A third house, different earth, new animals and crops. Perhaps new friends. And what of Anton? Would he ever come to be with her there? Would she see Adam Penfold and Olivio and Victoria?

A heavy splashing interrupted her. She turned her head and looked down at the river: Reilly. Gwenn felt fear and anger surge through her. Riding into the water on a sturdy Abyssinian pony, the big man forced the animal through the river with his spurs.

Gwenn leapt up and ran across the field to her new house. Compact, modelled after Alan's sketch, it had the thick stone walls of a Welsh farmhouse. Her heart pounded while she dashed through the sitting room into the unfinished kitchen. Not finding the shotgun, she snatched up a knife. Only hours before, she'd left the gun in the maize crib after driving off the starlings. One barrel was still loaded. She rushed out the back door, lifted her skirt and ran towards the open-sided shed.

Gwenn climbed the fence of the sheep pasture and jumped down among the merinos. She saw Reilly burst up onto the flat of the riverbank and start towards her. The sheep scattered when Gwenn ran between them. She arrived at the far fence just as Reilly, clumsy and heavy on his horse, made a shortcut through the young maize to intercept her.

Breathless, Gwenn entered the long thatched structure. She saw the gun leaning against a wooden rack near the far end. Light glinted on the bluish-grey finish of its barrels. She stumbled on the tools and sacks and ears of dry maize that cluttered the earth floor. She scrambled towards the gun and saw Reilly brutally pull up his horse at the same end of the crib. Almost in time, Gwenn dropped her knife and grabbed for the shotgun.

Reilly's hand closed over hers as she seized the gun. Panting, he kept his grip.

"Happy to see me, ain't you?"

"Let go of me."

"Mr. Fonseci sent me around to make sure you was off his farm. It's all his now. He's over at the plant. If your bastard friends show up, the greaser'll fix 'em nice, and he knows how close we are, dearie, now you've told everybody you was raped."

Reilly ran his other hand along Gwenn's shoulder and squeezed it with big fingers. She struck him hard with the back of her free hand.

"That's no way to greet an old luv." Reilly smiled. He lowered his hand to the front of her shirt. His other hand forced Gwenn's from the gun barrel. He tossed the weapon aside. She smelled his breath and sweat when he twisted one arm behind her and thrust himself against her, squeezing her back against the wooden rack. Gwenn struggled to free herself.

"Rape, was it?" Reilly pressed his hand between her breasts. Buttons tore from her shirt. She felt the scaly roughness of his touch. His hand covered one breast and her nipple hardened.

"I'll kill you for this, Reilly." Gwenn kicked his shins with her work shoes. This couldn't be happening to her again.

"That's my damned son out there somewhere with your niggers. Once you're used to me, you'll marry me, you stupid wench, and get your bleedin' farm back. That's what you'll do."

Thank God, Gwenn thought, she'd sent Wellie to the White Rhino with the Bevises.

Reilly ripped off her shirt. He ran his hand down across her stomach into the top of her skirt. Gwenn kneed him between the legs. He grunted, and together they fell sideways onto a pile of empty sacks.

His entire weight on her, Gwenn fought as she felt Reilly's hand push up under her skirt between her thighs. He tore at her underclothes. She thrashed and reached behind her head for the shotgun.

Groping along the ground, Gwenn's hand found no weapon. She clawed at Reilly's face and ripped the patch from his left eye. He struggled to put his mouth over hers. His beard scraped her, and her eyes almost touched his face. She saw the clotted pus that still leaked from his wound. Her other hand searched behind her.

Gwenn's fingers touched the side of a bucket. She plunged her hand inside and felt the powdery poisonous base of Cooper's Sheep Dip. The blue granules of arsenic and salt were gritty and dry between her fingers.

Reilly drew back his head and opened his belt. Gwenn smeared a fistful of dip across his staring eye and pressed it hard into his wounded eye and mouth.

Staggering to his feet, spitting and gripping his head, Reilly screamed like a man being quartered. Gwenn jumped up.

"God damn you!" Reilly raged. He clutched for her. "My eyes!" His nails clawed her bare shoulder as she burst past him out the end of the shed.

Gwenn grabbed his pony's reins and climbed shirtless into the saddle. At the riverbank she reined in for an instant and looked back while she gasped in deep breaths. Screaming, groping for the shotgun with one hand, Reilly clawed at his face with the other. He staggered about with small steps, his trousers about his ankles, his white belly free. "God curse you!" he yelled.

Gwenn turned the horse and urged him into the Ewaso Ngiro.

Breaking out of the river on the east bank, flushed and hot with excitement, she felt the cool spray on her bare upper body. She rubbed her cut shoulder with the water.

Frightened and angry, Gwenn pushed the pony hard, making for the shortcut that ran towards Anton's property and on south to Nanyuki and the White Rhino. She hunched her shoulders and leaned forward over the animal's neck, embarrassed by her nakedness.

As the horse tired, her thoughts turned over Reilly's words. What were Fonseca and the Irishmen planning for her friends? Of course they wanted Olivio dead because of his inheritance, and Anton gone because he owned the land under Fonseca's plant and was the only witness to her rape. Could she get to Anton in time to warn them?

Lathered and winded, the horse slowed to a plodding walk. Gwenn enjoyed the freedom of the fresh forest air on her chest. She stroked the horse and spoke to it. She smelled the animal's foamy sweat on her hands and turned her attention to her mount. The plucky horse had good bone and strong shoulders. Just what one needed in Africa. She reached into the single saddlebag, hoping to find some garment. Instead she found a whisky bottle, the end of a sausage and Alan's notebook.

Soon they came to the cedar forest that fingered down from the slopes of Mount Kenya. Gwenn felt the perspiration cool on her body and found herself distracted by the woods. The straight clear boles of the cedars lofted above her. She smelled the first stands of camphor trees and noticed the dark leaves of wild figs. Perhaps one day this forest would give her a wide bed of camphorwood. Gwenn closed her eyes and squared back her shoulders in the warming air. She felt the wind clean her body.

Crossing the trail before her, the round prints of elephants caught Gwenn's eye. Large fresh droppings were scattered among them, still dark with moisture, steaming with life, and thick with seeds and twigs.

She counted the days since Anton had warned Fonseca to get the plant off his land. The week was up today. She knew Anton would be back. Gwenn squeezed her knees together and clicked her tongue. She must save him. Agitated by the odors of elephant, the horse obliged and eased into a trot. Gwenn kicked with her heels and forced him to a canter.

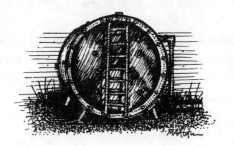

— 39 —

Anton unconscious at his feet, Vasco Fonseca stepped to the side of the saw pit and stared down at the bodies of Paddy and Slider. They deserved each other. He kicked in some sawdust and spat. He dropped the telegraph spar and looked at Anton.

"Now we'll pump your lungs full of boiling creosote," Fonseca said. He saw Paddy's blood smeared together with the sawdust that covered Anton's shirt. He watched blood ooze from the gash along the top of Anton's forehead.

Fonseca bent over and dragged Anton by his boots towards the cylinder. There the Portuguese dropped Anton's legs onto the bottom step and paused for breath. He mounted the steps. He would have to climb in first in order to drag Rider inside. Fonseca glanced into the interior of the steel cylinder and saw Paddy's shotgun resting on the sticky floor.

Outside, at the far end of the cylinder, the dwarf scuttled over to the metal ladder that rose eight feet to the top of the tank. He hauled himself up step by step, soundlessly, reminded of the bar ladder at the White Rhino Hotel.

Before bending to pull Anton inside, Fonseca walked deeper into the cylinder. The heels of his boots echoed against the curved metal walls. He lifted the dirty shotgun and tossed it outside. He looked up at the steel ceiling and ran his fingers along the punctured pipe that would fill the tank with hot creosote. "*Perfeito*," he said.

The door slammed shut behind him.

Too late, Fonseca threw himself against it with a curse.

"*Gaita!* Damn! What the devil!" he screamed, thrusting his shoulder against the door. "Who's there? Let me out!"

The outside latch was bolted. Fonseca heard small steps tapping along the metal roof above his head. A narrow column of light, perhaps six inches wide and three feet high, reached through the thick glass observation window mounted in the door of the tank. Fonseca wiped the top of the window with his sleeve. He put his round forehead to the glass and peered out.

Inches away, hanging upside down and set in a white face that was cut like a cracked eggshell, two eyes met his through the glass. One was milky-grey and glazed with death. The other, wide and unblinking, glared at him with wonder and ferocity.

Olivio lay on the roof of the tank. He was exhausted, battered by the crash of the wagon. His head hung down over the edge. His shirt was in shreds. His hands were raw inside their torn gloves. For a long moment the dwarf gazed into the apprehensive eyes of his cousin. He tapped the window twice with a forefinger.

Olivio descended the front ladder. He gathered himself step by step and placed both feet on each rung. Near the bottom, he balanced himself and stopped near the metal wheel that tightened the door for a perfect seal. It was within his reach. He pulled with both hands on the ribs that crossed the center of the wheel. He felt the contracted skin of his chest stretching cruelly while he strained. Slowly he revolved the wheel clockwise around the greased screw at its core. The door tightened.

The dwarf paused to rest on the bottom rung. Gritting his teeth, he stepped to the ground and examined his unconscious friend. A thick rim of blood was clotting along the edge of Anton's forehead. Olivio opened one of Anton's eyes. The dwarf removed his own torn shirt and dipped it in a nearby bucket. He bathed Anton's bleeding face and left him with the moist cloth under his head.

Olivio walked with painful steps to the base of the elevated second cylinder. He studied the simple mechanism of the pumping tank. He looked up and saw dark smoke rising from the boiler. One glove stuck to the reopened wounds of his right hand when Olivio struggled to pull the red-handled control lever to the OPEN position. The weakened muscles of his arms could not give him the strength he required. Without the shield of opium, his hands cried to him as the rebuilding nerves delivered their pain to his brain. The dwarf suppressed his agony and tried again. The lever would not move.

Olivio lowered himself to the ground and lay on his naked back in the dust. For once he was doing a man's work.

The dwarf extended his arms to either side. He heard Fonseca pounding against the wall of the lower tank. With his knees touching his chest, Olivio braced his feet against the lever. Straining until he felt his neck and unsweating face would burst, he straightened his legs. The lever moved. The dwarf lay still on his back. He heard the hot creosote flush down through the pipe from the pump tank. He watched the gauges while the pressure and heat needles rose.

When the temperature reached one hundred and eighty degrees, Olivio stood. He walked back to the first cylinder. There both gauges were shattered. He paused and placed his right hand on the feeder pipe. He waited. At last he could feel the warmth through his frayed glove. The pipe grew cruelly hot. Ignoring the pain, smiling thinly, Olivio kept his hand on the metal. Again he climbed the ladder.

He paused to breathe and to taste the moment. If they all could see him now! The boys in Goa, Lord Penfold and Mrs. Llewelyn, Mr. Anton and Mr. Slider, and Kina. And his grandfather himself. How proud of him the archbishop would be!

Olivio reached the top of the tank and lay on his naked chest. His head looked down over the edge. He felt the rivets of the steel roof plates punching into his scars. Olivio opened his right eye wide. He set his face against the narrow window.

Vasco Fonseca stared up at him. His eyes bulged under the high forehead. His mouth twisted silently. Olivio felt the tank tremble under him when his captive pounded on the door. The dwarf put one ear against the crack where the door met its steel frame. He heard the echoing shrieks. He put his eye to the window and gazed again into the raving eyes of his cousin. Upside down, Olivio smiled and wagged his head from side to side, his face several inches from Fonseca's.

The dwarf made out the dark shadow of the scalding creosote as it rose around Fonseca. He imagined it filling Fonseca's boots, then penetrating his trousers and shirt and clinging to his skin. Jumping desperately, his cousin danced about in the thickening mass, sometimes moving away and denying the dwarf his view. Feeling the tank grow warm beneath him, Olivio recalled the slow weeks imprisoned inside the gauze. The unending pain, his flesh flaking away like the breast of an overcooked chicken, and the scarred lavish body of his bride. And he remembered the dock in Goa where his boyhood friends tortured him in the olive barrel.

Suddenly Olivio became aware of a distracting movement near Anton on the ground below him. He watched Rafiki nuzzle his injured master. Anton moved. When he awoke, Olivio thought, he must send him on at once to see about Mrs. Llewelyn.

Topping up, the cylinder grew hot. Olivio felt his chest suffer through the scars. He put his good eye to the steamy window. His wide nose was flat against the glass, like a boy peering into a candy shop.

Fonseca's head was barely visible above the thick blackness. Were his eyes alive or dead? His mouth, nicely open, moved slightly as if sipping when the first oil slopped against his lips.

Gwenn sensed the pony take alarm. Staring ahead, she heard a large animal rush towards her through the woods. Anton and Rafiki dashed around a turn in the trail, almost crashing into her.

The two horses came together and pulled up. Nervous but friendly, the animals sniffed each other nose to tail. Anton reached across and hugged Gwenn with both arms. Shocked by the blood that covered him, she dropped the reins and put her hands to his battered face. She felt her eyes fill.

"Do you always ride like this?" he whispered in her hair.

"An old friend of yours tore off my shirt."

They dismounted and tied the horses in a cedar glade well off the trail. Anton unbuttoned his shirt and handed it to her. She bunched it in one hand and stood on her toes to kiss him.

Like a gunshot, a tree snapped in two.

"Elephant," Anton said softly, his lips against her ear. Limbs broke nearby. Above them, birds and monkeys twittered and cried and grew silent. Crouching, Anton led Gwenn by the hand to a patch of soft ground sheltered behind two rocks and a tall cedar. They lay down on Anton's shirt. Small forest mushrooms and yellow wild flowers grew beside them. They listened to the horses whinny in fear before the creatures bolted. From time to time, while the elephant advanced through the forest, Gwenn and Anton heard measured shufflings and snapping branches when the smaller trees were pushed aside.

A deep rumbling, the relaxed sound of digestion, came to them. Slowly, setting her feet with dignity as they swung from her knees, a cow led her young calf into the glade before them, occasionally shepherding it with gentle stroking movements of her trunk.

Pressed together with his arm around her bare shoulders, Anton and Gwenn lay on their stomachs. They watched the mother touch her baby's sides and forehead with her trunk as it staggered about between her front legs. The chin and upper forelegs of the calf bristled with stiff hairs. The mother slipped the tip of her trunk into the calf's mouth. The young elephant moved under its mother and began to suckle. Behind the mother, other elephant walked calmly through the cedars, like old farmers at home in a field of tall corn.

Freeing one hand from Gwenn's, Anton turned on his side. He reached to his belt and drew out the blood-stained blade. His other hand rested on the smooth skin of Gwenn's back. Feeling his hand brushing along her side, Gwenn watched him, absorbed by the blue of his eyes. He raised the knife to the old leather cord that hung from his neck and sliced through it. A gold ring fell between them.

EPILOGUE

1921

— 40 —

Sounds rather exciting," said Adam Penfold, sniffing the mushroom samosas. "Bit hard luck on the old Portagee, though. Shame there wasn't someone else about to help you let him out. Couldn't free up that wheel on your own, eh, Olivio?"

"Just as you say, my lord." The dwarf rubbed the bar with his glove. "I have so little strength in my hands."

"Von Decken and I better ride on up and decant the poor devil, though he should keep forever in that stuff. Remind me to take along some old canvas so he won't soil the wagon on the way home. Perhaps we can rinse him off in the river."

"I found this timepiece among Senhor Fonseca's effects." Olivio handed Penfold a gold fob watch. "Shall I set it against the value of his bar chits, my lord?"

"Why not, old boy?" Penfold wound the familiar movement and held the half hunter to his ear. "Why not? Good thing he didn't have it on him."

Penfold sipped his gin and tonic and splashed in another nip of Corry's Lime Juice. He picked up the platter of Indian pastries and limped over to the repaired square table.

"Hot samosas, a touch of tamarind chutney?" Penfold asked the three guests. He admired the high-heeled French shoes and fashionable pleated silk skirts of the ladies. Before either woman could select a pastry, their heavy-set escort reached between them to pluck one of the puffy triangles from the dish.

"Ladies first, Captain von Decken." Penfold pulled back the plate and offered it to the man's graceful companions.

"*Non, merci,*" one said while she struggled to open a shallow round Balkan Sobranie tobacco tin.

"For eight months in the bush, when this English gentleman was helpless and all prickly with good German shrapnel, General von Lettow and I fed him." Von Decken snatched up two samosas. "Now he starves me."

"Our Prussian friends never know when they've lost a war." Penfold watched Wellington Llewelyn offer a centipede to Nappy. The banded mongoose gobbled the long wiggling insect with one swift bite and licked its lips. Penfold handed Wellie a hard-boiled egg from a dish on the bar.

"There's always another campaign," grunted Ernst. "You'll see."

Nappy turned his attention to the egg that Wellington rolled towards him across the floor.

Ignoring the chatter, the boy went behind the bar and climbed the ladder with a little help from Olivio. Wellie paraded an Argyll and Sutherland bagpiper along the gleaming leadwood. The dwarf studied the miniature figure and marvelled again at this British foolishness. How could grown men wear skirts in those freezing island hills? He examined the two-inch Highlander with his good eye. Now that he was rich, perhaps he should get one of these blue, green and yellow checked skirts for his wife. Short and pleated. And one never wore anything under them, it was said. Perfect for Kina. The dwarf pinched the open loops of his ears. He must have his tailor copy one from the little soldier.

Penfold saw the mongoose struggling under a table in a fury of concentration. The curved shell of the egg was just too large for Nappy to bite open. The animal rolled the egg towards one wall. The mongoose turned its back to the wall and lifted the egg with its forelegs. It separated its hind legs and tossed the egg between them against the wall. The egg cracked open and the mongoose turned to eat it. Rather like a backwards jump shot at croquet, Penfold thought.

With Fonseca dead, Olivio reflected, the Portuguese's share of the estate must pass to Anunciata. She would be even more desirable than before. And soon he himself would be richer than the Governor. There rose in his mind the image of his new ambition, the Olivio

Alavedo Pavilion for Orphans of Mixed Race, attached to the College
of St. Paul in Goa. The donor's name would look down from the
limestone lintel while grateful girls passed beneath, chattering about
their patron.

This German seemed to have a little money now, too. Why else
would these beauties sit so close to the enormous coarse man? What
did he have in those old cigarette tins? The dwarf looked under the
table. One lady rested a hand at the edge of von Decken's leather
shorts. Her other hand, more active, hidden under the silk skirt,
stroked the second woman's thigh. The dwarf extended his thick
tongue and licked his lips.

At that instant the Balkan Sobranie tin slipped from the table and
popped open when it hit the floor. Gold dust spilled out as it rolled
across the line of the equator.

A hundred silver bells tinkled when the Black Tulips leapt up.
Quick as cats, they were on the floor, collecting the hard dust in a
saucer and ashtray. But their long scarlet nails prevented them from
gathering many of the elusive shiny grains. The fine golden trail
extended across the floor of the bar, filling a knothole and lodging
in cracks between the uneven mahogany planks.

"Don't worry, my darling *Schätzchen,* it wasn't one of mine." Von
Decken sucked his fingers and admired the firm pear-shaped der-
rieres of the scrambling women. "Half of these tins belong to our
young *Engländer.* That was one of his. The boy can dig up the floor
when he returns. Never did his share of the work, anyway."

Olivio scuttled down the ladder with three smooth linen towels
and a bottle of Fonseca white port. He laid the towels over the line
of gold and splashed the sticky liquid onto them. When he lifted the
towels, the precious dust clung to them. Only the knothole retained
its gold. He rolled up the towels and placed them on the empty
platter.

"After the alcohol dries, my lord, I shall shake them out in her
ladyship's bathtub." Thank heavens, the dwarf thought, rolling his
eye, this time she will not be in it.

"Where's your wife, Adam?" said the German.

"In Nairobi, at the races. Our English girls adore horses."

"And where's my *Engländer*?"

"On safari with his true love. About time, too. They're by themselves in a fly camp wandering about among the cedars on the lower slopes. Travelling light. No tent. Want to see the big tuskers trekking across from Mount Kenya to the Aberdares."

"Foolish way to spend their first time together," Ernst said. "They should be eating Russian eggs and bathing in champagne."

"We are in Africa," said the dwarf.

A Note About the Book

In 1910 three distinguished Kenya pioneers, Berkeley Cole, Lord Cranworth and Sandy Herd, founded at Nyeri, in British East Africa, a hotel called the White Rhino. Apart from that name, this book bears no relationship whatever to that hotel, or to those gentlemen or their families, or to any other actual person.

All rhinoceros are grey. Of the two African species, the black rhinoceros is smaller and more aggressive and browses with its pointed prehensile lip. The white rhinoceros is the largest land animal in the world after the elephant. It grazes with its broad flat-ended jaw, which caused it to be described as the *wid,* or wide, rhinoceros, in Afrikaans, hence "white" in English. In 1927, the Society for the Preservation of the Fauna of the Empire declared that the white rhino was in danger of extinction. Approximately 4500 white rhinoceros survive today in Africa. South Africa is their principal sanctuary.

I have knowingly taken one factual liberty. Tusker beer did not exist in 1920. Founded by Charles and George Hurst, Kenya Breweries made its first nineteen cases of lager in December 1922, all of which were consumed by Major Ewart "Cape-to-Cairo" Grogan at the long bar of the New Stanley Hotel. In 1923, Charles Hurst was killed by an elephant, and his brother named the beer "Tusker" in his memory.

B.B.

Acknowledgements

The *White Rhino Hotel* demanded a diversity of expertise sometimes beyond the gifts or knowledge of its author. Friends who generously provided specialized assistance were: Robin Hurt, Terry Mathews, Theodore Roosevelt IV and John Sutton on wildlife and Africana; Michael Blakenham on naturalist details of English wildlife; Anthony Hardy on shipping; Dr. Thomas R. Kuhns on wounds and medicine; Regina Kettaneh on German usage; David Fonseca Guimaraens on port wine; Michael N. Teague on Portuguese usage; James R. Houghton on industrial glass in 1920; Stuart H. Johnson III on classical references; Andrew Carduner on automotive matters; Alex Brant on firearms; William Gavin on New Zealand; Alan Delynn and Bobby Short on period music; and Walter L. Foulke and his colleagues of the Thanatopsis Literary and Inside Straight Club on the mysteries of poker.

I owe debts of inspiration and information to writers from H. Rider Haggard to Elspeth Huxley and the old journalists of *The East African Standard*, and to my companions of many African campfires.

At the creative and critical level, my thanks to Constance Roosevelt, Winfield P. Jones, Wendy Breck, William vanden Heuvel, Patricia Beard and Gene Stavis, all sharp-eyed readers; to the late Marietta Tree, for her encouragement; to Dimitri Sevastopoulo and my son Bartle B. Bull, who both toiled through every draft; to F. William Free, for his artistic eye; to my spirited agent, Ed Victor; and, first and last, to my friend and demanding editor, Peter Mayer, for making me do it.